From Windy Ridge to the Flint Hills

LEE ANNE WONNACOTT

DEDICATION

Just win, baby. Al Davis 1939 - 2011

ALSO BY LEE ANNE WONNACOTT

Newton Cutter
Iron and Rawhide
Rage at Rancho del Oro
Nick Stolter

Kelly sat on the grassy bank and watched younger brother, Colton throw rocks into the flowing river. The daughter of Nick and Marianna Stolter was tall for a fifteen-year-old girl and was growing into the image of her mother. She dragged a stalk of thick grass from hand to hand with a frown as she bit her lower lip. Earlier in the day, Kelly had put the two young fillies through an hour of rope training. The young girl had a knack for feeding apples and carrots to the horses in the next corral to keep their attention on the training. Her mind kept straying over to the thirteen-month old black colt who liked to nudge her around the corral.

Five feet six with shoulder length dark brown hair, dark brown eyes and a wiry strength and a quiet attitude. Even at her young age, she was aware that trained horses were far more valuable than simple broke horses. She had known that her parents had kept the money side, the business side of the family away from the children. There was money for all the things they needed, without the visible wealth of some families she knew.

A sudden cheer from Colton brought her out of her reverie. The young boy had been struggling to get flat rocks to skip five times across the water. A flat rock made a couple of splashing bounces, some skipped and rock after rock plunked into the water. His happy dance of celebration brought a chuckle from Kelly.

Hours earlier, her father, Nick Stolter and mother, Marianna, had packed saddlebags with gear and food. They had stood on the porch and watched him trot down the driveway following his long-time friend, Ginger Whelihan. A week, maybe ten days he had said. But Kelly had an ugly feeling crawling up her back it would be longer, much longer before he came back home.

Nick Stolter, Kelly's father had a keen eye for horseflesh. From an established Texas ranch, Stolter had grown up buying and selling excellent stock. Stolter had begun instilling the same knowledge and intuition to his eldest daughter. Two months ago, Nick had allowed Kelly to ride with the four sold fillies being taken to the train for shipping to Texas. Sassy and smart, the fillies had been favorites for Kelly and she was saddened when they were sold to a large cattle ranch. But that was business and she squinted in the afternoon sun.

The first few days of March had been chilly with clear, bright days bathed in sunshine. Kelly breathed in the smells of earth, grasses and animals and let it out slowly. A motion to the right caught Kelly's eye and she could see younger sibling, Lola walking up the river bank from where she had been digging. Earlier, the younger girl had been focused on excavating a hole in the riverbank about fifty yards upstream.

"You sure there's no gold around here, Kelly?" Lola's voice had a childish musical quality to it. The older sister sat up straight and reached out to take the dirty clump. It was a grimy brown rock with hints of something dull underneath the muddy sludge.

"No, Pa said there was no gold known to be around here. Maybe a winter storm washed this down from somewhere up in the hills." Kelly handed it back to Lola who studied it for a moment.

"Colton could be tossing gold nuggets into the river and we wouldn't know it." Lola lifted a strand of the reddish brown long curls back out of her face and watched her brother.

Kelly leaned back on her arms and squinted in the warm sun. "Take it up to Ma and see if she thinks its gold. If it is, we'll come back and look for more."

Lola shoved the clump into her pocket. "You think Ma knows what gold looks like?" Kelly nodded without a word. Lola sauntered towards the house.

To help a friend. To payback a personal debt. Kelly clenched her jaw with nervous energy as she brushed down two of the fillies, muttering her secrets to the horses before turning them out to pasture. She had oiled the bridles and cleaned the saddles. She had used the heavy brush to sweep off all the saddle blankets. She could not concentrate for very long on one thing and finally sat at the river watching Colton throw rocks into the water.

The muddy green water eased by the children. Twenty-five feet across to the other side was the flat valley and bumped up against a range of low hills. The children had crawled all over the hills, finding crevices and sandstone formations carved by the wind and water. Down the other side was scrub brush, cacti, lava outcroppings and the edge of the desert that went east as far as the eye could see.

She was still a young girl the first time Kelly had seen Lola start stacking rocks. Over the years they had contests to see who could stack the flat rocks highest. It was always interesting to see which stacks still stood when they wandered back into the arid landscape.

***

It was Wednesday when the mail rider usually came and for some reason it made Stolter's wife, Marianna stand wringing a dishcloth in her hands as her eyes scanned for the horse and rider. They had been married for almost twenty years yet she fretted every time Stolter left for more than a day. If they had been friends for so many years, why had Whelihan not been by to visit before now?

It was almost a quarter mile from the porch steps down the broad driveway that curve slightly east to the front gate. From the wooden mailbox, she took out three newspapers, a couple of magazines and one letter from a family friend farther south. The strain of worrying had deepened the lines around Marianna's eyes and forehead. It was a slow walk back to the house as her thoughts tumbled. Marianna sat down on the cushioned bench on the porch holding the envelopes and looked out at the waving grass.

It had been the simple life that she wanted. Land, horses, a loving husband and family to cherish holidays, birthdays, and anniversaries. She felt like she had a true partner in Nick. Someone she could share the work with and build a future. But money had been tight this last year. Marianna had kept quiet about needing fabric for sewing or trips to Los Angeles for shopping because the money was not there.

They had started they had started their married life living on Marianna's family ranch, the Flint Hills Ranch. Glen and Anna-Marie Richardson had plenty of room in the large house and life was good. When pneumonia claimed their first-born son, Charlie, Nick had grieved deeply. Marianna began to believe he would never recover from it. Her husband spent more and more time away from the ranch until one day when he took Marianna out on a picnic and told her he wanted to move away from the memory of Charlie.

When Nick and Marianna moved to Yucca Valley, the soreness and the ache of their son had begun to ease. Their daughter, Kelly, was born a year later. Once again, the joy and happiness brightened their lives and brought a contentment the married couple had lost.

Lola came up the steps of the porch and held out a muddy clump to her mother, bringing Marianna out of her reverie.

Marianna considered her daughter for a moment and then smiled. "What do you have for me today, Lola?"

"Pa says there's no gold around here. But I think it's just hiding, waiting for me to dig it up. I think that the river washes it down from far away, where the river runs through canyons and valleys, and it just lands right here with us." Lola rolled the clump over in her grimy hands.

"Oh alright. Let's take a look. Go get me a little bucket of water so I can wash this off. You'll need that little steel hammer that I keep in the kitchen." Marianna watched the young girl scamper inside the house. She should have stopped encouraging this gold foolishness a long time ago.

Lola was by far the most unique child that Marianna had ever known. She said things about people she met that she could not possibly have known. She could track and find animals by what she said were the feelings they had. At ten years old, Lola at times sounded and acted like an adult of thirty and other times like the young girl she was.

Marianna washed the grime and dirt off the rocky chunk. Several strategic taps with the hammer split off three pieces. "Looks like iron pyrite. Are there more chunks like this one? We can get one of the small wood crates in the barn and you can start saving them. I've often thought about making a bracelet of those pretty pyrite pieces, but I don't know how to do it. Your pa will know for sure when he gets back and takes a look."

Lola pulled one more rock out of her pocket. It had dulled yellowish flecks embedded in the stone and it made Marianna gasp. "Yes! This is gold, honey! Do you remember where you found it?"

Lola smiled and nodded. "It's the first time I've ever found it. I don't know if there is any more out there." Marianna hugged her.

"You and Colton both like to dig in the dirt. Has he found anything interesting, honey?" The mother looked at the daughter's reaction.

"He likes to dig for those colored rocks. The ones with the little fires inside them." Lola turned the chunk over in her small hands.

Marianna frowned. "What colored rocks? How does fire get inside rocks?"

Lola shifted her weight to her other foot in exasperation. She frowned. "Well, not real fire inside the rock. It just looks that way when you look at the rocks. They're pretty."

Marianna grinned. "Well, go out to the barn and find one of those small wooden crates. Put it to the side with a sign on it for your rocks so it doesn't get tossed out. We'll have dad take a close look at your rocks when he comes home."

Lola stopped and turned around to look at her mother. "Pa won't be home for a long time."

Marianna said, "No, he will only be gone ten days at the most, honey."

The young girl turned and gazed towards the valley. "There will be snow on the ground when he comes home, ma. The ground is white when he comes home. He is going to go to a lot of places and see a lot of people before he comes home." Marianna opened her mouth to say something and then stopped as her mind raced.

Lola bounded down the steps. "I'll have Kelly help me dig for more gold." The ponytail swung as the girl ran down the yard.

Marianna's brow furrowed with an immense twitch. She unconsciously held her breath. Lola had to be wrong. Snow on the ground meant it would be winter before Nick came back. He couldn't be gone that long. Not unless something had stopped he or he was hurt. Marianna wiped her hands down the front of her skirt as if to cast off the thought but it nagged at her.

***

On Thursday, the four Stolters drove the carriage into town and bought supplies. Marianna left the children to chat with their friends and she slipped across the street. The creaking door brought up the doctor's head and he grinned. Marianna Stolter shrugged out of her coat and tried to smile. "Something's wrong. I don't normally feel like this." Doctor Collins asked her to sit up on the examining table.

"Well, let's figure out what the matter is here with you, Marianna." He frowned then. It was a troubling inspection to her eyes and ears.

"This cough won't stop. My chest feels like there is a belt around it getting tighter all the time." She put her hand over her heart.

The doctor listened again to her chest and then again on her back. "You've got a deep wheezing in your lungs. You are most likely spending too much time out in the cold weather." She nodded.

"My husband, Nick, has been gone two weeks. The wind is chilled but the sunshine is warm when we work outside. Since Nick has been gone, we've had three mares foal. I've spent some long days and nights out in the barn." Her eyes dropped to the floor and her shoulders hunched.

Doctor Collins wrote several sentences on the sheet of white paper. He took off his glasses and rubbed them with a soft white cloth. "You are to get yourself home, get into bed and drink plenty of water. Those children of yours are growing up, they are smart and they can share some of the work. You must rest, Marianna, or this wheezing will turn into something serious."

She glanced at the doctor and then looked away. Her forehead wrinkled up and her eyebrows twitched. She clasped her hands together tightly. The doctor put down his glasses and sat down on a short wooden stool in front of her.

"Nick tried to tell me that it was a simple ride to go get new stock. This was an old friend who had come asking for Nick's help." She coughed into a green bandanna painfully hard.

"Nick wouldn't answer my questions about the danger. He was evasive with me, trying to shield me from something he didn't want me to know."

The doctor nodded. "We are all guilty of doing that with our wives, my dear. I don't talk with my wife about the different maladies I see in my patients because I don't want her worrying about how they are healing."

Her brown eyes were watery and she wiped her nose. "He hasn't sent word yet. I don't know what he is going through. But what's worse, is that I don't want him to suddenly stop and race home because of me." She coughed several times. The doctor tried to calm her.

"I want you to remember that you have children to think of, Marianna. Regardless of what is going on with Nick, you must be strong for your children while he is gone. They depend on you. In years to come, they will leave, marry and have their own families and then it will be just you and Nick together." She nodded and wiped her eyes.

He said, "I want you to go over to the restaurant and get some hot soup in your belly before you ride all the way home. I'll be out on Tuesday to check on your condition. You go home, get into bed and get some rest. No working out in the barn. Let the kids do it. You rest. Understand?" She nodded.

At the Ridgewood water hole, Kelly saw her mother grip a hand to a heaving chest as her mother turned her head away to cough. Lola and Colton chatted between themselves and seemed to not notice. The daughter caught the mother's eye, who simply shook her head and urged the horses on towards home.

***

On Saturday, Marianna called Kelly, Lola and Colton into the big bedroom where she struggled to sit up. Kelly helped Marianna sit up with a couple of pillows behind her.

Kelly looked at her mother's pale drawn face. "Lola, in the attic, there is a big steamer trunk. Inside it are some things that I need to tell you three about. The first thing is the red metal box with the leather handle. Go get it and bring it down to me, please."

When Lola brought in the metal box, the three children climbed up alongside their mother as she opened it. She unwrapped a thin suede square of leather and held a single white pearl mounted in a gleaming silver ring.

"Kelly, this will be yours on your wedding day. It was my mother's. Something old." She handed it to Kelly who marveled at the small band.

Next, Marianna took out a cloth sack and opened it up. Dozens of blue, red and purple award ribbons felt out in a heap along with three small brass medals. "These are my ribbons from when I rode in competition." A cough overtook the frail form and they waited until she had caught her breath.

"One of you should be able to win as much as I did and then go on to win more, if you practice and keep the horses in good shape." Colton carefully laid out the first, second and third place ribbons. Marianna then lifted out five thick heavy envelopes and laid them alongside her on the covers.

"Two years after your father and I were married, our first child was born, Charles Ross Richardson. We called him Charlie. He became sick right before he was a year old and died from pneumonia." Marianna paused and took a sip of hot tea.

Kelly put her hand on Marianna's shoulder. "Ma, you should rest. This can't be good for you." Her mother nodded and smiled weakly.

"Just a few more minutes and then I'll get some sleep. This is important right now, honey." Marianna wiped her mouth and her eyes scanned form child to child.

"We were living at my parent's ranch, the Flint Hills Ranch, farther south towards Mexico. Charlie is buried there." For the next few minutes, Marianna tried to describe the wide blue eyes and the curly reddish-brown hair and how Charlie liked to coo and laugh. She dabbed her eyes several times.

She gently opened the first envelope and brought out a legal-looking document. "My father, Glen Richardson, your grandfather died six years ago. Kelly and Lola, you might remember him as you met him a few times. I received this certificate from the lawyer who handled the will. I am the sole heir to the ranch at Flint Hills." Marianna wiped her eyes again.

The frail woman opened the second envelope. She unfolded the large square of brown paper to show the children a pencil drawn image of the Flint Hills ranch house. "This is what it looked like then. I'm sure it's changed by now. Nobody has lived there for several years. The cattle and horses were sold off to pay debts and bills. My father told me that he had set up the account of the funds into the bank in Los Angeles."

Lola frowned as she drew one of the purple ribbons back and forth through her hands. "We have an older brother?"

Kelly put her hand on Lola's shoulder. "Yes, before we were born. But he's gone now, Lola."

Lola shrugged away and with a frown said, "How are we to live there without you and pa?"

Kelly blurted, "What?" Her mouth hung open and her eyes were wide.

Colton stood up. "What?"

Marianna was racked with a coughing spell and laid back to rest. "I want the three of you to understand what I'm saying now. So, listen to me carefully."

"Your pa and I bought this ranch, Windy Ridge Ranch, here in Yucca Valley. We don't own it outright yet. There is still five thousand dollars owing on it. Every month we pay eighty-five dollars to the man who we bought it from. Mr. Jessup over at the Yucca Valley bank collects the payment each month." She laid back and put her hand on her chest to catch her breath.

"I believe your pa will come back in another few days. But if he doesn't, I'll need you to ride into Yucca Valley and make that land payment on the ranch." She gasped as she tried to catch her breath.

Colton asked, "What day? I can do that, Ma."

"Thank you, honey. I thought you might like to see some of your friends in town when you ride in." Marianna opened the third envelope. When she spread it out, the children leaned closer to see little images of trees, rocks, a river, fences, and footprints.

Colton exclaimed, "It's a map!" Marianna smiled.

"Not just any map, honey. Look again. It's a treasure map." Kelly, Lola and Colton took turns pointing out landmarks and objects.

"That one looks like a flower, Ma. What does that mean?" Kelly frowned as she asked the question.

"My mother was a very good seamstress. She used to make fancy dresses and pretty skirts for ladies in the county and for a while had a little shop in Bradford. She didn't spend hardly any of the money she made from sewing. My father wouldn't let her and told her to keep it all for an emergency."

Lola asked, "This is a map where she buried money?" Marianna nodded.

"Yes, and I helped her. You see, my folks did not trust the banks there. I think there was a bank robbery where my father lost quite a bit of money. He bought a safe in Philadelphia and had it shipped to Flint Hills and built into his study. The deed to ranch was kept there as well as important ledger and record books. I can remember very clearly them talking about not trusting people at the bank."

"You see, my mother Anna-Marie, had been an independent woman with her own money when she met my father. She was used to having her own money and not relying on anyone, except maybe her parents. She always told me to have a secret stash of a few dollars for emergencies." Marianna patted the map with a smile.

"Every time we buried a small jar or a leather pouch, I wrote it down on this map. I think I remember the first time when I was about six, maybe seven and mother had made a game out of it." Marianna sipped the tea.

Kelly looked at her mother. "Nobody knows the money is buried there?" Marianna shook her head.

"The last jar I buried at Flint Hills was the week that I married your father. I was nineteen. It is old and faded but it still shows where the money was buried. But the ones my mother buried, well, I don't know where or how much money. There are over a dozen that have twenty or thirty dollars though." She took another sip of tea.

Kelly asked, "I don't understand why you didn't put it in the bank? Wouldn't it be safer there?"

Marianna nodded. "Mother didn't trust banks. She told me a story about when she was a little girl, a crooked banker that ran off with all the money that was in the bank. Her parents were left with only a few dollars that they had in the house." Marianna coughed again and wiped her eyes.

Lola leaned forward. "So, you have your own little buried treasures at Grandpa Glen's ranch. The you and Pa moved all the way to Windy Ridge and left them there. Don't you want to go dig them up and take them?"

Marianna shook her head. "No, honey. I'm too sick. I could not make that long ride like this. My mother had a heart condition that flared up from time to time that made her very tired. I had come in from riding one day and found her on the floor struggling to get up. Later that night, I was sitting with her and she squeezed my hand tightly and told me to not forget about the jars. She died in the night." The four of them were quiet.

A tear slid down Lola's cheek as she slid her small hand under Marianna's. Kelly's throat tightened as she watched as her sister blink back more tears.

Marianna cleared her throat. "You must take care of each other now. You are family and strong if you are together. Help is in those jars that I left back there so long ago. Don't forget about the jars. This map will help you find most of them. I'm sure that Mother buried more, but I don't know where they are," she said with a gravelly voice.

Colton looked confused. "Are you telling us we have to go to the Flint Hills Ranch?" He pointed to the picture of the house. Marianna reached for his small hand. She looked first at Kelly and then at Lola.

"Bad things happen to good people, my sweet children. You must understand that something bad might happen to your father and he can't come home. If this sickness takes me and I'm not with you anymore you have to be brave and have courage to help yourselves." She clenched a handkerchief while she coughed heavily.

After she caught her breath, she continued. "You won't be able to stay here on Windy Ridge because you won't have the money to make the land payment. Mr. Jessup will want his money and if you can't pay, you'll have to move out."

Lola jerked upright. "Move out to where? Oh, you mean to Flint Hills." Kelly and Colton had a surprised look.

"Yes, I own that ranch free and clear, and I have proof here in the certificate. Nobody can ever take that ranch from this family. Plus, there is money there. You just have to dig it up and find it." She leaned back on the pillows and closed her eyes for a moment.

Kelly said, "Flint Hills Ranch reminded you of Charlie and it hurt so bad that you and pa moved away?" Marianna nodded and wiped her eyes.

Marianna put her hand on the next envelope. "These are your birth certificates. When each one of you were born, I sent a form over to the courthouse in Los Angeles. I had a birth certificate made for each one of you. It is proof of who you are. You have to keep these safe, like I have by putting them away where they won't get harmed."

Lola tapped the last unopened envelope. "Are you going to open this last one, ma?"

"No, not today, honey. I hope I don't have to open that one for many years from now," she said with a hoarse voice.

"Kelly, please put this all back into the box. Lola, honey, if you would put the box back into the trunk in the attic, please? I need to get some sleep right now." Colton helped her pull away the big pillows so she could lay down.

After sunset, the children bundled up in quilts and sat out on the porch looking at the first stars in the darkening sky.

Kelly said, "Maybe she was so sick she didn't know what she was saying." Lola shook her head.

"No, ma told us the truth, even if we didn't want to hear it."

Colton said, "You think pa will come home soon?" Again, Lola shook her head. Kelly sat up a bit straighter.

"Well, if pa doesn't come home, at least we know what to do now." She put her arm around her brother and hugged him.

2 MRS. SHERMAN COMES TO HELP

She had grown pale and weaker overnight. The deep coughing racked her body and left her gasping for breath. She tried to sit up and read but it proved too much and she laid back on her side. The doctor had sent out one of the ladies from the church to help Marianna.

Lola, Colton and Kelly sat on the porch looking out at the valley. The sounds of pots and pans banging around and dishes being moved came from the kitchen.

As a young girl, Lydia McGuire had trained in Boston Hospital as a nurse's aide. A quick wit and curious eye had made her a doctor's favorite on rounds. That was where she met Thaddeus Sherman, a seminary university student who had contracted pneumonia. It was love at first sight. Thaddeus brought his blushing bride west twenty years prior and she blossomed to be the partner he had always wanted.

Just then the door opened and the gray curly haired Mrs. Sherman leaned out. "She's sleeping right now. If y'all will come in and sit down I'll put lunch on the table." It was a warm smile that greeted them. Kelly gestured toward the door and the children walked into the house.

Lola had put her right hand on her chest and rubbed back and forth slowly. "It feels like pa's leather belt it around your chest and it's being pulled tighter and tighter." Lola's voice was nearly a whisper as they sat down at the table.

"I feel so bad that I can't do anything for her." Colton squeezed Kelly's hand.

Kelly cleared her throat and took in a deep breath. "Mrs. Sherman will get the house in good order and make soup for her and us. We can't let Ma get up and try to do stuff. The doctor said she has to rest."

At the sound of the voice, Kelly stood up and went to the window, wiping off her mouth as she walked.

"There's a man on a horse coming up the driveway."

Mrs. Sherman held the dishcloth tightly with the look of alarm as she peered through the door. "Do you recognize him? Do you know who he is? I wasn't told there would be visitors."

Kelly put her hand on the woman's arm. "I think I know who it is, Ma'am. I'll go talk to him." The young girl walked out and stood on the top step. A tall, lanky man in gray jeans and a plaid shirt under a thick coat walked an Appaloosa into the yard.

"I'm Mike Johnston from Cave Junction. Is your pa around? I'm here to pick up a horse." The man dismounted and stood holding the reins.

Kelly smiled. This was the man who had bought the young filly Kelly had been training. Kelly walked down the steps and reached to shake the man's hand.

"Yes, sir. My pa isn't home right now, but your horse is ready. If you want to come on out to the barn, I know which filly is yours."

"Very good. Thank you, miss." He followed Kelly back down the driveway and out to the barn.

An hour later when Kelly walked back to the house, Lola and Colton were sitting on the bottom step. She jingled the coins in her hand and showed her siblings.

"He had paid half when he bought the horse and then paid the other half today for the training." Colton's eyes were wide.

Kelly put her hand on Colton's shoulder. "Keep this to yourselves. We don't want other folks knowing we have cash. We don't know who we can trust right now." Lola nodded.

"We'll talk to Ma later tonight and tell her the man came." Mrs. Sherman bustled onto the porch with a quick smile.

"Is everything alright? Who was that man?" Kelly noticed that Mrs. Sherman blinked very fast.

Kelly said, "That was Mr. Johnston from Cave Junction. He had bought a horse from my pa a couple of weeks ago. He came to take the horse home." The woman nodded.

"Is he still out there or did he leave already? I still have hot coffee and pie if he'd like a bite." Mrs. Sherman craned her short, thick neck trying to look down the drive.

"No, Ma'am. He left. Cave Junction is almost sixty miles northwest of here so he wanted to get up the road before he stopped for the night." Kelly smiled to Lola and Colton who smiled back at her. Then all of them smiled to Mrs. Sherman, who looked puzzled at the three children all smiling at the same time. She shook her head and walked back into the house.

"Have you always lived in Yucca Valley, Mrs. Sherman?"

"Oh no, honey. I was born and raised in Texas. A small town of Rio Linda. We used to laugh and say when the rodeo happened each year the size of the town doubled in size. I went up to the eighth grade there. My ma was Raylene Ringman and my pa, James Rosen, are buried there. My oldest brother now runs their farm."

"What kind of animals were on your farm?"

"Well, it wasn't a real farm like what is here in California. It was a fruit orchard of apples, pears and cherries. My pa kept hogs, too. And we had a milk cow and a couple of those all black steers with the horns."

"Black Angus."

"Yes, those. When I got big enough, my mother took me out of school so I could help with the fruit from the orchard. My ma had grown and nurtured a big blackberry patch that always had great big fat berries. My pa built some wooden frames for the berry canes to grow on and keep them up off the ground."

"I like berry jam."

"Yes, my ma used to sell almost every berry she grew. But sometimes she kept out enough to make a couple of jars of jam. It was delicious on fresh bread."

"When did you come to California? How did you end up here?"

"We were at a church social one Sunday and I met a boy from the next town over. It was William Sherman and I thought he was so handsome. We got to know each other and over the next few years we fell in love. We got married when we turned eighteen. He had been studying for the ministry and wanted to be a preacher."

"We were living with his folks when he heard about the pastor in Yucca

Valley getting ready to retire. He wrote a letter to the pastor asked if he could come to Yucca Valley to learn about being a pastor. So here we are."

"Why didn't Mr. Sherman stay in Texas and start his own flock. He could have built a nice church with you to help him."

Mrs. Sherman smiled. "We talked about that. But for twenty miles around his folks' place there already were four other churches. There just wasn't room for another church or another pastor. It was a big gamble, but it came out alright in the end."

"Do you ever go back to Texas to see your families? You must miss them."

"Yes, sometimes I do miss them. I had an older brother and sister and a younger brother. They all still live around Rio Linda. They have come out to visit me in the past. We have gone back there and I'm always glad to get back home."

"Do you have any children, Mrs. Sherman?"

"Yes, we have a son. He had gotten very good marks in school and we had wanted him to go back east to Chicago or New York to the university. He is a very bright boy. We were disappointed when he decided to go in with a couple of other boys from school up to the gold fields in northern California."

"There's no gold here. We've looked."

"No. I've heard other people say that there is no gold in Yucca Valley, too. I've listened to the stories about men digging narrow, deep holes in the mountains and dying in cave-ins. I can't imagine risking my life to dig rocks out of the ground."

"Our family raises and trains horses. Pa says we are pretty good at it."

"Well, if you are good at something and you enjoy doing it that is probably where you will happy in life."

"Do you know the other ranches around Yucca Valley?"

"Oh yes, of course. The Billingtons own Blue Valley Ranch. They planted several acres of blue grass seed and in the late fall it turns a pretty rust color. Let me see. The McGregors own the Flying J Ranch. There is this huge lake where Canadian Geese fly in every year on their way south each winter. And then there is Greystone Bluffs, but nobody lives there."

"What happened to the people who owned it?"

"Rutherford Stone married Emma Gray and they bought the ranch many years ago. They had six children. Mr. Stone wanted his children to grow up out in the country. Not like he did in the city. Mr. Stone bought and sold goods from all over the world and brought them in on freight wagons. I'm sure you have met those men who drive those big wagons pulled by those big horses."

"Ma always finds something to buy when Mr. Lucci comes by. This tablecloth came off Mr. Lucci's wagon."

"Well, Mr. Stone owned five of those freight wagons and hired men to drive them all around. It's a good business, I imagine."

"When the war started, Mr. Stone went to fight for the North and he was wounded badly in his leg. He limped and used a cane after that. That was when the bad luck started for Greystone Ranch."

"What bad luck?"

"A string of bad luck hit that family something horrible. He decided to take Emma and the children to the Orient on a tour and to see what he could buy, I guess. The ship hit something and it sank. One of the children drowned. Then once they got on land they all got sick. It was six months before they felt well.

"That's horrible."

"Once they were well enough to travel they came right back home to America. Except on the crossing, another ship of dastardly thieves set upon them and robbed everyone on board. They hid their money in their children's shoes."

"In the shoes?"

"Yes. Once they arrived in San Francisco they must have thought everything would be alright. But it wasn't. While they had been gone, part of their house at Greystone Ranch had burned down. Neighbors came and saved a small part, but everything was damaged. They had lost almost everything."

"That is bad."

"Two of the children were still sick. I heard a story that one of the children felt like there was snakes under their skin. The doctor ordered them into a sanitarium." She shivered.

"Ick."

"People said he looked like a different man when he came home from the Orient. Emma was friendly and smiling and very generous volunteering to help others. After they came home, she wouldn't look you in the eye and maybe came into town once in a blue moon. Maybe three times a year she'd come into town and then she'd go right back home."

Colton asked, "Did something happen to her?"

"We don't know. She took to using laudanum. She used a lot of it. Rutherford had been trying to repair one of those freight wagons in the barn on the ranch and it fell off the blocks and crushed his chest. Killed him. Emma didn't know for three days because she was out of her mind sipping laudanum."

Kelly cringed. "Those poor people."

"At Rutherford's funeral, she sat like a stone statue. No tears, no words. She just stared at the casket. You can imagine the talk it caused." The older woman wrung her hankie in her hands.

Lola asked, "What about the children? What happened to them?"

"The oldest boy and youngest girl had gone back to her sister's home in Illinois. We never saw them again. The younger girl and boy were the ones who were terribly sick and they had been put into a hospital in Los Angeles. We never saw them again either." Mrs. Sherman slowly shook her head and she cast her eyes down.

Lola's mouth hung open in shock. "There were six children? What about the last one?"

"Bobby Stone. One of Rutherford's brothers came out to the ranch and helped run it. There was some animosity between the Bobby and his uncle. On top of that, Emma got on a horse one day as if she was going out for a ride. She never came back. Just disappeared. That's what I heard."

Lola's eyes were big. "She disappeared? What do you mean?"

"Search parties went out looking for her. Folks said that she was out of her mind in grief over Rutherford. But I think she was out of her mind with laudanum." Mrs. Sherman nodded as if she had other hidden information.

"They never found her?" Kelly sat back and looked at the older woman.

"No. Bobby drank everything in sight. He was drunk all the time after that. They told some wild, outrageous stories about the trip to the Orient. Folks never believed them. They even went so far as to claim the people who came back weren't their ma and pa."

Lola nearly shrieked and clamped her hand over her mouth. "Oh, my gosh!"

"Nobody has lived at Greystone Ranch for over ten years that I know of. There's been no word about what happened to Bobby Stone. Nobody knows."

"That is so sad." Kelly looked at Lola who had wide eyes.

Mrs. Sherman nodded vigorously. "Oh, I know. Before he left on that trip to the Orient, there had been talk that Rutherford might enter politics and run for the governor's seat. People knew him. People trusted him. That was all gone after he came home from over wherever it was they went."

Kelly said, "My goodness." It was a shocked look on her face. Mrs. Sherman stood up and straightened her dress. She patted Lola's head.

"I'm going to go up and check on your ma, then I have to get home. I want to be home by dark. Mr. Sherman will think highwaymen stole me away if I'm not home tonight." The three children grinned as they watched Mrs. Sherman hurry into the house.

Kelly had saddled the gray mare and helped the portly Mrs. Sherman mount up. "I'll let the doctor know how she is doing. He'll be coming out tomorrow to check in on her. You keep her warm and resting." She waved her hand as the mare began to walk down the drive.

4 DOCTOR COLLINS EXAMINES MARIANNA

It was a little after ten the next morning when the creaking buggy of Doctor Collins rolled up the drive. In the bedroom, he held the small tin horn with extra care to Marianna's chest and listened. He grumbled something under his breath and then told her to sit up. He then listened again to her back.

"I don't like that wheezy rattle in your chest, Marianna. You've let yourself get run down and weak."

Marianna's eyes were half closed. "I'm just tired, Doctor. I need a good night's sleep and some soup."

The doctor raised his eyebrows and stared hard at the sick woman. "No. If we were in a bigger city, I would admit you to the hospital and keep you there until you were well again."

Kelly had listened to the cough become more frequent and longer over the last week. She knew that her mother had caught cold but was not aware of how serious it was.

"Nonsense. Kelly, Lola and Colton are a big help to me. I'll be good as new in a few days." Again, the strained cough.

The doctor made a sweeping gesture to the room. "Children should not be tending to sick adults. I'm going to send a couple of folks over to help you. You are not to go outside in the cold air. You are to rest."

Lola hugged her legs as she sat up on top of the dresser chest. Colton sat in the window seat and watched the doctor listening to the stern tone. Kelly blinked several times and took in a deep breath as the doctor caught her eye.

"Kelly, your mother is not to go outside or stand on her feet longer than five minutes. The liquid accumulating in her lungs is keeping her from breathing. It's making her weak." His brows furrowed together and the girl visibly flinched.

"I understand, Doctor. We'll keep her down and warm and make her rest." The gray-haired man with the round spectacles gathered up his gear into the brown leather satchel. Lola went to sit beside Marianna and Kelly took the physician downstairs followed by Colton.

He stopped on the porch and turned to look at the two children. "This is serious. Her life is in danger and she's refusing to admit it."

Colton's voice seemed small. "One of us stays with her all the time. We make sure the house is warm. She sleeps a lot." Kelly hugged her brother.

"Did you already send word do your pa?"

"We don't know where he is at. We don't know how to find him. We don't have anyone to help us find him." Kelly gave the doctor a quick run-down of Nick leaving with Ginger Whelihan to get work. Kelly frowned when the doctor rubbed his face vigorously at the sound of Whelihan's name.

"I'm going to send out either Mrs. Sherman or Mrs. Walker to help with the laundering and cooking the meals. Kelly, as I understand it, you and Colton are taking care of the horses and livestock?" Kelly nodded.

"I'm going to order supplies from the general store for the house and send them out. People understand that you can't pay right now because your Pa is away and with your ma sick, well, they'll just have to wait."

The doctor rubbed his face and leaned against the tie rail. His eyes found Kelly and he cleared his throat.

"Kelly, you should know a couple of things now because you are the oldest and you have been put in charge while your mother is ill. Sit down on the step here." He motioned for them to sit and then perched on the step.

The gray eyes looked at the girl. "Your father told you he is an old friend of Mr. Whelihan?" Kelly nodded.

"Mr. Whelihan's reputation precedes him."

The brow frowned. "What do you mean?"

The doctor cleared his throat again and wrung his leather gloves in his hands. "In the last few years, Mr. Whelihan has been linked to several robberies over in Merced. Folks have whispered about him being connected with cattle rustling in Arizona and Texas. There's no proof, but folks say others have seen him do things that were not exactly to the law."

Kelly's mouth fell open. "Are you saying that Mr. Whelihan has taken my pa away to do something against the law?"

The doctor shook the grayish mop of curly hair. "No. Your ma told me that Mr. Whelihan came to ask for help and your pa was his good friend years ago. Your pa felt obliged to help. But I can't say what that help was for."

Kelly and Colton looked at each other with wide eyes. "Was Mr. Wheli-han running from the law when he came to get my pa?" The doctor stood up and dusted off his black slacks. He shook his head.

"Not to my knowledge, my dear. But he is a known card sharp and confidence man. He is lightning fast with his Colts and often takes work as a bounty hunter for other criminals. I've heard stories that he even has worked as a bounty hunter for the Texas Rangers."

The doctor tied his satchel to the saddle straps and mounted up. "I'll be back day after tomorrow to check on her. If she gets worse, one of you ride for town and I'll run out here. Understand me?" Both Kelly and Colton nodded vigorously.

They watched him ride down the tree lined drive and disappear around the bend. "How would Pa not know those things about Mr. Whelihan, Kelly? He was his friend," asked Colton.

"They hadn't seen each other in a long time. Pa doesn't tell us all about all the people he meets and talks with, honey. Maybe Mr. Whelihan has visited Yucca Valley without coming out to the ranch to see Pa. Maybe Pa went into town to meet him. I don't know."

Colton frowned. "Do you remember when Mr. Whelihan first came to the house last week? Lola stood back from him and wouldn't shake his hand. She didn't like him then. She said something was wrong about him."

Kelly nodded. "I remember, honey. There's nothing we can do. Pa left with him and said he'll come home in a few days. Come on in the house. I want a slice of pie." Colton nodded and they walked up the porch steps.

***

Marianna pulled her long robe about her tighter as she walked into the kitchen. "The doctor told you to rest in bed and stay warm." Kelly got up from reading the book on the sofa.

"I wish your father would send word of how he is and where he is." She wiped tears away. "Kelly, I worry that he's been thrown from his horse, broken his leg, someone tried to steal the stock and he's been shot." Her voice trailed off.

"Ma, do you want a cup of tea or a cup of coffee? I've got hot water there in the kettle."

"Coffee, honey. Please." She sat down in the wooden chair at the kitchen table, trying to get her breath.

"It's my lungs, honey. I can't seem to cough the icky good out of them. It's getting worse, I can feel it. Monday wasn't too bad. I felt sort of dizzy when I got home but I laid down and felt better that night. Tuesday, I was scared because it hurt to breath and I couldn't catch my breath."

Kelly spooned ground coffee into the kettle and stirred it. She put two white mugs on the table.

"I am so sick of being in this pain all the time. I can't think clearly. I feel as weak as a newborn kitten." She coughed into the cloth and watched

Kelly pour the steaming black coffee into the mug.

"Kelly, the worst thing is that I don't know what is going on with your father. I don't know if he is sick or hurt and laying out in the middle of land where no one will find him. I don't know if he made it there and is now coming home." She choked and wiped her eyes.

Kelly sat down next to Marianna and laid a hand on her arm. "The mare that foaled last Saturday is doing very well. The colt is scampering around like a bumblebee. They get out in the corral during the day and I lock them in at night. I wrote everything down in the log." Marianna nodded and sipped the coffee.

"We're going to do the laundry tomorrow, early in the morning. Lola will give me a hand with that and I'll get the things up onto the clothesline so they can dry during the day." Kelly bit her bottom lip.

"Pa is good with his gun and he doesn't do risky things. He can bring back a couple of head for new stock alone without any worries. He'll come home, Ma. He always does." She watched her mother drink a gulp of coffee.

"Where are Lola and Colton?" Marianna looked around the room.

"They're outside digging the dirt or looking for rocks. I don't know. Lola sat with you earlier while you slept. I thought she was reading but she was watching you. She's very sensitive to you being sick." Marianna smiled weakly.

"Would you build up the fire in the fireplace, honey? I want to rest on the sofa for a while." Kelly went out to the porch and brought in three big chunks of wood. She positioned those into the fireplace and soon they started to crackle.

Kelly helped Marianna wrap up in a quilt and angled the sofa towards the fire. Her mother fell asleep quickly. Kelly sat down on the floor and leaned back against the sofa. She watched the flames licking at the wood and listened to the crackle of the embers.

It was at that moment that she realized that she had never seen her mother sick with more than a cough and runny nose. Her mother had always been able to shake off illness and get back to her day to day life. But this was different. Kelly leaned closer and could hear the gurgling breaths as her pale mother struggled to breathe. Kelly tensed up and felt helpless.

5 ANOTHER VISIT FROM MRS. SHERMAN

It was just after breakfast, about eight thirty when they heard the buggy coming up the drive.

"Mrs. Sherman is coming and it looks like she brought Mr. Sherman. I think that is him," Lola stepped inside the front door and alerted Kelly. The two girls walked out onto the porch.

"Hello Mrs. Sherman. How are you?"

"I'm doing very well. I brought my helper, Mr. Sherman, with me today so we can get more things done." She got down out of the buggy and smoothed down her dress. Mr. Sherman pulled on his work gloves.

"Howdy, Miss Stolter. How is your ma doing? We've been worrying about her." His bushy black eyebrows wiggled and bounded when he talked. Along with serving as the Yucca Valley minister, Sherman built and sold wood furniture in his store in Yucca Valley.

"She's resting right now in her bedroom. It's like herding cats to keep her in bed, though. It pains me to see her like this," Kelly smiled.

Mrs. Sherman beckoned to Lola. "Miss Lola, if you'll help me carry this food into the house, please. I'll be making a pot of soup and I brought a small ham and potatoes for your dinner." Lola ran down the stairs and over to the buggy.

Kelly called out. "Mr. Sherman, I'll help you unhook your hook and turn him out in the pasture."

"Much obliged, miss." After Lola and Mrs. Sherman took the pots out, Kelly led the gelding over to the barn. She guessed the animal was twelve, maybe thirteen years old and still strong enough to pull the light buggy.

It took an hour to heat the water for the laundry on the outside fire. They washed all the bed linens and everyone's clothes. Kelly and Lola peeled potatoes and carrots for the soup. Mrs. Sherman baked two loaves of bread.

Lola watched Mrs. Sherman form the loaves and use butter to grease the pans. "Mrs. Sherman, at the bakery in Yucca Valley, they have a chocolate cake that we really like. Kelly and I want to learn how to make that cake. Do you know how? Can you teach us?" The older woman listened and then smiled.

"I love that cake, too! And you know, it is just as delicious without the frosting as it is with it." Mrs. Sherman clasped her hands together.

"Kelly, if you'll get a pen and paper, you can write this cake recipe down. I'll tell you how I do this. It may not be just exactly like the one in the bakery, but I like it just the same." For the next hour, the girls listened, watched and wrote down all the details about Mrs. Sherman's cake.

"The flour that you have here is good for bread and cookies. But you need a finely ground flour for the fluffy in cakes like the bakery. The cocoa at the general store is good, but there is no sugar in it. You should add in what's called powdered sugar. It's what the bakeries use for all their fancy frostings. Using a mortar and pestle, you can grind up sugar really fine until you get like a powder. I know, it takes forever." She laughed and dragged the back of her hand over her forehead, leaving a white smudge.

Colton and Mr. Sherman chopped and stacked a half cord of firewood. Together, they got the weeds cut down in the garden patch. Colton helped steady one of the barn side doors so Mr. Sherman could reset the screws in the hinge. They kicked the dirt off their boots on the porch and came into the kitchen.

"That is a good looking chestnut colt with the white stockings out there in the barn, Miss Kelly. I know a young lady up at Big Tree who has been looking for pretty colt like that. Would you mind if I sent word up? She might want to come give a look." Mrs. Sherman poured a hot mug of coffee for her husband.

"That would be right kind of you, Mr. Sherman. That is a nicely marked colt and we're hoping that he turns into a good-natured yearling. Go ahead and give that young lady our address and have her send a letter," Kelly smiled.

Lola came back into the kitchen from checking on her mother. "She doesn't have much of an appetite, Mrs. Sherman. She said a bowl of your soup would be good, though. I'll take it into her when it's ready.

"You are such a good girl, Lola. Hang on just one second and I'll get a small bowl of soup and a slice of warm bread ready." The woman bustled about getting a tray ready. Lola grinned.

At three o'clock they all washed up and sat down to a ham dinner with sweet potatoes and fresh bread. "Mrs. Sherman, your ham is sweet and spicy. How do you make the sweet honey glaze for it?" Colton shoved a big chunk into his mouth and chewed happily.

"I use a specialty spice I buy when I'm in Los Angeles. It's called cloves and I buy at this little spice shop over there. We went out to dinner a few years back and I was so impressed with the ham dinner I had, that I asked them how they did it. The chef came out and told me how he crushes up this spice and it makes the ham so good." She smiled and took another bite.

Lola said, "It's delicious. We'll have to get some of those cloves spice." Kelly and Colton both nodded.

After the buggy had been loaded and the gelding hitched up, the three children watched Mr. and Mrs. Sherman climb in and sit down.

"We cannot thank you enough for coming out to help us. We very much appreciate you putting aside time for us. We could not ask for better neighbors than you, Mr. and Mrs. Sherman."

***

Doctor Collins held his breath and listened to her lungs and heart. "Yes, it is pneumonia in your lungs. Three days ago, I had hoped it was just a deep chest cold. But it is pneumonia. That gurgling feeling that you can't cough up, that is the pneumonia. It is dangerous because the air cannot get inside the lung because the fluid is there."

Marianna wiped her eyes and said, "Yes, it hurts to breathe and I can't take a deep breath."

The doctor listened again to her chest. "Your heart is beating faster than it should because it is trying to get rid of the infection. Don't get up out of bed unless the house is on fire. Only if it is absolutely necessary. You must get as much sleep as you can. That is when the body heals itself."

Marianna said, "I've been in bed and resting, but I just feel so exhausted and tired all the time. I wake in the night because my chest hurts. I can't stand up for more than a minute because I feel so weak."

He had a grim look. "When you cough, it is the body's way of trying to force out the infection. Keep a soft cloth handy and cough into the cloth. That will keep it from spreading to the children. I can arrange to have you moved into the medical suite in my office, if you would prefer. This is very serious, Marianna."

"No, I want to stay home. The children can care for me. I'll be better little by little. I just need to rest."

"Have you been eating as normal?"

"No, I've lost most of my appetite. I have been sipping vegetable soup. I've had water and some apple juice. There is nothing I want to eat."

Doctor Collins frowned and scribbled another note on the paper. "You will need beef broth and chick broth. I'll send over two pots this afternoon. You still need to eat, but the broth will give you nourishment until you can sit up at the table."

Marianna asked, "I don't understand why I haven't healed and felt better. Usually I can get up and get everything done around the house. Now I lay here, doing nothing and shiver with cold or fan myself because I am so hot."

It was a stern voice. "Marianna, you must stay warm. Don't get chilled. Fresh air is alright, but no wide-open windows. I want your bed linens changed so you rest in a clean bed. Have the children boil those linens to clean them with soap outside away from the house. Don't take any chances."

In the living room, he sat down at the table and made three lists, one for each child. "Kelly, I want you to ride back into town with me. I'm sending out soups and broths for your mother. Mrs. Morgan at the restaurant will give you a bundle of things you'll need to make more."

"Lola, I want you to make sure she drinks water and keeps sipping apple juice. She must not suffer because she isn't getting enough water. Can you do that for me, please?" Lola nodded.

Doctor Collins looked at the young boy. "Colton, you might have the most important job to do for your mother. She does have to rest and sleep. The urge in her is strong to get up and work in the house. You'll have to tell her about all the small work you children are doing to keep the house tidy and all the chores done." Colton nodded.

The doctor wiped his face. "Get one of your books and read to her. Tell her small stories that she can listen to you. The three of you can sing to her but only for half an hour or so. Don't wear her out. A person who is sick in bed wants to get better and get up. She has to rest." All three children nodded. The doctor handed the sheets to them and they read silently.

He said, "This is Tuesday. I'll be back on Friday to check on your mother. Understand?"

Kelly said, "We've felt kind of helpless to do anything for her. Yes, Doctor Collins. Thank you for coming out."

6 ONE SOLD FILLY

It was a cool, clear day in the small country town of Yucca Valley. Kelly had come to town for supplies and was in a hurry to get back home, but the small boy sitting on the bench in front of the store busily licking a candy on a stick caught her eye. She smiled. A shaggy coated dog under the porch chewed on something between his paws.

"Kelly! Kelly Stolter!"

She turned around to see who was yelling for her. It was Georgie running towards her in that long stride lope. He had a big grin on his face.

"I was hoping I would catch you."

"Hey Georgie. What's the matter?" He shook his head. At fifteen, he was six feet tall with brownish red curly hair, light green eyes and broad across the shoulders.

"Do you still have that black and white filly for sale? There's a lady over at the hotel asking about horses for sale." He blinked a couple of times and stood up straight.

Kelly sat down on the wooden porch of the general store. "Yes, we still have her. I'd like to get another week with her though. She's a feisty horse but strong and attentive."

Georgie scratched his head and shifted his weight. "How much do you want for her? I know your pa don't sell his horses cheap." Kelly smiled as she pulled off her gloves.

"Pa was asking $45 for her. She comes with all the riding gear and we'll put a one year guarantee on her for cutting. Do you want me to wait here while you go tell the lady?"

Georgie's eyes opened wide and his mouth dropped open about the same time. "Oh, my goodness. Yes, if you'll stay here, I'll run over and let her know. She may want to come talk to you."

"I'm headed out to the ranch, if she wants to come along. I can saddle up that filly and put her through the paces, if she wants," said Kelly. A big forelock of Georgie's dangled down over his forehead making him tug at it on and off. He nodded with a quick smile and then turned and took off running down the street. Kelly grinned as she watched him.

***

The scrape of a boot made Kelly turn around. "Hello, I'm Rebecca Hunt." The woman wore tan slacks with short boots and a green knitted pull over sweater. Her short brown curly hair was pulled back in a ponytail. Georgie waved and trotted back across the street to the station.

"Hello Miss Hunt. I'm Kelly Stolter. I understand you are looking for a filly." Kelly guessed that the young woman might be in her early twenties.

Rebecca gestured to the porch. "Please sit down, Miss Stolter. It feels like I've been on my feet for a week." The two young women sat down on the rough plank bench.

Rebecca said, "My family run beef up in the Sacramento Valley. I've been looking for a cutting horse for a while. It seems like all the good ones are down here in the southern part of the state." Kelly nodded.

"The trouble I've been having is I want to find a horse that has been trained by a woman. It will be my horse alone and I don't plan on anyone else riding it." She smiled brightly.

Kelly nodded. "The filly we have for sale is a little over two years old. She's mainly black with three white stockings and a white mark on her chest. I've put her against calves and steers and she's proven that she can think to cut."

Rebecca raised her eyebrows and said, "I'm glad to hear that."

"About six months ago, we took her down to San Miguel to work her on sheep. That is about thirty miles to the southeast. Pa knows the ranch owner and he felt it was necessary for her training to work the sheep. The first day it took about an hour for her to calm down and start working. I think those white fluffy critters got the better of her." Kelly laughed.

Rebecca giggled. "Yes, you never know when you'll have to herd reindeer or cats!" Both girls laughed out loud.

Kelly said, "We're asking $45 for the filly, complete with gear. If you have time, the ranch is six miles out east of here. I would be happy to saddle her up and show you what she can do."

"I was hoping I could see her. If you don't mind waiting, I need to go tell my family where I'm going. Don't be surprised if they want to tag along," she said with a grin.

Kelly stood up and smiled. "They are very welcome to come out with us." She watched Rebecca run across the town square and up the steps to the saloon. A few minutes later, she came walking out followed by an older man and another boy.

"Kelly Stolter, this is my father, Carlton Hunt and this is my brother, Kody Hunt." The man's handshake was firm and his bluish gray eyes crinkled up at the corner. The younger Mr. Hunt wore dusty black jeans, a long sleeved white shirt under a cloth suit jacket. He touched the brim of his hat and nodded his head.

"Miss Stolter, pleased to make your acquaintance. My daughter says that you have a filly she'd like to look at. We'd like to come along, if it is no bother." He inclined his head forward to ask the question.

Kelly smiled and nodded. "Please do. It's always prudent to have another set of eyes looking over a horse when you are looking to buy. My horse is in the corral at the stables."

They had been trotting for about half an hour. Carlton Hunt made a brief wave towards the valley. "Miss Stolter, this is your father's ranch?"

"Yes. My father and mother bought it fifteen years ago right before I was born. My father has been breeding, raising and training cutting horses for over twenty years. He used to ride in rodeo competition. That's how he met my mother. She beat him for the blue ribbon." They all laughed.

"Nick Stolter is your father?"

"Yes, sir. Do you know him? He is away right now on a stock buying trip in Phoenix." Kelly looked inquisitive to the older man.

"I believe your mother might have been the only one to beat him in competition. I know my younger brother got beat three times by a Stolter up in Reno and twice in Denver." He raised his eyebrows.

"Yes, that was most likely my father. I've never had the desire to compete. I pay more attention to the breeding lines and temperament of the animals," she said. Out of the corner of her eye, she saw Mr. Hunt nod to Rebecca.

When Kelly trotted up the driveway, Colton and Lola walked out onto the porch and down the steps.

Kelly smiled and gestured toward her siblings. "Mr. Hunt, this is my sister, Lola and my brother, Colton. My mother is not feeling well lately and she's most likely resting."

"Good afternoon, Mr. Hunt. Welcome to Windy Ridge," Lola called out. Mr. Hunt touched the brim of his hat in greeting.

"Lola, untie my saddle bags and take them in the house. If you would put on water for coffee, we'll be back in a few minutes. I'm going to show Mr. Hunt the black filly." The younger girl pulled the leather ties and handed the first set of bags to Colton. Lola took the heavier set to the house.

Kelly nodded to Mr. Hunt. "If you'll follow me down to the barn, we can water the horses down there." They followed Kelly down a slight incline to the east.

For the next forty minutes, Kelly put the filly through her paces. Kelly dismounted and offered the reins to Rebecca who lightly climbed into the saddle. While Rebecca rode, Kelly explained about the pedigree, the gear and the guarantee. A smiling Rebecca got down and wiped off her jeans.

"Pa, she is exactly what I want. I barely touch her neck with the reins and she turns. She backs quickly and pivots just right." Rebecca nodded and patted the horse's neck.

"It's a bit unusual to offer a guarantee on a cutting horse, isn't it?" Kody Hunt sounded skeptical.

Kelly smiled. "Not for us. We'll take back any of our horses that can't do the job. They are one hundred percent healthy and in top shape when they leave our gate. If you take good care of them, they will be good horses."

Kelly watched as Mr. Hunt ran his hands over the filly, lifted her feet and looked at her teeth. "She is a nice, strong horse. Young, though."

Kelly leaned on the rail. "Several of our horses have gone to Texas and Louisiana. There are a couple of big ranches down there that have our stock. But to tell you honestly, if we don't sell her, it won't break my heart!"

Mr. Hunt looked over the filly, then looked at Rebecca and smiled to Kelly. "Would you give us a minute to discuss this, Miss Stolter?"

Kelly gestured to towards the house. "Yes, of course. I need to go see to my mother for a few minutes. Please come up to the house when you are ready."

When Kelly got to the house, she was surprised to find Marianna dressed and sitting on the bench. She coughed twice into a handkerchief.

"Lola said you were trying to sell the black filly. How much did you tell them she was?" Marianna nodded as she listened to Kelly talk about how Georgie had caught her in town.

Twenty minutes later the three Hunts walked up to the house where Kelly sat chatting with Lola and Colton. Marianna stood up and smiled.

"Good afternoon, Mr. Hunt. I am Marianna Stolter." They all shook hands.

"So, what do you think of our filly?"

Mr. Hunt put his boot on the bottom rail of the porch and smiled. "Mrs. Stolter, you've sold your filly. Seems that my darling daughter has fallen in love with a horse." He chuckled.

"Can you make out a bill of sale on the horse and we'd like to take her with us, if it is convenient?" Kody Hunt smiled at his beaming sister.

"Lola would you bring out the coffee cups and the coffee, please? Kelly, if you will go get the ledger and the papers." Marianna gestured for the Hunts to be seated.

An hour later, Kelly stood with her arm around her mother's waist. Marianna smiled and waved as the black filly trotted behind Rebecca Hunt down the driveway.

"Kelly, your father is going to have heart palpitations when he finds out how much you sold that filly for. He's never asked that much for a horse, no matter how good they were!" Kelly grinned and helped her mother back into the living room where she took off the coat.

"I didn't want to sell her. I had this idea of training her up in time for the rodeo in September. I was thinking that I'd put my blue ribbon next to yours and pa's." Marianna started to laugh, but her cough took over. Kelly helped her back into the bedroom where she took off her clothes and got back into bed.

***

The gray dawn of the next morning brought agony. The tears sliding down Kelly's cheeks would not stop. She held her mother's cold, still hand in her own and stared at the slender fingers. The dark lashed eyes were closed; the skin pale. Kelly motioned for Colton to slide up alongside their mother.

"I have to ride into town and get the sheriff and the doctor. I know there's some sort of paper the doctor needs to fill out." Kelly looked at the red-eyed Lola and then stepped to the doorway. Still a young woman at thirty-six, Marianna Richardson Stolter lay on the bed, a victim of the rattling wheeze of pneumonia.

Kelly could not remember the temperature, or if there were birds, or if anyone else passed her on the road. It was as if she was in a smoky haze. The sheriff tried to get her to sit down while he sent for Doctor Collins. As she and the doctor galloped back to Windy Ridge Ranch, Kelly's vision blurred with tears that just wouldn't stop.

The doctor came downstairs to where the children sat around the table. He wiped his face off with his handkerchief and sat down.

"I cannot tell you how sorry I am. I had hoped she would regain her strength and health," he said in a strained voice.

"I'll fill out the paperwork once I get back to my office. Did you want to bury her here, Kelly, or in the Yucca Valley cemetery? It's a damn shame your Pa ain't here to make these decisions for you kids."

Kelly rubbed her eyes, sniffled, and then took in a deep breath. She looked through the open door to the porch were the sheriff stood with his hat in his hand. She stood up and went outside. Colton and Lola followed.

"We don't own this land, Sheriff. Pa was buying it, but we don't own it.

I don't want her buried where we might not be at, so take her into Yucca Valley and we'll bury her there." Kelly turned, as hot salty tears streamed down her cheeks. She let herself be distracted by two crows arguing somewhere overhead in the old cottonwood branches.

"Sheriff, we don't even know where to start looking for my Pa. We don't know where he went or what he was going to do. You know more about this sort of thing than we do. We're just kids," she said as her voice started to break. She could feel his strong hand grip her shoulder.

"Would you notify the people who should be notified? Put the word out that my mother has died and we need Pa back home quick as possible, please?"

"I already did that, Kelly. I sent word to Santa Fe, San Francisco, Denver, Chicago and New York. When I get back to the office, I'll send word on to Dodge City, Dallas and New Orleans. If he is in trouble or locked up, we'll find him, honey." The doctor released his grip on her shoulder and took out his handkerchief to rub his eyes.

The next day the three Stolter children stood next to the freshly dug grave and watched the long, wooden box be lowered slowly down into the ground. People walked past and murmured condolences.

Kelly whispered, "Lola, tell her goodbye and that we love her." The young girl slid her hand into her sister's.

"I did, Kel. She knows. She's sorry she cannot be here with us. But she said we will be alright." Lola rubbed her eyes and sniffled.

Colton said, "I'm not ready to go. I want to stay here with her for a while." Kelly looked at the young boy and then gestured to a nearby tree.

"Alright. Let's get comfortable. Everything else can wait," she said with a catch in her voice. Kelly gave permission for the dirt to fill in.

They walked the horses over the entire thirteen-mile distance back to the ranch. The house was cold and dark when they entered. Colton and Lola started a fire in the hearth while Kelly heated water on the stove. Kelly warmed up the beef and gravy dish that was sent back with them and they silently stared into space while they ate.

Kelly felt powerless to stop the jagged, twisting knife slashing through her heart. Life would never be the same again. In the dark, the three of them curled up together in Marianna's bed. The faithful lab, Dusty, nestled in on the foot of the bed as their sentinel against the night. Slowly, they drifted off to sleep.

7 LETTER FROM NICK'S FAMILY

"Kelly, wake up!" Lola stood next to the bed as her sister sat up and rubbed her sleepy eyes.

"What? What's wrong?"

"Nothing's wrong. In the mailbox, there was a letter from New Orleans. It must have come yesterday while we were town. It's from Pa's family, isn't it?"

Kelly looked at the envelope. Sarah Stolter Michaelson. Pa's sister.

"Aunt Sarah. She doesn't know Ma died and that we don't know where Pa is at." Kelly threw back the covers and frowned at the dancing dust mites in the streaming sunlight. Kelly looked at Lola and Colton.

"What time is it? You two eat? How long you been up?" Lola looked at Colton and nodded towards the kitchen.

"There's eggs and taters still warm on the stove. There's a little gravy from last night that's good with that loaf of bread from Mrs. Johnson." Lola got a plate and began dishing up food while Kelly sat down at the table.

**

Dear Nick and Marianna,

I hope my letter finds you and your family well. I do miss you so.

I'm happy to hear about how well the horse business is doing. I do love to ride and get out in the fresh air.

**

Kelly read on silently for a few minutes. "She says that everybody is doing well. They had eleven new calves last month and three of the sows are due to have piglets. I'm sure Pa knows these people she talks about, but I don't know them." Lola started heating water for coffee and then sat down next to Kelly.

"There's nothing any of Pa's kin can do for us all the way from New Orleans. It would take them a week just to get here on the train." Kelly chewed on the savory potatoes.

She said, "I'll have to write back and tell them what has happened. I fear that there will be this rush of concerned adults coming to the ranch trying to do something for us. We don't need that right now."

Colton looked up. "What do we need? We have chores we have to do. We have things we can do to pass the time. The real thing we have to do is wait for pa to come home."

Kelly looked off in the distance. "If we tell them what happened, they'll come out here. I don't want them here. So, I say we don't tell them."

"Isn't that the same as lying to them?" Colton asked. Big brown eyes looked from sister to sister.

Lola asked, "How long does it take for a letter to get there?" Kelly dumped coffee into the boiling water and then picked up the envelope.

"The letter is dated the twentieth. Today is the fifth. That's fifteen days. If we write today, we'll have to ride into Yucca Valley to get it on the stage tomorrow. It will get to New Orleans on the twentieth of next month. We could write it like it was the day before ma died."

Colton said, "So we write that pa is off on a trip? Which he is on a trip, so it's the truth. And we just don't say anything about ma. It's not the same as telling a lie, it's more like we just don't tell them everything." Kelly nodded.

Colton stood up. "I'll ride into Yucca Valley for the stage after I'm done with the chickens. I'll need money for the postage. Maybe there's cake in the restaurant. If there is, I'll need money for that, too. Okay?"

Kelly nodded as she poured a steaming cup of black liquid. "I don't want to ride into town. I don't want to see people look at me and feel sorry for me. Lola, do you want to go?" The younger girl shook her head.

"People have hugged me enough to last a year. I don't want any more of that. Colton can ride alone. Or take Dusty." Kelly nodded and took a sip.

"I'll start writing. It should be ready in about an hour. The stage runs at three o'clock so we have plenty of time. I just want it done and over with." Kelly forked in another mouthful of her breakfast and chewed. Colton pulled on his coat and headed out the door with a bucket. Lola shook her head and went to her room.

***

Colton had ridden out to Yucca Valley an hour earlier with the letter. Kelly dragged the small cart out to the wood stack and was loading wood chunks when Lola scampered around the side of the barn.

"There's a stranger coming." Kelly straightened up and looked toward the driveway. She and Lola walked toward the house as a rider appeared.

"Halloo there! Anybody home?" The rider had a full, bushy brown beard and was wearing a torn and patched jacket, dirty black jeans and boots with run-down heels.

Kelly fussed with her leather gloves. "Good afternoon, mister."

"Hello miss. My name is Vern Stanton. I'm a friend of your pa's. Well, at least I think I'm still a friend of his. Is he here?"

"No, we expect him home this afternoon." Lola stepped to the left of Kelly to look at the man.

"I heard about the passing of your ma. My condolences." He dismounted, took off his hat and dragged the back of his glove over his mouth.

Kelly said, "Thank you, mister."

"Here's the thing. I've been meaning to come by and pay your pa for the ten dollars I borrowed off him awhile back. I'm headed for Louisiana and I don't plan on being back this way for quite some time. Maybe never."

Lola took a step forward and stared at the man. "If you don't mind me asking, mister, why did you borrow money from my pa?"

The gruff man seemed taken aback at the question. "Well, I'm ashamed to say that the sheriff fined me ten dollars for trespassing. I stayed a few days in a barn on the other side of Yucca Valley. I borrowed the money from Nick to pay the fine. I told him I'd pay him, but I ain't had any work." The man gripped the edge of his hat, dug his heel into the dirt and looked at the ground.

Kelly started to speak, but Lola reached out her hand and put it on her sister's arm. "Where was this barn at, Mr. Stanton?" Kelly looked at her sister and then at Stanton.

"I thought it was abandoned because most of the house had burned down. The garden was all overgrown. The barn was still standing and pretty weather tight so I stuffed some old hay into some canvas and made a bed. I'd been there four days when the sheriff found me." Lola listened for a moment and stared hard at the man. He started to shift from foot to foot.

Kelly asked, "Did the sheriff tell you the name of the land you were on?"

Stanton rubbed his forehead. "He said it was Grey Rocks or Grey Bluff, something like that."

Lola said, "Greystone Bluffs Ranch."

"Yeah, that's it. Why did you ask, miss?" Lola shook her head and turned away, rubbing her eyes as if in a sudden pain.

Kelly said, "It might be a long wait for my pa to get home, Mr. Stanton. Or you could give the money to me and be on your way. It's your choice." The man dug a hand into a jeans pocket and brought out several coins. He held them out to Kelly who stepped forward and reached for them.

"I'll be moving on. I don't want to disturb you young 'uns any more. It's mighty hard to deal with someone dying. You tell your pa thanks for me, will you? And I am sure sorry for your loss." Stanton was quick to mount up, he touched the brim of his hat and turned his horse.

Kelly stood and watched until the man rode out of sight on the road headed west. "That was an odd man." Lola shook her head.

"He didn't owe pa any money. He felt bad for us because ma died. His ma died when he was young and he felt bad for us. He remembers that pain, Kelly." Lola raised her eyebrows and shrugged as she took in a deep breath.

"He didn't have anything to give us to show the respect he had for Ma and Pa. All he had was money. He'll never be back again. It's like making sure a story is all done before you close the book cover."

Kelly shook her head from side to side slowly. "I never paid attention to how people treated me every day when I would meet and talk with them. They treat me, treat us, differently now. Like we are different people or something."

Lola took her hand. "And it's just started, Kelly. Come on, let's go have something to eat. I think there is a slice of pie left." They walked back to the house.

That night as they sat at the kitchen table, the two younger children played a game with tiny twigs and colorful rocks. "Colton, do you remember how ma told us about burying little pouches and jars of money out in the yard at the old house?" Kelly threaded a needle and began mending the seam on a shirt.

The young boy frowned. "Did you believe her? That it was real?"

Lola guffawed. "Yes, it was real. I believe her. She had no reason to lie about that, Colton."

Kelly looked up at the sky. It was warmer today. Several sparrows flitted in the grass around the barn.

"The one thing she didn't tell us was if she also buried money here, at Windy Ridge. There may be money in the ground we have been walking on and we don't know it." Kelly pushed her needle into the fabric carefully. "I say we take day or two and dig up the yard to see if we find anything."

Colton looked at the yard from the steps out to the gate at the driveway. "Where do we start? That money could be anywhere."

Lola sat down on the top step. "We divide the yard up into three parts. Whoever gets done with their part first goes to help another." Colton nodded.

Kelly said, "We want to find enough money for that eighty-five-dollar land payment. We need to stay here long enough to figure out what to do. And to buy the things we need to get by."

Colton asked, "What if someone comes by and asks what we are doing? Mr. Lucci would ask. He's nosy."

Lola laughed and said, "We're kids. We don't have to know what we are doing. Tell them that we just wanted to see what it would look like."

Kelly laughed, giggling at her sister. "We're going to need shovels and pickaxes. And I want to set up three jars in the house so we can see who finds the most money. Sort of like a contest."

Colton and Lola got up and walked towards the barn musing about what might lay under the hard-packed dirt in the yard.

It was Lola that found the first pouch. Buried about a foot deep in the flower bed next to the house, a soft leather pouch was pulled up. Sixteen dollars and a small folded paper that listed things to buy. It was their mother's handwriting, which brought tears to their eyes.

Colton sat on the step. "If ma buried the money here, do you think she had planned on living here a long time?"

Lola looked at her brother. "Yes. When Grandpa Glen died, maybe ma and pa talked about selling that ranch and living here."

Kelly came out of the house with a paper and a pencil. The loose board squeaked as she walked across it and she frowned and stopped to look at the culprit. She shook her head and put the items on the rough wooden table.

She handed a broad brimmed hat to both children. "Okay, Lola found the first one. Now we get to see who finds the next one and who finds the most. Let's get back to it."

A little after mid-day, Kelly's pickaxe hit an object. With the shovel, she dug out a small round tin that had been used for candy. Inside was an old leather bracelet with a greenish stone woven into it, and five dollars in coins. None of them recognized the bracelet.

Lola shook her head. "That tin isn't ours. It belongs to someone else. Someone who used to live here a long time ago. It's not Ma's." In that moment, the children realized it wasn't just their mother who buried things.

For three solid days they dug, starting right after morning chores. The yard looked like a battlefield with all the holes and piles of dirt. They found buried jewelry, books, bibles, an iron ring with three keys, letters, six dogs, and five cats. Kelly had gathered forty-nine dollars, Lola found seventy-three dollars and Colton had dug up eighty-two dollars.

Colton asked, "What are we to do with the other stuff we dug up?"

"I'll put it in the steamer trunk in the attic with a note about how we found it." Kelly said, looking at the items on the table. "The important thing is we have enough for the land payment now."

Lola stood up and rubbed her hands together. "We haven't dug up around the garden or around the back of the house yet. Ma used to spend a lot of time in the garden. I would think there would be a couple more pouches and jars out there." Colton perked up and nodded.

Kelly frowned. "I remember her planting those climbing roses along the fence posts, too. I wonder if she used that digging to hide something." She raised her eyebrows. "If you two want to explore the garden area, I'll start digging up around the roses after lunch."

That afternoon Kelly was excavating around a yellow rose bush when Colton Ran over to her. "You should come see this. We found an old copper pot." Kelly sat back on her haunches while taking off her gloves. Then she frowned and followed Colton to the back of the house.

Lola stood at the southwest corner of the garden plot looking down into a hole over a foot deep. When Kelly looked down, she could the glint of copper where the shovel had scraped against the pot.

"What is it, Lola?" The young girl was shifting her weight back and forth from foot to foot. She had begun clenching and unclenching her fists.

"There's something under the pot that's not supposed to be there." Lola started to tremble.

"I don't want to see what's there. I want to be far away when you take that pot out." Tears welled in her eyes.

"Okay, okay honey. We'll saddle up your mare and you can go up on the ridge where you can't see this. You wanna do that?" Kelly hugged her sensitive sister. Lola nodded.

Lola brought out several chunks of beef jerky and a canteen from the house while Kelly saddled the horse. "I'll send Colton up to get you when we figure out what this is."

"It's not a what, Kelly. It's a who." Lola mounted up and clucked her horse into a walk.

Two feet down farther, they found a small bundle wrapped tightly in old yellowed muslin. It was a grave of a baby or very small child. With slow care, Kelly and Colton dug down another foot and then took care to place the small form into the hole. A thick, flat stone settled over it. After they had filled in the small grave stamping down the disturbed soil, Kelly placed a cross to mark the site.

Kelly and Colton rode double up to the ridge and down to the springs. Lola had been stacking rocks. She stood up as they came to meet her.

"Someone's baby died. They dug a grave and buried it there. We dug the hole deeper and then settled it down farther. I made a cross to mark the site." Kelly spread out the blanket in the grass and sat down.

Lola had a mean edge to her voice when she said, "I don't want to dig anymore if I'm going to find things like that."

Kelly said, "You didn't feel it until you started to move the pot. You haven't found anything else like that aside from the dogs and cats. Those didn't bother you, honey." Lola shook her head. Strands of hair had escaped her ponytail and fluttered about.

Colton said, "We only have the other side of the garden to dig up. And the flower beds at the back of the house. If you don't want to dig anymore, Kelly and I can do the rest."

Lola wiped her eyes. "If you'll do the garden area, I'll dig up the flower beds. Seems farfetched that someone would bury a body right up next to the house. Is that alright with you?" Kelly and Colton nodded.

Colton asked, "Do you think Ma buried things right underneath the carrots and potatoes, Kel? We'll have to wait until late fall to completely dig up the vegetable patch."

"It's a possibility. As we pull up the vegetables we can take a look. I'd rather dig it all up at the same time, though. I'm tired of digging, honey," she said with a tired voice. "Tomorrow we'll start filling in the holes and raking the soil back level. See if we can get the yard back the way it used to be."

Together they walked the horses back to the barn. At sundown, they had accumulated more trinkets, jewelry, books, and tins of letters, two more books and twenty dollars more from the flowerbeds. One silver bracelet had a silver heart charm with the letter "D" engraved on it.

***

At the dinner table, each Stolter ate with their mind in a different place. Kelly could see that Lola stared off into space with assorted frowns as she worked her thoughts through something. Colton alternately ate, and then fussed with a piece of wood that laid next to his plate.

Lola brought up Flint Hills Ranch. Kelly was stunned and dropped her fork.

"You want to what?" Kelly had to wipe the butter off her chin that she'd spit out.

"I want to see the ranch. I want to see where Ma grew up. I want to know why it was a great place for a family. I feel like I'm torn in half. I'm afraid if we go, pa will come home and not know what happened to us." Lola chewed a mouthful of rabbit.

Kelly put her fork down and glared at her sister. "It's just land and trees and grass and a house. And well, barns and corrals." She could see her younger sister had not heard a word and was back to other thoughts.

Colton pushed his sliced carrots around on the plate and said, "Is there a swimming hole? It would be great to have our own swimming hole. Every time we go down to the river to swim, there are always other folks there." He wiggled his fork back and forth while he looked at Lola.

Kelly looked at Lola with a frown. "It's a long ride, Lola. Over 125 miles. We'd be nine days getting there. I don't know how long we would be there and then another nine days getting back."

Lola gasped and swallowed as she quickly looked at Colton. "Ma said there was a swimming hole there, Colton. Maybe there are big trees and pa can build us a big tree house. We could play castles and army." Colton cheered.

Kelly picked up a slice of bread and started to smear butter on it. "Ma said it was a horse ranch. There must be plenty of grazing land and water for a horse ranch." She took a bite and chewed in silence.

Lola said, "We could leave a letter for pa on the table."

Kelly's mouth hung open in amazement. "What? Pa would come home to find all of us gone, the house dark, and some note about us running to southern California. You can't just get on a horse and go for a ride to Flint Hills."

Colton shook his head and held up a hand. "I want to stay here. I don't want to ride a horse for nine days and then another nine days to get back. You go." He took a bite and chewed while he looked at Lola. His older sister wrinkled up her nose at him.

Kelly looked at her brother and struggled to find words. "Colton, you're nine years old. You can't stay here all by yourself. A hundred things could go wrong and you could get hurt and then we'd be in real trouble."

Colton put down his fork and glared back at Kelly. "I'm better with the rifle than you ever were. Me and Mr. Remington will just sit on the porch and keep rocking. Without you two to bother me, maybe I can get some good digging done over at the creek."

Kelly rubbed her forehead in exasperation. The thought of her nine-year-old brother alone on the ranch for half of a month made her want to tear her hair out. She pushed her chair back and went to put the kettle on the fire.

Colton said, "This is my home. I like it here. I have friends here in town. If Pa says we must go, then I'll saddle up and ride. But I'd just as soon stay here so if Pa comes home I'll get to see him. You girls will be off riding down the road somewheres and me and Pa will be here."

Lola looked at Kelly. "Ma said there was a lawyer that took care of the ranch after Grandpa Glen died. Can we write a letter to him? We should tell him what happened to ma and how pa has not come home yet. He could help us decide if there is anything we should do."

Kelly thought about it and nodded. "I didn't think that a lawyer so far away could help us."

Colton said, "That's a good idea, Lola. If I remember right, his name is Doyle. Doyle like those playing cards in the drawer." Lola giggled.

"You've got butter on your chin, Kelly." Colton giggled.

Kelly groaned and wiped the gooey clump off her chin. "After supper, I'll get out some paper and we'll write to him. There is a noon stage tomorrow so we'll ride into Yucca Valley to put the letter on the stage. And….." her voice trailed off with a grin.

Colton hooted. "We can stop for cake at the bakery!" They cheered.

Thursday was mail day, but the rider didn't stop. He just rode on by. The children were still lounging on the front porch debating their next move when a familiar clanging sound was heard.

Colton stood up on the porch railing. "Mr. Lucci is coming."

"So, what do we need?" Kelly took in a deep breath and let it out.

Colton said, "Socks. All mine are worn out."

"Anything else? I'll go put on the water for coffee." Kelly stood up and went into the house.

Huge, strong Percherons walked up the driveway and Mr. Virgil Lucci waved his hat in greeting. After the horses were unhitched and turned into the pasture, he sat down on the bench on the porch. He tousled Colton's hair who sat on the top step.

"So, have you traveled the mountain high and the valley low since the last time we saw you, Mr. Lucci?"

Lucci wiped his forehead with a grin. "I don't know why folks choose to build houses at the top of hills. Maybe they just want a view. The trouble is, the road going up to the house is more of a narrow dirt path. And they don't think to grade the road. The rains cut big ruts into the dirt and it makes it hard to haul vehicles up. Charles Rossberg put in a huge log home with five bedrooms and three fireplaces up at Spanish Butte. From his home, you can see probably twenty miles on a clear day."

Lola asked, "When it rains around here the roads get bad, thick with mud and very slippery. You probably have to roll through a lot of mud or do you stop until it dries?"

"Oh no. I came through Freshwater in axle deep mud. I had to rest the horses for a full day because of the strain. For a light buggy or a cart, the mud would not be too bad. But this big wagon tends to sink down. I'm very lucky in that I've never had to unload my goods to get a wagon unstuck. I've had other teams help pull me out, too." Lucci motioned with his pushing hands.

Kelly said, "Pa used to tell us stories about the cattle drives and about how the trail that was there two months before was completely gone down a bluff or something. You ever find where the road is just gone?"

Lucci put his hands up as if to pray to the deity. "One year I came down the Cimarron cutoff and half the road washed out when the Canadian River flooded. Thirty-foot-deep chasm, and I was glad my horses were walking. They saw it before I did and came to a halt."

Colton asked, "Do you have a lot of trees that fall over the road? Every occasionally, we have to chop up one of the alders that fall down from the wind."

Lucci pointed to his left hand, splaying out his fingers. "Nicked my finger too many times doing that. I've had to hack up, chop and saw my fair share of trees. It got so bad one year I paid a lumberjack to come along with me. We must have cut up over one hundred trees that winter. In the spring, I came back through and sold them all as cords of firewood to folks out in the desert."

Kelly said, "You are the only freighter that comes around. There must be more, but maybe we are too far out of the way."

The freighter rubbed his chin. "Some of the other freight haulers sold out and started shipping on the railroad. They don't even run their wagons anymore. There have been a few that once they have broken down, they just don't fix them."

"Up around Tompkins Junction I have seen the broken, shattered wagons that couldn't get around a bend on a mountain road. I've spent too many hours letting myself down a cliff on a rope to help folks out and haul merchandise back up to road." He laughed.

Colton asked, "What is the biggest thing you've hauled? A piano?"

Lucci slapped his knee laughing heartily. "The one thing I won't try to haul or rescue is a piano. Had a man ask me about broken pianos once and if I knew where they were. Took me a month, but I wrote out a map of six pianos that had fallen off on the trail. That man came and got them. One by one. Probably took him ten months to get them."

Lola said, "People ride wagons, stages, horses and the train. Do you ever get people riding with you?"

Kelly interrupted. "Mr. Lucci, it's that time where we start getting ready for dinner. If you want to wash up over at the bucket alongside the kitchen, please help yourself. We can continue talking over dinner, if you'd like." Lucci nodded and stood up.

At the dinner table in the house, Lola passed a bowl of mashed potatoes to Mr. Lucci. He put down his biscuit and took the bowl.

"Yes, Lola. People ask all the time to ride with me. They don't realize it's that much more weight on the horses to pull. I mean, if the folks were going to help me make money, I might consider it. Most people just want to go for a ride and see the country. It's a lot of secluded country in a slow-moving wagon. The one woman that I allow to ride with me is Miss Marilee Petit. Pretty spinster schoolteacher rides with me from Denver to Dodge to go home for the summer months."

Kelly smiled and said, "Your horses seem to like Windy Ridge. I see them rolling around in the grass and wading in the river to drink. I imagine it's hard to get them to slow down once they start running."

Lucci chewed on a mouthful of food. "My Percherons are faster than oxen. I tried them big beasts and once they decide that they are tired, they stop. Nothing can get them going again until they decide. The horses take two steps to every one of theirs. They may be stronger, I give you that. From time to time, I'll swing in at the back of a caravan and follow along. Most times though, they all stop and I keep rolling on."

He ran gnarled fingers through his hair and said, "Well, my horses are strong and I rely on them a lot. A while back one of my mares was getting ready to foal and I stabled her. I still had sixty miles to go. It's a rough pull for just three so I pastured them. I hired a mule driver and his ten mules to pull me the rest of the way. Mean, cantankerous, bellyaching all the way and I was never so glad to get that trip done."

Lola grinned as she buttered a biscuit. "Aren't you afraid of men robbing you? There are many not very nice men out there. Sometimes do you get scared?"

Lucci nodded vigorously. "Yes, from time to time some fool decides he's going to pull a gun and take my money. They all think I'm rolling along carrying hundreds of dollars and truth is, I may have ten to fifteen dollars on me. They don't see the money when they look at the merchandise on the wagon."

Kelly stirred the food on her plate. "How far do you get in one day? I think that the number of people that you stop to see depends on where you are."

Lola picked up her plate and carried it into the kitchen. Colton took his in, also. Kelly scooped the last ladle full of stewed beef onto a grateful freighter's plate.

Lucci nodded and said, "When I'm up in the hills, I only get about fifteen miles a day. I have favorite places I like to go. Out on the prairie, desert or flatlands, I can usually get in twenty-five miles a day. Folks live a little farther apart. The widow Virginia Stein lives on a bend in the trail. She always buys firewood when I have it and every year she buys a new rug for the living room."

Dinner was over and the dishes were cleaned. Lucci went out to make his bed under the wagon as he always did. For Lola, time seemed to slow down when Mr. Lucci stopped to visit. There was never enough time to ask him all the questions that rolled around inside her head. There was so much she wanted to know about. That was why she always looked forward to him rolling that big wagon into the yard.

The lanterns were turned down. The candles blown out. In the distance owls called out as they hunted. There was a gentle scratch of the cottonwood leaves against the roof. Overhead, the glittering stars twinkled against the inky black sky.

***

The attorney stared at the pages lying on his desk in the dawn light. Doyle had read the letter from the Stolter children several times. Each time he read it, he became more determined to track down Nick Stolter. The attorney had spent a week sending out a dozen wires trying to find some traces of Nick Stolter. Nothing. He suspected that nobody wanted to give word to a lawyer about a missing cowboy.

The entire western half of the U.S. was quiet about Nick Stolter. Not in jail anywhere, not in a hospital anywhere, not arrested anywhere. The attorney had sent a letter to the U.S. Marshall's office in Santa Fe and Los Angeles to explain the children's situation and the disappearance of Nick Stolter.

Doyle leaned against the window sill and looked out at the waving trees in the distance. There was a horse and rider walking in on the west road. Stolter had no criminal background, didn't associate with known criminals and had been leading a clean life. Wherever he was, there was a good chance he was not near a Western Union station or even had the thought that there were telegrams waiting for him. Hundreds of miles of scrub brush, arroyos, and mesas. Perfect for the man who doesn't want to be found.

10 DOYLE SENDS A TELEGRAM TO NICK

The attorney stood in the small office in the Bradford Hotel with Tommy Boardman. "His wife died while he was away for work. His three children are alone on that ranch in Yucca Valley, and nobody knows where he is."

Boardman had owned and operated the Bradford Hotel for fifteen years. A tall, slender blonde man with a mustache and a strong jaw, his was the only live Western Union connection for the surrounding thirty miles, save the disconnected key machine at the Faraway Inn at Williams Creek. Boardman raised his eyebrows as the attorney paced back and forth.

"Merle, if you don't have the key code for the station where he is, that telegram has to go general delivery. It means everyone will see your message." The attorney nodded. On a half-page sheet of white paper, he carefully wrote down the words.

"My condolences. Please contact attorney Merle Doyle, Bradford. Urgent. Merle Doyle, Atty."

Doyle rubbed his face with both hands. Somewhere out on the range, there was a man who was about to get the most terrible news.

***

Kelly paced into the living room and then all the way back to the kitchen wringing a small towel in her hands. Lola had read the letter twice while Colton shook his head.

**

Dear Kelly Stolter, Lola Stolter and Colton Stolter:

First, allow me to offer my condolences on the passing of your mother. She was part of an excellent family and she is a great loss to those who loved her.

I am happy to help try to locate your father, Nick Stolter. His traveling companion, Ginger Whelihan, is known to me and while I do not know the nature of their business, I will say that your father is most likely in safe hands.

I have sent messages out to the larger jails, hospitals, medical clinics and Marshall's offices in Arizona and California. I have not yet notified the Texas Rangers as they would only be involved if a crime has been committed. I have no information or evidence of that. I do have a number of responses back and unfortunately, there is no word on your father. If I hear anything about Mr. Stolter, I will send a telegram.

I must say that your personal living situation seriously concerns me. I will send an immediate notice from my office to the landlord and the bank to explain the situation. As of this letter, I am to be considered your personal attorney of record regarding any monetary transactions. It would seem a visit would be in order so you can be aware of the condition of the Flint Hills Ranch.

Please write to let me know your intentions.

Yours truly,

Merle Doyle, Attorney at law

**

Kelly leaned against the counter. "That's a relief. I never thought of just talking to the bank about the payment."

Lola put down the pages. "I still want to go. It's a visit to the Flint Hills. If we get there and see that it's smaller and in worse shape than Windy Ridge, we can come home and find a way to keep living here."

Lola turned a small shiny stone over in her hands as she sat at the kitchen table. "Remember how Mrs. Sherman said that family came home and found half their house had burned down? What if Flint Hills house is all torn up and we can't live in it?"

Kelly nodded and put more wood into the cook stove. "Then we come back to Windy Ridge and figure out a way to live here. That attorney fella should be able to help us sell Flint Hills and that money could pay off Windy Ridge."

Colton sat on the floor in the living room leaning against the sofa, ruffling the yellow lab's thick coat. "What about the other? What if the house is twice the size of this one, the barn's bigger and there's more acres of grazing land and good water? It would have to be really something special to make me want to leave Windy Ridge."

Kelly filled the kettle with water and put it on the stove for coffee. "Another thing to think about is how many other horse ranches are down there? Maybe there is nobody down there that wants to buy cutting horses. It might be a nice place to live, but if we can't sell the stock, it's useless to move."

Lola pushed the little stone with her spoon, rolling it across the table and back. The light glinted dully on the shiny bits. "Alright, let's say that we are going to go visit. Colton wants to stay here, so that means Kelly and I ride for Flint Hills." She turned in her chair to face Colton.

"I'm afraid if we leave you here all alone something bad will happen to you. We've already seen strangers come walking up the driveway. We can ask one of the neighbors to come stay with you while we are gone." She looked at the boy.

Kelly measured coffee into the bubbling kettle. "Or you could go stay with someone. But then they'll want to know where we went and start asking questions. And there will not be anyone to feed the rabbits and chickens."

Colton nodded. "Kelly, you'd need to cook up some food for me to eat during those nine days. I can get the carrots and apples raw so that's okay. Every other day I could ride into Yucca Valley and eat at the bakery, and bring something home for the next day. That means you'll have to leave me a couple dollars."

Kelly took down a thick mug and put it on the counter. Carefully, she spooned in sugar. "That's a good idea. Folks don't make a fuss when we ride into town now so you should be able to mosey on in there alone with no problem. You just have to be careful what you say to folks."

All of them were quiet for a few moments letting thoughts drift through their heads. Lola saw that Kelly stood in the kitchen silently staring out the window in thought. "The next land payment isn't due to be paid until the thirtieth of next month now. If it takes nine days to get down to Flint Hills and back, that leaves us twenty days to figure out what to do."

"Kelly, after we pay the next land payment, how much money will we have left?" Lola dropped the spoon and sat up straight in the chair. They watched her do the arithmetic in her head.

"We should have about one hundred twenty dollars left. If we must make the May land payment subtract out another eighty-five. That leaves us forty." Kelly rubbed her face with both hands.

Lola had gone back to rolling the little shiny rock back and forth with the spoon on the table. "When we go to Flint Hills, let's take that map ma made and see if we can dig up two jars. See if we can find some more money."

Kelly narrowed her eyes for a moment. "I just thought of that. The problem is, we don't know who is watching that ranch. And the minute we leave they would flock to the yard and dig it up after they saw what we did. But we'll have to try it."

Colton said, "You have to figure that attorney man will want to be with you all the time. You being kids and all. You can't very well run off and start digging up the yard. He'll think that's mighty strange."

Lola had her chin on her hand. "Ma said Grandma Anna-Marie also buried money so there might be quite a lot." She paused with her mouth open mid-sentence.

"How much money is owed on Windy Ridge? How many more land payments do we have to make? Will Pa own it after all the payments are made? How does he own it if he's not even here?" She rubbed her eyes. "I've got so many questions."

Kelly brought her cup to the table and sat down. She was distracted as she watched the little shiny rock roll back and forth. "I want to talk more about us making the trip. We'll have to pack bedrolls, food and the rifles and the Colts. We'll have to plan on sleeping out two nights on the way down and two nights on the way back. Be sure to bring a couple of flints and matches."

Lola watched the steam drift up from the hot coffee and nodded. "We should pack slickers in case we run into rain. I don't want to get held up in a cave hiding out from the rain. We should check over both saddles, blankets and bridles to make sure nothing will break on the way down."

Colton said, "We need to ask someone about the stage route. It might be easiest to follow a mile or two back from the stage so you won't draw attention. You'll have to ask at the hotel in Yucca Valley for the map the stage takes. Don't be running out across open ground where you might run into trouble."

Lola started asking questions again. "Can you ask the attorney man to find out how much is owed on Windy Ridge? If we stay here, we'll know how much money we'll need."

Kelly took a sip of the hot liquid. "We have questions with no answers right now. We must be as prepared as possible for what we don't know might happen. We have to pay attention to our own business and keep moving towards what we want." Kelly frowned.

"Do you remember what ma used to say about that?" Together, almost in unison, they said, "Do the best you can with what you have." They all smiled and laughed.

Colton went to stand next to Kelly's chair. "And what pa used to say. 'One Stolter alone is a formidable opponent. Three Stolters is a force to be reckoned with.'" Again, the children laughed.

A few hundred miles away the skills of that formidable opponent were about to be put to the test.

11 WAYS AND MEANS

The kitchen table was cleared and a large piece of brown paper spread out. The children sat around the edge.

Lola asked, "Should we take a pack horse for what we need?"

Kelly thought for a moment and said, "No, there are small towns all along the road. We'll have food and water on us, too."

Colton twirled his pencil. "What you should do, the easiest way to go, would be to just follow the stage down to Bradford."

Kelly's eyes went wide and she smiled. "Of course. They know all the waterholes. They know when to stop at night. We'd always be safe riding with them."

"Smarty pants," teased Lola. Colton smirked.

Lola leaned back in her chair and dropped her pencil onto the paper. "The stage is heavier, though, and slower than just us on a horse. You sure you want trot along behind them?"

Colton said, "You're gonna need a map. Something that shows the road all the way to Bradford. Once you get there, that attorney man can take you to the ranch."

Lola sat swinging her foot looking at the blank page. "We'll need to get some target practice in before we ride. Shooting cans, dirt clods and bottles is different from shooting people." Kelly nodded.

"Somebody tries to kill you, you try to kill them right back." Colton held his fingers up like a gun and blew the pretend smoke away.

Kelly said, "So we each take a revolver, a rifle, the knives, flints, and ammunition. We'll take two sets of saddlebags, a bedroll, and a blanket."

Lola said, "I'm taking my slingshot and my field glasses." Lola drew a dog face on the paper. "How much money will we need?"

"I don't know. A dollar a day, nine days, two people. What? Eighteen dollars. That's just to get us there."

Colton said, "Better add in a little more just in case you have to buy something you need. Plus, you will need money to get yourselves home, too."

The young boy's eyes twinkled. "How much you got, Lola?"

"I've got five dollars." She smiled. "That's twenty-three."

Colton leaned on the table. "If you're leaving me here for almost a whole month, I'll need money, too. I'd like to get a good meal in town when I go in."

Kelly stood up and went to the window. "We've never ridden like this before. We don't know what we'll need."

"It's not real good spring weather yet so plan on getting caught in the rain. You'll need a canvas cover or a tarp. Some way to keep dry. And you better carry rope. You never know when you'll need rope."

Kelly said, "I want to take a small kettle and coffee. Take some beef jerky, too. I hate being hungry out there."

Kelly sat down and drummed her fingers on the table. "It's a long ride. We'll need to take the endurance horses. Strong ones." Lola nodded.

"That big dun buckskin gelding would be a good one. I like him. He's strong. That Appie cross gelding might be a good one." Kelly rubbed her eyes.

"No, I want to leave that Appie cross for Colton while we're gone. You like him, don't you, Colton?"

Colton shrugged. "They're all the same to me. If I can throw a halter on them I'll be alright. I'll probably ride in and see Georgie, too, while you're gone. Oh, and especially when they have cake at the bakery."

Lola nodded. "I think that black mare with the two front white stockings would be a good one. I like her."

Colton yawned and stood up. "I'm tired. I'm going to bed. Good night." He hugged Lola and then hugged Kelly. He walked over to the doorway as he rubbed his eyes.

"Come on, Lola. Let's lock everything up and go to bed. We can work on this tomorrow." The girls walked around, locking windows and both the doors.

After the lantern had been turned down, Kelly laid in bed under the blankets and watched the moonlight stream in and light up the floor. Her chest tightened as she uttered a small sob. A lone tear slid down her cheek.

The next morning Kelly went to the desk in the corner and pulled out the calendar. She stood looking at it for a few minutes and then brought it to the table and laid it down.

"We don't have time to write a letter and get a response. It cuts down the time we have before the next land payment." Her face had a serious look.

Lola asked, "Then how do we tell him we are coming to visit?"

"Telegram." Colten said. "We have to send a telegram. It'll cost money, but it's the only way he'll know you're coming."

"Words cost money. What do we put in the telegram?"

Kelly sat down at the paper and pencil. "Today is the seventeenth. If we leave tomorrow on the eighteenth, that will put us, hopefully, in Bradford on the twenty-seventh. If we don't have any trouble. Now, we've never made this ride, so let's add on one more day just in case something happens. That puts us in Bradford on the twenty-eighth."

Lola put her arms on the table leaning forward. "So, write, 'Coming for visit. Arrive 28th?"

Kelly put down the pencil after she wrote out the message. "There's one more thing, Colton. If we run into trouble and don't think we'll be home on time, I'll send you a telegram."

The young boy nodded. Kelly continued. "Let's figure Lola and I arrive in Bradford and stay three days. That should give us plenty of time to find out what we need to know and get advice from the attorney. If everything goes fine, we'll leave there on the twenty sixth."

Lola said, "For the next three days, check at the telegraph office when you come in to eat, and see if we sent you a message if something bad happened. If you don't get a message, we're alright and coming home."

Kelly said, "If anyone asks, just say you're expecting word from pa." The oldest sister looked at her siblings for a quiet moment. Lola sat back and rolled the little shiny rock around.

Colton giggled. "Ooh! Cake for three days! Yum!" Kelly chuckled and shook her head at the one-track mind of her younger brother.

They saddled up and rode into Yucca Valley and sent the telegram. As they sat in the bakery enjoying plump slices of chocolate cake, the telegraph clerk walked in with a folded sheet. He handed it to Kelly. She read aloud.

"Expecting you 28th. M Doyle attorney." Kelly grinned. Lola held up her glass of milk in a toast. "Here's to safe journey."

Kelly lifted her glass. "Here's to the Flint Hills Ranch."

Colton made that little boy giggle sound as he lifted his glass. "Here's to more cake!" They burst into laughter.

12 THE STAGE AT YUCCA VALLEY

Out on the boardwalk, Kelly and Lola took their horses to the water trough near the stables. Half an hour later the big Overland Stage rolled in pulled by six horses. They watched while five passengers got off the stage and went into the lobby.

"Kelly, five people got off the stage and there were nine waiting in the lobby. How are they all going to fit on the stage?" Lola frowned as she watched the people step down off the stage.

"Some passengers might change to another stage here. There is another one at four o'clock that takes people up to Nevada and Utah. There's seats up on top, too, for people who don't like to sit inside. Pa has told a couple of stories about twenty people crowding onto a stage in Dodge City."

The girls watched the team get unhitched and walked to the corral. The girls backed their horses away from the trough and into the shade. A station tender leading a fresh four-horse team headed toward the stage followed by a younger boy leading two more big horses.

"Kelly, isn't that Georgie Hailey? I didn't know he worked with horses." It was the bouncing mop of reddish blonde hair over a tanned face and the white smile that gave him away. His bare arms were muscled, and the horses obeyed his commands. Kelly's eyes lit up and she grinned.

"Yes, that is Georgie. His uncle is the blacksmith on the other end of town." They watched the young man lead his team over and help hitch up and settle the horses. Once the passengers started loading, Georgie trotted over to the girls in the shade.

"Hi Kelly, hi Lola. You ladies look like you are ready to ride. Where you going?" At two months older than Kelly, Georgie Hailey towered nearly a full head above her. He had the broad shoulders, lean physique and narrow hips of the traditional western man.

"South a ways. We have to go see an attorney about some land down south." The strong hand patted the neck of the dun. "Georgie, what's the name of the drivers of the stage? We're gonna follow it south. I'd like to know who we are following."

"That's Benny Worrell, the driver. Riding shotgun is Mike Knepler. Benny will take the stage down to Helton Corners, then he gets off and another driver will come on. Mike is hired by Overland so he stays right through to Santa Fe."

"I don't see Colton. Is he staying at the ranch?" Kelly nodded.

Lola said, "He didn't want to ride all that way. Plus, we need someone at the ranch in case pa comes home." Georgie nodded.

"Hey, I'm really sorry about your ma." He ran his hand back through his hair. "Do you want me to get out to the ranch and check on Colton while you're gone? He might get lonely."

"If you go out to the ranch, stop at the gate and yell a couple times for him and tell him who you are. I don't want him to shoot you and then ask your name." Kelly grinned. Georgie chuckled. "You might see him in town once or twice. He has a fondness for the chocolate cake over at the bakery." They all looked up at the sound of the stage driver urging the horses to walk on. Georgie helped Lola up onto her dun.

"Hey, when you ladies come home, how about coming over for supper one day and bring Colton? I'd like to hear about your trip." Kelly looked at the icy blue eyes and nodded as the horses started walking.

On the outskirts of the small town, another rider came galloping up behind them. He reined up and trotted alongside.

"You ladies must be Kelly and Lola Stolter. I'm Dex Hamel. I'm the outrider security for the stage. Georgie said you two were headed south with us. If you hurry, you can ride with me." He grinned and tapped his mount with his spurs and the horse went into a gallop. The girls followed.

After about nine miles, Hamel shouted to Kelly. "Up ahead is the turnoff for the first waterhole. We'll be stopped for about twenty minutes." Kelly nodded and waved a gloved hand.

At the river, the girls led their horses downstream to stay out of the way of the teams. Lola was adjusting the strap on her boot when Hamel came running over.

"The number three black gelding is going lame. We're going to turn him loose here and someone will pick him up and take him back to Yucca Valley. Has either of your horses ever pulled in a team? My horse has never pulled." Hamel's chest heaved as he panted.

"Yes, my dun has pulled wagons in a team. We use him for dragging logs and such. It's been a while, but he will do it," Lola said as she stood up.

"Would you allow him to pull up to the next town? It's six miles. We could pay two dollars for him to pull and you can ride up on top with the driver. Or you could ride double with your sister," Hamel said.

Lola looked at her sister. "You'll have to hitch him up. I'm all right with riding up on top of the stage. I'll have a stage story for pa when he gets home." The young girl grinned.

Kelly nodded. "Two dollars for having a talented horse. Who knew?" Kelly laughed out loud as they stripped the gear off the saddle and stowed it in the boot. Ten minutes later, the stage rolled back up onto the road with Lola's dun in the third position.

Hamel told Kelly to pull up her bandana because of the dust. At the little town of Serra Mesa, Lola's dun was wiped down, watered and brought over her at the corral. Kelly cut up two apples and fed the horses their treat.

"Thank you, Miss, for letting us use your horse. He's a nice animal." Hamel dropped two dollar coins into Lola's hand. Lola smiled.

"Where is the next stop?" Kelly asked.

"Another seven miles at Helton Corners. We'll change teams there and then run right into dark as we roll into the last stop of the day at Columbia Junction." Hamel waved as he walked back to the stage. Lola chattered on about the ride up on top. Kelly saddled up the dun and they fell in behind the stage when it rolled back onto the main road.

***

Hamel dropped back to trot his black gelding alongside the girls.

"We're coming up on High Man Falls. It is a big water hole with plenty of room. Benny and I will unhook the team and let them water. You getting along alright?"

Kelly smiled as they rode along the dusty road. "Oh, yes, Dex. This is a bit different from just riding to get somewhere. We've had a chance to look at the scenery and the places pa has talked about."

The wide drive took a right turn down a slight incline to a fifty-yard square clearing. Elm, oak and weeping willow surrounded the south and east side of the water. To the far west end was a waterfall that tumbled over a sandstone cliff about a hundred feet up. The splashing water coated the rocks with a fine mist.

Lola nudged Kelly towards the trees. "Someone has camped in here. There's an old fire ring there." Kelly nodded and knelt to look at the deer tracks.

"Looks like about six deer have been here recently. Those smaller tracks must be fawns. Goats would have made noise by now, so those must be fawns." Kelly stood up and looked around. One of the women from the stage had wetted down a handkerchief at the water's edge and was wiping her face and neck.

"Lola, if you were going to hide here, where would you hide? It's all open here." Kelly looked at Lola. The young girl was the family champion of hide and seek.

"That's easy. I'd hide behind the water fall or up on that cliff. Why do you ask?" Lola had a puzzled look on her face.

With a lowered voice, Kelly casually walked to the other side of Lola and knelt again. "We don't know what the ride will be like coming home. We might not be able to follow a stage back this way. If we need a place to hide, this might not be a good place." Lola nodded slowly and looked around again.

"Alright. I see what you mean. I'll start making a note of those places, just in case." Just then they heard a loud whistle and saw Hamel wave them over. The team was hooked up and when the stage door closed, Benny urged the team back onto the road.

Kelly groaned as every muscle protested her moving when she woke. She was surprised to see Lola's bedroll empty. She wound her hair up into a bun on top of her head and pulled on her boots.

Nearly all the passengers and crew were in the restaurant eating breakfast. Lola had a plate full of pancakes, eggs and sliced steak. A hand set a cup of coffee down in front of her and she turned to see Dex Hamel smile and wink at her as he chewed on a chunk of pastry and then moved to another table.

"I bought some food to go with us, Kel. We won't be hungry at all." Lola wiggled her eyebrows and made the still sleepy Kelly smile. The coffee tasted delicious, the pancake was soft and fluffy and she was suddenly ravenous.

As they walked back to camp, Hamel trotted up alongside them. "So, are you riding with us today?"

Kelly folded up the canvas sheet with Lola. "We'll ride as far as the first water hole. I want to make some miles today and I plan on riding for as long as possible." She smiled at the kind man.

Lola smiled, too. "We appreciate you watching out for us, Mr. Hamel."

"Well, take good care of your horses and they'll get you there." He headed for the corral. Kelly and Lola led their horses out of the corral just as the stage began to roll out onto the south road. They mounted up and trotted after it.

Lola said, "The map says there is a big waterhole up ahead on the right. From there we go another four miles to water then there is no water for seven miles." Kelly nodded.

The road took them into low, rolling hills where the stage slowed as the team worked hard to ascend each hill. Kelly began to feel the frustration of being slowed down by the heavy stage.

"Mr. Hamel, is it okay if we ride on ahead, around the stage? We'll be at the next waterhole waiting," Lola asked the security man with a smile.

"Sure, go ahead. Just be careful. You see any strangers, just keep shy of them. Don't use your guns unless you have to." Hamel waved them on.

The girls eased by the stage on the left-hand side waving to the driver. They broke into a gallop as they crested the hill and loped down the other side. The brush was thick on both sides for over a mile and then it thinned out as the road took them amongst large boulders. On the left were glimpses of high mesas with cacti and scrub pines.

Lola shouted, "That should be the road to the waterhole." She pointed ahead at the wide, rutted drive. They slowed to a trot and turned in on the gently sloping drive, going to the north side where they jumped down so the horses could water.

***

"Colton, you there?" Georgie Hailey dismounted and brushed the dust off his pants. When Georgie looked up he could see Dusty, the yellow lab running down the driveway.

Georgie knelt and ruffled the dog's fur. The happy lab's tail wagged furiously.

"Hi, Georgie!" Colton climbed up onto the fence from the tall grass.

Georgie grinned. "I thought I'd come say howdy to you. Must be mighty quiet around here with the girls gone and all."

Colton jumped down and opened the gate. Georgie led the dun through and after Colton closed the gate they walked up to the house. "I brought you a treat from the bakery. I snagged the last piece of apple pie for you." Georgie hugged the young boy and laughed.

"That was nice of you, Georgie. Kelly makes pie but doesn't make them sweet enough. She uses honey instead of store-bought sugar. We always argue about it. That's why I like cake so much. It's hard to mess up a cake." The young boy laughed.

When Colton came out of the house he brought out two glasses of lemonade and handed one to Georgie. A flock of noisy crows complained in the tall grass. Bees hummed amongst the wildflowers.

"So, what have you been doing to keep yourself busy out here?"

Colton grinned. "Not too much. Dusty wakes me up at sunrise, so I can't just lay in bed and be lazy. I feed the chickens and the horses. We've got a mare that is due in two months. I check on her and feed her carrots from the garden."

"You get any fishing in? You have time for fishing now." Georgie winked.

"Lola is the one who likes fishing. I like digging in the water. She says it disturbs the fish and they won't bite. Besides, I like eating the fish but not cleaning them." Both boys laughed.

Georgie leaned back on his elbow and looked out over the softly waving grass. The gentle air was warm and smooth.

"When my pa died, I thought my mother would never stop crying. I think she felt that he ran off and left her alone. My ma was a city girl born in North Carolina and she had never lived on a ranch or farm." Georgie was quiet for a moment.

"It was a few months after pa had passed when I came into the house one day and my uncle was sitting at the kitchen table. My pa's brother. My ma had been writing back to her family in North Carolina and she had decided that she wanted to go back.

"What happened?" Colton's brown eyes watched Georgie.

"My ma asked my uncle to take me in until I was old enough to run the ranch by myself. My pa wanted me to have the ranch. I didn't know. He never told me."

Colton blinked fast a couple of times as he looked at Georgie. "I am afraid of that the most. That pa won't come back. We'll end up having to go live with family we don't know. This is the only home I've ever known."

Georgie nodded. "At first I didn't know why my ma didn't want me to go back to North Carolina with her. That she didn't love me anymore or thought I would be a big problem to her. Then my uncle explained that I would grow into a man and own land that my father used to own."

Colton watched the thin blade of grass drag through his fingers.

"My uncle has been very good to me. He's helped me learn a lot of things that my pa would have taught me. Colton, I have my own ranch and I'm only fifteen. I'll have a home for when I get married and have kids like you." Georgie ruffled Colton's hair, who laughed.

"So, your ma went back east? Did she ever come back?" Georgie shook his head and rubbed his hands together.

"She writes once a month to tell me what she has been doing. She's happy with her sisters and friends back there. It turns out that when my ma and pa were married, her parents made them write up a paper that paid money if my pa died."

Colton sat upright. "What? What does that mean?"

"It's called insurance. When someone dies, the money is used to pay off the bills and debts and for the funeral of the person who died. It sounded to me like they were planning on my pa dying, but then the lawyer man told me that my pa wanted us to have money in case anything happened to him."

Colton nodded. "I understand. Men get kicked by horses and they break legs or die. One man we know up north fell into a well and was killed.

Trace Jordan's pa fell off the roof and broke his neck and died. People die by accident all the time. Pa used to tell us all the time that the West is a dangerous place to live."

Georgie wiped off his forehead with the tattered green bandanna. "My ma will never come back to California. If I want to see her again, I'll have to go there. I sort of figure when I get married, part of the honeymoon will mean I go to North Carolina to see my ma."

"You have a couple of years before that happens, huh, Georgie?" Colton grinned. The two young men laughed together.

A few minutes passed and then suddenly Dusty's ears perked up and he bounded down the steps into the grass. They could see the grass moving as the dog searched.

"I wanted to be here if Pa came home. It would have been sad if he came home and nobody was here. Georgie, my pa is going to be sad for a long time because ma died. I don't want him to be even more sad because we weren't here." Georgie nodded as he listened.

"I've got ham, carrots and potatoes for dinner, Georgie. I'll split that piece of pie with you, too. Let's go eat." Colton grinned.

"You are a right and proper host, Colton Stolter! Let's eat!"

It was a bright blue sky with only a few puffy clouds hugging the western horizon. The limbs of the big oak behind the house gently raised and lowered in the breeze. Amid that natural beauty, two young men had come to know each other better.

***

Helton Corners had been built into the northwest corner of the Helton Ranch. It was renowned from California to Texas for champion Black Angus beef cattle. The air was heavy with the scent of open flame cooked beef when the stage rolled in. Kelly's mouth immediately began to water.

When the girls walked into the restaurant they were stunned to find long tables packed with people eating dinner. One of the waitresses gestured them over to the counter.

"Were you ladies looking for dinner? The stage doesn't stop very long and we usually pack up a dinner for each passenger," she said with a big smile.

"How much for the dinner? We don't have very much money." Lola was digging in her pocket.

"It's a dollar for your two dinners. We wrap them up in paper and a cloth so you can eat them later if you want to."

Lola nodded and handed over a few coins. They moved over against the wall and watched folks come in to order food.

Benny Worrell took of his hat as he came in and slapped it against his thigh. "Thank you, ladies, again, for the loan of your gelding. You helped us out of a tight spot."

"You are very welcome, Mr. Worrell."

"This is where I climb down. Day after tomorrow, I'm getting onto the driver's seat of the Overland headed for Los Angeles. I'm going home to see my wife and children and get a few days' rest." Kelly took off her glove and reached to shake his hand.

"Thank you for helping us understand more about how the stage goes from station to station, Mr. Worrell," said Lola. "We had no idea of the danger of what you do all the time." Lola shook his hand.

"You young ladies be careful out there on the road. It's a good road all the way into Bradford where you're headed. The new driver is Ernie Hopkins. I'll send him over to say hello. He's been driving longer than I have and has made this run probably a hundred times. Mike and Dex will be with you so you don't have worry about much. I hope to see you again some time." He smiled and waved.

***

A tall, heavy man with a pronounced limp in his left leg walked in and glanced around. When he saw the girls, he nodded and walked over to them with black spurs jingling. He took off his gloves.

"Ladies, you must be the Stolter girls. I'm Ernie Hopkins. I'll be driving the Overland on in to Bradford. I wanted to introduce myself before we roll out. We leave in about ten minutes."

"Yes, sir. I'm Kelly and this is my sister, Lola. We're going on to Bradford to see an attorney about the estate of my mother." Hopkins looked them up and down.

Hopkins ran his hand back through his brown hair. "I see you ladies are carrying Colts. I take it, you know how to use that iron?"

Lola grinned. "Yes, sir. We know enough to keep shooting until it stops moving. Whatever that may be." Hopkins raised his eyebrows.

He leaned closer. "You ladies ever want to ride security, you look me up. Them bad guys would never suspect pretty things like yourselves." He started to chuckle as he put on his hat and winked at them..

He said, "Dex Hamel and Mike will be riding ahead as security. Will you be riding on ahead with them or following the stage?"

Kelly said, "We prefer to follow back a few yards, but within eyesight of the stage, Mr. Hopkins."

"I like him." Lola nodded with a smile and a wink to her sister who simply grinned.

14 MEETING MR. HELTON

"Ma'am, do you know if any of the Helton's are around? I'd like to speak to one of them, if I could." Kelly's eyes were hopeful. The waitress held up a finger and then turned and disappeared into the kitchen. She came back a minute later with two parcels followed by a man about the age of their father.

"I'm Victor Helton. You ladies wanted to see me?" Tall at six feet four and well over two hundred pounds, Victor Helton was an imposing figure with swept back black hair and dark eyes.

"Yes, sir, Mr. Helton. My name is Kelly Stolter and this is my sister, Lola Stolter." She took off her glove and extended her hand. The man grinned and gently shook her hand.

"Stolter. Now why does that name ring a bell?"

"Our ranch breeds, raises and trains champion cutting horses. I wanted to find out if you were looking for any horses for your cowboys on the ranch." Kelly kept her voice low and her eyes on his.

"That's where I know the name. Yes, about five years back we bought a cutting horse from your father, I believe. That horse thinks on his own. Excellently trained animal. We've often talked about getting two more. Do you have any with you?" His dark eyes looked from Kelly to Lola and then back.

"No, Sir. Not with us. Right now, we have a completely trained eighteen-month old filly and a two-year-old gelding that has just finished his exercises. If you'd be interested in either one, we'll be back on the ranch in about ten days." Kelly smiled.

"I would be interested. If you don't mind, what are you asking for them?" The tall man crossed his arms over his chest and stood with his feet apart.

Kelly smiled. "We're asking sixty dollars for the filly and seventy for the gelding. We've had a couple of low-ball offers on the filly but she's worth the money."

"Don't you think that price on your filly is a bit steep?" He sounded gruff.

Kelly pulled on her glove. "No, not at all. Her mare was a blue-ribbon prize money champion cutter. If we don't sell the filly, I'll put her on the rodeo circuit next year. After she wins, I'll double her price and one of the big Texas outfits will buy her." Hamel flagged down Kelly's attention and signaled it was time to go.

"Mr. Helton, thank you for your time. If you are interested, write and let us know when you want to come see her." Kelly reached to shake hands with the man who reluctantly smiled and nodded.

The stage had just started to roll when the girls walked onto the porch. Hamel waved them on and they mounted quickly and trotted past as a perplexed Helton stood next to the rail.

Lola rode closer to Kelly. "You sounded just like pa back there. How'd you know to ask for him?"

"I remembered ma and pa talking about delivering a gelding to the Helton Ranch. They were impressed that such a ranch would buy one of our horses. So, I decided to take a chance. What's the worst thing that could happen? He could have said no. But he didn't." Kelly grinned to her sister who laughed out loud.

Five miles down the dusty trail the sun turned into a reddish orange ball that hovered an inch above the horizon. Hamel dropped back in between the girls.

"In another mile or so we'll pull into Shea for the night. You're welcome to camp out with us if you're gonna stop." Hamel looked first at Lola and then Kelly.

"Lola, do you want to stop at Shea or do you want to ride on? I'll stop. I'm tired of being in the saddle." Kelly shouted to Lola.

Lola nodded affirmatively. "Yes, stop. I'm tired, too."

Hamel said, "The restaurant has other food to go with your dinner packs from Helton Corners. They've got cold drinks, too, and fancy desserts." He laughed.

***

The sun disappeared into the hills and a purple gray wash had crept up the hills. After the horses were turned out to graze, Lola and Kelly cleaned up and went into the restaurant. They sat down at a rough table to eat just as the waitress stopped by.

"Lemonade, milk or beer. I really don't think you two pretty ladies drink whiskey or tequila." She giggled. The girls laughed with her.

"Lemonade, please. Do you have a little sugar for it, too?"

"Yes, miss, we surely do."

Lola tapped the table. "We heard a story that you have some fancy desserts."

The waitress laughed again. "Yes, miss. One of the girls spent over a year in Paris, France to study at some fancy art school. She worked part time in a bakery there and came back knowing how to make all these fancy things. I can't even pronounce them properly. I'll bring the tray out when you're ready for dessert so you can see them." She bustled away and brought back two glasses of lemonade.

Hamel came in looking freshly washed. "May I join you ladies? I washed up." Lola nodded.

"Of course. Please sit down, Mr. Hamel."

He leaned forward and lowered his voice, saying, "I wanted to tell you that one of the men passengers asked to speak to you about your horses. Not the ones you're riding. The ones you were talking to Vic Helton about."

Lola sat up straight. "What does he want? Who is he?"

Hamel's voice got even quieter. "His name is Dunbarton. He's traveling home to Texas. That's all I know. I've never seen him before." The girls were quiet for a moment. Just then the waitress brought out the drinks and plates and set then on the table. Hamel gave his order and she returned to the kitchen.

"We'll speak to him after dinner." Lola nodded and bit into the flaky crust containing the tender beef with savory onions and peppers. She groaned. Kelly stared at her sister.

"You have to learn how to cook this, Kel. I could eat a bucket of this!" She smiled and then took another bite.

Kelly took a bite and closed her eyes chewing happily. She groaned along with Lola. Hamel laughed out loud. "I tried to tell you it was good."

"They make a pie crust and then load it up with this beef and onions stuff. Then they fold the crust over, seal it and bake it. It's good," Kelly said, licking her fingers.

Hamel swallowed and took a drink of his beer. "They also serve spicy ones with jalapeno chilies and tomatoes. Your mouth feels like it's on fire, but boy, it tastes so good."

"My little brother Colton would like that. He likes spicy stuff. Ma used to make spicy hot chili and Colton would nearly eat the whole thing." Lola said and then bit off another mouthful.

Kelly saw the waitress approaching with a long wide tray that she set on the edge of the table. Hamel laughed.

"Ladies, for your enjoyment we have a fine selection of desserts," she said happily gesturing to the tray.

"Apple, peach and berry turnovers. Cream and berry stuffed croissants. Cinnamon pecan sticky buns. Then there is the cake, a cream and custard combination called terra me two. Or something like that. This is chocolate shortcake. That is from the east coast and has whipped sugary cream in between layers of cake and it is called Boston Cream Pie." She smiled. Hamel winked to her.

"Oh, my gosh, Kelly. I want one of everything." Lola burst out laughing. Kelly laughed and gently pushed Hamel's shoulder.

"Evil, wicked people tempting two delicate young ladies with these obviously sinful yet sweet masterpieces." Kelly laughed.

"Delicate young ladies with big Colt guns strapped on their thighs," Hamel held his stomach while he laughed. The girls giggled.

After desserts were enjoyed the three stepped out on to the broad porch and sat down. Hamel lit a cigarette.

"So, where is this Mr. Dunbarton?"

"He is either in the saloon or in the hotel. There's not a lot of entertainment in this town," Hamel said.

"Okay, we'll go down to the saloon and see if he is there. If not, we'll try the hotel." The girls stood up.

"I ate too much. My pants are tight, Kel." Lola rubbed her tummy with a small grin.

"Yeah, I know. I'm like a baby. You feed me and I want to go to sleep. We'll go find this Mr. Dunbarton and then head for camp." Kelly rubbed her own tummy.

Hamel stood up. "If you will wait on the porch, I'll go into the saloon and ask for him." Kelly nodded. They walked two doors down and stopped in front of a saloon with loud piano music and the laughter of men and women drifting out the doors onto the porch. Hamel looked in, then walked to the bar. The girls watched him look around and then he came back out shaking his head.

When they reached the lobby of the hotel, the girls were surprised at how quiet it was.

Lola whispered, "I think we should whisper so we don't disturb anyone." Kelly raised her eyebrows. She stepped to the registration desk where the man frowned at her.

"If Mr. Dunbarton is a guest here tonight, would you kindly tell him the Stolters are here to consult with him, please?" Kelly clasped her hands together and smiled.

The clerk raised his eyebrows and started to write. "Miss, please spell your name for me." Kelly obliged the clerk who curtly nodded and headed up the stairs.

In less than five minutes a tall slender man in his fifties with a gray goatee and mustache came down the stairs and into the lobby, closely followed by the clerk. He wore gray, freshly pressed slacks and a white, open collared shirt. He walked towards Kelly with his hand out.

"The Misses Stolters. I am most pleased to meet you finally. I am Mick Dunbarton." His hand was cool and dry as his soft grip held her hand.

"The pleasure is ours, Mr. Dunbarton. I am Kelly and this is my sister, Lola." Again, the man shook hands with the younger girl.

Would you like to sit down?" The blue eyes nodded towards a group of chairs near the windows.

After he sat down in the easy chair he cleared his throat. "I must start with an apology. I overheard your conversation with Mr. Helton at the last stop. My curiosity was stirred by your words, Miss Stolter. You are a younger version of your lovely mother, Miss Kelly."

Kelly smiled and nodded. "You are very kind, Mr. Dunbarton. Our family breeds, raises and trains cutting horses. My mother had been teaching me everything she knew about training."

"Yes, I am ecstatic that I found you. What you might not know is that I met your mother in Denver when she was very young. She had won a couple of cutting competitions where she bested my family's horses." He smiled and rubbed his hands together.

"Somehow over the years I thought I would get a rematch, but it never happened. And now she is gone. I am so very sorry for her passing. I feel the loss of a passionate competitor," he said. Kelly and Lola both smiled at the same time and said nothing.

"Neither of you ladies know me. You don't know anything about me and you might even think me forward. But I felt strongly enough about this to risk your offense and speak my mind. You see, I suspect you are traveling to the Flint Hills Ranch because it is part of your mother's estate." He looked for a reaction and saw none.

"Don't let anyone talk you into selling that ranch. Your mother was a champion partly because she lived there and walked that land. When you go there, you'll feel the strength and vibrancy of the trees, grass, hills and the river. While you've never seen it, you will come to love that land as she did." Before he could continue, Lola interrupted.

"Pardon my interruption, Mr. Dunbarton. You feel people, don't you?" She had leaned forward slightly to look at him intently.

"Yes, Miss Lola. I sense things about people." He smiled and blinked. The young girl smiled and nodded.

Kelly leaned forward slightly. "Mr. Dunbarton, where are you from? What is the name of the place you live in Texas?"

Dunbarton shifted in his chair slightly. "My permanent home is in Hattiesburg, Mississippi, but I have a considerable amount of land near D'Angelo, Texas, which is where I'm headed on this trip. I run longhorn cattle, Miss Stolter, and cutting horses are extremely valuable to me." Kelly and Lola exchanged a look.

"If either the filly or the gelding were trained by your mother, I would like to purchase them." Dunbarton arched his fingers together. "It would give me a somewhat emotional opportunity to enjoy her company one last time, so to speak. Would you accept one hundred fifty dollars for both horses?"

Kelly started to speak, but Lola stopped her. Without taking her eyes off Dunbarton Lola said, "Sell the horses to him, Kelly. He wants them because they were the last horses that ma trained. And he loved her like we do." Kelly raised her eyebrows and looked at Dunbarton. The man rubbed his hands together and cleared his throat as he averted his eyes to the floor.

"Mr. Dunbarton, if you are serious about purchasing those exact two horses, I'll instruct our attorney in Bradford to draw up a bill of sale and arrange delivery. When the stage stops in Bradford, go to the offices of Merle Doyle. He will have the contract and documents waiting for you. Once he lets me know that payment has been made, I'll notify the ranch that those horses are sold." Dunbarton rubbed his hand over his mouth and stood up. The girls stood up.

"I'm very happy, Miss Stolter. I never in my wildest dreams thought I would own a Marianna Richardson horse, but now I will own two. Thank you," He reached his hand to shake Kelly's hand. With Lola, he held her hand just a moment longer and then smiled with her as if a secret had passed between them. He then bowed slightly and walked up the staircase.

Hamel was sitting on the bench on the porch when the girls came out of the hotel. "You alright? He didn't upset you, did he?" Hamel stood up. Lola shook her head.

Kelly waved her hand. "No, we're alright. He just wanted to buy the horses." They stepped down into the dusty street and walked towards the stables.

"No, Kel. He wanted to buy ma's horses. He and ma knew each other for a long time. When she married pa, it just made him very sad. He is very happy now that he'll have ma's horses." Lola smiled.

"Maybe your ma was the first girl he ever loved. I can still remember Susie Anderson clear as day. Fifth grade. She broke my heart." He laughed out loud. Lola and Kelly giggled.

The night had cooled down and the half-moon shined a cold yellowish light. The grass held the song of crickets and the scent of earth. As Kelly's eyes grew heavy, she pulled the blanket a little closer to her chin and smiled, knowing that many had loved her mother.

15 DUNBARTON MYSTERIOUSLY DISAPPEARS

There was a stronger breeze blowing the next morning. The washed out blue sky still showed a tinged reddish stain near the horizon.

Half an hour later the connecting stage came in and Hamel and the driver unhooked the team. Just then Kelly remembered her interesting conversation with the Texas land owner. When she scanned the group of passengers, she did not see Mr. Dunbarton.

Hamel trotted over to them. "So, you two are taking off from here? You'll go another seven miles and then there will be a turnoff to the left that does down a slope. Quarter mile on there is a big water hole. It's a well-known water hole so you'll most likely come up on other folks there. Be sure and fill all your water canteens there."

Kelly fussed with her gloves. "Three days riding under your protection, Mr., Hamel I think we can do seven miles on our own today."

Lola said, "Mr. Hamel, I don't see Mr. Dunbarton on the stage. Didn't he get on?" Hamel shook his head.

"No, miss. In the night, he hired a horse and rode out, real quiet like. I didn't hear a thing so he must have been careful. There was a message left at the desk that he would not be continuing on the stage." The outrider raised his eyebrows. Lola looked at the ground for a moment and then took in a deep breath.

"Thank you for all your help and friendship, Mr. Hamel," Kelly said with a genuine smile. Lola swung up into the saddle. Hamel held the horse while Kelly mounted up.

"Hope to see you ladies again sometime. Happy trails!" He held up his hand and waved. Kelly and Lola waved again before they climbed up to the road.

Seven miles went by at an easy lope. They saw several deer scamper across the road ahead and disappear into the brush and trees. The road had turned into a hard-packed surface. As they came down off a small hill they saw off to the right a rounded depression that must have been a water hole, but now was dry.

The turnoff was loose gravel and sand that crunched under the horse's hooves. It was a wide place in the river sheltered by weeping willows and a couple of old cottonwood trees. Several blackened rings of rocks were set back from the water for folks who needed a fire. There was no one there.

"Okay, Lola. Let's fill everything up and we're going to ride for quite a time from here on." Kelly filled two water skins and both canteens.

As they walked back onto the main road, two riders on paint horses trotted past them. Bandannas were pulled up over the nose and mouth and with low tan broad brimmed hats, Kelly couldn't make out the men's faces. It was only a lifted gloved hand in greeting as the men turned their horses down into the water hole.

***

The day was coming up on noon. The breeze was warm, yet when they rode through shade there was a coolness about the air. At the last water hole, they had taken off their dusters and rode on comfortably in their jeans and the black sweaters their mother had knitted for them.

They had startled a flock of quail, passed an older man and woman hauling something under an old patched canvas in a rickety, swaying wagon and been chased by three mangy dogs. The sky had been clear with only a few puffy clouds hovering around the mountains in the north.

Lola edged her horse a bit closer to Kelly's. "The map shows a hazard up ahead. Maybe we should stop, because those people in the wagon won't be able to get by." Kelly nodded and slowed to a trot.

Another two miles went by and the girls saw nothing in the road or anything that had been pulled off to the shoulder. Lola shook her head and shrugged. Kelly gestured ahead and the horses went back to a gallop. Another five miles went by and Kelly's horse slowed down to a trot and nickered several times. Kelly gave the animal his head and it turned around and trotted back to a narrow footpath.

Brambles and brush blocked the way, so Kelly used the small machete she's brought along and hacked away limbs until the horses could get through. A sandy path led around fallen boulders and stopped at a deep, clear spring with cool water that was surrounded by poplar and birch trees. Both horses waded in and drank long.

Lola took off her gloves. "Well, it looks like we're stopping here for a while." Kelly looked around.

"Look over there." Kelly pointed to an area nearby.

At the west end of the spring was a makeshift lean-to that had partially fallen in from the weight of the overhead tree limbs. About six-foot-wide and five-foot-deep, Kelly knew someone had taken the time to craft the shelter. To the right of the shelter, about ten feet away, was a ring of rocks obscured with piled brush.

Lola nosed around. "We weren't supposed to find this lean-to. Someone went out of their way to cover that path pretty well with brush and hide this fire spot." Kelly nodded.

"Are we on someone's land? Do you want to go?" Kelly asked.

Lola shook her head and rubbed her forehead. She pulled the map out of her saddlebag and spread it on the soft sand. "It doesn't show a water hole here. And it doesn't feel like anyone's land. We might as well rest for a while and have something to eat."

"I want a fire and coffee." Kelly broke small twigs over her knee and re-stacked a few of the rocks into the ring. Lola brought over the saddlebags. Both horses had started to nibble on the tender green grass at the water's edge.

Kelly asked, "How do you think Colton's doing? You think he's alright?"

"Sure, he is. Colton will hide first and try to stay away from anyone. If anyone surprises him, he'll shoot them and then try to figure out who it is." Lola pulled off her black sweater.

"You know, before ma died, I mostly thought of him as a little boy. In the last month, he's grown up a lot. He does all his chores now without being told to. He brings in firewood if he sees there's none in the kitchen." Lola walked over to the springs and filled the tin pot.

Wispy white smoke curled up from the small fire. After the larger wood pieces caught and burned, the pot went on and the girls sat down.

"Kel, do you think pa is alright? There must be something important to keep him away like this." Lola leaned back on her sweater and looked at the fire.

"I think he must be alright, honey. If he was hurt, he'd find a way to tell someone who'd send a telegram, or write a letter or come by. I know it's gonna hurt him a lot when he finds out ma died."

Lola shook her head. "He's going to blame himself for not being here."

"Doc said there was nothing nobody could do for her. She got sick and we did our best. We would've done the same if it had been him instead of ma." Kelly dumped a small amount of the coffee into the pot and put it back in the fire.

They unwrapped pieces of soft bread covering the thick slab of tender beef. They split a sweet roll for dessert and shared two cups of coffee. Kelly was licking her fingers when Lola silently nudged her and nodded toward the horses. Both animals had stopped chewing and were looking with ears pricked forward towards the grassy area on the other side of the springs.

Kelly saw her gelding's ears go back and she imitated a pistol with her hands. Lola went up onto her knees and both girls drew their guns. A few minutes went by and then the gelding snorted and went back to grazing.

Lola had a deep frown on her forehead when she softly said, "It's time to go." Kelly nodded and began to spread out the embers. Lola dumped out the last trickle of coffee and then plunged the pot into the springs to cool it down.

Kelly led the horses over to the narrow path and handed the reins to Lola. "I'm gonna drag some branches over the dirt and mess up our tracks. Stay right here while I try to get that camp back to the way we found it."

Lola nodded.

Kelly piled twigs and brush back over the fire and dragged a leafy branch over the soft dirt smudging the horse tracks. There was nothing she could do about the clipped grass from the horses' grazing. She backed out scraping a branch after herself.

After they were back out on the road, they pulled the loose brush back across the narrow path. As they mounted up, Kelly looked at the obscured path. She knew it was there, but most folks would ride right on by and never know it was there.

Two miles of trotting on southward, Kelly pulled closer to Lola. "So, what was it back there?"

Lola shook her head. "Something silent getting closer. It wasn't a good idea to stick around and have a look."

Kelly nodded. She had learned to accept Lola's need to move and not argue about what should be done.

"Okay, Lola. You've got that map memorized by now. You lead and get us to a good camp by sundown," she said with a smile in her voice. Lola grinned and both horses lengthened out into a loping gallop.

16 THE STAGE STOP AT RUSSET HILLS

It was over an hour later that the big rumbling stage trundled into the small area. Hamel waved his hat at the girls.

"I see you young ladies made it just fine. Did you stop to do any sight-seeing?" The man chuckled.

Kelly laughed. "No, not even a traveling circus."

"Hey, Dex. Why is this called Russet Hills?" Lola called out to the out-rider.

Over his shoulder, he called out, "Potatoes."

Lola looked at Kelly and then said, "What? Did you say potatoes?"

"I was told the first time I stopped here that the hills were curved and flattened into terraces. There used to be a big family out here that planted potatoes, and they built little canals up on the mesa for the river to feed down over the potato plants and water them."

Kelly went up on her tip toes and shielded her eyes from the sun. "That's gotta be a mile long. I can see how someone graded the hill up like big stairs."

Lola asked, "What?" She grunted in frustration and climbed up to stand on the top fence rail. Hamel dashed over in a panic to catch her, but she waved him away.

"Dangit, Lola. You'll fall if you're not careful." Hamel looked up at Lola balanced on the six-foot-high rail.

Kelly put her hand on the shotgun rider's arm. "She's alright, Dex. She's got good balance like a goat." Hamel started to calm down, but he wouldn't take his eyes off the young girl.

"You're right, Kelly Someone spent a lot of time leveling out those terraces. There's four of them. That's a lot of potatoes. Four miles of potatoes." Lola shrugged her shoulders and climbed down.

Hamel visibly breathed a sigh of relief. "They aren't just any watery, mushy potato either. Their firm and white with a thick, dark brown skin on them. And they taste really good."

Lola pulled on her gloves. "I thought all potatoes tasted the same."

"Nope, red-skinned potatoes are almost sweet, and white potatoes are like the russet, but they've got softer insides and a thin, white skin. Then there's gold colored potatoes that are yellowish. When you cook them, they turn golden." Hamel rubbed his belly with a big smile.

"You have got to get out more, Miss Lola. You have to experience more potatoes in the world." The man giggled.

When they walked into the station, Ernie Hopkins was sitting at a table eating a huge baked potato smothered in butter, onions and bits of crumbled bacon.

"This is just heavenly," he said with his mouth half full. The girls snickered.

"I wish we had more time. I'd like to walk up there and look at those plants." Lola smiled.

"Good luck with that, Miss Lola. They don't allow anyone not family up there. I've tried. I've begged to see those plants. They don't let nobody up there." Hamel crossed his arms over his chest.

Kelly asked, "Are any of the family here? I'd like to meet one of them." She looked at the empty counter. A younger girl came out carrying a tray of the freshly baked potatoes. Kelly walked over to look.

"These are a dime each, miss. They're fully cooked. We charge more for the toppings." Reddish curls bobbed around on the hair pinned up on top of her head. Greenish eyes were clear and bright.

Kelly asked, "What about the cold, raw potatoes? Do you sell those?"

"From time to time we sell ten pound sacks of them. We don't have any right now. It's still early in the growing season. These ones we just cooked were from the hot house." She dragged the back of her hand over her forehead and smiled.

"I think we might stop and buy some when we ride back through next week. My name is Kelly Stolter. Can I pay you for the sack now?" Kelly started to pull off her glove to fish out her coins. The young girl stopped her.

"Hello, Kelly Stolter. I'm Virginia Magrin. Please don't pay now. I would feel awful if I had to refund your money when you stopped by because we didn't have any."

Mike Knepler leaned in the door. "Come on, Ernie. Eat up! Horses are hitched and ready to go."

Lola walked over to Virginia. "So, if I wanted to go up and look at a couple of those plants, who would I ask?"

Virginia shook her head with a pout. "Oh, nobody is allowed near the plants except for the family. That's the Beaulieu family. They are protective of their land and keep people from trampling over the ground and the plants." She smiled and took Hopkins' plate as he handed it to her going out the door.

Lola turned sideways as she nodded. "Okay. Well, thank you. We'll have to stop on our way back." Lola quickly eased out of her right-hand glove and reached to shake hands with Virginia. After a few seconds, Lola let go of her hand and the girls went out the front door after Hopkins.

A mile down the road, Kelly pulled up alongside the trotting Lola. "So, what was it back there?"

"They're hiding something up there and they don't want anyone near it." Lola looked at Kelly who shrugged.

"Everyone has something to hide. Maybe they are just private people."

"The thing is, Kelly, there aren't any fences around those terraces. I got up high enough to see. Not a fence in sight. If you want to keep people away, you build a fence. The Beaulieu family ain't got no fences."

Kelly said, "Well, one thing is for sure. We're stopping back here and taking a sack of them potatoes home with us." Lola nodded.

"Ma used to make some really good baked potatoes. I miss those. I wish I knew her secret on how she did that." Kelly urged her horse into a lope to catch up with the stagecoach in the distance.

The stage started down the trail along the edge of the mesa. A brilliant streak of red clay contrasted sharply with the sandstone. At the bottom were white, gritty patches of tiny rocks in amongst the fat stubby cacti. Around the final bend of reddish boulders, they saw the far eastern hills painted with dots of gray and lavender.

***

At the Shea station, the girls helped unhook the team and rubbed down the horses. The black mare and the dun gelding shook and rolled into the soft grass in the corral. They paid the fifty cents for a bucket of oats and corn as extra feed for the animals.

"Are you girls gonna stay in the house there? They have a real nice sleeping porch with cots and blankets. The stage folks generally pay extra to sleep in the rooms on the beds." Hamel took off his gloves and gripped and flexed his hands.

Kelly looked at Lola who looked at Hamel. "Where you bedding down at for the night?" Kelly nudged her and hissed something. Hamel's mouth dropped open.

Lola frowned and squirmed around to look at Kelly. "What? I just asked him where he was going to sleep at tonight." A husky-lab mix station dog trotted up to Lola and she scratched him behind the ears.

Kelly whispered, "Girls don't ask men about sleeping arrangements, Lola. It's not polite." Lola looked up at the night sky and let out a big breath of exasperation. Kelly knelt to scratch the friendly dog.

Lola slightly bowed to Hamel. "I'm sorry, Mr. Hamel, if I made you uncomfortable."

The man held up a hand. "It's alright, miss. I'd probably be safe bedding down near you girls anyways. Ernie, Mike and I usually sack out in the bunkroom in the barn. It's quiet and we don't stay up chattering all night like the stage passengers do."

"I can't think straight when I'm hungry. I need to get some dinner in me. Then after that, I'll figure out where to sleep. Something smells good in there. Where can I wash up?" Kelly rubbed her face with both hands. Hamel gestured to the side porch.

The three men and the two girls walked around to the back porch of the kitchen. Inside the door were two rough wooden tables with oilcloth covers. They all sat down to a hot meal and the girls drank milk while the men had beer and whiskey.

Lola asked, "How's your beef, Kelly? It looks good." Kelly's plate was brimming with sliced roast beef in a brown gravy, mashed potatoes and small ears of corn.

"Soft and tender. They must cook it all day to get it like this. The potatoes are good, too. How's your chicken dinner?" Lola's plate had sliced chicken breast, mashed potatoes and sliced carrots in a sweet honey glaze.

Lola held up a bite of chicken. "Crispy on the outside and juicy on the inside. The biscuits are soft and very good. If I eat too much of this, I won't be able to get on my horse." The men laughed.

The cook came out of the kitchen and sat down on the wooden chair in the doorway to smoke. "You boys have an easy trip this time?" They all nodded with their mouths full.

Hamel wiped his mouth off. "We had a horse go lame up at Sera Mesa. Miss Lola let us use her dun gelding and we made it into Helton just fine." Lola smiled and wiggled her fingers in a wave.

"Where you girls from? We don't get many traveling ladies coming through." The cook blew smoke out into the night air.

Kelly chewed a mouthful and pointed for Lola to speak. "Yucca Valley. Our folks have a ranch on the east side about six miles out. Windy Ridge Ranch."

Cook nodded. A stubbly black beard covered a heavy jowl, and his thick black eyebrows hung out over a pair of dark brown eyes. He wore a long sleeved white shirt with the sleeves rolled up to the elbows and a white apron that went to his knees.

The waitress came to get another order and he stood up to fill plates. Lola split a biscuit with Kelly and let honey drizzle on it from the little pot. The cook brought back the pitcher and refilled their milk cups.

"So, where you ladies headed to? Santa Fe? Dallas? Chicago?" Lola chuckled and then had to wipe her mouth.

Kelly said, "No. Nothing so exotic. We're going down to Bradford. Our family owns a ranch down there and we're going down to take a look."

The heavy man pushed himself back up to standing once again. "Well, happy trails to you. Stop back by if you get the chance." He waved and walked through the kitchen doorway.

Hamel gestured with his fork. "I don't believe I've ever heard him say more than two or three words. He was a magpie around you girls." They all chuckled.

After dinner, Kelly and Lola carried their saddle bags around the side to the screened porch. Wide alder pole benches were spaced about six feet apart with a folded quilt at the foot of each. A lone man in the end cot was lightly snoring.

"What do you think, Lola? Sleep near a stranger or go out to the barn and sleep near people we sort of know?" Kelly looked at the cots.

"The barn." Lola picked up her saddle bags and walked down the steps to the yard.

Hamel, Ernie and Mike were standing next to the corral rails when the girls walked around the corner of the barn.

"Well, this might seem just a bit unusual. We'd rather bunk down with people we know than sleep six feet away from a total stranger. Is that alright?" Kelly put down the heavy bags.

Knepler nodded and said, "Sure, you ladies are welcome. But I'll warn you. Mr. Ernie here snores." Hopkins swatted the back of Knepler's head.

He whined, "Don't be telling personal things about me to the young ladies, now." He followed that up with a wink to the girls, who laughed.

Hamel gestured towards the barn. "Come on, I'll show you where you can sack out. You both can sleep in the same big cot or one in each cot. You'll need your bed roll as the blankets are pretty thin."

The bunk room had divided alcoves with double wide cots. The lumpy mattresses were covered with a loose flannel blanket. Kelly told Lola to wait a moment and she dashed out into the dark night. A minute later she reappeared carrying four of the quilts from the sleeping porch.

Just as they got comfortable, the station dog walked in and whined softly. Lola patted the top of the quilt and the dog climbed up on the cot. He turned around three times and then laid down with a plop. Kelly grinned at Lola who tried not to laugh out loud. With the dog to keep them warm, they were asleep in minutes.

In the restaurant dining room, Lola heard a familiar laugh. She turned around and grinned a brilliant smile.

She waved and called out, "Mr. Lucci!"

"Well, it's the young Stolter ladies! Good morning, good morning! Imagine running into you out here," The big man hugged both and gave them kisses on their red cheeks.

"You ladies didn't decide to run off and see the world now, did you?" The freight wagon driver winked at them.

"You mean like join a travelling show or become a vagabond?" Kelly shook her head. "You can't very well be a vagabond when you have to be somewhere on Mondays."

The man laughed. "Please sit down. Tell me where you are going and where you have been!"

Kelly took off her jacket and put it on the back of the tall wooden chair. "We've been following the stage south from Yucca Valley. We're going to Flint Hills to see where ma grew up."

Mr. Lucci got a sad look on his face. "Ah. Your poor dear mother. I'm so sorry for your loss. She was a dear woman. Very kind to me."

"Thank you, yes. We miss her terribly." Kelly smiled gently as she fidgeted with the edge of her shirt. She cleared her throat. "Where are you headed to, Mr. Lucci?"

His gray blue eyes gleamed. "I'm waiting on the rumbling wagon of Bartholomew Van de Greuden that is due to arrive from Denver in the next three hours. I made better time than he did this trip. Usually he waits on me here and I'm the tardy culprit. He is bringing in a dozen rolled up carpets from a hotel up there in the Rockies. The men who own the hotel decided to toss out the old furniture and rugs and bring in new. We got those carpets for pennies."

Lola nudged Kelly. "We could have used a carpet on those cold wood floors this past winter. There were some mornings I couldn't put my toes on the floor it was so cold." Lucci laughed and rubbed his belly. The stage crew came in and Kelly introduced the men.

Over their meal, they talked about the condition of the road going south and west. They exchanged stories and gossip about different people they knew. The waiter brought a platter of eggs, sliced beef steak, and ham along with potatoes, biscuits and cobbler. The peaceful chatter was suddenly shattered by a blaring trumpet outside. Lola's fork clattered against her plate.

"And that, my good ladies, is the sound of Bartholomew Van de Greuden. He heard once how famed Roman Marcus Aurelius was announced by trumpets. He's been doing it ever since." They all laughed and walked out onto porch. While Lucci and Van de Greuden unhooked the team from the parked wagon, Hamel and his crew smoked at the end of the porch.

"While they're busy with the Percherons, let's look at those carpets? Want to?" Lucci gestured with his hand towards the huge wagon.

"Sure!" Lola and Kelly nodded happily.

The girls climbed up on the wooden tailgate of the big wagon. In the dim light, long curled rolls were stacked five across and five high.

Lola leaned to run her hand over one of the rolls and suddenly jerked back as if a snake had tried to bite her. She jumped down off the tail gate and shook her hand.

Kelly climbed down and tried to grab her hand. "What is it? You get caught on a nail?"

"Shh." Lola gripped her hand as if she had been stung. Kelly tried to see the injury but Lola pulled away.

They walked around the end of the wagon and watched the freighter walking across the yard. Lucci introduced them to the big, muscled Swedish man.

"We were just looking at the size of your wagon wheels, Mr. Van de Greuden. It rides pretty high." Lola peered up at the big man.

"You have a good eye, miss. Yes, in the winter I have the tall wheels on the wagon to help me get over the snow and through the creeks that run deeper than other times of the year. I have another, wider rimmed set of wheels in Tucson that I put on for the run in the desert towns." Van de Greuden's eyes crinkled up at the corners when he talked.

The girls lifted their heads when they heard the two-tone whistle from Hamel. "Oh. We're being called by the stage crew. I would like to talk with you more about your wagon sometime, Mr. Van de Greuden. Goodnight!"

Lucci gave the girls a quick hug. "Say your prayers for a good smooth road tomorrow, ladies!"

Kelly and Lola waved as they trotted away towards the corral.

At the water trough, Kelly put her hand on Lola's shoulder and stopped her. Her eyes were wide with concern. "What was that all about? You acted like something tried to bite you when you touched that carpet."

Lola nodded and shifted from foot to foot glancing back over her shoulder. "I know why they got those carpets so cheap from that hotel. Kelly, people died on those carpets. Every last one. They've been cleaned up and washed. But you can't wash away death from carpet." Kelly made a sour, disgusted face and then shivered.

"Eww." She shivered again.

"Hey, come on you two. It's time to get some shut eye and we want the door locked on the inside tonight," Hamel called out. Quickly, Kelly and Lola ran over to the old barn and stepped past Hamel who closed the door behind them.

Twenty minutes later, in the darkness of the barn, Lola nudged Kelly. The older sister turned to see Lola's wide eyes filled with tears. "He will come home, won't he, Kel? Dad will bring those horses and come home?"

Kelly pulled Lola into a hug under the quilt. "Yes, honey. Pa told us stories about running one hundred head of stock down out of Canada with only two other cowboys. He's good at this, honey."

Lola's whisper shook with emotion. "But there's bad people out there, Kel. I see more and more every day, every mile. I want him to come home safe." The young girl's voice broke as Kelly shushed her.

Later, after Lola's breathing became deep and even, Kelly turned on her side to look up through the window into the inky blackness. Tiny diamonds twinkled. Was her father safely camped for the night? Would he make it home to them?

As her eyes became heavy and sleep called to her, one tear slid down the soft cheek.

***

When she stepped out of the old barn the next morning Kelly shivered in the cold and pulled her coat tighter. The eastern sky showed a wash of pink below the deep blue higher up. In the west one lone star still twinkled. Knepler's jangling spurs announced him as he stopped at the foot of the stairs to the yard. Five days of riding with four more to go. Silently, she marveled at the crew who did this for a living.

"Before you girls go over to breakfast, I need to tell you a couple of things about the road ahead." Kelly buttoned the cuff on her shirt as she and Lola sat down on the step.

The heavy brow furrowed as the man glanced at the girls and then glanced away. "There has been some trouble at Rim Rocks the last few times we've been through there. A man was shot there a month ago. Some outlaw was on the run from authorities. They caught up to him in the saloon there and he tried to shoot his way out and died." Ernie twisted his bandanna around in his hands.

Dex Hamel leaned a bit closer. "The Rim Rocks restaurant is run by a woman, Megan Silva, whose husband ran off with one of the women that was on our stage. Megan was never quite right in the head after that. And now she thinks all the women who travel alone on the stage are, well, of ill repute." Kelly gasped and raised her eyebrows.

"What does that mean?" Lola asked with wide innocent eyes.

Hamel cleared his throat and avoided her eyes. "Well, we'd like to not even let Megan see you two young ladies because she gets angry and upset really easy. If you stay in the bunk room over at the corral, we'll bring you over a couple plates of food. Or you can go sit out of sight in the back room at the saloon and eat over there. Bob, the bartender, usually has chili and cornbread along with good cold beer. I'm sure we could get you glasses of milk or lemonade to drink, if you wanted." Hamel tried to smile but it looked more like a painful grimace.

Lola laughed and slapped her knee as Kelly stared. "I can just see us telling Pa about how we got to Bradford. Oh sure, we just stopped anywhere and sat in the town saloon eating chili and drinking beer." Kelly began to giggle and then laughed so hard she had tears in the corners of her eyes. Knepler's mouth fell open.

"Fifteen years old and already consorting with questionable men of ill repute in dens of inequity," Kelly started laughing all over again. Lola fell over against Kelly in giggles.

"What?" It was Hamel's turn to ask for the explanation. Lola giggled as Kelly wiped away tears of laughter.

"We read a lot of different things, Mr. Hamel. We were taught to read everything and then ask questions to help us understand things in the world. Our mother used to explain certain, ah, phrases and words to us so that we could understand about folks in the big world." Lola giggled again.

"What's a den of inicky? Or whatever she said?" Hamel frowned and shifted his weight to his other foot. Ernie and the other security rider leaned in closer to hear.

"Den of inequity. It is the polite way of talking about bars, taverns, saloons, lounges. Places where men spend their hard-earned money on drink and colorful ladies and lose their common sense," said Kelly. The men nodded, looking at each other with a murmured acknowledgement. One by one, the men started to laugh behind their hands.

Ernie cleared his throat to be more serious. "We're gonna stop ahead at two waterholes where you may see Mexicans camped out. They're friendly and usually have their kids with them. They ride big, powerful paint mustangs and those horses are sensitive about having other horses around. So, it's okay to say hello. Just keep your horses back away from the mustangs." Ernie slid his gloves through his hands. Then he winked with a grin.

Hamel said, "Thirty-five miles south of Bradford is the border with Mexico. We'll start seeing more and more Mexicans on the road. They may come riding up behind you fast, so from time to time glance around to see what's coming along behind you. If they do, just edge over to the right and they'll run by on the left."

Kelly smiled and said, "Lola can speak some Spanish." They all looked at the younger girl slapping her gloves against her leg.

Lola put out both hands as if to stop the conversation. "Don't get them thinking that I can carry on talking in Spanish now. I know enough Spanish to order some food and ask for the ladies' room."

Kelly laughed and Lola glared at her sister. "In other words, I know enough words to be dangerous," she said with an exasperated face. "Don't count on me to be carrying on about the state of the roads or the price of beef."

Ernie asked, "Where did you learn Spanish?"

Lola started to blush and grinned. "One of the boys I was in school with, Pepito Romero. I asked him one day what he had said in Spanish and he told me. I asked him to teach me a few words so the other kids wouldn't know what we were saying." She shrugged and wiped her mouth on her sleeve.

Kelly perked up and said, "So that means that we should make sure our guns are locked and loaded in case we get in the middle of a shootout?" Ernie's hand slapped his forehead and groaned. Hamel grinned. Kelly winked at Hamel who giggled. Lola started to laugh.

"No! No shooting!" It looked like Ernie was ready to tear the bandanna to shreds.

Lola asked, "Can we eat now? I'm hungry enough to eat my gloves."

Kelly laughed and said, "Better feed the children."

Ernie threw his hands in the air like he had given up and headed towards the low-slung wooden building. Lola and Kelly giggled along behind him, followed by the laughing stage crew.

An hour later, the big Overland stage pulled out with four additional passengers. A woman headed east had gotten ill and spent the previous day in bed there. She had recovered enough to get on this Overland. She had black curly hair, dark brown eyes and a pasty white face. She held a thick white cloth to her mouth.

Hopkins stood next to the open door. "Ladies and gentlemen, this is the stage headed towards Santa Fe in the New Mexico territory. We are not carrying any payrolls, bank deposits or gold. We should not be the target of highway robbers. Please keep your arms and head inside the stage if it is moving. We cannot guarantee your safety. We have security riders in the front and back. We know you have many choices on how you get from one place to another. Thank you for riding the Overland."

The three riders stood watching the passengers load on. Lola said, "She's not sick." The young girl pulled on her gloves and then knelt to tighten the buckle on her boot.

Kelly buttoned up her heavy sweater. "Well, she sure looks sick to me. I wouldn't want to be in that stage with her." Lola shook her head. They watched her husband stand off to the side smoking the last stub of his cigarette.

Hamel sat on his horse and watched. "What do you mean, she ain't sick?" Lola looked up at the outrider.

"She's going to have a baby. It looks like she doesn't know it yet, or at least she is acting like she doesn't know. Maybe she doesn't want her husband to know." Kelly murmured something and then checked the cinch on the saddle one more time.

Hamel said, "Yeah, I've heard about women getting sick to their stomach when they first expecting."

"Who are the other two men?" The first man was in dark cloth slacks, a white shirt and a leather jacket. He carried a soft leather portfolio with handles, like a businessman, and short lengths of salt and pepper hair were visible under the tan Stetson. His boots looked like they had never been worn. He glanced around with a pair of cold, gray eyes before loading on.

"I didn't look at the list." Hamel patted the neck of his black gelding. The second man smiled and waved and thanked Ernie before he got up into the stage. Dark blue denim jeans, a red plaid flannel shirt, and a deep faded scar from above his ear down to his right jaw.

Lola said, "I'm just a nosy Nelly this morning. There is just so much I want to know here. I'm feeling sassy, Kelly!" The young girl walked over to the stage and looked up at the man sitting next to the window. She pulled out the Colt revolver, checked the chambers, and holstered it. Then she walked on past to say something to Mike. She stepped back and the big coach started to roll.

The young girl shook her head as she hoisted herself up into the saddle. She glanced at Kelly. "Check your Colt. There is something not right about that red plaid shirt man. I wanted him to see that I was carrying a weapon." Kelly immediately pulled her revolver and checked the chambers. She slid the gun back into the leather holster and settled back in her saddle with a frown.

***

The coach had been rolling for almost an hour over hard-packed sandy clay mixed with dirt. The team slowed to a walk and then turned into a drive-way, heading for the water hole. Kelly and Hamel helped take the team to water and stood talking with the crew. Most of the passengers had gotten out to get some air and to smoke. When she turned around to look for Lo-la, she saw the young girl had drawn her Colt and was holding it in both hands down in front of her body. She was slowly backing towards a patch of brush.

"Dex! Trouble! Get everyone in cover!" Kelly drew her Colt, crouched and sprinted around some rocks, heading towards Lola. Three men rode into the clearing with bandannas over their faces and guns drawn. One of them fired a warning shot over his head and everyone ducked down. Eve-ryone except Lola, who stood up and put a bullet through the man who fired the shot.

Kelly pulled her back behind the rocks. "Damnit, Lola."

The young girl whispered, "It's war games time, Kelly. Lock and load. They shoot at me, I'm gonna shoot right back. They better learn."

Kelly gripped her sister's sweater. "You go east, I'll go west. Take down the horses if you have to. If we let them go, they'll just come back and try it again down the road. You know what to do. Got it?" Lola nodded and scampered into the brush.

Kelly could see the woman was still huddled on the stage with her hus-band shielding her. She could not see any of the other passengers. Another ten feet and she had a line of sight on the short man with the bandanna over his face. Dust drifted from the passengers scuffling for cover.

A man's voice called out, "You there in the rocks. We've got guns on your passengers. Throw down your iron and come out." A shot sounded and a man screamed, gripping his chest before he fell into the dirt.

It was a young girl's voice that yelled out the warning. "Anybody else want to shoot at me? I've got twenty more shots just waiting and I'll make you late for dinner."

Kelly began to ease up for a better look when a man in black jeans and worn-down boots stumbled into the brush. Then he fell over the stump and his pistol tumbled from his hand into the briars.

His eyes saw her weapon and they got big. "You're just not having any luck today," Kelly said as she pointed her Colt to his leg and fired. A blood-curdling scream came from him and he gripped his leg. Kelly kicked his gun out of the brush and picked it up her left hand. She looked up when she heard the two-toned whistle. She stood up and backed out into the clearing.

Hamel called out, "Kelly, Lola? You all right?" Lola trotted out from behind a boulder. She had a dirt smudge on her forehead. Kelly nodded briefly to her sister.

"That's three up, three down. Anybody else?" Kelly's voice was low and cool. Lola shook her head and holstered the Colt. "We're done here."

Kelly turned towards the brush and called out. "It's okay now. Come on out, Dex, Ernie."

Mike trotted over. "All the passengers are all right. But I can't find the one man. Where's the man in the red plaid shirt?" They all glanced around. No red plaid.

Ernie ran over to the man with Kelly's gunshot in his leg. "His papers in his pocket say he is Vee Mills. He's bleeding pretty badly. If he makes it to his horse, he might be able to get into Rim Rocks. There's a doctor there."

Hamel had a frown on his forehead as he asked, "Lola, where'd you learn to shoot like that?"

The younger girl rubbed the barrel of the revolver against her pant leg to clean it off. "We play good guys, bad guys all the time. I really like all those old-time books about how wars were fought and won. I have Kelly and Colton play war games with me all the time. It takes a while, but we get it sorted out."

Hamel rubbed his head trying to understand. "You play war games with guns?"

Kelly nodded. "Pa taught us how to handle and care for guns. They are tools just like hammers and plows. But there are times where people just need to be shot. Like this time here."

Mike walked over to Lola and gently put a hand on her shoulder. "Thank you, Lola. Thank you, Kelly. We weren't expecting any trouble right here."

Kelly handed the man's revolver to Mike who looked it over. "Be sure to tell Overland that it was us that shot. We'll take the credit or the blame for this. I don't think any of you got a shot off."

Ernie yelled out, "Everybody get back on the stage. Dex, Mike, let's get the horses hitched up and get the blazes out of here. Everyone move!"

Lola looked at Kelly and gestured with her chin towards the eastern boulder cluster. "What about the dead man over there, Ernie? What are you going to do with him?"

The stagecoach man shook his head and struggled with a glove. "Overland says we let them lay where they fall. We don't have time to be digging holes and saying prayers, missy. We've got jittery passengers and a schedule to keep. We're rolling now!"

There laid the dead man. The girls walked over to the body and Kelly knelt. She rolled him over and searched his pockets. She handed two envelopes to Lola. Then she searched his other pockets.

"Ten dollars, an old picture of a woman and a little boy, and a letter to Daedelus Maximillian Burendson." Lola raised her eyebrows. "That's a big impressive name for a man who'll be late for dinner."

"Unsaddle their horses and turn them loose. Stack the gear behind these rocks. Someone will find it. They got nothing we want." Once turned loose, the outlaw horses freely nibbled at the short grass around the water hole.

On the road headed south, Hamel dropped back in between the girls. "That was a close call. You girls sure you're all right?"

Kelly and Lola both smiled. "We're alright. Mother taught us that once all the upset is over, there's life to get on with."

Hamel thought for a moment and then asked, "Why'd you take all the gear off them horses?"

Lola frowned and then snickered. "None of them men are going to be able to get into a saddle. It's not the horse's fault they have fools and dunderheads for riders." Lola waved a dismissive hand.

They watched Hamel urge his horse on ahead of the stage. There was a flurry of black feathers from the tree tops along the road. Crows had been perched calmly watching the action. Kelly twisted around in the saddle and gave a glance back to the empty road. Quarter mile back there stood the lone red plaid shirt on the side of the trail.

The scent of sage was strong when they trundled up the wide, sandy drive.

"It's the old Clearwater Ranch. Overland has a contract to stop here because there is a natural spring that comes up. The water troughs are always full no matter what time of year."

"If nobody lives here, who keeps filling those troughs?" Lola stared at the old two-story house. "What happened to the Clearwater family?"

Hamel said, "I've heard four different stories about what happened. We should ask Ernie if he knows exactly what happened." He whistled and waved Ernie over.

Ernie shook his head. "The person on the contract was Victoria Clearwater. She is or was the last known member of the family to actually live here. One story I heard was that Apaches came over the Mexican border, killed everyone, and took the cattle and horses." Lola shook her head.

"Another story I heard was it was plague or sickness that killed everyone. A hundred yards to the north there's a graveyard all grown up with grass and weeds. You can see the headstones of the family. Like that black death in England many years ago that killed half the people." Ernie shrugged. "All these years, I've thought that Miss Victoria grabbed everything she could and ran back to the east coast."

Kelly asked, "Is it haunted? Have you heard anything about that?"

Hamel said, "No, I don't think so. Nobody I've ever talked to about it has said anything about it being haunted."

"Not haunted. Just empty. Who owns it now?" Lola asked. "It's out here in the middle of nowhere. Nothing around it, except the spring." Lola leaned over looked down into the water trough. She turned her head like she was listening.

Ernie shrugged and shook his head. "I don't know. You'll have to ask in Rim Rocks about it. I'm sure there is a deed somewhere. Maybe it's recorded in Los Angeles."

"On the way back home, Kelly, I want to stop and look at the house," said Lola. She had knelt and squinted her eyes as she let a handful of the sandy dirt slide through her fingers.

Kelly frowned as she looked at Lola. "It looks like there are five clear trails leading north and east. Like single footpaths. Animals must use those to come in and drink."

"I can see a lot of footprints. There are people who walk through here and stop for the water. There are children's foot prints, or a grown-up who is really small," Lola had stepped over to the scrub brush.

Ernie said, "We can't stand around here all day. We've got a schedule to keep and we're ten minutes late. Get these horses hitched up and let's get moving." The men headed towards the team and Ernie asked the passengers to get on board.

After the men went to the horses, Kelly asked, "What is it, Lola? I can see that a lot of people come through here. A lot of them walking, not riding."

"You remember in school how we learned about birds flying the same route every year to get somewhere?" Lola pointed to the sky.

"Yes. Migration."

"The people that come through here are doing the same thing. They come through at certain times of the year more often than other times. They don't stop and stay here. But they know it is safe to stop here and get water." The young girl laughed. "I'd like to have a hunting blind to watch the people come and go. See who they are."

"The west is a horse culture. Men die without their horses here. That's why we have a good business. I don't understand why all these people walk through here," Kelly scratched her head and then stretched out her arms.

Lola shook her head. "Maybe they are walking to get horses. This is going to bother me for some time until I figure it out." Kelly laughed.

"Lola, you've turned into a sightseer. You want to stop and touch and taste and listen to everything. I'd bet that if there were a photographer on that stage, you'd be wanting to get a picture of every place we stopped." Both girls laughed.

"Hey! Don't laugh. Someday someone will build a little hand-held camera that everyone can have and take pictures any time they want," Lola said.

Kelly doubled over laughing. "I can just see you now. Hey honey, get a picture of me standing next to this rock." They giggled.

"And there will be this little shack that will sell food and snacks while people take pictures with that rock." They laughed as they walked back to their horses.

After they got back on the road, Hamel dropped back to ride with the girls. Lola had him laughing until he had tears in his eyes about the pictures.

***

The stage began a switchback descent down the side of a mesa. Wooden buildings of a small town could be seen in the distance. Flickering lights dotted windows.

"Must be Rim Rocks."

"Yep."

"Wonder if I can get pomme frites here."

Kelly looked at her sister. "What?"

Lola gestured dramatically with her arms. "You remember Ma talking about those fancy little stick potatoes she had that time we went to New Orleans? I got to eat two of them before she ate the rest. They were really good. Crispy and golden on the outside and soft and mushy on the inside."

Kelly groaned. "Again, with the potatoes."

"Colton likes his cake. I like potatoes. You? You eat anything, Kelly Stolter." Lola grinned.

Kelly looked offended. "No, I don't!" After she stopped to think for a moment, she said, "Well, yes, maybe I do."

As the road flattened out on the desert floor, Kelly saw tall saguaro cacti, mesquite scrub brush and lizards scurrying around rocks. The afternoon sun was about a foot above the horizon.

Lola asked, "So are we going to hide out in the barn with the horses or do we get to become ladies of ill repute hanging out in the back of a saloon?"

Kelly grinned. "I'm all for the ill-repute. I don't care if it ruins my chances for a good marriage into high society. If I get my nose that high, I'll drown in a rainstorm." Lola laughed out loud with her mouth open.

"I hope the chili is good!" Kelly laughed.

Two small children played in the dirt under a big cottonwood on the north end of town. They stood up and waved as the stage rolled by.

"Hey, Kelly, look! There's a gunsmith here. We can get our guns cleaned." Lola craned her neck to get a look at the double open doors and the shop.

"Our guns aren't dirty, Lola. Don't be spending our money where we don't need to."

"Yes, but we can still walk over and look at the guns. I'm a sightseer, remember?" Lola giggled.

Kelly rubbed her forehead as she shook her head with a groan. Hamel brought his horse to the left of Lola.

"On the far south end of town is the stables and the corrals. Go on down there and stable your horses for the night. Mike and I will bring the team down after all the passengers are off loaded. You decide what you wanted to do about dinner?" Hamel grinned.

"Saloon." Kelly nodded.

The man nodded with a grin. "I figured that. Get washed up. You look like a couple dirty saddle tramps." Hamel laughed and rode towards the stage. Kelly frowned and looked at Lola who frowned and stared back at her sister.

"Ill-reputed, gun slinging saddle tramps." Kelly snorted.

Lola chastised her older sister. "No, not yet, Kelly. You have to wait until you pass through the doors of the saloon before you can call yourself ill-reputed." Kelly snapped her fingers in disappointment and laughed.

The broad street went straight through the heart of the town, and lining it were a dressmaker shop, two general stores, the infamous Megan Silva restaurant and five saloons. There were two stately hotels on opposite sides of the street, both in whitewash with black trim.

Lola casually mentioned her shopping intentions. "After dinner, I'm going over to the gunsmith shop and take a look at what he has. I don't care what you say, I need to do this."

"Alright."

"What do you mean alright? You're not mad?" Lola's mouth hung open.

"I got more important things to be mad about than you lollygagging over some revolvers and knives." Lola looked smug. "Besides, a professional gunsmith is not going to entertain the shopping notions of a nine-year-old girl." Kelly raised her eyebrows.

"Hey! Professional gunsmiths don't turn up their noses at cold, hard cash, Missy. As Pa says, 'I'm a one-man Stolter force to be reckoned with.' Besides, I'll be ten in just a couple of weeks." Kelly laughed.

The girls paid for corn, oats, and hay for their horses. Behind the barn there was a trough and the girls dampened their bandannas and wiped off their faces. A cloud of dust flew when Kelly shook out her hair. The old oak tree hid cackling crows in the branches overhead.

Hamel came around the end of the barn. "You girls ready? Let me wash up."

Bob Gandy's saloon was told to be the oldest saloon in the area. Thirty feet wide by one hundred feet long, it had a main bar on the left-hand side and round wooden tables scattered to the back wall. The wide plank floor was polished smooth from years of feet.

Hamel guided the girls around the side porch and came in through the solid back door to a big room with hanging lanterns overhead. On the walls were painted portraits of prize bulls and men with horses and dogs holding the pheasants they'd shot.

Two women holding knives and forks in their hands sat at a corner table talking. One was a blonde with a mass of curly hair piled on top of her head. The other woman had one side of her long auburn hair pulled back with a glittering comb. They both wore low cut dresses and a considerable amount of lipstick, rouge, and mascara.

At a table for six, the girls pulled out chairs and sat down. Hamel disappeared through the door into the main saloon. He came back shortly followed by man in a black shirt and a bolo tie with a long white apron about his waist. He looked over the group and smiled.

"Welcome ladies and gentlemen to Bob's. My name is Harry. What can I get for you to drink?" Harry looked at Kelly.

"Glass of milk, and a glass of water, please." Kelly smiled.

"Yes, miss. And for you, miss?" Harry smiled to Lola.

"The same for me, please." Harry nodded and went back into the saloon. Before the door closed, a tall, muscular man came in carrying two heavy trays of sloshing drinks. He set them on the table and gave beers and whiskies to Ernie, Mike and Dex.

"Ladies, I'm Bob Gandy. Welcome to my saloon. Did you have a good ride?"

Kelly inclined her head towards the man with a gentle smile. "Yes, sir. Thank you. It has been an interesting trip."

Bob nodded. "We've got beef steaks on the grill along with home fried potatoes. I have a pot of chili and cornbread if you'd like something simple. I can get lamb chops for dinner or the ham dinner from Megan's, if you would rather have a bigger dinner."

The girls and the stagecoach crew ordered dinner. Harry came back with the drinks for the girls along with fresh bread and butter.

"I was just thinking that I'd probably have to pay extra at one of those hotels to have a dog come sleep on the bed with me." Kelly winked. Ernie almost spit out his beer.

Hamel said, "Overland has its own bunkroom here. There are two other stages in town so that means there are six other men in the bunkroom. There's twelve bunks, so there is room if you want to rest over there." Hamel took a drink of his beer. A hand appeared on his shoulder. It was the auburn-haired woman. She held her napkin in her other hand.

"Dex Hamel, don't you make these sweet, young ladies get into one of those wooden bunks behind the station. Mandy and I can set up a bed for them over at The Cosmopolitan." White teeth, brown eyes. The taffeta of her dress rustled.

She introduced herself. "Ladies, I'm Kassie and this is Mandy. It's not a big room, but the bed is downstairs in the back and it's comfortable. You'll be safe and won't have to listen to these men snore all night."

Mike nodded approval to Kelly. "Thank you, ma'am. You are generous with your offer. We accept."

"Excellent. Dex, if you'll show them over to the hotel desk when they're ready. I'll let them know to expect you." She waved and smiled as she walked to the door where Mandy waited. Lola nudged Kelly and raised her eyebrows.

Bob and Harry brought in the trays of dinners for them. Everyone concentrated on their food and little was said.

"I've eaten so much, I need someone to carry me over to the hotel," Lola said with a laugh.

"I was just thinking that I'd like some of that ham cut up in my scrambled eggs tomorrow with a handful of those home fried potatoes. But then, I'd like to taste a couple of those big biscuits with ham gravy over them." Kelly grinned and rubbed her belly. Mike's mouth dropped open.

"Why is it you don't weigh three hundred pounds, Kelly Stolter? You can eat twice as much as any one of us and you're like a twig. Where you putting it?" Ernie laughed. Kelly shook her head.

Bob came back in. "More bread and butter? Or are you ready for dessert?"

Lola perked up. "You have dessert?"

"Oh yes. Do you have a craving for anything in particular?" Lola looked at Kelly who shrugged.

"How about chocolate cake?" The three men leaned forward.

"I believe they have a chocolate and a yellow cake over at the restaurant. Apple pie, peach cobbler, or bread pudding, too." Bob took their dessert orders and left.

Ernie said, "Tomorrow we'll go eighteen miles, change horses twice and then stop for the night in Bluewater. After that it's three water hole stops and then we're in Bradford. That's where you ladies leave us."

Kelly said, "There is an art and science to running that stagecoach. You should be compassionate and caring about the passengers so they'll come back again. You have to know how to repair and fix the coach and tend to the horses so the stage continues on."

Ernie said, "There's a lot more people helping us that you don't even see, too. There are big offices in Los Angeles, Dallas, Dodge City and Chicago that set up the routes, hire drivers like me and security like Dex here. There's a big company in Missouri that builds the coaches. There are a lot of local ranches that supply the horses at the stops."

As they discussed all the organization for the Overland to run, Bob and Harry brought in the dessert plates. Kelly and Lola both gasped at the four-layer tall chocolate cake with chocolate frosting dripping down the sides. Harry refilled the milk and water glasses.

"Well, we figured it out. Just put chocolate cake in front of them and they'll shut right up." All three men chuckled. Kelly took a drink of the milk to wash down the cake.

"Lola, this chocolate cake is forty miles north of Bradford. Make a note of that for Colton." The older sister wrinkled up her nose and smirked to the younger.

Lola swallowed and looked at the men. "Colton, our younger brother is crazy for chocolate cake. We promised we would scout all the cake places on the way here for him." Kelly put her fork down and pushed the empty plate away.

Mike and Hamel stood up. "We'll be out back smoking when you are ready." Kelly and Lola nodded. They closed the door quietly.

Lola wiped off her mouth. "Ernie, do you know the man who runs the gunsmith shop?" Ernie frowned.

"Yes, that's Alex. You want to buy a gun?" There was a worried twitch in the man's brow.

"No, I just want to go look and see what he has for sale." Lola smiled. "I want to stop in there before we go to the hotel."

Ernie nodded. "Oh. Alright. Well, if you're done, I'll walk you over there. I wouldn't mind seeing what he has."

Forty-five minutes went by inside the gunsmith shop while Lola talked with the owner. In his late seventies, Alex was mildly irritated by a young girl talking about weapons and knives. Ernie assured him that she was very capable. As the five of them headed across the street to the hotel Mike commented that he had never seen Alex so touchy.

The double bed in a small back room was warm and comfortable with two quilts. The girls washed up, brushed out their hair and got into bed. In the dark, they whispered back and forth about what they had seen and heard. As the whitish moonlight began its walk across the floor, they drifted off to sleep in peace and comfort.

***

In the cold morning light, the new team was jittery and had trouble settling into the pace. One of the spotted geldings fought the bit, tossing his head and whinnying. Five miles out, the stage pulled over to the side of the road.

Mike said, "I checked him. I don't see what's wrong."

Ernie said, "Well, we can't go on like this. They won't move to a gallop with him acting up."

Lola and Kelly got down. "What's the matter?" Several of the passengers had gotten out to see what was happening.

"That spotted gelding is acting up. We don't know what's wrong. We can't turn him loose right here because we wouldn't make it to Bluewater. We need him for the hills." Ernie rubbed a hand over his face.

"You mind if I take a look?" Kelly asked. "I know a couple things about horses."

"Yes, but be careful. I don't need one of these horses stomping all over you." Ernie gestured to the team. Kelly nodded.

After a few minutes of Kelly going over the horse, she turned to Ernie. "His bit is too narrow. Whoever geared him this morning forced a narrow bit into his mouth. Inside of his mouth is bloody where it's cut into him."

Ernie's shoulders slumped. "We don't have another bridle. He can't run without one." Kelly took a couple of steps to where Lola was holding the horses.

"Lola, the dun is running with a wide bridle. They need it on this gelding. Would you run your dun with just a halter until Bluewater?" The younger girl nodded without a word.

"Mike, can you take that bridle off him, gentle and easy, please? I'll put the other on him after I've cleaned it." The security man began unbuckling the fasteners and pulling the straps.

A few minutes later, after some coaxing, the gelding accepted the dun's bit and the bridle was buckled onto the horse. Kelly patted the strong animal, talking to him quietly.

Kelly pointed to the road ahead. "Ernie, see if he will move out with the team now."

Ernie announced. "Okay folks, everyone load back up. We're ready to roll."

The tall, thinner man with the Stetson walked over to Kelly and held out his hand. "You're a good judge of horses, miss. I'm Reg Blackner." His gray eyes gleamed.

"Thank you, Mr. Blackner. I'm Kelly Stolter. My family breeds, raises and trains cutting horses. I know what to look for when a horse is in pain, sir." She shook his firm grip. He let her hand go and loaded up into the stage. Blackner nodded curtly and pulled on the heavy glove.

Kelly and Lola mounted up and trotted along behind the stage. The team lengthened their stride and went into a gallop. Ernie signaled a thumbs up back to Kelly who smiled and yelled a thanks to a smiling Lola who lifted a hand in acknowledgement.

Three miles later they climbed a small hill and turned into a clearing off the left-hand side of the road. On the south end, there was a Mexican family around a campfire who stood up and waved. When Kelly dismounted she saw Lola had walked over to say hello. Kelly looked around to see any paints but saw none.

"Miss Stolter, may I have a word, please?" Mr. Blackner walked over to her.

"I'd like to hear more about your family business of horse training. I know of three ranches around Santa Fe that may be interested in your horses."

Kelly described the stock, the ranch and the previous horses. For the next ten minutes, she talked and answered questions about the family business. He once again shook her hand and then walked back to the rest of the passengers.

Kelly took a few minutes and checked the bridle on the gelding. The bleeding had stopped and the horse's mouth would be sore for a few days, but he was alright. She patted him.

When Lola came back she told Kelly the family was headed for Tucson. "They live down in Baja, Mexico. They stopped to see a family around San Diego for a week and now they are on the road to Phoenix."

Kelly asked, "Where are their paints?"

Lola put a hand on Kelly's arm and leaned closer. "They're walking to Bluewater. They'll get horses there."

"What? They're walking all the way to Bluewater?" Kelly was surprised.

"Well, actually no. There is a big freighter coming along behind us about a day back that they will get on for the ride. But to us, it's like walking."

She asked, "How do you get up one morning and decide to walk twenty-two miles?"

"They aren't in any hurry, Kelly. They've got family and friends along the way to visit. They get horse rides and wagon rides from place to place. I don't understand a lot of it." Lola shrugged.

Kelly sounded exasperated. "Did you ask who they are?"

"Alberto Zendejas and his wife, Antonia and two of their children, Carlos and Omar." Kelly shook her head and shrugged. When the stage rolled out, Lola called out goodbye and the Mexican family waved.

Kelly tried to reconcile walking and riding for a family with children. She felt that to be without a horse was to be stranded. She shook her head and rode on.

Six miles had gone past when the stage slowed down to a walk. Kelly rode up alongside the coach and asked the driver if anything was wrong.

Ernie said, "This is the only water hole where we unhitch the team up on the road and take them into the waterhole. It's a tight fit to get this big stage into that small clearing. It's easier to just walk the horses in."

She and Lola took the back team into the clearing and waited while the animals drank. She smiled as she watched Lola dig her toe around in the water's edge. Mike brought two big pieces of beef jerky for them. They all chewed while the horses watered.

Lola looked at Mike and said, "So you know the road really well from here on to Bluewater?"

Mike nodded. "Yes, it's really wide so three stages could drive side by side. And people take good care of the road, too."

Ernie said, "The horses know the way from here, too. They know that the day doesn't end for them until they stop at the station."

"It's a long day for them so they want to get there as well as we do," said Hamel. After the teams were hitched back to the stage, the big coach began to roll again.

As Kelly rode she watched the tops of the trees light up with the last rays of the sun. Gray and purple crept up the hills to the east. The heat waves from the sun still shimmered in the western distance, then all at once, they were gone.

The road had followed along a sandstone mesa for two miles. A sharp pass cut into the grainy dirt and the road passed north through two cliffs. A grassy valley was ahead. The road slowly descended to the green flatland below.

Dozens of lights burned in windows of the shops, restaurants and saloons. Loud piano and violin music came from the saloon doorways. The stage rolled to a stop in front of the Bluewater Inn and the passengers disembarked.

Mr. Blackner touched the brim of his hat at Kelly before he walked up the steps into the Inn. Kelly smiled and waved a gloved hand from the back of her horse. Kelly's watch read seven forty-five.

"I'm tired. That was a long ride." Lola took off her glove and rubbed her eyes. "I don't know how those people stay cooped up inside that coach like that."

"We might have to cut our ride home into different lengths than the stage water holes. Some of the distances are too long and some are too short," said Kelly. When the stage rolled once again, the girls followed at a walk. The big stage turned right and went about one hundred yards to the station and the tenders took over from there.

Hamel yelled, "Bring your horses down to the stables and unsaddle them." Kelly ordered extra hay and grain for the tired animals. There was a bench in the back with basins of water and towels where the girls washed up. Kelly wrapped her long hair into a bun on the top of her head and wrapped a leather tie around to secure it. Lola brushed out her hair and tied it up into a ponytail.

"Mike and I are going over to the saloon and have a couple of drinks before dinner. The restaurant has a really good chicken fried steak in a cream gravy," Hamel said.

"Oh, my gosh, that sounds good." Kelly could feel her mouth starting to water. "We'll be over there if you want to come join us." They waved and walked back up to the main street.

The Bamboo Restaurant was decorated with fine paper screens, brightly colored fans and tall reeds of bamboo in colorful pots. The small Chinese woman asked if they wanted hot tea or coffee when she laid down the menus.

Lola frowned. "I don't know what these dishes are, Kelly."

"Turn the page. You'll see the steaks." Lola nodded.

The Chinese man bowed slightly as he filled the water glasses. "Are you ladies familiar with Chinese cooking?"

Kelly shook her head. "No, we've never had it."

"I will bring out a sampler plate for you to try. There is no charge for tasting. Then I will come take your orders." He smiled and left.

"Do you know what you want? It all sounds so good," asked Kelly. She measured out two spoons for sugar for the hot coffee.

"If I don't like the Chinese food, I'll have baked chicken and potatoes." She smiled tiredly.

Several of the passengers came in and sat down for dinner. There were mainly couples eating dinner in the restaurant. At the back of the room there was a couple eating dinner with two small children.

The waiter brought out a tray of many small dishes. As he set them on the table he told the girls the name of the dish. Kelly smiled at Lola. He said he would return in a few minutes after they had a chance to taste everything.

"What is that one called? I like that one."

"This fried rice is so good. You have to try it."

"This is like a crunch pastry wrapped around chicken and squishy little vegetables."

Kelly smiled. "Lola, go ahead and order the Chinese food. I'm having the chicken fried steak. I'm so tired, I just want to eat what I know." The waiter came back and bowed again after he had taken their order. He smiled a big smile when Lola ordered the Chinese dishes.

Halfway through dinner, the stage crew came in. They sat down at the next table. "I see you are having the Chinese food, Lola. Do you like it?" Ernie grinned.

"Yes, it's pretty good. I've never tasted anything like this. You gonna have it?" Lola's eyes were wide open.

"No, I don't eat Chinese food. I eat American food." Lola rolled her eyes.

Kelly looked at Lola and held up both hands with her palms out. "Don't start." Three of the waiters came a bit closer to listen.

"So, Ernie, the next time I see you eating a taco or quesadilla, I can knock it out of your hands because you only eat American food?" Lola waved her fork.

"Knock my food on the floor is a good way to start a fight with me," he said as he laughed. "Just for that, no more potatoes for you!"

"I've got this Colt .45 revolver on me that says I can eat any food I want." She grinned and started to stand up.

Mike looked at Ernie. "A gunfight with a nine-year-old girl over food. You idiot. I'm gonna have your head examined by a doctor when we get to

Santa Fe."

Ernie laughed and wiped off his mouth as he stood up. Carefully, he walked in between the chairs and gave Lola a kiss on her cheek. She blushed bright red and laughed.

Kelly said, "See? Den of inequity. You men have lost your minds." They all laughed.

After dinner was done, the men walked back to the saloon. Kelly and Lola went over to the hotel and paid for the sleeping porch cots.

"What time do we ride in the morning?"

"I don't know, but it's going to be too early."

Bradford was a small country town organized around a town square centered with an old oak tree. Coming in from the south, a rider saw Goldman's Saloon first with its freshly painted sign of "Hot Food and Good Whiskey." If a man were to relax back in a comfortable chair on the wide boardwalk out front it would only be a matter of minutes before he would know the goings on in the small town.

About thirty yards away to the east were the offices of Merle Doyle, Attorney at Law, conveniently located across from the rowdy Chick Miller Saloon.

At the corral, they turned their horses in and paid for a small bucket of oats and a sheaf of hay. Kelly took off her gloves as she and Lola walked across the square. Lola grinned and pointed to the close-set iron bars covering the two small windows in the building next door which bore a sign of the gunsmith. A small door opened to the dusty stairs going up to the second floor. A tall, heavyset man opened the door and frowned at them.

"Good afternoon, sir. My name is Kelly Stolter. This is my sister, Lola Stolter. I'm looking for Merle Doyle, Attorney at Law."

The big man smiled briefly. "Good afternoon, Miss Stolter. I'm Merle Doyle. I've been expecting you. Please come in." He stepped back and held the door wider open for them. Kelly saw the black mustache, a freshly laundered white shirt and black bolo tie. After he shut the door, his shiny black boots thumped on the glossy wood floor. He gestured to two chairs across from his desk.

"I hope your travel here was safe and not too difficult. Your younger brother did not come with you?" he said in a low voice. Kelly shook her head and smiled, aware that she was still covered in dust from the road.

"Mr. Doyle," said Lola as she slowly took off her gloves. "We are children. We don't understand a lot about the law or the business of adults. What we do know, if that our mother who recently died had inherited a ranch here and we want to take a look at it." She took off her bandanna and wiped her face thoroughly.

Doyle frowned again as he listened to the young girl and opened his mouth. He suddenly shut it. "Thank you, miss. I can understand your eagerness. While I am confident you are the daughters of Marianna Richardson Stolter and Nicholai Stolter, I need to see proof that you are who you say you are." He looked at first Kelly then back to Lola.

Without taking her eyes off the attorney, the younger girl held her left hand out to Kelly. The attorney frowned again as he watched Kelly's response.

From the duster left pocket she fished out a soft leather portfolio wrapped with a slender leather cord. Lola took it and unwrapped it and laid one document on the desk and then another. Doyle put his small spectacles on and peered at the documents.

"May I?" He gestured as if to pick them up. Lola nodded.

"These are birth certificates. How did you get these?" Doyle yet again frowned. Lola sighed and looked at the floor.

Kelly said, "Mother registered our births in Los Angeles at the court house."

"I see. That's unusual." Doyle gently laid the certificates down on the desk. He then lifted a heavier paper stack wrapped with a cord from the side table and set it in front of him. "What is this other envelope? It is sealed."

Kelly's eyes filled with tears and Lola squeezed her hand. "The night before our mother died, she said that she had hoped she would not have to open that envelope for many years to come. We talked it over, Mr. Doyle, and we think Pa should be the one to open it up. With you." Lola watched the attorney lift the envelope up to the light in an attempt to see the contents.

The attorney took a sip of the water. He tucked the envelope underneath the birth certificates and then placed both hands flat on the desk. He looked from child to child. "Your grandfather, Glen Richardson, did in fact, bequeath the Flint Hills Ranch to his daughter, your mother, the now deceased Marianna Richardson Stolter." He cleared his throat.

Lola lifted the certificates, folded each one and slid them back into the leather portfolio which she handed back to Kelly.

"There are a couple of things that I want you to understand. First, in California your mother would now be the legal owner of Flint Hills Ranch. But, as she is deceased, it is your father who is now the owner as he is the legal husband of Marianna." He wiped his forehead with a white handkerchief from his pocket.

"The difficulty here is that your father has not returned home and you have no knowledge of his whereabouts or the time when he may return home. So, before I can go any further, I will have to file a notice with the court regarding your missing parent." Doyle stopped speaking abruptly as he saw Lola stand and dig something out of her pocket. With a small smile, she took a step forward and laid a dollar gold coin on the desk.

Kelly said, "With this money, Mr. Doyle, you are officially our legal representative in this matter. This coin is payment as our attorney. Is this satisfactory?" Doyle took of his glasses and sat back in his chair.

The left corner of his mouth curled up. "For children who claim they do not understand a lot about business of adults, both of you understand a great deal."

"We read a lot, Mr. Doyle. And mother explained a lot to us before she died. Still, we are just children and need someone to help us work through this problem. We can't do it alone," Kelly explained.

The attorney reached across the desk and picked up the coin and then opened the portfolio. "When your Grandfather died, the livestock was sold per his last will and testament. There have been no tenants on the land that I know of but I have reports of trespassers and squatters that stay out there for a couple of days and then move on. I'll say that it's been over a year since I've seen the property so I cannot tell you what shape or condition it is in." He flipped over a couple of pages. He looked quickly at the girls and then down at the white page.

"Your grandfather left a rather large financial estate to your mother. As Glen's attorney and now as your attorney, I can authorize money to be made available to you, if needed." He stopped and looked up to see both girls shaking their heads.

"I don't want to disturb mother's money from her father. We have money. We don't need that just to get by while we are here." Kelly twisted her leather gloves in her hands. Kelly's eyes misted and she dabbed at them with her handkerchief.

Lola watched her sister's distress. "Our mother told us that if pa does not come home before the next land payment on Windy Ridge is due, we'll have to move."

For the next half hour, Doyle listened to the worries and concerns of the girls and began writing notes on the sheet of white paper. From time to time he nodded.

The attorney put down his pencil and took off his glasses. "Well, there is another option, another solution you might consider."

"What is that, Mr. Doyle?" Lola asked.

The attorney nodded with a quick smile. "I would want an exact dollar amount of what is owed on Windy Ridge Ranch before it becomes free and clear. If it is not a large amount, you might be able to pay off the loan using your grandfather's money. You, or rather your father, would own Windy Ridge and Flint Hills Ranch."

"We don't know exactly how much is owed on our home. We haven't tried to talk to Mr. Jessup, the landowner of Windy Ridge yet. We didn't think about that." Kelly shrugged and looked at Lola.

The attorney shook his head. "It would be best if you did not try to talk with him. I can send him a letter as your attorney and ask for the payoff amount. I'll put a letter on the nine o'clock stage tomorrow. Please be at ease, ladies. I'll handle this matter for you."

Kelly gestured to the side. "That's all I had to talk about. Lola, what did you want to talk to the attorney about?"

Lola shook her head. "We want to see the ranch. It is part of the decision we have to make and we can't know what to do until we see it." The younger girl had relaxed back in her chair and was swinging her boot back and forth.

"Are you hungry? Do you want to go over to the hotel and eat before we ride out to the ranch?" Doyle stood up and went to stand near the tall dusty windows. He watched the girls stand up and stretch.

"We've ridden 125 miles, Mr. Doyle and we have thirteen more to go. We aren't stopping now, so if this is a good time for you to take us now, we'd appreciate that." The attorney nodded and ushered them to the door.

On the ride out the East Bradford Road, Doyle pointed out the landmarks and neighbor's properties. Finally, about two o'clock, they turned onto the long driveway that lead up to the Flint Hills Ranch.

***

Doyle and Kelly lifted the tattered ropes from the gate and dragged it into the tall grass so the horses could get through. The girls walked the horses up into the driveway and the closer they got, the more damaged the house appeared to be.

"The stone walls are upright and strong. Folks say it was Phineas Rideout, Foster Rideout's brother, who designed and had it built for the original owner." Doyle sat on his horse at the gate into the yard alongside Kelly and Lola and described the area around the house.

Doyle said, "It is a post and beam house. It's very solid and sturdy. You can see the upper story has some damage. The roof is gone over two of the bedrooms and sitting room. It shouldn't be too hard to fix."

Kelly and Lola got down off their horses. The younger sister was the first to step foot up onto broad stone patio. Kelly walked past her and stood in the doorway. The door creaked open slowly. Doyle took off his hat and walked in behind Kelly.

Lola was in awe of the size of the house. "This is where my mother lived and grew up? It's huge!"

"This room was used by Glen Richardson as his office. There used to be a big oak desk in the center. I was here half a dozen times over the years," said Doyle with a lowered voice. "He liked to smoke cigars out on the patio."

Kelly ran her hand over the empty gun cabinets on the left of the stone chimney. Lola came into the doorway. "There is another room like this on the other side of the kitchen. It's open all the way to the roof." Kelly saw the south family room with a towering river rock fireplace with tall windows. Dust mites danced in the gentle light.

Doyle sat down on the bottom stair tread. "This was the Richardson family home. Glen's father, your great-grandfather, guided the construction of this house along with Glen's brothers. On the other side of the big barn is where the original house used to stand. It had been torn down to help build this house." Doyle looked up at the squared trestle timbers that supported the second story.

"Down to the west of the house there are big, twin, two story barns. I haven't been inside either one in years so, when the carpenters come out to work on the house, have them take a look at the barns." Doyle wiped his face with the white handkerchief. There was a fine coat of dust on his black pants and jacket.

"Kelly, we could live out in the barn while the house is rebuilt and repaired. There are four bedrooms on this floor. There is even a bunkroom with four twin beds." The older sister nodded.

Doyle looked at the girls. "Your mother told you about your nearest neighbors, Mary and Foster Rideout. They are to the northeast about eleven miles. When you are ready to meet them, I'll escort you over there. I took the liberty of sending word to Mary that you would be visiting. They are good neighbors and watched your mother grow up."

Kelly slid her hand over the heavy wood of the massive door. "How many acres is this?"

"One hundred ninety, close to two hundred if you count the hill country. This ranch comes right up against the Ladd Ranch." Doyle gestured to the southeast.

Lola looked at Doyle and said, "We had chance to meet a Ladd descendent on the way here. He told us if we had the chance to send his regards."

"Who was that?" Doyle had a frown.

"Jacob Sanderson. His mother was Viola Ladd until she married Mr. Sanderson."

"Oh, yes. I remember Viola. She had gone back east to study arts or something. There was talk that the family knew she'd marry some political bigwig. But she came back here one summer, fell in love with Sanderson and got married." Kelly and Lola nodded slightly.

"Lola, pa lived in this house for a couple of years with ma. He'd know exactly what it looked like back then. And we have ma's picture." Kelly looked at her younger sister.

The disappointment in Lola's voice was evident. "Somehow I thought it would look like ma remembered it." She took in a deep breath and shook her head. She took off her gloves and walked into the kitchen. Kelly and Doyle followed her around looking in closets and touching the walls.

Doyle said, "Most of the other big ranch houses are like this one. Pretty much the same size. Some are only one story. I'll think you'll have enough room." He turned and saw both Lola and Kelly staring at the trestle ceiling two stories up.

"Come on. Let's go walk out to the barn. We'll need to figure out if we can all fit in it." Lola nodded and rubbed her eyes. The three walked through overgrown weeds and grass. The wagon wheel ruts in the drive led to the left of the house and on around to the barn.

Kelly stopped at the corral and her mouth hung open. "That is a big barn." Lola ran up the broad plank steps up to the doorway and peered into the dimness.

Doyle pointed out. "Yes, but there are two. The second one on the far side was used as the bunkhouse for the hands when Glen had horses on the land." Doyle opened his mouth to caution the young girl, but she had already gone inside.

Kelly stepped up onto the heavy plank wooden floor. "Do you have any idea how many hands were working the horses?"

Doyle shook his head. "I'd guess about twenty. I'd been in Bradford about a year, I guess, when one night I went over to the saloon. It was louder than it had been and some of the Ladd hands were drinking pretty good and got liquored up. Fight broke out with the Richardson hands and they rolled out into the street. Someone fired a gun and it all broke up." Doyle rubbed his chin.

Lola's voice sounded far away. "Our house at Windy Ridge would fit up here!" They heard her running feet overhead.

Kelly turned and looked at Doyle. "Ma said Grandpa Glen had over two hundred head on this land. There must be water somewhere." Doyle nodded and stepped back out into the sunlight. He pointed to the southeast.

"Yes. The Rio Linda River runs by in the northeast acres and Wilkes Creek runs through the south were most of the grassy valley is situated." Lola walked out near the old water trough followed by Kelly. Next to a crumbling fence they stopped. Doyle gestured to the distance.

"I can get a surveyor out here and set the posts if you want to mark the boundaries."

Doyle frowned and glanced at the silent girls as they walked back to the house. Kelly walked to Lola's saddlebag and pulled out a wrinkled brown paper. Lola nodded and clapped her hands. From the other saddlebag, the younger girl fished out a small shovel.

Again, Doyle frowned. "What is this? What are you girls doing?"

Kelly shaded her eyes from the sun. "You might want to sit down and make yourself comfortable, Mr. Doyle. This might take a few minutes." Curious, the attorney sat on one of the low stone walls of the porch in the shade.

Lola backed her boot heels up to the bottom stone step of the porch. Kelly had her turn a couple inches to the right. The young girl measured out twelve steps towards the driveway.

"Wait. I can't see the fencepost. Let me try this again. That didn't feel right." Lola went back to her starting place and began taking bigger steps.

"I don't understand. What are you doing?" Doyle took off his hat and rubbed his forehead with a green bandanna.

Kelly put her hand on her hip and took in a deep breath. "Our mother and grandmother, Mr. Doyle, both despised banks. Said there was no telling when some crooked banker would decide to dump everyone's money into a bag and sneak off into the night. She had her own way of, well, putting money aside." The attorney shrugged.

"How many now?" Lola anxiously waved her hand.

Kelly squinted at the pencil drawn paper. "It shows six foot prints coming towards me, but I'm not sure that's right. Come look." Lola quickly ran over to Kelly and examined the paper.

"No, it's more west than where you are. Move over there." Lola pointed to a spot about two feet farther west.

Again, Lola paced off the twelve steps and then turned and made six more steps towards Kelly. The young girl knelt and drew a large circle around herself in the dirt with the shovel. She handed the implement to Kelly who groaned.

"You wanted to do the first one. Go ahead," Lola said with a grin and stepped carefully out of the circle.

Ten minutes of stabbing the little shovel into the ground later they both heard glass break. Lola shrieked and just about gave Doyle a heart attack. Kelly whooped and dug faster until she had cleared away the loose dirt. Carefully, she lifted out the shattered Mason jar and laid it in a clear spot.

Doyle walked over and knelt.

"Hold out your hand, Lola." Kelly lifted out dull coins carefully letting the glass shards fall to the ground.

"That's five dollars in gold coins she buried." Doyle's face had a stunned expression as he stared at the coins and the smiling girls. "How many did she bury?"

Kelly grinned. "That, Mr. Doyle, is a family secret." Lola laughed.

"Before any work starts on that house, this entire area is going to look like a herd of gophers came through it. Ma's map only shows her little treasure spots. It's going to be a big job for the three of us to dig up every inch to find Grandma Richardson's, too." Kelly laughed and hugged her sister.

Doyle shook his head in disbelief. "I'll be damned."

"I wanted to make sure that this ground wasn't that rocky clay that is out in the desert. It's good soft soil," said Kelly. "We're going to need five pickaxes and maybe six shovels. And a couple of buckets to haul dirt around."

"How about a little wheelbarrow so we don't kill ourselves carrying buckets, Kel?" Lola pointed across the yard at an old wheelbarrow.

It was a laughing, smiling, joyous face that looked at Doyle. "Colton, our little brother, loves to dig things up almost as much as I do. He's gonna love this!" Lola giggled. Kelly giggled at her delighted sister.

"Well, we spent five dollars on food getting here so this five dollars means we paid that back into the wallet." Kelly let the coins fall back and forth between her hands.

Doyle cleared his throat. "I do understand about crooked bankers and that. Bradford had less than reputable banker fall in league with a criminal a few years back and attempted to clean out the safe. We caught him in time though." Kelly and Lola looked at the attorney.

"I have a big Milner safe in my office in Bradford I use for important papers and files. I'll give you young ladies a leather portfolio so that if you decide you want to lock up anything you find, just bring it to my office." Doyle gestured with his hand.

"Now it won't be the most convenient because I'm not there all the time and I do travel to Chicago, Los Angeles and San Francisco each year. But it's there if you need it." Doyle turned away shaking his head.

Lola nodded. "I'll want to lock up all those things we dug up at Windy Ridge. Remember, Kel, you put them in the steamer trunk up in the attic?"

Doyle turned around with a puzzled look. "What things?" The girls told him the details of the digging adventure they had at Windy Ridge Ranch.

"Are you girls going to dig anymore? Maybe you want to ride out around the ranch and look at the land?"

"No, sir. We needed to see the house and barns so we know what we are up against. That and this beautiful yard." Lola smiled.

"No, we had promised ourselves to dig up one just to prove ma wasn't telling us a tall tale." Kelly wiped her hand over her forehead and laughed again. "We got the proof right here."

Kelly helped Doyle drag the pole gate back across the drive and tied the rope to the posts. After she mounted up she sat with Lola and looked back up at the slight rise to the house.

"Is it what you expected, Lola?" The young girl nodded and pulled on her leather gloves.

"It is now. Seems like it could be home." They both nodded and then reined their horses on down the driveway and headed for the main road.

Three hours had passed like wildfire on a dry prairie. Doyle pointed out different landmarks as they rode back towards the small town. As the horse's hooves thudded on the wide oak bridge a small flock of ducks chasing bugs quacked noisily in the water underneath. Lola pointed out deer that stood in a copse of trees on the eastern hills. They arrived back in Bradford just as the orangey gold sun started to sink below the horizon.

An hour later Kelly and Lola sat at a corner table in the Hotel Bradford dining room with a sheet of plain white paper and a pencil between them. Between mouthfuls of food, they discussed what they had seen at the ranch.

They looked up when the door opened and Doyle hurried over to their table. He waved a piece of paper.

"I have news of your father. A telegram came in earlier this afternoon while we were at the ranch. Last night, Tommy, er, Mr. Boardman brought it up. It seemed important."

Texas Rangers advised Kelly, Lola and Colton Stolter that Nick Stolter is traveling home. Signed, Henry Elliot, Texas Ranger.'

"What does this mean?" Lola sounded exasperated.

Doyle looked at the young girl. "That means he has stopped traveling east and is now coming home."

Kelly asked, "Why did this come from the Texas Rangers? Why didn't Pa send the telegram?"

Lola took the telegram and read it. "Is Pa in trouble?" Doyle held up his hands palms out to try to calm the girls. The waiter brought over a white cup and the pot of coffee. Doyle motioned for him to pour.

Kelly's voice started to break. "Who is Henry Elliot? Can we send another telegram to Pa?"

Lola asked, "What does it mean that he is traveling home? Is he bringing stock with him?"

Doyle cleared his throat. "Alright, just hold on a minute now. Yes, write out what you want to say and I'll have Mr. Boardman send it. Remember now, we just don't know where he is so the telegram will have to go general delivery. Everyone who gets the wires will read it so think carefully about what you want to say."

For the next half hour, they bantered back and forth over the wording for the message. Doyle explained that he had requested the aid and assistance of the Texas Rangers to track down Nick Stolter. In the hundreds of miles between Phoenix and Yucca Valley, the Rangers had successfully found the man. The paper in their hands became the thread of connection to their father.

Doyle handed the telegram message sheet and several coins to the waiter who disappeared into the small office next to the registration desk. Ten minutes later, the waiter put the signed receipt and several coins on the table. Kelly grinned at Lola who smiled. Doyle breathed a sigh of relief. Everyone went to bed much calmer and happy.

***

When Doyle checked for the girls the next morning at the hotel he discovered they had left an hour before and headed for the Flint Hills Ranch. A growl found its way from his throat as he spurred his horse up onto the east Bradford road.

Doyle reined his spotted Appaloosa to the rail at the trough. He smiled wryly as he saw two makeshift chairs leaned against the wall on the slate patio. There was a small fire going in the patio fireplace.

"Hello, Mr. Doyle!" As he dismounted the girls came out of the barn. They had smudges on their faces, dirty boots, and the energy of a playful pack of puppies. They chattered on about the nooks, crannies and surprises they had found around the house.

"Mr. Doyle, we want to ride home knowing what to do about living here or staying at Windy Ridge. The ride from Tucson to here could be a month, especially bringing fifteen head," Kelly said with a serious look. "You have to tell us what to think about. You have to help us look at both places and help us determine which one is the best for us." Doyle sat down on the patio bench and grimaced in thought.

He brought his eyes up and looked at Lola. "I'm not going to sugar coat this because you both have proven that you can understand plain talk. You could survive easily at both ranches. I have been thinking about what would happen if, like you say, your father did not return. Your grandfather's money would be disbursed to you as needed, regardless of where you decide to live."

Kelly watched Lola swinging her foot in thought. "Lola, I'd really like to live in the place where ma grew up. I'd like to live on the land where she was happy. I'm not sure about Colton. I know he loves Windy Ridge. My question for you is, can you live here knowing Charlie is buried here?"

The younger girl swept back straggling ends of reddish blonde hair and squinted at her sister. "Charlie is not a stranger, Kelly. He is our brother,

106

alive or dead. It feels kind of good with him here in this place, like our family is together." Kelly nodded.

She then turned her eyes to the attorney. "We have to make us live where it will be best for all of us. Pa wants us to be safe, healthy and happy. If Pa never comes back, we must make do with what we have. He'd want that. So would Ma."

Doyle straightened up and took a deep breath. "You leave day after tomorrow and I should have some more information for you. The situation is that your mother was executor of Glen's estate and she never formalized it while she was alive. Your father should be the executor but he is, well, in absentia, meaning missing. The court might feel that there should be another blood relative to Glen governing the estate."

Kelly rubbed her forehead. "This makes my head hurt thinking about all this. Were you going to take us over to meet the Rideouts today?"

"Yes! Yes, I wanted to take you over there so you could have at least another friendly face to know while you are here. Mary and Phineas knew Glen and your mother very well for many years so you might get a bigger picture of what life was like here on the ranch." Doyle stood up and gestured to the land.

That afternoon Doyle escorted them out to their nearest neighbor. It was a tall, white Victorian house complete with ornate carvings and decorations. The windows and doors were in stark black and only the solitary stained glass in the second story window showed color. Kelly whispered to Lola that it looked brand new.

"Please do come in. I've been so looking forward to meeting you." Mary Rideout's hazel eyes were bright and held a steady gaze. Her blondish gray hair was swept back in a straggly bun that bounced when she moved. She wore tiny pearls in her ears.

Mary had been a good friend of Glen Richardson's and knew Marianna as a young girl. For several minutes, she listened as Doyle explained the current Stolter situation. Mary looked at the thin, heavily veined hands in her lap and then looked up.

"Your mother and I used to go blackberry picking several times each year when she wasn't off at a rodeo or something."

They had all talked for about an hour when Doyle stood up. "I'm going to leave and ride back to town. I have a dinner appointment that I don't want to miss." He smiled and bowed to Mary. Then he turned to the girls and patted his pocket where he had put the message. Doyle reminded the girls to come into his office anytime and that they should be cautious at Flint Hills.

"When you go back by the ranch later, be sure to draw the gate closed and rope it shut. It may not keep out all the wild things but it might stop the one critter that is the worst." Mary followed him to the door.

"Thank you, Merle, for bringing the girls out here. We have a lot to talk about." The door closed quietly.

***

It was the deep growl that brought Colton's head up from his book. Dusty was standing now, looking at the door. Again, the growl.

"What is it, boy?"

It was an easy step up onto the chair rail and Colton balanced on the window ledge to look outside. The yard was empty. Not even a crow digging in the dirt. The young boy frowned and looked at the yellow lab. The dog was not trying to get out.

"Is something coming our way, boy?" Colton lightly leaped to the rug and trotted around the stairs to the closet. Gently, he lifted the Colt from the holster and checked the chamber, then locked the barrel.

"Dusty, if I let you out, you'll run them off and I'll never know who it is out there. But I don't want them coming up to the door, either." Colton frowned.

At the top of the stairs, Colton eased over the rail and his toes gripped the narrow ledge as he sidled around to the window. Nobody. Nothing there.

Colton held his breath and did a slow scan from east to west like Kelly had taught him. Then he let his breath out.

Back on the stairs, he pulled on the low boots and a forest green barn jacket. The young boy knelt before the lab.

"Don't kill it. Don't bite it and don't let it hurt you. You have to be quiet, boy. Real quiet." Small fingers ruffled the coat. "Let's go see what it is."

Between the kitchen and the back bedroom there was narrow door that had rarely been used. Colton struggled to push a heavy trunk to the side and then turned the knob with a squeak. The hinge protested, but gave way letting Colton and Dusty squeeze through.

The variegated slate patio was six feet wide and ran the length of the back of the house. Beyond the short grass were four apple trees and then the wood post fence fifty yards out. Dusty headed straight for the fence and Colton ran behind him in a crouch.

Colton crawled through the rails and then paused to listen. Dusty growled louder now, twenty-five feet ahead. Colton saw the dog's hackles were up. That was when he heard the voice.

In the tall grass, next to the rail fence lay a man gripping his bloodied right leg. Colton started to say something, but the man motioned for him to be quiet. Dusty licked the man's face. The young boy knelt.

"Is that you, Colton?" the gravelly voice said. The deeply lined face grimaced in pain

"Yes, sir. Who are you? What happened to you?"

"I'm Ray Chapman. You probably don't remember me. I was here last year helping brand stock with your pa." The man made a deep groan and writhed in pain.

"What happened to you?"

"Colton, I need to get inside so I can bandage up my leg. It hurts something fierce. I might need stitches. Are your sisters here? I can use some help."

"Mr. Chapman, they are gone on a trip. It's just me here. What do you want me to do?"

"When I was here in January, I saw the bunk cot in the record office in your barn. Do you still have that cot set up in that little room under the loft?

"Yes, sir."

"I'll tell you what happened, but I have to get somewhere safe and inside your barn is as good a place as any. I know your Pa is away but I need your help, Colton."

It was another slow sixty yards to the barn. Colton brought in a lantern and soon the room was bathed in a yellow gold light.

"I come down through Tollson Pass and I had been meaning to cut over and head east. Two men on horses were laying low in the brush. They must have been holding up folks on the road. One of 'em shot me off my horse." Chapman struggled to steady his right leg on the stool and pulled up the pant leg.

"I've got to get the bullet out, Colton. I need a thin knife and some alcohol like whiskey. If you can find your ma's sewing box I can use that needle and thread." The bloodshot eyes pleaded with the young boy. Colton nodded.

Colton took a deep breath. "I'm going to leave Dusty here. He'll let you know if someone comes into the barn. I must go up to the house and get those things you need. I might be a few minutes."

It took just a few minutes to gather the supplies. Colton also grabbed the small sack of cloth scraps and the pint of liquor.

The wound trickled blood. For twenty minutes Colton watched as the man explored it with the tip of the knife.

"It's in too deep for me to get it out with the knife. My fingers are too big for me to grab it. Colton, I need your small fingers to take out the bullet, please. I wouldn't ask you if I thought I could do it myself."

"You want me to take out the bullet?" Colton's eyes were wide. Chapman nodded.

"If Dusty had a bullet in him, you'd reach in there to take it out, wouldn't you, if it would save his life?" Colton looked at his lab and then nodded.

"Just pretend that it's Dusty and you want to get it out. You'd help butcher out the chickens and rabbits around here. This won't be so bad for you, boy. I can put a cloth over it so you don't have to look, if you need it, Colton."

A few seconds later, the young boy dropped the slug onto the table. Chapman rinsed the wound with the liquor and then took the threaded needle from Colton's hand.

Colton watched the first stitch go in. Chapman grimaced and his hands trembled with the effort. "I've seen men lose a leg because they left the bullet in too long."

"Where are you going to go from here?"

"You know the Milton Ranch about nine miles to the southeast?"

"Yes, I know Savannah Milton. We are in school together."

"Her pa still owes me wages from work I did for him over the winter. They hit some hard times and he couldn't pay me everything he owed me. I'll go there and see if they have a horse I can take in trade for what he owes me."

Colton watched Chapman slice off the thread from the second stitch. "I think my pa would want me to ride you over to the Milton's place tomorrow. You ain't thinking of trying to walk out there tonight, are you?"

Chapman shook his head as he tightened the third stitch. "No. If it's no bother to you, I'll rest here tonight and head for the Milton place tomorrow. You've done me a huge favor, boy, and I'm not sure if I can ever repay it."

"Tell you what, Mr. Chapman. My ma taught me to pay a favor to someone who needs it, but might not have earned it. Somewhere out there on the road, you may come up on a boy like me who needs help. You help him, like it was me."

Chapman grimaced as he knotted the fourth stitch. "Your ma was a good woman and a fine mother, Colton."

"I miss her a lot. Every day. We did everything we knew to try to help her get well, but it was not good enough." Colton rubbed the tears away. Chapman averted his eyes back to the thread.

He cleared his throat. "I was mining for gold up in the hills in northern California when my ma died. Her heart gave out. She was close to sixty years old and had raised six kids. We were all grown, married and gone. The letter my older sister wrote said that ma felt she had done her duty and lived a full life."

The boy's voice sounded small. "You have brothers and sisters, Mr. Chapman?"

"Yes, I have three older brothers and one older sister. I have a baby sister, too. We used to have some good times when we were young, like your age. I can remember the looks and the smells and the taste of my ma's cooking."

"A friend of mine from town, Georgie Hailey, his pa died when he was my age. He felt lost until his uncle took him in. His uncle is helping him grow up to be the man that his pa would have wanted." Colton turned a small chunk of wood over in his hands.

"I haven't thought about them in many months, Colton. Thank you for helping me remember my roots."

Colton nodded and smiled.

"Last one. I need some long narrow strips of cloth to cover up these stitches, Colton. Can you tear some for me, please?" Chapman focused on inserting the needle.

The wound was wiped with alcohol and the bandages tied on.

"I'll get a quilt and some food from the house. I'll bring down a pitcher of water so you can wash up, too." Chapman nodded.

"That would be much appreciated, boy." Colton smiled and stepped out the side door of the barn followed by the dog.

***

It was just about nine o'clock the next morning when Colton's buckskin walked up to the Milton Ranch gate. Colton had a few minutes to chat with Savannah who got an abbreviated version of the events.

True to his honor and word, Mr. Milton saddled a horse for Chapman. Back out at the front gate, Chapman reached to shake Colton's hand and again thanked the boy for his generosity.

Chapman rode east and the young boy rode north. Colton went home having learned the importance of helping his fellow man and Chapman had left a small bit of himself for the boy to ponder.

***

Mary told the girls about their mother as a younger girl and the sad story about their first son, Charlie and how he died. Both girls sat examining their hands as they thought over what Mary had said.

Brilliant gold and red light from the late afternoon sun shone on the tops of the trees at the edge of the yard. They drank hot tea on the porch while Mary talked about her four grown children living around the world. Dinner was baked chicken, soft potatoes and crusty, seasoned bread. The girls told her about their general life, some of their dreams and the deep sadness of losing their mother.

"I made up two rooms upstairs for you. I'm afraid I get to bed early. I like to read myself to sleep most nights." The woman stifled as yawn as she stood up.

"There are blankets on the chairs. If you want a nighttime snack, there is fresh bread, pie and ham on the counter." She paused at the foot of the stairs.

"I know it's a lot to take in and I'll try to make it a bit easier for you while you are here visiting." She smiled and climbed the stairs.

Kelly woke up the next morning in the soft, warm bed. She could smell bacon cooking and fresh, rich coffee. When she walked into the kitchen in her bare feet, Lola was shoving a forkful of pancake into her mouth.

Mary smiled warmly to Kelly. "I don't want to put a lot of things into that barn right now because you'll only be here a few days. I know you could probably use a few things to be more comfortable," she said with a smile.

Lola spoke up. "Yesterday we found an old campsite up on the ridge in the valley a ways from the house. It looked like it was maybe a month ago that it was used. Someone has been camping up there." Lola and Kelly looked at Mary who looked at her two hands. She rubbed them together.

In a low voice, she said, "It's coming up on six years now that Glen has been gone. I know there have been people cutting across the property going east. You'll probably come across a couple of old campsites like that when you walk around the property." Lola squinted her eyes and watched Mary fidget.

Kelly watched Lola and just before the younger girl spoke, Kelly said, "Mrs. Rideout, we understand that sometimes bad things happen. Men become desperate and do stupid things. It is part of living life. As the children of Marianna Richardson, we have inherited that land. If you know something about those acres, I want you to tell us, good or bad."

Mary eyes opened wide and her mouth dropped open in surprise as she looked at the girls. "Well, you do have a way of speaking boldly. Glen was never one to mince words either, so perhaps you got that in the bloodline." She nodded and took a deep breath.

"On the far north edge of the property is the old mine. Some say they took all the gold out years ago. There used to be a wooden barrier across the front, but I imagine it is long gone now. It's dangerous to go into it. You have to take in a torch and tie a couple of ropes together so if you fall down a shaft, someone can haul you out." Mary took a sip of tea.

Kelly sat back in the chair and relaxed. "Mr. Doyle told us that Glen's family built that big house. And that Foster Rideout most likely built the big fireplaces there. Is that true?"

Mary nodded with a gentle smile. "Yes, Foster was the oldest. Fifteen years older than Phineas. Their father was a trained mason in England with his father. When Edmund came to America, they started cutting granite, marble and slate and establishing quarries. Pennsylvania, Arkansas, Missouri and way up in Colorado."

"The patios and fireplaces are the biggest I've ever seen. It must have taken them months to do it all," said Kelly.

"At first, we thought it was a hunting lodge for rich easterners to come out and use. There were so many rooms it could have been one of those high mountain hotels. But it was built specifically to Glen's father's instructions. Somewhere in the house is a leather sleeve with rolled up drawings of how the house was built." Mary rubbed the corner of her eye.

A moment of quiet passed. Lola blurted out, "The house doesn't feel like anyone died in it. Most houses feel like someone passed away in them. Flint Hills doesn't feel that way." Mary frowned at Lola.

"What do you mean, dear?" Mary sat up a little straighter and clenched her hands.

Kelly took in a deep breath. "It doesn't smell old. It doesn't creak or groan like an old house would. We sort of heard stories about houses where people died in them and there was talk that the house was haunted by ghosts." Mary shook her head.

"No. Anna-Marie was killed in a strange accident where a wheel came off the coach and flipped over. She died right there. Glen was out fixing a fence or something and the one of the hands found him. They said his heart gave out."

Lola looked at Kelly and gestured with her chin towards Mary. "Before ma died, she told us she wanted us to know what it was like to live at Flint Hills. She had many happy memories of that place and since then, we've been very curious about it. That's why we came."

"Oh, I understand that. My own children are scattered all over the world and I doubt any of them would ever come back here to live the rest of their life. They're all used to more hustle and bustle, more people and excitement." Mary waved a dismissive hand. "It's hard to get excited over spring calving and putting hay in the barn when you've watched buildings and bridges being built."

"It would be kind of lonely at first if you were to live here. Well, you don't know anyone around here. It might be hard for you children to make new friends." The older woman paused a moment to see if the girls would respond. They simply looked at her.

Mary continued. "Flint Hills is quite a ways away from town and the nearest school is at Beatrice which is six miles south of Williams Creek."

Kelly made a little snort and a giggle. "School. I won't miss that." She looked at Lola who shook her head slowly.

"I like to read," said Lola with an exasperated look at Kelly.

"Well, there are plenty of books in that big library at Flint Hills. Anna-Marie brought in big wooden crates of books for the boys when they were younger. She made them read at least an hour every day. Have you seen the library?" Mary leaned forward with a smile.

Kelly frowned. "How did we miss a library? We didn't even see it!"

"What?" Lola started to stand up and then sat back down with a stunned look.

Mary stood up and poured another cup of tea for Kelly and herself. She handed the plate of cookies to Lola who took one and gave the plate to Kelly.

"Anna-Marie was a highly educated young woman when she married Glen Richardson. She had toured Europe and Asia with her parents. She had studied painting and sculpture in Italy. She spoke fluent French and a smattering of Latin. And she sang like dove. She played piano and violin."

"Really?" Lola had an incredulous look on her young face.

"Oh yes. I know that she taught Marianna songs to sing while she played the piano. People always asked your mother to sing when we'd have the big dances out at the grange hall." Mary nodded.

Kelly looked dejected and said, "I sing and all the dogs howl." Lola partly spit out her cookie and had to wipe it off her shirt with a napkin while she giggled.

Lola grinned. "You know who sings really well?"

"Colton." They both said it at the same time. "He sings those silly little songs ma taught him all the time. To the dog, to the fish, to the horses. Sometimes even at night when he is in bed you can hear him humming something."

"He would sit with ma and sing with her while she cooked, when they rode together. Ma used to put him in the laundry basket when he was a baby and sing to him while she hung out the clothes on the line." Kelly and Lola smiled at each other.

Mary held up her hand. "On the other hand, you have neighbors in The Ladds, The LaCostas and us. Furio LaCosta bought up the land to the south of Flint Hills and he runs some black angus but his main work is cultivating and planting those wine grapes."

"I've never tasted wine. Whiskey, yes. Wine, no," Lola swung a foot back and forth as she munched on the cookie.

Kelly nodded. "I like beer. But it must be really, icy cold beer. And then I can drink a cup of it. If it's not cold, it tastes like something you'd use to clean a saddle with." Mary laughed and slapped her knee. They all laughed.

"Now if you young ladies will help me load the buggy, I'll show you that library," Mary said with a wink.

Lola stood up and bowed with a grand flourish of her hand before Kelly. "Miss Stolter, after you, my dear." Kelly stood up and frowned.

"Where do you learn these things?" Kelly looked exasperated.

Lola grinned. "From a book." She winked at Mary, who laughed and took the cups and tea pot to the kitchen.

With Mary in the black buggy and the girls on their horses they trotted the nine miles to Flint Hills. The older woman pointed out the different trails and paths that cut off the main road and twisted around trees and boulders over the hills. Finally, the road curved to the right and started up a gentle rise. The deep, crumbling ruts of the driveway made the buggy bounce and jostle, and Mary had to hang on with both hands while Kelly led the black mare up to the house.

***

After the buggy was unloaded in the barn, they walked up to the ranch house. "Do you see those tall panels on the right side of the gun cabinet?" Mary stood in Glen's office with the girls.

"Yes." Kelly looked at the carved oak panels.

"Push on the left ridge of the farthest panel to the right." The girls exclaimed as the two-hinged panel slid to the side with a deep groan. Behind it was an old oak door, carved and ornate, with a brass pull handle. Kelly tugged and the hinges groaned as the door moved.

Inside, the small glass windows let in streams of light. Bookcases fifteen feet high spanned the entire interior of the room.

"There must be a thousand books in here!" Lola walked around the room, dragging her hand along the spines.

"Glen's books, his father's books, most of your mother's books are right here."

Kelly grinned. "Lola, you're going to have to have a strategy and a plan to get these read." Lola laughed out loud.

"To anyone walking into the house, this library looks like the side wall of the kitchen. From the kitchen, it looks like one of the walls to Glen's office. It's sort of hidden alongside the fireplace, the office and the kitchen."

Kelly walked through the doorway followed by Mary and then into Glen's office. She looked up at the wall.

"Those small square windows up on the wall look like decorations from here. Like pictures hanging on the wall. But they are really the windows that let in the light for the library." Mary nodded.

When they walked back into the library, they found Lola perched on a small wooden ladder paging through a book up on the fourth shelf. "I'm going to need a dictionary to figure out what some of these books are about. There's French and German, and there's a whole shelf of books with these funny little curly lines." Kelly grinned.

Mary wiped off a wooden chair and sat down. She watched Lola browsing books. "So, you've had a chance to see some of the ranch. There is a lot of work to be done to get it back to a livable, working horse ranch again.

When your father comes back, he'd take over doing most of it. But until then, you'd have to start with food and shelter."

Lola looked at Mary and Kelly for a moment and then shelved the book she was holding. She climbed down to the floor and pushed the small ladder back to the corner. She wiped her hands off and went to stand near Kelly.

The focal point of the north family room was the stacked stone fireplace. There was room enough for a big sofa with a big covered porch for sitting and reading. This had been Mrs. Richardson's room with double doors that opened onto the porch. The long kitchen had a large French oven and a wide cook stove. There were two big cabinets back-to-back with a slab of black stone over the top.

Near the kitchen was an oblong room with windows facing north. Lola walked around the room and said that was where the table used to be. She murmured about getting another table. On the other side of the wall was where the secluded library was, behind the two doors.

"It does get warm here in the summer and autumn and that is why Anna-Marie had the outside kitchen built. It used to have a long, iron grill where Glen grilled beef. There used to be a dozen benches, chairs, and rockers. It looks like birds have made a home in the outdoor fireplace." Mary smiled as she looked over the stonework.

"The roof on the barn looks in pretty good shape. We can't find any holes up there and if we did, those are pretty easy to patch. Both front and rear doors can be locked with sliding blocks from the inside. The door into the bunkroom has a hinge missing and that can be fixed. We don't have any hired hands so that outside door would be nailed shut." Lola crossed her arms over her body in thought as she looked through the doorway.

Kelly watched Lola thinking. "We found the big garden patch out to the northwest of the house. It's overgrown with weeds and some old plants have seeded into the ground. We were tending ma's garden patch up at Windy Ridge and we would want to have the same plants here. Lola and Colton have spent a lot of time in the garden because I was always working with the horses with Pa."

Mary nodded. "I could bring you some things to eat from time to time. When the local ranches butcher a steer, sometimes they bring by a few good-sized pieces of beef. Here at Flint Hills you are farther from town than you are at Windy Ridge so you'll have to plan your rides into town."

"Is there a construction man in Bradford? Someone who builds houses or fences?" Kelly asked.

"Yes, I believe Clay Dunagan does carpentry work. He's the blacksmith in Bradford and he makes nails and such in the forge. I know he helps put up barns and helps build houses when there is a need." Mary waited for Kelly to speak.

Lola said, "We need a carpenter to look at the roof and those two bedrooms upstairs. They'd be able to tell us how to go about getting that repair done. That way we could see how much money it will take to fix the house."

Kelly said, "It might be a lot of money to fix the house so it would mean we stay at Windy Ridge." Mary was silent as she watched the two girls.

"We still have to talk with Mr. Doyle about all the land and what he thinks we should do. He was very insistent on us learning as much as we could."

Mary asked, "What about your horse breeding and training business? Do you think you could sell your horses around here?" Kelly straightened up and gestured to the door. Lola and Mary followed her out to the front patio.

"Many of our horses go to Texas to the big ranches down there. We sold two on the trip here and the buyers will pick those up while we are here. Mr. Doyle is handling the contracts on those for us. We also have a delivery of three head to make to Santa Fe next month," said Kelly as she sat down on the stone bench.

Mary rubbed her hands together. "You girls are much braver than I was at your age. I lived under my parent's roof, very protected and sheltered until I met Phineas. I wouldn't have dreamed of riding all the way from Yucca Valley to here alone." She smiled.

Lola swung her foot as she sat on the bench. "We'd need help bringing the herd down from Yucca Valley. The road is good all the way so loading the house stuff on a couple of big freight wagons would be enough."

Kelly shook her head. "No, there are some things that we might not want to bring all this way. We could sell off some things that we don't want any more. We'll have to talk it over some more," said the older sister.

Mary smiled brightly. "Well, moving your horses would be the easy part. I'd send five of my hands up to help. That way you could choose to either ride the wagons with your things or ride the herd with your horses." Kelly smiled and nodded.

Lola looked long at Mary. "You are generous to us, Mrs. Rideout, and you barely know us. We're strangers to you."

Mary stood up and pulled on her gloves. "Not exactly strangers, no. I can see something of your mother in you. The way you hold your chin or the color of your hair. I have missed her these years. I hope by helping her daughters and son, Marianna can rest a bit more comfortable in heaven." She turned away as she wiped the corner of her eye.

Kelly and Lola stood waving until the horse and driver had disappeared into the road headed east.

That night the girls laid out their bedrolls in the loft of the big barn. They braced the doors closed and watched the white moonlight slide across the wide plank floor. Hundreds of crickets serenaded them. The rustle of feathers preceded the hooting call of an owl.

***

"What did you want to do here today, Lola?" In the dim morning light, Kelly squinted at her sister.

Barely above a whisper, Lola said, "I wanted to dig up another jar, but I'm suspicious of people watching us do it."

"I know. I was thinking about that before I went to sleep last night. I think if we started digging up the yard without Colton, he'd be pretty mad. He is a champion digger." Both girls giggled. They pulled on their socks, slacks and boots along with thick sweaters. "We'll need a lantern and a couple of good shovels."

After they had unblocked the door, Lola said, "There are a couple of trails leading south from the barn. We could follow those and see where they go."

Kelly stretched with a yawn and rubbed her eyes. "I need to get a fire going because I want hot coffee. Mary left food in the basket for us. Honey, I'll need you to help me set up a table over on the patio so we can eat. I want to see the water on the ranch."

Twenty minutes later the drifting scent of strong coffee floated about the patio. Kelly had watched Lola's eyes gaze out over the waving grass in a long stare. It was easy to imagine her mother wrapped in a thick sweater standing here. Kelly shook her head to pull herself out of the reverie.

"Get your Colt and put it on, Lola. I don't want to take any chances while we're out walking around the ranch." They put on denim jackets and each one took a canteen.

At the end of two hours of walking, the girls had found where some trails dead ended at rock outcroppings and creeks. Other trails had gone unused and only the depression of the ground under the overgrown vines and grass gave away their presence.

The Flint Hills were named for the thick slab deposits of the black stone. The girls found an outcropping with chisel marks where people had splintered off chunks. There was an underground spring gurgling out in a weak stream on the north side about halfway down the hill before making its way to the valley below. This was the beginning of one of the sources of the river. Kelly bent to taste the chilled water and nodded with a smile to Lola.

They perched up on boulders and looked ten miles out into the valley. From their vantage point, they could hear anyone riding up over that trail. The big cottonwood leaned out over the spring and helped the water stay cool all year round. Off to one side of the cottonwood they found a blackened ring of rocks.

"It's not a stranger that stopped here. I can't tell how long ago that campfire was used. Maybe a month. The marks from a pan or a pot are there." Lola poked the center with a long stick as if trying to get the ground to give up its secrets.

Kelly pointed to the other side of the clearing. "Someone bedded down over near that tree. There is a worn-down spot there. If we move in here, we'll have to tell this camper to move on."

Lola walked over and knelt to slip into the sleeping spot. "It's very quiet right here. It's open and calm here in the hills. It is two miles to the east road from here," said Lola. "It's not a stranger who has been here. It is someone who knows this place, like they are here to hide. Or maybe just getting away from people." Lola dug out a little hole with the tip of her knife and sifted the dirt through her fingers.

Kelly frowned. "Let's walk back and saddle up. I want to see the boundaries of the grazing pastures. If we move the horses here, they need to graze." Lola nodded and they began the long walk back to the house.

It was close to noon when they stopped their horses up on the ridge. "The land on the other side of that river is the Ladd Ranch, according to Mr. Doyle. Theirs is the biggest ranch in the county." Kelly watched the sparkling water shine in the sunlight.

"Maybe we can swim in that river in the summertime." Lola grinned. They watched the gentle breeze ripple through the green grass in the pasture.

"There's another river on the north side of the ranch. We'll head over there." Kelly urged her horse back onto the trail.

The sun glinted and reflected off the water, stabbing bright light into their eyes. It was like thousands of liquid diamonds shone at the same time all around them. Kelly saw little bright spots dance over a laughing Lola as she stood next to the water.

A big cottonwood tree hung out over the river, its leaves sounding like gritty scratching as the wind rustled through them. Occasionally, a couple of papery leaves dropped off and floated away. A couple of crows barked at each other somewhere out of sight.

"This is a lot closer to the house than the other river. A couple of those boulders are pretty big. We could dive off those when we came down to swim. Sitting in the shade under that cottonwood in the summertime will be nice and cool." Kelly looked at Lola who had knelt to pick rocks out of the water.

The younger sister blinked a couple of times. "There are no fences to ride here. We'd have to tend the garden just like Windy Ridge. There's nothing to take you away from working on the training, Kel," she said. She brought up another dripping handful of dirt and sand from the water.

Kelly tossed away the twig she had been twirling. "Okay, Lola. Let's say that we've decided to move here. The first thing we should do is tell that attorney, Mr. Doyle, so he can send a letter to the man who owns Windy Ridge. Grampa Glen's money will pay it off and Pa will own that ranch free and clear. Like he said."

Lola held up a hand to stop Kelly. "If we are supposing that we've decided to move, we should ask Mr. Doyle to find someone to start working on fixing the house. We don't know what needs to be done, we've never built a house, so all that can be done while we are on the way here with the horses. He said he knows some men who build stuff so we don't have to be here for that."

Kelly nodded raising her eyebrows. "You're right. Mr. Doyle can use Grandpa Glen's money to hire the people to fix the house. That way if it was all fixed, we wouldn't have to live out in the barn when we get here. I mean, we could if we had to, but it sure would be nice to move into the house the day we came." Lola watched Kelly for a moment and then moved to another spot in the river to hunt for rocks.

Kelly grimaced and shook her head momentarily. "I was just thinking that it will take more than a couple of days to look over all the stock to figure out which one is which, check their feet and make sure they are good to travel. Maybe we should ask Mary if any of her cowboys could help us go over the stock to check them."

Lola dug her boot heel into the soft dirt and twisted it back and forth. "Pa kept a ledger in the desk at Windy Ridge. You saw him making notes in it when a mare foaled or we sold one. We'd have to start with that to make sure we have all the horses. Kelly, if you find a horse that won't make the trip, you'll have to sell it in Yucca Valley."

Kelly scratched her chin. "I'd ask Georgie Hailey to come out and give us a hand. If any of the stock couldn't make the trip, I'd give them to Georgie. He'd know what to do. He might be busy working, but I'd ask him anyway." Kelly snapped her fingers quickly.

"That reminds me. Mr. Dunbarton should have gone to pick up those two fillies already. I want to send a telegram to Colton and ask him if Dunbarton took them. It was sort of odd the way he rode out from the coach that day so I wonder if he went through with buying those two. You'll have to remind me to ask Mr. Doyle when we get back to town."

Lola stood up. "I'm hungry. Let's go back to the house and eat. We have to start writing this stuff down before we forget about everything we have to do, if we are going to move here." She looked quizzically at Kelly.

Kelly shook her head and took in a deep breath. "I can't start thinking about the what-ifs here, Lola. What if Charlie hadn't died? What if Pa had never left on the trip? What if we had never come to see this ranch?" She rubbed her fingertips hard onto her forehead.

Lola smiled. "Come on, Kel. You'll feel better after you eat. You always do. Over lunch we can talk about the what-nows. You know, the list of things we have to do now that we are going to move." She poked her sister, who laughed. With one last look at the lazy river, they mounted up and walked back to the house.

"We should take a ride over to see Mary Rideout, too. If she really meant that she'd send up her cowboys, we should talk more with her, Lola." Kelly took in a deep breath and let it out slowly.

Lola nodded. "Later today. After we eat."

20 MARY RIDEOUT OFFERS COWBOY HELP

It was shortly after three o'clock that afternoon when the Stolter girls walked up onto the porch of Mary and Phineas Rideout. Both girls sat down at the kitchen table. "You've thought this through? Have you seen the entire ranch?" They had told the elderly couple of the decision to start the move to Flint Hills.

Lola pulled off her dark leather gloves. "We've seen the two swimming holes, all the pastures, we found three tree houses, four old camps, and a sandstone pit where someone had dug up something. We climbed both barns and the house and we're going to have Mr. Doyle find a builder to fix the roof on the house."

Mary poured three cups of hot tea and offered the small sugar jar to the girls. Mary poured a small glass of whiskey for Phineas who brought in a cup of hot coffee from the kitchen. For the next two hours, Kelly and Lola laid out the lists of work and showed her the map of the ranch they had drawn.

"We found the old mine. It will have to be boarded up again. We found Charlie's grave and cleared away the grass and weeds. We also found a narrow road that cuts off behind a landslide from the East Bradford road. It comes from the north over the behind the house and stops on the ridge." Kelly spooned two measures of sugar into the tea.

Lola said, "When we get home we'll make a list of what we will sell or give away and what we will bring with us. Everything else we have to move is small compared to moving the stock. It's our business, and our work. We can pack everything up and send it on ahead. The three of us want to ride with the stock."

Phineas took a sip of the coffee and put the cup down as he smiled grimly. "We have five men who can ride the herd with you when you bring them down. They'll be ready to ride to Windy Ridge ten, maybe twelve days from now. I've got several things I want done here on the ranch before I release them to go north."

Kelly sat quietly for a moment looking down at the twisted glove between her hands. She had just taken in a deep breath when Lola's foot nudged hers."

"I must tell you, one thing about my riders, though. They'll be in charge of bringing in the horses. The men will have their instructions from me. The foreman will decide when and where to stop for the night and what to do if any of the horses comes up lame or gets hurt." Kelly and Lola nodded as they listened.

"I would go with you myself, but I have business coming up and I need to be here." Phineas stood up and went to the cabinet and took down a leather portfolio. "I have to ask you a difficult question now and I want you to think about your answer carefully." Lola frowned.

Phineas laid out two sheets of paper on the table along with a small pencil. "If anything happens to you three children along the way, if you simply vanish, or heaven forbid, you die, what is to happen to the herd?" Startled, Kelly nearly knocked over the small cup.

"What?" Lola started to stand up and then Kelly's hand held her arm. Kelly could feel her heart racing wildly and Lola had started to tremble.

Kelly's voice had lowered and became quieter. "Pa is still out there. We've asked Mr. Doyle to try to find him. The Texas Rangers have told us he is moving west, but they don't know where he is. We can only believe that he has gotten word about Ma. If we are gone, the herd must go on to Flint Hills for Pa. If God calls us to Heaven in the middle of this ride, everything must go on to Flint Hills. Once Pa gets to Flint Hills and finds out what happened to us, he can then make the decision about what he wants to do from there." Lola jerked her arm away and went to stand next to the window.

Phineas had sat down and started to write on the paper. "When you go into town to talk with Mr. Doyle, please give him this paper. It authorizes the hands of our ranch to take temporary control of your stock for the purpose of moving it to Flint Hills. That way if any lawman questions whose stock it is, this will prove who owns and who controls the stock." He slid the sheet in front of Kelly who leaned over to read it slowly. Lola stepped over to her sister and leaned her head down to read the sheet.

"Any sensible lawman won't believe the word of young children owning a herd of that size. This will protect you and the stock, as well as the hands." When they were done, Foster folded it up and slid it into the portfolio.

Mary stood up and walked around the table to hug first Kelly and then Lola. "Our hands will be ready in about ten days' time. You won't need to rush to get back to Yucca Valley. If you would prefer, I can send one of them over to Flint Hills to ride back with you. There is a considerable amount of work and planning to do to move a herd of that size on the return trip." She smiled gently. Lola closed her eyes and hugged the woman.

"We're going to say goodbye right here. We wish you safe journey and best of luck. You have good people to help with the horses so it should be a good ride." Mary stepped back next to Mr. Rideout.

It was Lola who stepped over to Mary and Phineas and held her small hand out to the man. As he shook it, she said, "Thank you, Mr. Rideout, for helping to take care of us. I'm glad I came to know you and will always remember your generosity to us." The older man's mustache twitched and he smiled back at the young girl.

Out on the porch, there was a man waiting in leather chaps holding his hat in his hand. "Kelly, Lola, this is Doug Langdon. He is the foreman of the hands that will be moving your stock. Doug, this is Kelly Stolter and Lola Stolter. You'll be moving their stock for them to Flint Hills Ranch from Yucca Valley. We'll leave you here to get acquainted." Mary and Phineas watched the girls shake hands with Langdon. The Rideouts nodded and walked back into the house.

Langdon gestured to the wooden chairs on the veranda and the girls sat down. A barrel-chested man with black and gray curly hair, he had gray eyes and the tanned, deeply wrinkled skin of a western ranch hand.

"You are bringing your stock a long way, Miss Stolter. I was told there are about 135 head. I wanted to bring up a couple of things before you ride out, if that is alright with you?" He had a deeper, gravelly voice and looked from Kelly to Lola.

Kelly said, "Thank you, Mr. Langdon. Yes, I am grateful that your hands will be moving the stock. It's going to take more than a couple days and there are bound to be things that come up that we hadn't thought of ahead of time. Please tell us what is on your mind." Lola nodded.

For the next half hour Langdon told the girls about checking over the stock, nightly stops and how the hands would generally pitch in to lend a hand. He was a pleasant man who had a job to do and showed patience in answering their questions. "Vern Dixon is my ramrod for the drive. I make the decisions and he makes sure those get done. I'm not anticipating any trouble on this drive, but just in case we'll be carrying weapons. Your horses are carrying rifles. I take it you can shoot?" Both girls nodded.

"We both have Colts in the saddlebags. The Rideouts don't like guns in the house so we aren't wearing them." Lola gestured with her chin towards the horses at the rail. "Our younger brother, Colton, shoots also. He's soon to be ten and I've seen him miss once with the rifle."

Langdon said, "Well that's good to know there will be other guns on the ride." When they stood up to leave, they shook hands again and confirm leaving later the following week.

"The Richardson place has been empty and cold for too long. I'm glad you are going to bring life back to it. I'll see you in a few days, miss."

About two miles out from the Rideout place, Kelly twisted in the saddle to look at Lola who had been silent. "You said something odd to Phineas, Lola. What's wrong with him?"

Lola slid the leather reins through her left hand. "He won't be here when we get back. He'll be gone. Not just away. Gone, like gone to Heaven gone. Colton will never get to meet someone who loved ma." The blue eyes were watery and the younger girl sniffled.

Kelly said, "He doesn't look sick. This must happen fast?" Lola nodded.

"Everything comes to an end eventually. People die. It's the way life is. Charlie died. Ma died. And now Phineas will die. We all go on. We live our lives and go on. That's all we can do, Kelly. I don't know how else to explain it." Lola shook her head and wiped her eyes.

"I understand that part, honey. Part of me always wishes that I had more time with people," Kelly said.

"I wish I could find someone that I could talk to about this and who would understand. Ma used to listen to me. Pa thinks I'm just a small girl with a wild imagination." They rode along in silence.

"I know this is the way you are. I may not understand it all, but you are my sister and I love you.

Lola, maybe once we get moved here and start meeting people, maybe then you'll find someone to talk to." The younger girl nodded and turned her attention out to the trees and hills along the road.

The western sky had begun to show orange and gold streaks across the deep blue as sunset approached. The chunks of wood in the patio fireplace crackled merrily. They climbed up to the western eaves and sat on the roof to watch the sunset. The grays and purples slowly crept up the hills to the east. The cool breeze carried the scent of earth, trees, sage and animals. The bottoms of the western clouds looked like someone had thrown pink dust up onto them. The two sisters sat huddled on the shake roof as one last burst of golden sun gleamed and then it was gone.

***

The town was bustling with activity. Three ranch wagons sat in front of the general store. The doors to the gunsmith shop were locked with a heavy chain and padlock. A lone woman swept the front porch and walkway of the church. Two small children took turns throwing a ball for a dog to fetch.

At the top of the stairs, the wood and glass door to the legal office was locked. Nobody answered the door when they knocked. The blacksmith's

125

doors were closed and the corral had three buckskins chewing on hay. Around behind the building was a footpath that went down into the marsh. Kelly followed Lola around to a broad wooden bench under a weeping willow tree. They sat down and watched a couple of ducks diving in the water.

"This is kind of nice right here. Read a book, write in a journal or just watch the ducks." Kelly looked at the floating plants and cattails. Lola lifted a long thread of wool yarn.

"Some people knit sweaters here." They both laughed. After a few minutes, they climbed back up the footpath and walked over to the hotel.

The girls sat down on the chairs on the hotel veranda. "You see that big house on the other side of the river over against the hills? It looks deserted and abandoned. There must be a bridge somewhere to get to it." Kelly nodded.

Impatiently, Kelly said, "Go in and see if Chrissy, the waitress has seen Mr. Doyle." Lola took off her gloves and walked into the hotel.

"No, Chrissy hasn't seen him, but they have doughnuts!" They went in and sat down to eat a couple of doughnuts. When Chrissy brought over the plates, Lola asked her about the big Victorian house on the other side of the river.

"It's been vacant and abandoned as long as I've been here. Coming up on three years now," she said with a smile and then turned and headed back to the kitchen.

A deep voice spoke from behind them. "You saved me a ride all the way out to Flint Hills." Merle Doyle stepped around to the side of the table. They gestured for him to sit.

After Lola took a sip of milk, she said, "We're going back to Yucca Valley tomorrow. Do you have any news for us?"

He nodded. "Yes, but we should go up to my office to discuss it. There are too many listening ears here." They looked around at the women chattering, men reading newspapers and folks eating.

As the office door shut, Doyle lifted the shades and gestured them to sit down. "I have word from a judge in Los Angeles that as your attorney, I can access Glen Richardson's estate. I took the liberty of having a copy of your mother's death certificate sent to the court in Los Angeles along with the telegram from your father. I have been designated temporarily as the executor of Marianna's estate." Doyle paged through a stack of papers on the table alongside his desk.

Kelly brought out the leather portfolio of the papers she had been keeping. "We've come to the decision that we should move our home from Yucca Valley to Flint Hills Ranch. There are a few things that we need done to start this move."

For the next hour, the girls told Doyle what they had found, seen and heard at ranch. They handed over the Rideout papers to Doyle who initialed them and wrote out another copy. Doyle made notes on repairing the Flint Hills ranch house and clearing out the damaged rooms.

"What happens to Windy Ridge now?" Lola swung a foot idly as she listened to the attorney.

"There is a stage leaving this afternoon. I'll put a letter on it to your landlord, Mr. Jessup explaining that I will need a letter of the final payment amount on Windy Ridge. The Richardson estate will draft a check and it will pay off the mortgage on the ranch. Most likely, your father will lease it out, if a suitable tenant can be found. That way if Colton decides later on that he wants to go back and live permanently at Windy Ridge, it will still be in the family's hands."

Kelly and Lola looked at each other and nodded.

"How much money do you think you'll need to make the trip back to Yucca Valley?" Doyle had drawn out a heavy leather pouch from the top drawer of his desk.

Kelly shook her head. "None. We have money."

"You shouldn't try to make that trip with anything less than fifty dollars. Do you have that much?"

"Fifty dollars? What are we supposed to do with fifty dollars?" Lola's mouth hung open. She then stood up and emptied her pockets onto the corner of the desk. Coins, buttons, a shell casing, a stubby nail, and three small rocks rolled on the smooth polished desk. Doyle chuckled.

"I keep forgetting you are still children and prone to pick up things that you find interesting." He had an amused look on his face when he reached to gather up the coins. He looked at Kelly who pulled off a boot and dumped out a handful of coins. Then she dumped out her jeans pockets. Red and blue string, three silver tinged buttons, four screws, and several more coins. Doyle grinned and picked up the coins.

"I think I have two more dollars in the bottom of one of the saddlebags." Kelly shrugged. Doyle looked at them.

The attorney frowned. "You've got nineteen dollars between you."

"Wow! That much? Lola, I thought you spent more than that?" Kelly started to laugh.

"Oh no, the hat I saw was so last year's style. It wasn't me." Lola flipped a strand of hair back in a haughty manner that made Kelly laugh.

"We haven't used much ammunition so we won't have to buy any. Aside from food, we won't have to buy anything else." Both girls shrugged with calm eyes.

Doyle's mouth hung open. "How much did you have when you started out?"

"Twenty-two dollars and fifty cents. Colton counted it twice." Lola smiled. Doyle put his palms flat down on the desk.

"Do you mean to tell me you started out 135 miles with just twenty-two dollars?"

"Yes, we spent maybe six dollars on food but got that back from the jar in the Flint Hills yard. Oh, and that reminds me. We'll dig up a couple more tonight and see what we find." Kelly grinned and winked.

"Mr. Doyle, I forgot to ask who is paying those five hands to ride up and bring back the stock. How much is that going to cost?" Lola started swinging her foot again as she rolled the three small rocks around on the desk.

"Phineas Rideout is sending them so he is paying them for the ride. I would think each man would get about thirty dollars. I don't know." Doyle frowned and sat back in his chair to think about it.

Lola slowly put the items on the desk back in her pocket. "I want you to give each man an additional twenty dollars when they get back with the stock to Flint Hills. Separate from what Mr. Rideout is paying them."

"What? Why?" Doyle sat up.

Lola let out her breath and rubbed her face with her small hands. "They will come home to a much different ranch, Mr. Doyle. We have no idea what sort of difficulty they will come across getting our stock safely moved here. I want them to have something extra to help them get by."

"What are you talking about? That's one hundred dollars for those hands." Doyle stared hard at Lola.

Kelly said, "Can you pay them or not? If you cannot, or won't, we'll find a way to put a little extra money in their hands when we get back to Flint Hills." She turned to watch Lola rolling the three small rocks around.

Doyle chewed on the corner of his mouth for a moment while he looked from one Stolter to the other. He took out a sheet of paper and scribbled out the instructions. He drew two lines beneath the paragraph and handed the quill to Kelly.

"Sign there so I can prove you instructed me to pay those hands. Lola, you'll sign below Kelly." Kelly quickly signed and then handed the quill to Lola. After the younger sister had signed, Doyle blew on the ink to help it dry and then laid the document off to the side.

The girls stood up. Doyle looked at them. "Anything else?" He handed the leather wallet to Kelly. Lola carefully nudged the three small rocks closer to the attorney who squinted at them.

"I want you to send those off to an assay office. I want to find out the purity." The corner of her mouth curled up in a smile. Kelly wiggled her eyebrows.

"What is it?" Doyle peered at the stones.

"Gold. There's gold on the Flint Hills Ranch. It's just lying there in the river on our land, Mr. Doyle. Miles of it in the water running across the north part of the ranch." Doyle's mouth fell open and he picked up a shiny rock. He swore.

"When we get back and move in, Colton and I will dig up every inch of that river and take out every speck of gold. So, keep this quiet, Mr. Doyle. We don't want anyone getting nosy." The girls left the attorney rolling the small rocks around in his hand.

***

Just after sunset, in the graying light, Kelly and Lola turned off the east Bradford road onto the long drive up to the ranch. From across the clearing they could see the big house sitting cold and silent over a quarter mile away. Kelly halted her horse.

"We're going to have to shield the lanterns tonight. Anyone sitting right here can see us in the front of the house." Lola peered into the gloom.

"Someone on top of the barn can see all the way out to here. That would be a good place to put Colton if we ever needed him to sit rifle."

"Let's go walk out the three places we want and put down a marker. Later tonight we can go take a look." Together they trotted to the house, unsaddled the horses, and turned them out to graze. Nothing had been disturbed at the house. All the little stacked stones still stood like silent sentinels around the patio.

For the next hour, they measured out and walked off the places where the jars should be buried. To an unknowing eye at a distance it looked like the girls were playing a game in the dirt. Then they went into the barn, shut the doors and from the vantage point of the loft they laid on their blankets whispering about the things they had seen and what they had heard.

"Kelly! Wake up!" Lola's voice was a whisper as she shook her sister awake.

"What?"

"Shhh! Quiet. There are two dogs down in the yard." Kelly rolled over onto her belly and slowly raised her head. Two black four-legged shapes sniffed around the patio and the yard. Kelly put her finger up to her lips to silence Lola.

Kelly scanned the grass beyond the yard fence but saw no movement. "They're coming this way. Did you lock all the doors?"

"Yes, the braces are on tight and I latched all the window shutters down. They can't get in." Lola whispered. Both girls scurried over to get their revolvers and then silently crept down the loft steps to the first floor. They heard the dogs sniffing around the front door and then they worked their way along the south side and then to the big double back doors. That was when they heard the long high-low whistle.

Both girls scurried back up the stairs and stayed back in the shadow from the loft door. They saw the dogs scamper across the yard, slide in between the fence rails and race east through the tall grass. They heard the whistle once more but there was no other movement. After an hour, the dogs had not returned.

"Maybe it was a traveler going cross country. There are men who walk everywhere," whispered Lola as she looked at her watch.

"Come on. Let's go get that digging done. I'm awake now." Kelly let her hand holding the revolver drop. They pulled on their boots and sweaters.

In the grass near the east fence, Lola stepped on the shovel and forced it down into the ground. She carefully lifted out the pile of dirt and laid it to the side. At sixteen shovelfuls, the tip something and she looked silently at Kelly who had been watching. It was a small metal box about three inches square, with a tied string around it.

Kelly walked it back to the barn, crossed the mark off the map and put the box up in the loft. She ran quickly back out to Lola and helped her put the small piles of dirt back into the hole. They moved on to the next spot near the water trough.

After a foot down, Lola shook her head. They walked back to the barn, lit the lantern and looked again at the map. "Maybe six inches to the right?" Kelly asked, "You want me to dig for a while?" The younger girl nodded.

Lola watched Kelly push in the shovel and lift the pile of dirt. "Stop! Look!" Lola brushed off a very small wrapped pouch. It was thick black fabric with cord wrapped over a dozen times around it.

Kelly pointed to the other piles of dirt. "Sift through the other dirt that you lifted out and see if there is anything in it." Quickly, Lola let the dirt slide through her hands, finding two more pouches. Kelly pushed them into her jeans pocket. They both pushed the loose dirt back into the hole. Kelly stamped down the dirt while Lola brought back three shovels of dirt from the yard.

Carefully, they walked around the side of the raised stone patio moving to the northwest corner near the steps. Just as Lola took her first step into the darkness, twigs broke on the other side of the small ravine. They both froze and put their fingers to their lips simultaneously. Kelly signaled for them to crouch and slowly they knelt up against the wall.

After a few minutes, another crunch broke the quiet and then the rhythmic walking of an animal moving away. Kelly grinned in the darkness and patted her heart. Lola smiled and nodded. After three shovels, full the blade hit glass, breaking it. Lola lifted out most of the glass with the shovel spilling it onto the stone step.

"We're going to need the lantern for this. I can't see anything. I don't want our hands cut up from that glass. I'll go get the lantern and gloves and come back. Stay right here and be quiet," whispered Kelly.

After Kelly came back, the lantern showed them the broken glass jar in the bottom of the hole. Kelly reached in with her glove and lifted it out.

There was a thick folded piece of paper in the jar that Lola shoved into her pocket. The clean dirt went back into the hole. Kelly put the glass pieces onto a tattered corner of an old burlap sack. They smoothed over the dig area and walked back to the barn.

From the tin can came ten dollars in gold pieces and a folded letter yellowed with age. The tiny writing read:

**

My darling daughter,

Find a man named Mick Dunbarton from Hattiesburg and ask him to tell you about me. We were in love at one time and I was sure we would marry.

Your Mother Loves You, Anna-Marie

**

"Wait! We met Mick Dunbarton." Kelly stared at the note and then at Lola.

Lola's forehead was wrinkled in a frown. "When you met Mr. Dunbarton, you thought he had been in love with ma. But it wasn't ma. It was ma's mother, our grandmother, Anna-Marie who he had been in love with."

Kelly shook her head. "We don't know what happened. We'll have to try to figure this out when we get home. Keep those gold pieces safe, Lola. Don't spend them. We may need those to figure out what happened between Mick Dunbarton, Anna-Marie and ma."

Lola asked, "But why would Dunbarton want those last two horses that ma trained?"

Kelly shrugged. "I don't know. I don't understand a lot about how people fall in love and stuff. We'll have to figure it out when we get home."

From her pocket, she pulled out the black fabric and used the tip of her knife to cut away the cord. A half-inch square of thin silver hung from a slender chain.

"A bracelet?" Kelly's brow furrowed and held it closer to the lantern. Lola leaned over her as she turned the square over and over.

"Wait! Look!" Lola pointed to the smoother side. "Letters. MD + AML. What does that mean?" Kelly squinted at the tiny marks.

Lola sat up and exclaimed, "Mick Dunbarton and Anna-Marie something. What was Anna-Marie's name before she got married?" Kelly's mouth fell open and she rubbed her fingers over the metal as if to force an answer out of it.

"Anna-Marie must have buried this. But it's beautiful. Why would she have buried a pretty bracelet like this?" Lola carefully wrapped it back into the black fabric. Kelly shook her head in silence with pursed lips.

"I don't know, honey. I don't know why adults do the things they do and never tell us about them. What time is it? I'm tired and all this mystery stuff is making my head hurt." Kelly rubbed her temples.

"Half past eleven. Time for bed. We want to be dressed and ready at sun up." Outside in the darkness, scurrying feet scampered amongst the leaves and twigs. The hooting owl called again. The thousands of gleaming twinkles shined on.

***

Nine days later, the girls walked their tired horses through the Windy Ridge gate shortly after midday. Dusty had come running and barking at them which brought Colton from inside the house. They washed up and ate a small dinner chatting about what they had found on the way down and answered dozens of questions from Colton.

"The house is twice the size of this one, Colton. There is a huge library that is locked in the middle of the house with a thousand books. There are four bedrooms upstairs. Or there will be once the roof and walls are repaired."

Colton asked, "What do you mean, big? Windy Ridge is a big house."

Lola shook her head. "No, I mean each room is big. And there are lots of rooms."

Kelly walked out carrying a steaming cup of coffee. "Really big, like it would be twice the size of our front room here, Colton." She sat down on the wooden bench and stretched out her legs.

Lola swung her foot. "Grandpa Glen's father built it for his family. They used to live in a much smaller house on the west side of the back barn. When they started building the big house, they tore down the old house and used it on the new one."

Colton asked, "So what's wrong with the place? What would stop someone from living there?" Kelly looked at Lola and then took a sip of the hot coffee. Kelly gestured with her head towards Colton.

"There's not anything there that would make it hard to live there," Lola said. "There's nothing in the house except dust and dirt. We'd need to take all this furniture and things.

"I found Charlie's grave up on the northeast corner of the property. Ma had buried him under a big old oak tree and pressed flat pieces of slate over the grave."

Colton asked, "Did it make you sad, Lola? Sometimes you get sad about people."

She shook her head. "No. Not sad. It felt like the family was together there. It's not a mean or bad place. I saw real fast why that was a favorite tree for Charlie." Colton nodded.

"What did the lawyer man say?" Colton looked at Kelly.

She smiled. "Well, I don't understand a lot about lawyers and such but he worked to help us understand the whole will and the ranch. He said that as our attorney he would work to make sure we were protected until Pa comes home. If something bad happens to Pa, Mr. Doyle will make sure we have a safe home to live in. He got a ruling from the court in Los Angeles so he can use Grandpa Glen's money to fix the Flint Hills house and pay off Windy Ridge."

"You mean, we'll own Windy Ridge and we don't have to worry about making the land payments?" Colton stood up and frowned.

"Yes. He has sent a letter to Mr. Jessup asking for the final payment amount. Mr. Doyle said that it should be about a month and the deed will be put into Ma and Pa's name." Colton sat and thought about what she had said.

Lola lowered her voice and leaned forward towards Colton. She told him about the midnight digging in the yard at Flint Hills. Colton's eyes were wide and he gasped.

Kelly said, "I talked to a Mr. Dunbarton from Louisiana at one of the stage stops. He was very interested in buying the last two horses that ma trained. That was a colt and a filly. I told him if he was interested in buying them to write and let me know when he wanted to purchase and take delivery. Did you hear anything from him?"

Colton went over to the desk. "All the mail that came is right here. Most of it is people saying how sorry they about ma dying, how they wished they could have seen her one more time and such." He put the basket in front of Kelly who started looking through the letters.

Lola said, "There is something else, Colton that we want you to know about. I have to go get something to show you. I'll be right back." The younger girl got up and went to the saddlebags lying on the porch. She fished around inside and brought out a folded dark green cloth with a leather strand wrapped around it. She laid that on the table. Colton looked questioningly to Kelly who grinned and wiggled her eyebrows. From the house, Lola brought out one of the big glass pie pans and the pitcher of water.

"We know you like to dig with us, honey. We found something wonderful for you to dig for at Flint Hills." Lola unwrapped the parcel and dumped almost a pound of dirt, sand, small stones, and some grass into the pie pan. Colton's mouth fell open and he leaned to stare at the pile.

"Watch this." Slowly, Lola poured the water over the pile of dirt, almost filling the pie pan. She put the pitcher on the table and then pushed the pie pan closer to Colton before she sat down. His eyes were wide and shining.

"Go ahead, honey." Lola smiled to Kelly who leaned on her elbow to watch her brother. He shoved both hands into the pan swirling the dirt into the water making a brown sludge. After a few minutes, he stopped as he held a handful of mud sifting it through his fingers. He looked at Lola.

"Is this?" The young boy trailed away to a squeak as he blinked several times and held up his hand. Lola nodded.

Colton shrieked making Kelly grimace and then she burst out laughing. Colton ran and hugged Lola happily dancing and then ran to Kelly and did the same. Both girls laughed at the small boy's delight.

"The north river that runs over the ranch is about four miles of digging for us." Kelly laughed again as she watched her brother whoop and holler dancing around the porch. Colton's yellow lab, Dusty, came running from the back of the house to bark at them.

Kelly said, "Lola waded into the river and picked up a couple handfuls just to look. She found a couple small rocks with gold in them. We asked Mr. Doyle to get those assayed so we know for sure that it's gold and to figure out how pure it is." Lola grinned at Colton.

"Do you remember Mr. Bloomfield, that junk man who was the gold miner? Do you remember the story he told us about making a long wooden box to wash the dirt in to find the gold?" Colton nodded plunging his hands back into the mud.

"We're gonna build one of those and start washing dirt at Flint Hills. Colton, you'll be in charge of digging out every inch of that river to get every speck of gold." The boy ran back to Lola and hugged her tightly.

Kelly said, "After we haul out our first shovel full of dirt, we'll be official gold miners."

Kelly watched Lola and Colton wash through the mud carefully tossing out the dirt. They found five more specks of fine gold. The girls told Colton more of the details about Flint Hills, the Rideouts and the town of Bradford. After Kelly had cleaned out a small glass jar, she watched Colton put the small specks into it and then fastened on the lid.

Kelly said, "Colton, I think it would be good for us to move our home to Flint Hills Ranch. Lola wants to live where Ma grew up. It's a bigger ranch and we could have more stock. Mary Rideout offered five of her hands to help us move the herd to Flint Hills. All we have to do is bring in one of those big freighter wagons, put our things on it and start riding."

Colton said, "So we don't owe any money on Windy Ridge? We'll own it all?" Kelly nodded.

"If we move, what happens to Windy Ridge?" His brown eyes were serious.

"The attorney said most likely we'll own Windy Ridge by the end of the month when the papers go through. He can help us find a tenant rancher to lease it out. I made sure that it won't be sold, Colton. Someday, if you decide that you want to have a ranch of your own, Windy Ridge will be yours.

Until then, we'll find someone to pay us to live here." Kelly tilted her head to look at Colton.

"This is the only home I've had. I don't want to leave it. I'm happy here. But I want to dig up all that gold, too. Four miles of river might take years to dig up. I want to go dig it all up." Colton rolled the small jar back and forth in his hands. "I don't know what to do."

"We will still be a family together. We'll still be able to read, and dig and ride any time we want. We'll just be doing it in a different place. That's why we wanted to talk to that attorney about everything." Kelly put down her coffee cup.

Colton held up the small jar. "This is why I want to go. And if you say that Windy Ridge will always be ours and I can come back, well then, I feel good about that. Sounds like we are going to move to Flint Hills." Kelly grinned and Lola hugged Colton.

That afternoon they started making lists of what they would need to do. Kelly and Lola told Colton more details about the different stops along the way.

***

Five days had gone by with more lists made, more planning and a lot of talking amongst the children.

"The cowboys arrive day after tomorrow. They will help us go over the herd and figure out how to take them south." Kelly laid out the calendar.

"They will take several days to make sure the herd can be moved and if the horses look good, they leave on Friday."

"Now that we know Pa is alive, how do we tell him where we are?" Colton asked. "What if he comes here and we are gone?"

Kelly stretched. "The attorney man will send a telegram that Pa will find if he stops in a town. That will tell Pa where we are."

"You know what would be best? If we could find Mr. Lucci and have him move us. He knows exactly where to go. He knows where the water holes are at." Lola nodded.

"Yes, but we don't know where he is at," Colton said.

"We should have Georgie come out and help look over the horses."

"Good idea. Someone ride into town and see if you can find him. Tell his uncle the blacksmith that we are getting ready to move the herd and we want them looked over before we move them."

Colton said, "I'm the easiest to pack. All I have is my bed, the chest of drawers and my clothes. Oh wait. I want to take my books, too. Oh, and all my digging tools in the barn. Oh, my gosh! The barn! How are we supposed to pack a barn?" Colton held his head in his hands.

"Alright. How about if one of us rides with the herd. One of us will ride with the freight wagon and another one of us will ride with the other wagon."

Lola exclaimed, "Hey! The mail man just put mail in the mail box! I'm going after it." Lola bounded out of the door and ran for the gate.

Kelly stood with her hands on her hips as she surveyed the room. "We need three more of those big steamer trunks like what ma has up in the attic. The attic! Oh, my gosh I almost forgot the attic. Come on, let's get everything down out of there."

Colton asked, "You sure all of this is going to fit in that house? How big is it again?"

Kelly poured another cup of black coffee and stirred in sugar. Lola came in the door waving a white envelope. "Mr. Mick Dunbarton."

"Oh, my gosh!" Kelly exclaimed. She looked at the handwriting on the envelope.

**

Dear Stolter Family:

I hope my letter finds all of you home and in good health. It was a pleasure meeting you and getting to know you both. I appreciate the short time you spent with me. Alas, business called me away and I left the stage suddenly to return to Los Angeles.

If you still have available the colt and the filly that were trained by your mother, Marianna Richardson Stolter, I still wish to buy them. Please send a telegram to my agent, Mr. Shawn Rollins, in Los Angeles, who will arrange to pick them up from either your ranch or a location you designate.

I cannot express my great joy over meeting you and learning of your family. I hope you will permit me to contact you from time to time to say hello.
Sincerely.
Mick Dunbarton

**

Colton listened with wide eyes. "You must have made a big impression on him. I don't understand."

"When Kelly and I first met him, we thought he had been in love with Ma before she married Pa. But Mick Dunbarton is a lot older than Pa."

Colton squinted as he looked at Kelly with a puzzled expression. "What are you thinking?"

Kelly looked at Lola. "I wonder if Mary Rideout knows Mick Dunbarton. She seemed to know a lot about the Richardsons."

"I don't know. I don't know how Mr. Dunbarton knew Ma. Or when he knew her. When Pa comes home maybe he can figure it out."

Kelly folded the letter and slid it back into the envelope. She turned it over in her hands several times. She opened the leather portfolio and pushed it in with the other letters. Kelly turned to see Lola sorting through a pile of rocks at the table and Colton turning pages in a book.

"We need to ride into Yucca Valley and send that telegram to the agent for those two horses. I need to tell Georgie's uncle that those two will have to stay there until the agent picks them up. Come on, let's get busy here." Kelly clapped her hands twice shooing the kids into action.

21 THE MYSTERY YEARLING

Saturday had come too fast for them. The biggest part of the house was ready to be loaded on the big freight wagon that stood parked on the right side of the house. Right at sunset five riders turned up the driveway and Dusty barked the alarm. The Rideout foreman and the cowboys for the drive to Bradford walked their horses into the yard.

The next day was busy from sunup to sun down. Doug Langdon and his cowboys pushed the seventy horses into three corrals and one by one sent them through a loading chute to check them over for the last time before the drive. Kelly sat on the top fence rail with her father's ledger and checked off the stock as they were identified. There were three horses over fourteen years old that were separated out. They found a black mare that was blind in one eye but still ridable.

One chestnut yearling shied away from the chute, whinnying repeatedly. Several times Kelly thought the horse would try to climb the fence only to fall and scamper away. Twice, she checked the log and could not find any record of the young horse. The cowboys got a rope on the animal which only made him panic more. Kelly asked the men to get the ropes off the scared animal and step away so it could calm down alone.

Kelly ran into the house calling for her sister. "Lola?"

"What's wrong?" Lola put down the book she was reading.

"We've got a yearling not in the log. He's scared to death and fighting everyone. Would you go take a look?" The young girl nodded and sat down to pull on her boots. She pulled her gloves on and followed Kelly down to the corral.

Langdon shook his head as Kelly approached. "He's tried to bite anyone that comes close. He's spooked or something."

"Gentlemen, if you'll kindly step over near the barn, Lola is going to spend some time with the yearling and try to figure out what's wrong."

Langdon took off his hat and scratched his head. "How's she gonna do that?"

"Mr. Langdon, please?" Kelly gestured towards the barn fifty yards away. Several of the cowboy sat down to roll smokes and talk. Two of them leaned against the barn and watched the young girl climb up onto the top fence rail. Kelly could see the agitated yearling pacing back and forth.

"Can you see what she is doing?" Langdon fidgeted with his belt buckle.

"That horse is getting closer to her all the time. It looks like she's talking to him." The cowboy glanced sideways at Kelly who nodded.

Several minutes had gone past. "Wait a minute. I think she's feeding that horse something out of her hands."

"That's the sign that she knows what the problem is. You only feed a horse as a reward for him behaving the way you want. That yearling did what she wanted him to do. She'll be over here in a minute," said Kelly.

"She's climbing down." The cowboys stood up and took a couple of steps towards the corral.

Lola smiled as she walked to Kelly. "He's deaf. He cannot hear anything and he's afraid. There is also green goop in his left ear that needs to be cleaned out. Burrs maybe. It's real sore."

"Let me go get the medical kit. We can get him cleaned up so he'll heal. Lola, I'll need you to keep him calm while I work on him." Lola nodded. Kelly opened the side door to the barn and went in.

"Miss, what were you feeding that horse? By the way he was acting, I thought he'd take off your hand if you tried to touch him."

Lola looked at the cowboy. "Carrots. Carrots and apples are like candy to a horse. Once they taste them, they'll do just about anything to get another one. It's too early in the season for apples right now so I pulled baby carrots out of the garden and shoved them in my pocket. Half the carrots in the garden every year go to the horses for their training."

It took an hour of patient coaxing for the yearling to let the sticky green puss be cleaned out of the left ear. Kelly smeared soothing salve into it and turned him loose.

Langdon leaned on the rail and watched Lola walking around with the yearling. "What do you want to do with that horse?"

"Georgie Hailey in town will train him to pull a wagon and a buggy. He'll make a simple riding horse or a wagon horse. He can't hear commands so everything will be hand and rein training. Georgie's uncle is the blacksmith in town. They rent and sell horses. I have a feeling that Georgie will take a liking to this yearling, though."

Kelly rubbed her head. "That's just it. That yearling is not on our books. He's not branded. He's not our stock. I don't know where he came from or why he is with our herd."

"There is still wild stock out there. Mainly in Nevada, out in the desert and some down south. You mind if I speculate a bit here, miss?" Kelly turned and looked at Langdon.

"Go ahead."

Langdon crossed his arms over his chest and chewed on the corner of his mustache. "I'd say that whoever owned his dam figured out the colt was deaf months ago. They didn't want him. They didn't want anyone to know their stock produced a deaf horse. Deaf horses are difficult animals. Lots of hammerheads are deaf and people think it makes 'em mean. This yearling here, I'd say his owner quietly mixed him into your herd knowing you'd take care of him. He's been living like a herd horse, growing up, and learning until today. I think he was put here."

"I never thought of that." Kelly looked back at the yearling and shook her head.

"I'd say your pa spent more than a couple hours a week riding out to look over the stock to check on them. He would have spotted this one quick. Right about the time that your pa rode out, this here yearling might have been moved in."

Kelly said, "I'd have to agree with you. He's got good markings, broad deep chest for endurance, and good strong legs. He does look like he might have come from a breeder somewhere. And you're right. I don't ride to look at the stock like pa used to."

Langdon squeezed Kelly's shoulder. "Okay. We have another herd to move in before it gets dark." The man winked and then walked back to the cowboys at the corrals.

Later that afternoon, the three children led the five horses into Yucca Valley blacksmith corral. The familiar curly redhead young man came out of the door with a big smile and took off the heavy gloves.

"Hey, you guys. You bringing me work?" George lifted Colton off his horse and tickled him. Colton giggled.

"Actually, Georgie, we want to leave these five with you and your uncle. Is he here?" Kelly climbed down and looped the reins over the post.

When Georgie's uncle came around, Kelly explained about the five horses and their individual conditions. Kelly discussed the transfer of ownership and that the attorney would provide a bill of sale. The man nodded in agreement and Georgie and Lola put the horses into the side corral.

"You might want to put your brand on that chestnut yearling, if you are going to keep him. Like I said, we don't know where he came from, Georgie, but he's yours now."

Georgie Hailey waved goodbye. "If I ever get down that way, I'll find you and say hello. I'm going to miss you Stolters!" Kelly felt a pang of separation. Georgie had always been congenial, understanding and patient around her. Colton adored him like an older brother. At that moment, she promised herself that she would find a way to keep up with how life was for Georgie Hailey.

***

It was the third day in the evening when the cowboys had stopped the horses half a mile north of Helton Corners. There was a big pasture and a shallow creek with a stand of alder trees on the east side of the road. The cowboys set up a small camp on the southwest edge of the creek.

Lola and Colton walked around the edge looking at the ground and trees. "Kelly, there is a wide alder pole bench over in the trees raised off the ground about a foot. It's about thirty feet set back and got marks on it where ropes were tied off over to the trees, like a canvas cover went over the top." Kelly nodded.

Lola frowned and then snapped her fingers twice in front of Kelly, who opened her eyes wide. "Kelly! Think! It's exactly like the one that was where we met the Zendejas family. Remember?"

Kelly grimaced and rubbed her face with both hands. She blinked a couple of times. "The Mexican family that was walking to Bluewater."

Colton said, "Mexicans were walking to Bluewater? What Mexicans? Where is Bluewater?"

"Yes! Them! When I went to say hello and all their gear was stacked on an alder pole platform just like that one. Well, maybe smaller, but still like it."

Kelly turned to Colton. "Yes, Lola found a Mexican family that had been walking along the road headed to a town we'll go through called Bluewater. When Lola first talked to them, she misunderstood that they had walked all the way from San Diego to where we found them."

Colton looked at Lola. "How'd you find Mexicans?" Lola shook her head irritably and waved her hands.

"They were camped at a water hole when we pulled in with the stage. Antonio Zendejas, his wife and two kids." Lola nodded.

Colton asked, "What happened to their horses?"

Kelly threw up both her hands, wide eyed. "There! See! I'm not the only one that thinks it's strange for people to be walking about California. That's what horses are for!" Lola groaned and acted like she was pulling her hair out.

"While I was in town one day, I stopped over at Pepi Romero's house to ask him if he knew the Zendejas family. He didn't, but his mother did.

141

Cousins. And there's this whole big story about the Mexican road that goes all the way to San Francisco. It's called El Camino Real. I'll tell you about it when we're up on the wagon."

Colton was indignant. "You said you told me everything you did and saw on the trip! You didn't tell me about that. You didn't tell me you met Mexicans! What else didn't you tell me?" Lola waved a dismissive hand and walked away.

Kelly chuckled and said, "Colton, your sister turned into a genuine sightseer on that trip. There were too many things and places she wanted to stop and look at. If she had, we would still be climbing over rocks or crawling through grass somewhere." Colton cackled with laughter. He shook his head and went to follow Lola into the grass.

Kelly climbed up into the back of the freight wagon to find the small book she had been reading. She might get a whole page read before she dropped off to sleep that night.

***

"Hello there!? I'm Vick Helton. I'm looking for Kelly Stolter, if she's here." Kelly held still when she heard her name.

Kelly jumped down out of the back of the freight wagon and brushed off her jeans. With a smile, she walked towards Helton holding out her hand.

"Mr. Helton. This is a surprise. Can I offer you a cup of coffee?" Kelly walked to the campfire.

"Thank you, no, Miss Stolter. I wanted to say hello and talk to you about your horses. Since the last time I saw you, I've had three of mine simply vanish, two I had to put down because of injury, and I've got a few that are just getting too old for the work. I was hoping to get out here before sunset and take a look at your stock, if you have any for sale in this herd here."

"So, you are looking for not necessarily a cutting horse, but more of a stock horse for working around the ranch and the cattle?"

"Yes, ma'am. That's what I'm looking for."

Kelly nodded. "Very good. There are five I have for sale right now in this herd. I'm going to have you talk to the foreman, Doug Langdon. He's been keeping a good eye on the herd. He might know where the ones are that I have for sale. They've all been running together coming down the trail so I don't know which horse is where right now." She smiled. "If you'll come with me, I'll introduce you and we can take a look."

After Helton had met Langdon, they went out into the herd to look over the stock. Forty-five minutes later five horses on lead ropes followed them back through to the camp.

Kelly smiled and leaned against the freight wagon. "I'll need to send a telegram to my attorney for an official bill of sale to you, Mr. Helton. He'll give you payment instructions and once I get unpacked in Flint Hills, I can send you copies of the pedigrees on the horses. Would you have a telegraph nearby?"

"Yes, ma'am. We have one in the small office behind the general store. I'll put these five in the third corral from the stables until I get that bill of sale. Would you like to follow me in or would you prefer to stop in the morning on the way through?"

"I've ridden sixteen miles today, Mr. Helton. I'd like to kill someone if they made me get back in the saddle right now. If it is convenient for you, I'd like to stop in the morning after I get everyone moving on the road," she said with a tired smile.

"I know the feeling, miss. Just go into the store and ask for the telegraph room. I'll leave word for them to send your wire for you. Again, thank you again for accommodating me this evening." He touched the brim of his hat and with a smile walked away to the horses.

Kelly went to stand next to the warm fire and enjoy a contented feeling of a job well done. Langdon came carrying his coffee cup and filled it up. "You did very well with Mr. Helton, Miss Stolter. He has a reputation of being hard to deal with in cattle."

"Thank you, Mr. Langdon. The Helton Ranch bought one of our top cutting horses last year. When I came down last month, we stopped in and I introduced myself to him with a gentle reminder about the quality of our stock. I told him when I brought my herd through, he might want to take a look. And he did," she said with a smile. Langdon chuckled and walked back to the cowboy camp.

It was an exhausted yet contented sleep Kelly enjoyed that night.

***

"That's not a house. That's a big wooden castle!"

Colton stood shielding his eyes from the sun. It was shortly after one o'clock when the Percheron team pulled the freight wagon into the yard. Kelly could see where the new shake roof had been put on. There was smoke coming from one of the chimneys. The main doors opened and Mary Rideout came out followed by Merle Doyle.

Doyle waved and said, "The herd ran in two hours ago. We figured you couldn't be too far behind." He smiled and helped Lola down off the wagon. He looked up at the young boy.

"You must be Colton. I'm your attorney, Merle Doyle, at your service," Doyle held his hands out to lift the boy down.

"How do you do, Mr. Doyle? It's good to see a face that goes along with the name." He grinned.

Kelly trotted over and hugged Mary. "That was a long slow ride. I don't know how those freight drivers do it."

"Hello, my dear. We've got a pot of soup on the stove and fires in two of the fireplaces to warm up the house." Kelly introduced Colton to Mary. Lola took Colton into the house for a fast tour.

"Let's get that wagon unloaded," Mary said with a squeeze to Kelly's arm.

Doyle and two of the hands began untying the ropes and peeling back the canvas tarps. Furniture, trunks and crates went into the house. The freight wagon was parked beside the barn and the big horses unhitched to pasture and water.

Mary cleared her throat. "Five days ago, my Phineas complained of pains in his chest. He took to his bed for rest. He never woke up and died in the night." She twisted the edge of her blouse and smile weakly.

Kelly stepped forward and put her hand on the woman's shoulder. Mary's eyes filled with tears and she struggled to maintain her composure. "We are so very sorry for your loss, Mrs. Rideout." A few minutes passed before anyone spoke.

Lola looked at Colton. "Mr. Rideout knew Ma when she was young, before she married Pa. His brother helped build part of this house." Colton nodded. There was a moment of silence.

"My sisters told me all about Mr. Rideout, ma'am. I was looking forward to meeting him. Someday you will have to tell me all about him," said Colton in a hushed tone. Mary reached and squeezed Colton's hand and sniffled into her handkerchief.

Mary then cleared her throat and stood up. "Have you heard any word about the children's father, Mr. Doyle?" Lola boosted herself up and sat on the counter. Mary handed her a small cup of soup and a spoon.

"I'm sorry, no. I check the wire twice each day. So far, nothing." The attorney shook his head with an uneasy look.

"Kelly, I heard about your sale of stock to Vic Helton up at Helton Corners. Very impressive. You are quite the negotiator," Mary said with a nod. "He has a reputation for buying at bottom prices and then bragging about it. How'd you do it?"

Kelly shook her head. "I just told myself every time he tried to lower the price, I'd raise it five dollars." Doyle laughed. Mary snickered behind her hand.

"He made payment and I processed the bill of sale on those head. I must admit, it went a lot faster than I thought it would. Some cattle sales take months to complete."

Kelly put down the cup. "I wanted to ask you, Mr. Doyle, if Mr. Dunbarton's agent completed the sale of the filly and colt." Before Doyle could respond, Mary Rideout jolted upright with an alarmed look.

Mary said, "How do you know Mick Dunbarton?" Her voice had risen with a tremble and her hands gripped her apron tightly.

Kelly frowned. "You know Mr. Dunbarton?"

"Yes, I am acquainted with him." Mary averted her eyes to her apron and rubbed her hands as if wiping them off. Doyle frowned as he looked at Kelly and then at Mary and then back at Kelly.

"Er, yes, the agent made a wire transfer into your account," said Doyle nervously. "They took delivery of the two horses day before yesterday. I confirmed it with a wire."

Lola jumped down off the counter and went to stand next to Kelly. The younger girl concentrated her gaze on the older woman. Mary brought her eyes up to those of the young girl for a few seconds.

"Merle, I believe I'd like to get home now. I'll leave you children to get settled in." Doyle helped Mary gather her things, and helped her into the black buggy.

The children and the attorney stood on the slate patio and watched the small vehicle roll down the driveway. Doyle rolled a smoke and watched the gray haze lift into the evening air.

"What was that all about?" His voice sounded gruff. "You touched a nerve in Mary Rideout."

Lola said, "Mary knows something about Mr. Dunbarton that she wouldn't tell us."

Kelly nudged her sister. "Lola, don't be rude. Mrs. Rideout has been very kind to us."

Lola climbed up and sat on the bench. "Yes, I know she has. And I am very thankful for the help to the family. But that doesn't change that she knows something that she would not say."

Doyle sat down next to Lola. "Tell me exactly what happened when you met Mr. Dunbarton." Doyle nodded from time to time as they went over the meeting. Lola and Kelly confessed their guesses about Dunbarton's role. Doyle was quiet for a moment.

He stood up. "Shall we go inside? I have some papers to go over with you."

Lola said, "I'll go see if Colton's stuck somewhere." The younger girl disappeared up the stairs.

Next to the fireplace at the table, Doyle had Kelly initial several pages from the sales, repairs, and transactions. Kelly opened her mouth and then closed it again as she changed her mind.

"Let me give you a piece of advice, Kelly. Whatever this situation is with Dunbarton, you'll want to hear his version completely. Whatever happened, he was there. Mary may wildly speculate about she thinks happened. But

Dunbarton was there. Only after you listen to everything will you be able to decide for yourself what the truth is." Doyle sat back in the chair and looked at Kelly.

"While I processed the contracts on those two horses, I decided to look up some information on Mick Dunbarton, just to find out who you were doing business with. Many times, when I'm doing legal work I look at the life and background of someone to help me figure out the type of person they are. What I found on Mick Dunbarton was rather surprising," said Doyle. "Would you like to know what I found?"

"Yes, please." Kelly curled her feet up underneath her.

"Dunbarton is one of the wealthiest men in America. He has stocks in all the major companies in the northeast as well as railroad stocks. The newspapers have article after article about his building something somewhere. One article did an interview that told how he is one of the few men who has been around the globe three times. Not even the Vanderbilts have done that." Doyle raised his eyebrows.

"What about his family, his wife and children?" Doyle shook his head.

"He never married. From time to time he was linked with different women, but he never made it to the altar. His life has been one of work and travel."

Kelly asked, "He said his agent was in San Francisco. Did the horses go there?"

"I don't know. Mr. Hailey, the blacksmith in Yucca Valley said that after the agent presented the bill of sale and the receipts, he took the horses and headed east." Doyle leaned his arms on his legs and stared at the fire for a moment. Kelly could see him thinking as the muscle in his jaw flexed.

"He told us he was headed to his ranch outside of Dallas. From there he was going to go home to Hattiesburg for a while." Kelly mindlessly twirled a strand of her hair.

"His ranch in Texas is noted to be over one thousand acres. The land in Hattiesburg is farmland and almost the same size. Kelly, it was like a thousand to one odds that he had been on that stagecoach that you followed down here. To me it was a pure accident you even met. He should have been in a railcar headed east."

Kelly shook her head and rubbed her face tiredly. "It's very strange why he wanted those horses that were trained by Ma. He was very insistent. I guess we'll never know."

"You've had a long day, Kelly. I'll be staying here tonight and tomorrow I'll help in any way I can. I must get back to Bradford for appointments in the afternoon. Get yourself to bed and get some rest. We can talk more tomorrow." He waved her up the stairs.

There was a lone lantern burning on the round table in the first bedroom. Lola was wrapped up in a quilt next to Colton, sound asleep. Kelly quietly turned down the lantern and closed the door. In her own room, her tired eyes found the twinkling stars through the window. Somewhere out there was her father, perhaps looking at the same stars.

22 SETTLING IN

It was the smell of coffee that woke Kelly up. She found a pair of clean jeans in one of the stacks on the floor and pulled on a black sweater and went downstairs. Doyle stood holding a spatula as he made pancakes and bacon. Lola and Colton sat like hungry birds at the table. They sorted through the dozen wooden crates against the walls to find plates and cups.

Doyle waved the spatula. "Tomorrow, bring in that freight wagon and those Percherons and I'll make sure they go back to Yucca Valley. That is a nearly new wagon and beautiful animals and I want them sent back as soon as possible." Kelly nodded as she forked fluffy pancakes into her mouth.

"We're a lot farther out from town than we were at Windy Ridge. We can't just ride into town anymore." Colton chewed on a piece of bacon.

"You don't have very much here in the way of food and supplies. I'll open an account at the general store. Be sure to start making a list of things you need. The closest store or food is six miles southwest at Williams Creek. The Faraway Inn serves good food and you can trust Gianni La-Costa. We call him "Papa". He is Italian, and a good man."

An hour later the three children stood in the middle of the bigger barn and started putting tack, implements, and tools into drawers and on hooks. "Kelly," Colton said with his eyes wide. "I didn't believe you when you said it was big as our house. It is." He grinned. Kelly tousled his hair and laughed.

"I'm going to need three big cabinets built in for the medicines for the horses and colts. Ten bales of straw, a couple of saddle blankets, and five sacks of oats and corn." Kelly wrote on a piece of brown paper.

Lola climbed up on a stanchion. "We've got to dig up a garden plot and get seeds into the ground soon. We can start that tomorrow. Colton, if you'll search around maybe you can figure out where Grandma Richardson used to make her garden."

"Alright, I'll take a walk around." Colton nodded.

"Kelly, put those seeds on the list so we can get them tomorrow. I'm going to need another pair of gloves, too. It's a bigger ranch. We're going to need more tools and equipment. We haven't come up on the work yet so we don't know what we'll need." Lola gestured to the open space of the barn.

"We need firewood, too. We need to take a ride into the trees and see if there are any dead trees or downed trees and drag them back," Kelly stretched her arms out to the sides.

"You said there was a room for me to use. Where is it?" Colton trotted down to the big double doors.

"Here, Colton. Look!" Lola slid a heavy wooden door on a track to the side and went into a twelve by twelve room. Built in shelves and a desk along with two broken windows and a door that went to the side yard.

"You've got an official office for papers and books. We'll make a big map of the river and mark it off as we work through it. We'll get a couple of tall stools so we can work in here." Lola watched Colton open drawers and cupboards.

"Wow! This is really good." He grinned. Kelly came in and sat down on the small bench.

Lola twirled a sliver of wood between her fingers. "What will Pa say when he gets home? What if he doesn't want any of this, doesn't want to live here?"

Kelly crossed her legs and swung her foot. "He'll live wherever we are, honey. If Flint Hills reminds him of bad things in the past and he wants to go back to Windy Ridge, he'll tell us. But we have decided that we want to grow up where Ma grew up."

***

As they walked back to the big house, Colton asked "Why haven't we heard from pa? Why doesn't he send word?"

Lola sounded irritated. "If he's lying somewhere hurt, he can't send word."

Kelly threw down the jacket on the chair. "Let's get you on a horse and go out in the south pasture, cut out fifteen head and then you move them at least a mile. All by yourself. Let's see you do it. It's not easy." She was exasperated.

Lola flung back. "I just want to get on a horse and start riding east to see if we run into him."

"So, what if we do. We get on horses and start riding east. Then someone shows up here with word from Pa. Or he does send word and he needs our help." Kelly could feel the hot pressure behind her eyes.

Colton walked in and sat down at the table. "Wouldn't Pa try to find another grownup to help him?"

Kelly shook her head and let out a big sigh. "He's done this before. He's run horses over miles moving them. He knows what he's doing out there."

Lola drummed her fingers on the table. "What about that man he's with? What about that Ginger Whelihan?"

"What about him? Pa said he was a friend." Colton looked at Lola.

Lola stood up and paced over to the windows. "What if Mr. Whelihan did something bad and Pa got hurt?"

Kelly exclaimed, "Oh, my gosh, Lola! Unless Pa tells us that, we don't know, Lola. It is a wild guess until Pa tells us." She hung the small towel over the back of the chair and then ran up the stairs.

The ugly feeling had been creeping up her back for a couple of weeks now. She kept telling herself that they were family, they had worked together, and been through things together. One would not abandon the other if the going got tough. She leaned her hands on the window sill.

The breeze blew the grass into gentle waves. Birds flew along the tree line. Two buckskins grazed near the edge of the pasture. Somewhere out there her father was moving a herd of horses west.

***

The sun had been up almost an hour. Kelly sat with a steaming cup of black coffee, reading next to the windows. She had a thickly knitted afghan wrapped around her and a book lay open in her lap. It was an old story of a little girl who went to live with her grandparents after her mother died. The hills of Switzerland became her home after living on the cobblestone streets of England.

"Kelly?" Lola called out.

"I'm in here." Lola came in, still in her pajamas, and sat next to her sister on the sofa. She held out a book.

"There was an old book in the library that I found. I think it is in French. Kelly, can you tell?" Lola handed the heavy leather-bound book to her sister. Kelly opened it up and flipped the pages to the center.

"Yes, it looks like French. Now I wish that I would have paid more attention to that lady that came in to teach French at school. I don't know very much, Lola. Who is Sun Tsu?" She handed the book back to her sister.

"I don't know. The next time we go into Bradford, I want to ask to see if anyone reads French. I'd like to know what this book is about. It looks important." Lola carefully turned the pages.

Kelly flexed her back and arms. "According to the calendar, today is target practice. An hour of target practice with the guns and knives. You and

Colton can set up the targets later. Is he still asleep?" Lola nodded.

She had a thoughtful expression. "He doesn't have the bad dreams any more. He sleeps in his own bed all night. It is good for him to be here. Every day he scoops up a couple of pails of dirt and washes them out looking for the gold. He is happier here, Kelly." She smiled.

Kelly said, "Yes, I can see that in him. This past week has been very tiring for him. He's been keeping himself busy until dark every day. He eats a big dinner every night. We'll have to start measuring him to see if he is growing." She laughed softly.

After a breakfast of eggs and pancakes, they went out to the garden and carefully watered the planted rows. It had taken a full day to pull out the weeds and grasses and turn over the rich, brown earth. The tiny seeds had been pushed in and the soil patted firm.

Up on the jagged ridge, Colton had formed round gobs of sticky clay and coated them with the sandy dirt from the north hills. These round orbs had been put in the crooks of trees, balanced on jagged rocks, and hung from tree limbs. Shots and booms echoed down the valley into the late afternoon.

"My two boxes are done. I don't see how I go through it so fast. It's like it only takes a minute," Lola shook the boxes and snorted.

Colton finished loading the Remington. "Get the glasses and spot me, would you?" Kelly nodded and picked up the leather case.

"Where is your target?" Kelly focused the lenses and scanned the ridge.

"A couple days ago at that old camp up on the ridge under that big tree I set up twenty-four targets of red clay. They should be dry by now. Let me know when you see them. The sun should be shining on them from this side." The young boy knelt down steadying the rifle over his knee."

Lola asked, "Had that campsite been used? Last time we were up there, it was dusty and the weeds had started to grow up around the sleeping dip."

Colton squinted at the gunsight. "No, it was old and cold. Nobody had been there. Do you think someone is coming back to it?"

Kelly said, "I see them, Colton. Go ahead."

The boy laid out prone and slowed his breathing. The long rifle jumped and the crack of the shot bounced off the flint in the hills. Four more shots rang out.

"Five down. You winged that last one, it wasn't a good hit." Colton grunted.

"Do you remember Mr. Guzman back in Yucca Valley?" The boy asked as another shot rang out.

Kelly said, "Yes, I remember him. Pa used to sit and drink whiskey and coffee with him. They were friends."

Two more clay balls exploded from rifle shots. "I had said that I wanted to shoot a new rifle to see what it felt like. I thought I could shoot better with a new rifle. Mr. Guzman told me something that made me think about the guns." Another shot.

Lola asked, "What did he tell you?" Three more quick shots.

"He said it's not the rifle, not the gun that makes the shot. It's the man holding the gun that makes the shot. He said to work at being good at shooting any weapon." Another shot.

Kelly said, "Colton, you missed that one." The boy grimaced.

"Mr. Guzman was in the army in the war. He used a rifle and was a sniper. He told me he killed people from far away before they could kill him or the other army men." Two more shots fired.

Kelly put down the glasses. "I don't see any more targets. You sure you put up twenty-four? Maybe animals, raccoons or squirrels knocked them around." Colton shook his head.

"I'll check them tomorrow." He pulled another handful of shells out of his pocket and loaded them into the rifle. Colton looked at Kelly and pointed to the west.

"To the west where that one trail ends, do you see those four posts that are stuck in the ground there?" He waited for Kelly to find them.

"Okay, I see them. What is that on them? Strings?" Kelly frowned.

"Yep. I pulled some strings out of the grain sacks and knotted them up. I wanna see if I can hit them." Colton worked on his aim.

"Colton, that's a long shot all the way over there." The young boy made a grunting noise and wiped the back of his hand across his mouth. He laid down on the ground and balanced the long barrel in a notched chunk of wood. He held his breath and pulled the trigger.

Kelly said, "You hit the post, but not the strings. Still a good shot though. I couldn't have done it."

Lola stood up and brushed off her jeans. "What's for dinner?"

"Chili. I'll make cornbread. I think we still have pie left unless you ate it." Kelly looked at her sister. A rifle shot rang out and Kelly checked with the glasses.

"You got one set of the strings. I think they have wrapped themselves around the post." Kelly put down the glasses.

"Lola, you want to try this shot? Colton did it, you should be able to." The younger girl shook her head.

"No. I like using the revolver or the knives. I'm not big enough or strong enough to throw knives so it's more of a sneak attack I'll have to make. You know, like an Indian slithers along in the grass and then jumps on you."

"Is that what they do? I had no idea. Where'd you see that?" Kelly tried to sound sarcastic. Colton giggled.

"You've been reading those penny story books again." Colton laid the rifle down. "Are we moved in now?"

Kelly thought for a moment and then nodded her head. "Yes, I'd say we're moved in. Why?"

"Are we still going to dig up the yard and find all Grandma Richardson's cans and jars?"

"At first, I thought that we'd have to dig up those cans and jars because we'd need the money. But we don't need it now. We sold horses and we're using that money to live on." Kelly knelt next to Colton. He nodded.

"And I thought you'd be spending all your time and energy digging in the river to find gold," said Kelly. "You have been pretty busy over there." Colton smiled.

Lola said, "So you think we should just leave 'em lay there under the ground until the time comes when we need them?" Kelly nodded.

Colton said, "I like digging in the river. I have that to do."

"I mean, look at the size of the yard and the back-garden area. It's three times the size of Windy Ridge, and it took us three days to dig up that. This will take a week, maybe two." Kelly gestured to the ranch.

"Alright. Alright. Just let them lie." Colton held up a small grimy hand to stop her.

Colton stood up and dusted himself off. Lola began putting her tools and boxes into the leather sling. Kelly picked up the three rifles. The breeze had picked up, making the girls' long hair flutter. Loose leaves rolled across the path pushed by the wind. Just as they came up over the ridge, Kelly froze and signaled for silence. There was a man standing next to a horse in the yard.

***

Kelly whispered, "Get the field glasses out and take a look." Lola knelt and opened the leather case and took out the lenses.

"I don't think I've ever seen him." She whispered as she handed the glasses to Colton who had laid down in the tall grass.

"Nope. We don't get a lot of visitors and that is a stranger. What do you want to do?" Colton looked through the glasses and then handed them to Kelly.

"Lola, get over on the north trail and come down behind the house from the trees. I'll go in on this trail. Colton, can you get a shot on him from here?" Kelly looked at the young boy.

"Easy. You think he looks like trouble?"

"We don't take chances. Grownups might think they can come in here and push us around because we're kids. We can take care of ourselves."

Kelly furrowed her brow. "Lola, be quiet getting around and don't let him see you. I'll signal when it's clear. Go." Kelly patted Lola's shoulder.

Colton said. "Alright. I see him put his hands on you, I'll shoot. See if you can stay out of my line of sight, too." Kelly nodded.

***

"What do you want here, mister?" Kelly's voice made the man jump.

Broad shoulders, thick through the body with black hair and mustache. "My name is Clay Richardson. I've got a claim on this land. Who are you?"

Kelly carried the Remington rifle in her left hand and her right hand was on the Colt in her holster. She stopped twenty-five yards away. "I'm Kelly Stolter. My mother was Marianna Richardson, daughter of Glen and Anna-Marie Richardson."

The man touched the brim of his chocolate brown Stetson. "My father is Birmingham Reginald Richardson, the youngest brother to Glen. We'd heard that Glen had died some time back and I came to see if the ranch was being lived in or if it had been abandoned." Richardson smiled and took two steps towards Kelly and started to hold out his hand. Quickly, Kelly held up a clenched fist to the east and then spread her fingers wide. Richardson stopped in his tracks.

"You'll want to stay right there, Mr. Richardson. We've got a couple of guns on you, just in case."

"Well, there's no cause for that. I don't mean you any harm here." Richardson had a somewhat shocked look on his face. He nervously looked around the yard and the hills.

"Is your Pa here? I'd like to talk with him about his plans for the ranch."

"My father is Nick Stolter. He's away bringing in stock and will be home in the next few days." Kelly took her hand off the Colt.

"I have questions about the ownership of the ranch. I guess I'll have to wait until your father gets home before I get some answers." Richardson rubbed his forehead.

Kelly shifted her weight to her other foot. From the corner of the house, Lola walked slowly with both hands gripping the Colt revolver.

"This is my younger sister, Lola Stolter. Lola, this is Clay Richardson, son of Birmingham Reginald Richardson, who was the younger brother to Glen. Clay is Glen's nephew." Lola blinked. Richardson started to back up and bumped into his horse.

"Good afternoon, Mr. Richardson."

"Hello, Miss Stolter." He started to touch the brim of his hat and then thought better of the movement. He looked from Lola and Kelly nervously.

"You can get answers fairly quickly about the ranch ownership from our attorney, Merle Doyle, in Bradford. You'll take the main road headed west thirteen miles. He has an office above the doctor's building. He can tell you about the will and the ranch." Kelly smiled.

Richardson cleared his throat. "I see. What about your ma? Is she home? Can I talk to her?

Kelly shook her head. "Marianna Richardson Stolter died earlier this year after a long sickness."

Richardson grimaced and shook his head. "My condolences on the death of your mother. I'm sorry I didn't get to see her in recent years."

"Thank you, Mr. Richardson."

"When you come back, you will want to bring Mr. Doyle with you so we can hear first-hand about any changes to the ranch ownership." Kelly nodded.

"Kelly, you best signal Colton to stand down. He'll get cranky if you don't," Lola said.

"Excuse me, Mr. Richardson. I have to get my brother's rifle off of you." She grinned and turned east holding her arms straight up over her head. Then she lowered them out to her sides so her arms and body formed a tee. Then she dropped them to her sides. Kelly picked up the rifle and turned back to Richardson.

Richardson asked, "There's three of you? Marianna had three children?"

"Our older brother, Charlie, died when he was very young. There is only three of us now." Kelly watched Richardson roll his shoulders and arch his back to relax himself. Twigs snapped behind Kelly and she turned around.

"This is our younger brother, Colton." The young boy stepped onto the hard-packed earth of the yard followed by the yellow lab.

When the boy got to Kelly he handed her the rifles and then wiped his hands on his jeans. He walked over to Richardson and held out his hand.

"Hello, Mr. Richardson. I'm Colton Stolter." The boy smiled as he shook hands.

"When you come back, we'd like to hear stories about Grandpa Glen." Colton walked back to Kelly and took his rifles.

"When my father married, he settled in St. Louis, Missouri. I haven't been here except once when I was a young boy, a little older than you, Colton." He smiled at Colton who smiled back.

"Thank you for the information. I'll ride into Bradford and talk with Mr. Doyle." Richardson swung up into the saddle. He touched the brim of his hat and reined his horse around. "I hope to see you again soon."

The children walked slowly down the drive about one hundred feet and stopped to watch the walking horse disappear into the trees.

Lola said, "Ma's cousin. I think we scared him."

Kelly asked, "You sure?"

Lola nodded and took in a deep breath. "Yes, he was telling the truth. Can we eat now? I'm hungry." Colton turned and walked towards the house.

"Me, too."

Did another Richardson have a claim on the ranch? There was a packet of letters in the steamer trunk from St. Louis, Missouri addressed to Marianna. Maybe those were from him. Kelly relaxed her shoulders and let some tension go out of her. She turned and felt the warm afternoon sun bathe her shoulders and neck.

23 THE CHILDREN MEET STENSON

The next afternoon Kelly leaned against the rail on the Bradford boardwalk. The front façade was thirty feet high. The tall narrow windows on both side of the door had drapes on the inside effectively shielding the buildings contents.

Kelly said, "This must be the place."

Lola sounded wistful. "I saw it the first time we came here to visit. We were so busy I didn't have a chance to even walk in."

"Lola, a gunsmith isn't going to give you the time of day. You're a little girl to them. First thing they'd ask is, where is your pa, where is your ma, stuff like that."

"Ma used to tell me that I would always be better with knives than guns. Because I was so little. She said I could hide a sharp little knife real easy. Said people would never think such a pretty little face would swing a knife at them."

Colton pulled on the door. The lock clanged, but the door did not move. "Locked. No one is in there."

"You children waiting for someone or you planning to knock over my shop?" The noise of footsteps to her right made her turn her head toward the noise. The man who had come out of the saloon took a couple of steps and then saw the children and stopped suddenly.

At age forty-two, Bruno Stenson was the sole weapons and arms dealer, selling shotguns, rifles, handguns and custom knives for the surrounding twenty-five miles. He was a serious, frowning man with a round-cheeked, smoothly shaven face. Very short sideburns, blonde hair with a side part combed over with a pomade cut short. Narrow short straight nose. He wore a black Stetson hat with a black beaded band. At six feet two, the gunsmith's broad shoulders and muscled arms towered over the children. Below his ample belly, hung a silver belt buckle. His black jeans were tucked into black boots with silver tips.

Kelly stood up and dusted off her jeans. "We're looking for Bruno Stenson, gunsmith." The blue green eyes looked at Colton, then Lola and then back to Kelly as he took out the ring of jangling keys. He squinted his eyes and took the cigar out of his mouth with his right hand.

"I am Bruno Stenson, gunsmith. Are you looking to buy, or are you looking to sell?" He bent over to grasp the heavy padlock, shoved in the key and the chain fell onto the steps.

Kelly said, "Neither. We've just always made it a habit of finding the local gunsmith in case we have need," she let her voice trail off. "In case we need gunsmith services." She smiled. Stenson opened the right-hand door and blocked it open using a heavy iron ball with a handle. He stood to one side and with a flourish of his arm, bade them enter.

"Ladies, gentleman. Please come in."

"Thank you, sir. I'm Kelly Stolter, this is my sister, Lola Stolter and my brother Colton Stolter." Immediately their eyes swung around the large interior.

Stenson took off the black Stetson and hung it on the top of the wooden coat tree in the corner. He unbuckled the gun belt and set the pistol on the table behind the counter. The shop was fifty feet long by thirty feet wide with polished narrow plank floors, and ten display cabinets. The tall, narrow leaded glass windows obscured the view into and out of the store. Colton had stopped to look at a tall bureau of small storage drawers. Kelly saw the shiny, four foot square 1850 Templeton safe sitting in the corner. Three intricate chandeliers sparkled overhead from the twenty-foot-high ceiling.

"I'm pleased to make your acquaintance. I had heard that you youngsters moved your horses onto the Flint Hills Ranch. Please allow me to express my condolences on the recent passing of your mother." Stenson bowed his head slightly.

As Lola took of her gloves, she said, "Thank you, Mr. Stenson. Mr. Doyle said you might have a selection of knives we might see. I'm looking for three filet knives for butchering." Stenson put both hands on the counter as he stood behind it and nodded.

"Yes, over here." Stenson walked down to the glass show case at the end. With a small key from his vest pocket, he unlocked the rear door and reached in to pull away the white fabric covering the knives. Lola immediately clasped her hands behind her back and leaned forward to look. Stenson had a puzzled look on his face.

"Steel handle, bone handle, wooden handle. Smooth spine and serrated spine. Some prefer a large, pronounced cross piece and others like a more decorative fitting like bone or ivory." Kelly could see Stenson moving along the back of the case as Lola moved along the front. She stopped and looked up at the gunsmith.

"I'm a young girl, Mr. Stenson. If I try to use a larger knife like a Bowie, I'm clumsy with it because my hands are not big enough to grip it properly. I tend to slaughter more than butcher. Now, on the other hand, I know I will grow and my hands will become stronger so I want to avoid tiny knives. My small problem." Lola stepped back from the case and smiled.

Stenson murmured something under his breath and nodded. "I see what you mean. The two steel Henckels knives might have enough weight, yet be light enough for your smaller hand." Stenson tapped the glass over the top of the knives. Lola smiled.

"No, it doesn't matter to me who owned them or where they came from." She smiled again. "Thank you, Mr. Stenson, for showing me the knives." The man's brow furrowed.

Stenson stopped for a moment. "Did you want to hold one to test the weight, Miss Lola?"

"No, sir. I'm not buying today. I just wanted to look. But thank you, for the offer." Stenson nodded and closed the case, locking the lock.

Colton walked over and put a hand on the glass case. "Our pa is away from home right now. He always did the butchering. Now we have to do it. We used to help him but we've never done it alone without him." Colton smiled. Stenson nodded as if waiting.

Kelly took two steps forward. "We've built a few hunting blinds around the property and we're hoping to bring down a deer in the next few days. I'm thinking that we have enough knives to butcher, but it is prudent to know what others are available. Mr. Stenson, what are you asking for those two Henckels?"

Stenson started to speak and then paused to clear his throat. "Well, I was asking nineteen dollars for the pair. That includes the leather cases and unlimited sharpening of them." Kelly nodded. She turned her head and saw that Lola had put her hand on the stock of a shotgun.

"Every gun, every rifle, every pistol, and every knife in here has killed someone or something. They are sure tools. They are tools of death." Lola clasped her hands together and turned as she walked nearer to Kelly.

"Young lady, I buy, trade, and sell instruments of injury and death. I'm a veteran of that horrible war and have seen enough of bloodshed and violence for my entire lifetime." Stenson crossed his arms across his chest. "Some folks aren't meant to have weapons. Others are. People bring them in and people take them out."

The door opened and an elderly man came in with several rifles wrapped in a cloth. His slow moving gray-haired wife with a cane followed him in. They looked at the children and then at Stenson.

"Thank you for your time, Mr. Stenson. I'm sure we'll come see you again." Kelly smiled and stepped towards the door. Colton walked to the gunsmith and shook his hand. Lola carefully took off her glove and held her hand out. It was only a second fingertip grip then he let go. Kelly closed the door after they had stepped outside.

As they stood under the old oak in the town square, Kelly looked at Lola. "What did you think?"

Lola smiled. "We can trust him. I'd say he has forgotten a lot of the secrets that have been told to him. He is a peaceful man and the time of war is in the past. He's looking for something and can't find it." She shook her head as she pulled on the glove.

"That's all I wanted to know." Kelly took in a deep breath and let it out in relief. "Alright, let's go eat and go home. Shopping makes me hungry." They all laughed and walked towards the hotel.

***

The weather had turned hotter. Every day, Colton found more specks in the newly constructed sluice next to the river. Lola and Kelly spent the time exploring the entirety of the ranch according to the surveyor map. Lola had been placing the slathered whitewashed rocks on the property line as markers. On the far eastern edge of the property one day she froze as she was placing a marker. Carefully, she nudged the overgrown weeds and plants out of the way and found a layer of river rocks pressed into the soil.

When the young girl laid her knapsack next to Kelly, she said, "I found a grave to the east side of the footpath. It's deep. It is a deep hole." Kelly stood up and looked at her sister.

Kelly looked at where the dry, crumbled dirt clods had been disturbed. They piled a layer of small rocks over it as a marker. They reminded each other to tell Doyle about it next time they went into town.

"Put your markers down, Lola. Then let's go wait for the mailman. Maybe there will be word from Pa today." The mail man told them to set up a mailbox next to the main fence down at the road so he would not have to ride up four miles to drop off their letters and packages on Tuesdays and Thursdays.

Kelly and Lola had started writing letters out to everyone they knew. They built a big wooden cubbyhole box and nailed it to the fence that they sat on to wait for the mailman. It became the thing they did on Tuesdays and Thursdays. Kelly and Lola liked to have balancing contests to see who could stand on the top fence rails the longest. One day they had been eating apples when the mailman came by and he laughed at them as they balanced on the thin boards.

The kids chopped down several young birch trees and built wide pole benches so they could sleep on the north porch. Kelly stitched up several thin mattress pads from the grain sacks and stuffed them with old clothes. Mr. Lucci brought by big length of dark green netting they nailed up onto the porch overhang. All of them started to live outside in the warm weather.

***

"Kelly, there's someone down at the front gate asking if anyone is home. Come on," Lola picked up the Colt and opened the front door. Kelly opened the closet door and pulled the Colt out of the holster and followed Lola out onto the front patio.

She waved, and then trotted down the driveway.

"Good afternoon. I'm Henry Elliot of the Texas Rangers. I'm looking for Nick Stolter." Elliot held up his leather encased Rangers badge.

"Wow!" Lola climbed up on the gate and reached for the badge. Elliot grinned and handed the leather sleeve to her.

Lola said, "Pa isn't home, but we are. You have found us, Mr. Elliot. What's the matter? You got bad news about our Pa?"

Kelly swung the gate open. "We've never seen a real Texas Ranger before." Her eyes were wide.

Elliot walked his horse on into the yard. "You haven't heard from him yet?" Both girls shook their heads. Elliot frowned.

"Well, I bring news of your father. I ran into him a month ago. If you have coffee, I'll tell you about what I found." His voice was gruff.

Lola exclaimed, "Where is Pa? Where did you see him?"

Elliot guided his horse to the water trough and dismounted. "I don't mean to alarm you, but I believe your father should have been home by now."

"When you saw him, Mr. Elliot, how many head did he have with him?" There was suddenly a barrage of questions from both the girls. Elliot grinned and held up his hands to stop them.

Elliot looked towards the house. "I believe you have a brother, Colton. Is he here? I don't want to tell all this twice."

"He's up digging in the river," said Kelly. "Lola, ride up there and bring him back. He'll want to hear this." Lola looped a halter over the head of the dun mare in the corral and headed around the side of the house. Kelly took the Ranger up the steps and into the home.

Twenty minutes later they all sat around the big kitchen table. Elliot told the children about how Nick had helped him track down two of three outlaws.

161

Colton asked, "Was he hurt?"

"It was the other side of Tucson, west of a little town called Red Springs. He had a bump on the head and his hands were scuffed. He was with good people, though. I'm sure he got by alright. The man he was with, Southcott, he was an Army officer that served with my partner during the war. Southcott was held in high esteem so I'm sure your father was alright."

Lola sat back in the chair and folded her arms over her chest. "Pa has fallen off horses, fallen off the roof, fences, and trees. He always gets back up and goes on."

Elliot leaned his forearms onto the table and squinted his eyes. "When I say him, he was running a couple of buckskins, two black colts and an older mare. I specifically remember those horses because they walked right over to me like they knew me." The Ranger shook his head with a chuckle.

The lawman cleared his throat. "It disturbs me that he isn't home by now. He said he was an experienced horseman and was headed west. I expected to see him here now."

All three of them then told Elliot very carefully and slowly about meeting Ginger Whelihan. Lola was very vocal in her doubts about the personality she met. Elliot listened and raised his eyebrows several times. Kelly perceived that there were words the Ranger held back.

Colton asked, "What are you going to do? Are you going out to look for him?"

Elliot said, "I have a home in Santa Fe, New Mexico. I was headed back there. I've got a few good friends in Bradford and I remembered that Nick said he was headed to Flint Hills. So, I decided to stop in here to see him."

Kelly said, "Then if he is on the road headed west and you're headed east, you should run right into him. He must have run into trouble because it is taking so long for him to get home."

Elliot stood up. "If I get all the way to Tucson and don't see him, I'll know something is wrong and I'll backtrack. It's pretty hard to hide a herd of horses like that. There's plenty of water holes out there that I don't know about. He could be at any one of them."

Lola stood up and rubbed her face. "When you say things like that to us, his children, it makes us want to saddle up and ride east. Ranger or no Ranger, you wouldn't be able to stop us, Mr. Elliot." The Ranger put both hands up with palms facing out as if to stop them.

"I'd do the same if it were my pa. I understand. But let me say one thing." Elliot looked at each of them for a few seconds. "There's a chance that trouble could be running after him. When he brings those horses through that gate, there could be men chasing him. He could be hurt. You must be here. And be ready."

Lola asked. "We do target practice twice a week, Mr. Elliot. We're ready."

"What do you mean, target practice?" Elliot frowned. Kelly grinned and told him about them keeping their shooting skills well honed.

Colton asked, "How did you find us, Mr. Elliot? How did you know we were here?"

Elliot nodded. "I've been reading the telegrams you've been sending. I'm sure your pa stops and asks for any messages when he sees those overhead wires."

"Then he saw the wire that Mr. Doyle sent. The one about Ma passing." Elliot nodded solemnly. The Ranger picked up his hat and walked out onto the slate patio.

"If I see him, I'll send you word where he is and that he's headed for home. Check over at The Faraway every day from now on. I'll tell Max to keep the telegraph machine on."

Elliot checked the cinch on his saddle. With a foot in the stirrup he lifted onto the horse.

"You've had a rough couple of weeks, I'm sure of it. Once your pa gets home, it will all get a lot better." He nodded and winked.

Fifty yards down the driveway, he twisted around in the saddle and waved a big hand. The children waved back enthusiastically.

***

The rest of the day was somewhat solemn and quiet. Each of them were preoccupied with their own thoughts and worries. Kelly stood with her coffee on the slate patio watching the front gate. The Ranger had been reading the telegrams she had been sending. But that meant that others had read them, too.

She heard Lola's voice and turned to go back into the house. Her younger sister and Colton were smearing jelly onto soft bread slices. They were arguing again about the positioning of the hunting blind.

"Foot paths, cattle paths, deer paths. We don't know what made 'em or what or who uses them. They're just there." Lola rolled a blackish rock back and forth between her hands.

Kelly said, "Come out here and show me what you are talking about." The three of them walked out to the eastern fence that separated the yard from the pasture.

Colton pointed up to the hill. "I want to set the blind back farther in those trees. I don't want us to be seen so easy. Someone walking along this path could gaze about and not see us sitting up there."

Kelly grimaced as she said, "Lola, have you been reading to Colton about camouflage again?"

Lola wiggled her eyebrows. "The fine art of not being seen in plain

163

sight." Colton nodded happily and grinned.

Kelly grinned. "Okay. Let me get my coat and gun. We'll go for a walk and figure this out." Twenty minutes later, the three of them stood on the east trail after it curved back to the north.

Colton gestured to the trail behind them. "From that slide area, the path curves first to the left around a clay ridge, then starts to come back west. Once it comes back and levels out right here, the path goes straight for about forty feet. If someone stops right there and looks around, I don't want them to see us."

Lola walked ahead another twenty yards. She turned to her right and pointed up the embankment. "We're going to have to destroy that footpath leading up into those trees. Once someone gets up there and looks back, they'll have a clear sight to us in that blind."

Kelly put down her knapsack and pulled on her other glove. Grabbing onto small shrubs and trees she pulled herself up to the top of the path. After five minutes, she came sliding back down the loose dirt. "Deer tracks up there. You can see where they've been nibbling. We going to have to plant clover down the other side of the path going down the hill. Make 'em stop to eat."

Colton nodded. They decided where to build the blind. Kelly pulled out a piece of brown paper and made a list of things they would need.

"I want to walk back and look at that slide again," Colton said. "Something about it bothers me and I need you to help me figure it out. I'm missing something there," the young boy said with worry in his voice.

Lola nodded. "The first time I saw that wide place on the east road it looked like a place where someone might pull over a wagon or a coach. It's big enough. Then I saw where there was a flat trail that followed the curve of the hill for about ten yards to the slide. It's not right."

Kelly picked up the knapsack and smiled. "We got a couple more hours before sundown. Let's go take a look." Colton let the way and they walked single file around boulders. They clambered over a downed tree and Kelly stopped to make a note about removing it.

A mile and a half later Colton stopped them and pointed to the sandstone ridge fifty feet above them. "I dig enough to know that ridge doesn't slide. There's no water seeping in to move this much dirt and rocks." Lola knelt next to the slide area and scanned across it several times. She shook her head.

"If someone has been coming through here, they have been doing a good job to cover up their tracks. If you look at the path we're on, it looks like it wants to take you up onto the ridge. The natural path goes over the top of that slide and curves west and then back to the north." Lola held her hand and arm straight out to line up with the path on the far knoll.

Kelly stood in thought for a minute. "Alright, let's think about this for just a second. Was the slide made to keep people from getting to the east road? Or was the slide made to keep people on the east road from coming down this path?"

Lola stood up and brushed off her knees. "Just looking at it, I'd say it was made to keep people on the east road from thinking they could cut up this path."

Colton looked to the left down into the gully at where the slide ended. "Someone with a pickaxe could carve out the new path up over the ridge and make it a little easier to follow. But it looks like animals still cross over the slide, just farther down."

Kelly held up a hand. "So, we agree, the slide wasn't made to keep folks from getting to the east road. Right?" Colton and Lola nodded.

"Alright, let's walk out to the east road and take a look from there. Maybe we can figure out why someone wanted to block off this path." Colton led the scramble up the rocky path. They walked along the rim. Just before they stepped down the narrow path, Lola held up a hand with a clenched fist signaling the stop and silence. They all crouched down.

Lola turned to the north and pointed her fingers to her eyes and then off to the distance. They waited for a count of one minute and then Kelly leaned closer to Lola.

"What is it?"

Lola turned her face closer to Kelly. "Someone has been camping over there. They're not there now, but they left recently." Kelly nodded.

"Colton, go left around that side and stay behind cover. Whistle if you see anything. I'll go along the right side. Lola, pull your Colt and go up the middle. You know what to do." They all nodded to each other and began the creep.

It took almost ten minutes before they all converged on the clearing. A blackened campfire ring, cold with white ashes and gnarled bits of burned wood. One alder tree on the east side looked like there had been a rope tied around it.

Colton knelt and looked at the fire. "The dirt is bare here. This is used often. There is a ring right here. I think it was where a pan was put down."

Kelly asked, "Lola, you've been out here putting those little white rocks up as markers. Where is our property line here? Is this camp on or off our property?"

Lola pointed the north. "Almost one hundred feet to the north is our line, as best I can figure. This camp is on our property."

"Alright, let's follow the tracks and see where they go from here." Kelly stood up. Colton found where a horse walked east through rocks and tumbled boulders and came out on a dry mesa.

"Why ride through all these rocks and out onto desert when there is a perfectly good road not half a mile away?" Lola shook her head.

Kelly looked at her sister. "Honey, if you are doing something wrong or if you have done something bad, you pretty much don't want people to see you. You ride off road. You stay off the main trail."

Colton said. "Or if you think someone is following you, you head up a trail that looks like it ends at slide, then cut up over the embankment and camp out at that clearing. You get off the horse until whoever is following you, goes right on by. Wait a couple hours. Ride on through the desert."

Kelly walked about fifty feet out into the desert until she came to a dried wash. "We'll have to check this campsite from time to time."

Colton said, "Come on. Let's go back to the road and see if we can figure out what happened." Slowly, single file they walked back down past the campsite, through the rocks and then to the ridge. Carefully, they slid down the embankment and came out on the east road.

Colton went out and stood in the middle of the dusty road. He pointed toward the raw dirt of the cliff. "You see the erosion of the water coming down that embankment. That will make part of the dirt start to wash away. That's normal."

Lola crossed her arms over her body. "Just looking at that wide place, I don't even see that path. The bushes and brush cover it up. Someone wouldn't even know it's there."

Kelly nodded. "So, you are saying that someone who knows the trail is there, uses it. Taking this path cuts about two miles off our time to get to the front steps. I don't understand why someone would work so hard to push all that dirt across the trail."

Colton said, "If you wanted to stop someone from using the path, why not fall some trees over it so a horse can't get through? Walkers coming through might do the same thing we did. Just find another path around and keep walking. The slide just makes it troublesome to get through on a horse."

Kelly shifted her weight to her other foot. "Alright. Here's the question. Does it benefit us to clear out that slide and make the path usable for us? Or is it better to leave it here even though it doesn't keep people out?" Colton shrugged.

Lola kicked at a dirt clod. "I'd say that someone has been using the path and doesn't want anyone else to use it. They pushed all the dirt in to stop folks from following. We don't use this part of the ranch or at least, haven't been using it. I say leave it alone."

Kelly looked at Colton. "Maybe the time will come, Colton, where we need this path cleared out. Maybe underneath all that dirt will be another reason why the dirt is there. Maybe someone dropped something and then filled in the dirt over the top to bury it. Grown-ups do stupid things, you've seen that."

Colton nodded. "I see what you mean."

Kelly took a couple steps towards the hidden path. "We've got three miles ahead of us. We should get back to the house just at sundown. We might see a couple deer as it is so late in the afternoon."

A covey of quail scurried across the trail. The late afternoon sun shone golden on the trees. Twice they paused to look back on the trail and found everything still. They stopped at the bottom of the path to look towards the house. Again, everything was still. Lola made a detour to check the mailbox, which was empty.

While dinner warmed up, Kelly brought her cup of coffee out to the patio and sat looking east. The grays and purples crept in to the base of the trees. The underside of the clouds were tinged with reds and orange. After a few minutes pink streaks in the sky disappeared into hills. Darting birds flitted after the last insects of the day.

***

In Bradford, Kelly had asked the blacksmith, Clay Dunagan, if anyone in town could do repairs. Construction work was the side occupation for the blacksmith so he agreed to come out to Flint Hills to take a look at what needed to be done.

"Mr. Dunagan, we don't know anything about building and constructing so you'll most likely be teaching us along with the repairs. I hope that is alright." Kelly leaned against the heavy wooden table at the side of the building.

"That is alright, miss. I'll put you to work running for handsaws, nails and the like." He grinned and winked. Around thirty years old, Dunagan had brown, curly hair cut short, a narrow face with a strong jaw and watery, gray-blue eyes. Aside from a mustache, he was clean shaven.

On Tuesday, Clay Dunagan showed up at the gate to start the repairs on the second barn. He stood in the kitchen doorway with his hat in his gloved hands. Over six feet tall, lanky, and with that wiry iron strength that many western men lived with. He nodded his head and looked first at Lola and then Kelly. "I found the stone foundation to the old house. It was about a foot down in the earth. You want to come take a look?"

The driveway continued west about one hundred yards beyond the second barn and was so overgrown it was indistinguishable. "I had to feel for the wheel tracks of the wagons. I looked pretty foolish crawling on my hands and knees, but I found it. I tied off a rag on the post that I set up so you can get an idea how big, or how small, this house used to be." He pointed to the small white rags waving at the corners.

Colton walked down to one corner, knocking down weeds and grass as he went. "I see it." The children walked around the outside edges.

Dunagan knelt and let a handful of dirt slide through his bare hand.

"This is not a rocky soil. There's trees to use in building. I'd say the builder set these stones as a foundation and then stacked stones in mortar up to the ground level. They took every board and put it in the new house where you live now. Well, it was a new house back then."

Lola asked, "Are all the houses built like this?" Dunagan shook his head.

"After a man would dig out a clean hole in the dirt, they'd find a broad, flat stone and tamp it down into the hole. Then they'd set up a tall wooden post or log in the corners. They'd spend a lot of time making that whole frame level and such. That would be the base and they'd build the house up on top of it. It's called pier and post. Both your barns are built on pier and post."

Colton asked, "Is there anyone around that knew what this house looked like? There are no pictures for us to see." Again, Dunagan shook his head.

"No. Well, the one man that might know would be Phineas Rideout. His brother, Foster did all the fireplaces and the slate work on the new house. Phineas might have seen this old house. But people's minds get fuzzy with age and he might not remember clearly." Lola looked at Kelly and nodded slightly.

"If you have questions, just ask me. I'd best get back to work on that second barn." He smiled and winked as he turned to walk away pulling on his heavy gloves.

When the children had looked over the second smaller barn, they discovered it had been mainly used as storage and a bunkroom. Roof shingles were missing. Two of the access doors were off the hinges. There were five broken windows. Originally, there had been ten bunks, but five had been removed. A thick layer of dust along with broken glass was scattered along the narrow room.

It was Colton and Lola who spent lots of time with the builder. Several of the rafters had to be torn out due to rot and insect damage. The three of them tramped around the west hills until they found the right small fir trees and Dunagan showed them how to fall the trees for the rafters and shakes.

The rafters on the south side of the barn were extended out ten feet to give shelter to a wood porch. Dunagan laid out the shakes and ran courses of the wood right up to the peak. Lola and Colton groaned over having to find and cut the firewood. Dunagan laughed.

The repair of the second barn took a solid week. Every morning just past sun up, the now familiar buckskin came through the gate and went directly to the barn. After turning the horse loose to graze, Dunagan quietly came into the house and started the fire to heat coffee.

"When you hire on your hands, you'll need that bunkroom to be water tight and warm enough in the winter. Hands won't stay on a job where they can't get a hot meal and have a warm bunk. Glen had built on that long bunkroom and his hands lived there. It's big enough that they had their own area and weren't falling all over each other," said Dunagan.

Kelly thought for a moment. "We've never hired hands before. It's always been just us."

Dunagan took a sip of the hot coffee and put his cup down. "I came out on that last week where they had to get the herd ready to sell. There were four of us blacksmiths going through the herd trimming hooves and putting on shoes. I remember a couple of the hands talking about going to look for work up in the Imperial Valley or moving to Texas to work on a big ranch."

Lola nodded. "When the herd was gone, the work was gone."

"That's right. Some men just want a simple life of working horses or cattle. Book learning wasn't meant for them. When you hire, you want men who have been doing this since they were boys. If they were a shopkeeper or a cook last week, you don't want them working your horses this week." Dunagan leaned his forearms onto his thighs, the slight smoke drifted from the cigarette.

Kelly said, "I want to double the size of herd we have. We brought those head with us from Yucca Valley. Pa might be bringing ten, maybe twelve head with him from Phoenix. We don't know yet. We'll grow slowly, though."

"Well," Dunagan stood up and crushed the cigarette stub into the dirt with his heel. "Let's get to work on the bunk room so those hired hands can have a place to store their gear." He smiled and winked.

From the barn loft opening, Kelly, Lola and Colton gazed out over the weeds and grass to the small rags waving in the breeze. Chances are they'd never know how the Richardson life used to be on this ranch. But they would have a future here and it was looking brighter all the time.

24 THE SWIMMING HOLE

The next day Kelly packed a lunch for them and rode along with Colton to help with digging in the river. He had accumulated enough specks to cover the entire bottom of a small jar and was finding more each day.

Kelly looked up river and then down the tumbling water. "I'd like to find a place where we could swim. It's too shallow here."

Colton stood up rubbing his hands together. "About a half mile downstream there's a place the water falls over a ledge. I think it's flint or granite. There is a pool there that I think we could swim and dive."

As small buckets of dirt and gravel were spread out over the long boards of the sluice, Lola ladled out water. Little by little the dirt washed away. Specks accumulated up against the small wooden treads. Kelly could see the discarded piles of dirt off to the sides.

Lola brought over two bluish green rocks that looked like they had a vein of gold going through them. Then she found a completely black rock with tiny gold veins. "Lola, we won't have to worry about rocks in the river, if you keep finding these pretty ones." The younger girl laughed.

Colton paused and looked at Kelly. "Every time the mail man rides in, I hope to see a letter from Mr. Doyle about the gold here. Part of me wants to know and part of me doesn't want anyone to know about this."

"Colton, when he finds out something, I'm sure he will tell us. I think it came as a shock to him that we found gold here. I kind of think that Grandpa Glen had looked for it before." Lola banged the metal ladle against the boards to get Colton's attention.

"You see any fish?" Kelly leaned to peer into the water. "It would be nice to fish for dinner once in a while."

"Yes, there are lots. When I push over a boulder and see the worms, I toss those out in the river for the fish. The fish hang around waiting for food." The boy handed another bucket of dirt to Lola.

At noon, Kelly spread out a small towel and unwrapped cooked beef and cornbread. Colton chewed his lunch. Lola swallowed and asked, "Kelly, when Pa comes home, will he make us go to school somewhere?" Colton stopped eating and stared at his oldest sister.

Kelly grimaced. "As far as I can tell, there is not a real school in Bradford. There is a big room in the back of the auction house that I think is used as a school, but I don't know for sure. I heard from Mr. Doyle that there is an elementary school out at Beatrice. But that is twenty-two miles for us to ride one way. That's too far."

Lola said, "Grandpa Richardson's books about science and the earth are very interesting. I'd like to learn what they mean. And that book in French, I still want to know what that is about. I need a teacher if I'm going to learn what I want."

Kelly said, "Colton, I could see how you would want to learn more mathematics so you could tell if someone was trying to fool you out of your gold with numbers." Colton's shoulders slumped, he dropped the bucket in the water and put his head back with a groan. Kelly snickered.

Lola said, "So maybe there is a teacher that can come by once each week or something like that?" Kelly nodded.

Next time we go to Bradford," Kelly said, "We'll ask Mr. Doyle who the teacher is and find out how to order a French dictionary. Alright?" Lola nodded.

Kelly glanced at Lola and said, "I can tell there is something else on your mind. What is it?"

Lola took a deep breath. "I want to dig a pit and see if I can catch a deer in it."

Kelly sat up straight and her eyes flew wide. "What? Dig a what?"

Lola repeated herself. "I want to dig a pit and see if I can catch a deer in it."

Kelly shook her head. "I heard you. How do you think you are going to catch a deer in a pit when they can jump twenty feet in the air?"

Lola nonchalantly smiled. "Not if they're dead, they can't"

"What?" Kelly looked incredulous. "You have got to stop reading those war books!"

Lola looked at Colton with a grin. "As you well know, deer are night animals. They get out and forage in the hour after sunset and in the hour before sunrise. Sometimes, they even get out in the middle of the night and eat the vegetables in our garden."

"Yes, I know. Ma used to complain about them all the time." Kelly waved her hand dismissively.

Lola said, "I want to dig down six feet and put sharpened spikes in the bottom so they'll bleed out and die."

"And just where did you get this idea from, Lola Stolter?" Kelly rubbed her eyes and shook her head.

"Grandpa Richardson has three books on warfare strategy up in the library. I've been reading those. There's a picture about digging a pit for a horse and rider to fall into, but I'd be using it for deer." Lola had a smug look on her face.

Kelly shouted over to her brother. "Oh, and Colton I suppose you agreed to help her dig in the dirt to build the pit?" He stood up, shaded his eyes from the sun and nodded.

"She's been helping me dig for the gold in the river. I can help her dig the dirt out for the pit." He shrugged and went back to scooping dirt. Kelly held her hands up to her face.

Lola wiggled her foot. "It should only take us a day, Kelly. You won't have to do anything. You can just stand and watch if you want."

"I'm sure that Ma is in her grave yelling about heathen little children running wild or something like that." Kelly groaned.

Colton yelled, "If we do get a deer or even a couple of rabbits, it will be worth it. No shooting, no danger. Good meat."

Lola smiled. "You train the horses. Colton digs for the gold. This is what I do. We all have a hobby, Kelly." Calmly, serenely, the younger sister outlined the details of the construction.

Colton dumped the bucket of dirt into the sluice. "I didn't think it would work either, Kelly. Then Lola showed me that it works in war where people fight back. Deer don't fight back. They just fall in and die. Then we get to eat them."

As if a foregone conclusion, Lola stood up and dusted herself off. "We start digging tomorrow." Lola took her bucket, waded into the river and filled it up with water for the sluice.

Kelly sat there listening to the splashing water in the river. Her two industrious siblings continually dumped dirt and rocks into the sluice and then exclaimed happily when they found a speck of gold. Part of her wanted to bury those warfare books. More than anything, as long as they were both alive and happy, that was really all she wanted. She grinned, stood up and went to scoop dirt out of the river.

***

The dawn rays of sun shone golden on the side of the kitchen wall. Lola walked in rubbing her eyes and sat down at the table. "I don't feel good. I feel like something is wrong and I don't know what it is."

Kelly nodded. "I had nightmares last night." She held up the coffee pot and a cup with a questioning glance. Lola shook her head.

"Can you make pancakes? I feel like I could stay in bed all day but I have things to do. I don't want to do anything," she said with a groan and put her head in her hands.

Kelly shook her head. "I didn't sleep very well last night either." She got up to get down the bowl for pancakes.

Lola looked around and asked, "Is Colton still asleep? I thought he'd be up and gone by now."

Kelly shook her head. "He was really tired last night. I don't want him getting tired like that. It's not good for him. Let him sleep."

Lola rubbed her temples. "I'm trying to get along. I'm trying to just get things done every day. But today is different. It feels like I should be doing something. Something good." Outside on the patio, Dusty barked three times.

Lola went out to see what he was upset about. She petted the dog's head. "What is it, boy? What's out there?" Her eyes scanned from left to right. She shrugged and went back inside the house.

A few moments later, Colton came down the stairs still in his pajamas. "What was Dusty barking about? He woke me up."

"I went and looked. I didn't see anything. He calmed down and went back to his box." Lola shrugged. "Kelly is making pancakes."

Colton climbed up on a stool. "Can I have a little coffee and sugar? I can't wake up all the way." Lola's mouth fell open. Kelly poured half a cup and then put in two spoons of sugar. Colton wrapped his small hands around the mug and smelled it.

"I just got done telling Kelly that I don't feel like doing anything today. I want to eat and then just go sit and read for a while," she said as she rubbed her eyes.

They were half way through the pancakes when Lola stopped and listened. "Dusty just growled." Kelly dropped her fork with a clang, startling Colton, who jerked around.

"I'm not in the mood for someone trying to sneak up on me. Lock and load!" She looked at her brother and sister struggling to swallow. "Now!" Lola's stool was knocked over in their haste.

Colton took the Remington and held the closet door for Lola. The younger girl handed the Colt .45 to her sister. They squatted down and went out the study door in a crouch.

Dusty barked three times with the fur on his hackles up towards the barn. He bared his teeth snarling.

"Colton, I'm going to put four shots into the barn. You knock down anyone or anything coming out of it. Lola, you empty that gun into the barn. Got it?" Kelly voice was low and guttural. They nodded. "Spread out."

From behind the stone pillar, Kelly brought up her gun and fired. Bullets thudded into the barn, Colton sighted in and watched for anything that moved. Lola had crept down the steps off the side. She knelt and fired all six shots into the barn. The blue gun smoke drifted up into the air.

Kelly could see Lola reloading from her pocket. Dusty barked and ran down the steps and across the yard headed to the barn. She waited two minutes and then leaned back to get Colton's attention.

"Call Dusty back. Make sure he's okay." Colton nodded and whistled three times. Within a minute the yellow lab trotted back to Colton with a bloody snout. The boy ruffled the dog's neck.

"We must have hit whoever it was. He's all bloody." Colton grimaced.

"Alright. Let's get dressed and get our boots on. Make sure you've got ammunition when we go down there. Colton, get up on the roof and knock down anyone coming at us. We'll have to start shooting if they decide to shoot at us." They all nodded.

The two girls spread out from the house and covered the two sides near the barn. Lola signaled clear first and then disappeared into the tall grass. Kelly watched for the crawling Lola.

The younger girl brushed the hair back out of her face. "Dead man lying at the corner of the barn. He ain't moving. One of us got him. There's nobody else out there."

Kelly groaned and sat back, rubbing her face with both hands. "All I wanted to do was have some pancakes and read a book today. And now someone has destroyed my calm. Arrgh!" Kelly stood up and signaled to Colton to come down.

An hour later their three horses pulled up at the north end of the Faraway Inn. The conspicuous form had been wrapped in a flannel bedsheet and tied down over the black mare.

The Williams Creek area laid up against a tumbling river almost six miles west of Flint Hills Ranch. It had always been known for good ranch land with expansive grassy meadows between the mesas of Beatrice and Three Corners. The Faraway Inn was an old stagecoach structure situated with its back up against a wide riverbank. Huge old cottonwood trees leaned over it, heavy branches splayed out dropping leaves and twigs onto the roof.

The Faraway Inn had a heavy, river rock façade, a jumbled mass of stones pushed in with mortar like an impenetrable quilt from foundation to roofline. It is a long and low old structure with a single pitched sloped roof, sections of shingles missing and mostly in disrepair. The Inn sat in general dilapidation, the six-pane windows like blank stares out at the world. The years had not been good to this local structure. The tall chimney of the kitchen trailed smoke meaning something was cooking. The building sat there like a huge rock beast sleeping in the morning air.

The heavy wooden door sported three brass bars stacked vertically above each other about a foot apart. In the center of the door were three interlocking rings, like the metal had been braided and formed into rings. Below that was a familiar carved wooden door pull smooth from years of use.

Kelly, Lola and Colton walked into the main room. A couple was sitting near the fireplace eating breakfast and looked up when the door opened. A tall, heavy man with a black beard and white apron came through the kitchen door with a broad smile.

"Welcome to the Faraway Inn. Are you folks here for breakfast?" His eyes looked at Kelly and then Lola. Kelly smiled and looked at her sister.

They walked over to the counter. "I'm Kelly Stolter. This is my sister, Lola and my brother, Colton. We had a bit of trouble out at our ranch and were told we could come here if we needed help." She smiled hopefully.

"Howdy miss and miss and mister. I'm Max. I'm the cook here. What sort of trouble? You're not hurt, are you?" Max had black straight hair combed back with a pomade for shine. His muscled arms looked more like a champion wrestler than a country inn cook.

Kelly leaned up against the bar and whispered to Max, "We shot a man and killed him. We have the body outside on a horse."

"You shot who?" Max exclaimed. Kelly, Lola and Colton all grimaced at the same time. The tableware of the diners clanged against the porcelain plates. Max held a hand up to reassure the diners.

A dark-haired woman came running through the doorway from the kitchen speaking rapid Spanish. Max answered her. Her eyes got big.

"Are you children okay? Well, I guess you are because you are the ones alive. Oh dear!" She ran around and hugged all three of them.

"My wife, Amanda. She can get a little excited." The cook looked at the ceiling. "I better take a look."

The three children and Max were followed by Amanda out to the hitching rail. Kelly unwrapped the head. Max and Amanda shook theirs.

"The scrap of paper in his pocket is addressed to Tom Scherol. Unless he was carrying a message for someone, I'd say this is Tom Scherol." Kelly shrugged.

"Where's your pa? He really should be handling this, not you children." Max had a suspicious look in his eye. They told him about Nick being away to get stock.

"Should we take him on to Bradford or can we leave him here?" Lola sounded exasperated. Max gasped.

Max tried to calm them. "Oh no! No! I'll put him in the barn and then I'll send a telegram over to the sheriff."

"Who is the sheriff? Where is he at?" Colton rubbed his right eye.

"Well, we don't rightly have a sheriff or even a Marshall here local. When we have trouble like this I send messages to any law enforcement via the telegraph." Max nodded.

Colton gripped Kelly's arm. "Wait! Could this be a wanted outlaw? Could there be a reward?" The boy's mouth hung open and he started to smile up at Kelly. His older sister started to grin then shushed him and shook her head.

Amanda said, "Well, he could be. You never know. Outlaws are everywhere. You could be standing right next to one and not know it!" She winked at Lola who giggled.

Kelly led the horse down to the stables as she followed Max. They untied the body and Max laid it along the wall. The bloody flannel sheet fell to the ground. Amanda brought a bucket of water and Kelly shoved the flannel into the cold water.

On the way back to the Inn, Kelly explained about Dusty barking.

Max was skeptical. "Your dog barked so you started shooting? How often do you just haul off and shoot things out there?"

Kelly said, "This is what happens when someone tries to sneak around our barn. If he would have come to the gate and hollered for us, none of this would've happened."

Colton added his two cents. "Besides, he interrupted our pancakes."

Amanda gasped. "Oh well, have a seat. We can make a couple of pancakes for you, seeing how yours are probably cold now." The kids climbed up onto the stools at the bar. Max disappeared through two glass and wood double doors.

The pretty dark-haired woman had a silver bracelet that jangled as she poured coffee. "I'll be right back with your pancakes. You stay right there."

There was a painting of a dog holding a duck in its mouth behind the bar. Near the fireplace there was another painting of a tall, black horse with a blue ribbon on its halter.

Lola nudged Kelly. "Look at the fireplace. It looks just like the one at the house." They all turned and looked at the river rock chimney that went up through the ceiling. Both diners saw them looking so they turned and looked at the fireplace, confused.

Colton said, "So Foster Rideout probably built that one, too."

Plates of pancakes, bacon and eggs slid in front of them. Colton took off his gloves, picked up the fork and immediately started eating without another word. Amanda winked at Kelly who chuckled.

Halfway through their second breakfast, Max came in through those double doors and held a piece of white paper.

"So, you know Henry Elliot, Texas Ranger?" They all nodded.

"Henry Elliot, Texas Ranger, answered my telegram. Tom Scherol was a wanted man for bank robbery in Denver. There is a reward." Max wiggled his eyebrows and laid the paper in front of Kelly and Lola who chewed and read.

Colton took a drink of milk and then asked, "How do we get the reward?" Max grinned.

"Well, first you have to eat your breakfast. I have to send word for the doctor in Bradford to come out and declare that Tom Scherol out in the barn is dead. Once the death certificate is sent to the Rangers, they'll send the reward money."

Lola patted her tummy and groaned. "And I didn't want to do anything or go anywhere today. Now I'm glad I did." Kelly smiled at her contented sister.

"Mr. Doyle was right. This is a good place to come," said Kelly with a nod.

"Oh! You know Mr. Doyle, too?" Amanda grinned.

"Yes, he's our attorney."

Amanda looked surprised. "Oh, you have your own attorney?"

"Oh yes. Doesn't everybody? They're very handy and smart!" Colton grinned.

Colton put his fork down and drank the last of the milk. "I'm so full I can't get on my horse." They all laughed.

"How much do we owe you for breakfast, Mr. Max?" Kelly started to fish in her jeans for coins. Max waved his hands and shook his head.

"When you get that reward money, come back for dinner. You can buy us a drink." The children waved goodbye and headed out the door.

Kelly squeezed the water out of the flannel sheet and tied it on behind her saddle. Much happier, and soon to be wealthier, they walked their horses the six miles back to Flint Hills.

25 WHAT HAPPENED AT SLAUGHTER CANYON

That afternoon they laid around the house on the sofas and the floor in front of the fireplace talking about what had happened. They drank coffee, read books and dozed under the light, cotton spread.

In the cool evening light, Dusty, stood up on his toes and barked. He ran down the steps towards the front gate. In the dark down the driveway came a familiar voice. "Halloo up there. It's me Vern Dixon, come to check on you children."

Kelly smiled at Lola. "Come on up, Mr. Dixon. Colton, take Dusty so he doesn't chase after Mr. Dixon."

The older black man walked up the drive leading his black mule. Painfully thin, but spry with wild tendrils of salt and pepper hair held back in a bandana. It was a white-toothed smile that greeted the children.

"Miss Kelly, Miss Lola, Master Colton. I see you young'uns are still faring well by yourselves." Colton reached and shook the leathery hand.

"After you settle your mule, Mr. Dixon, come on in the house. We've got some ham and taters left over from supper if you are hungry. Kelly made bread this morning so it's fresh."

"You are right kind. I'll be there directly." Kelly, Lola and Colton had greatly enjoyed the man's stories around the campfire during the drive to Flint Hills.

Around the table they chattered while Dixon ate a good-sized portion off the crockery plate. When the dishes were cleared away they went out on the wide front porch and Dixon rolled a cigarette. The crickets sang loud and long out in the grass. Something rustled the papery dry leaves in the old cottonwood.

Kelly looked at the old man. "Mr. Dixon, Mrs. Rideout has told us to stay away from the part of the ranch in the north that she calls Slaughter

Canyon. Can you tell us about that area?" She saw him raise his eyebrows and puff on the smoke.

Dark eyes looked at the children one by one. Gray smoke coiled up and then drifted away on the evening breeze.

"The main road used to go right straight through the four-mile canyon. It made the trip faster getting west. Nowadays, the road runs to the north of the canyon and few even know there is a little trail that leads down into that area. I think it might be only the locals that ride through there now, or folks who get themselves lost somehow." He leaned his forearms forward onto his thighs.

It was a low, gravelly voice that spoke. "People died in there. Outlaws kidnapped a young woman and her child. Held them for ransom. The family had no money, couldn't get any money as they were dirt poor. Outlaws killed them." Lola looked shocked and put her hand up over her mouth.

Kelly asked, "Who were they?"

"Constance Mueller and her son, Jody. He was five, I believe. After the slaughter, folks blocked off the entrance with boulders, fallen trees, and one crazy fool even tried a stick of dynamite to cave in the eastern sandstone walls. It didn't work."

Colton had made a comment but it seemed like Dixon purposefully ignored it. "It's not the only Slaughter Canyon I know about. There are several."

Colton climbed up and sat on the top rail on the porch. "Would you tell us about those Slaughter Canyons, Mr. Dixon?"

Dixon nodded. "The first time I heard about Slaughter Canyon was listening to my grandad and pa tell a couple friends about a herd stampeding and killing three cowboys who had camped down in a wash. You got to admit, it is possible. You hear about stampedes tearing up wagons and land and even other animals who can't get out of the way of them hooves."

Kelly shivered and said, "I've seen a stampede. Hundreds of cattle all running in the same direction. Godawful sound."

Dixon murmured agreement. "Another version I heard was three men out hunting took down an elk, a bear and couple wild boars. They called it a slaughter. Now that seems like it might have happened, too. Except nobody knew their names and you'd think folks would've put in names on a tall tale like that."

Lola said, "That sounds like a story my pa would've told from someone he heard it from." There were a few quiet moments while they let other thoughts run through their heads.

Dixon blew smoke high up into the air and watched it float away. "There's another Slaughter Canyon in Montana territory where Indians cornered a couple of covered wagons and killed everyone. It was written about in the papers in Denver, New York, Los Angeles and Chicago. Everybody knew somebody that was riding in one of those wagons."

It was a solemn look he gave the children. "Same thing with the Northwest territory. Settlers and homesteaders getting killed by the Indians. Everyone isn't a kind, gentle, God fearing' Christian out there. Friend of mine told me he was sure that several prisons back east were emptied out and all the convicts sent out west on wagon trains. Some didn't make it. Some disappeared. Those prisoners formed gangs and now they roam around the west."

"I spent a couple years down in the Mississippi Louisiana bayou when I was younger. Had a shack down there where I could drink hootch and eat all the shrimp I could catch. One of them old Cajun boys I used to drink with, he was a character. One glazed over whitish eye, ugly wrinkled knife scar from his forehead down the side of his face. He had that dark brown mestizo paper-thin skin and you could see where he'd had tattoos on his arms. He was missing three fingers on his left hand."

Kelly chuckled. "Sounds like he had seen his share of good times."

Dixon sniggered. "He told me a story about a Slaughter Canyon south of Dodge. He had helped bring in about three hundred head to Abilene. The riders laid over for two days resting and sleeping. Four of them had work in Mississippi so they rode out. My buddy rode with them, thinking that he'd try to get on at a ranch."

"If you ride eight miles south back down the Red Rocks Trail, you'll see a wide area in the road where there's like a dozen weeping willows clustered around a spring. I've been down that trail, so I knew he was truthful with me. The other side of the springs is a trail that cuts off over onto the Cimarron. That will take you south to Mississippi and the delta.

"They took the cutoff and rode for a couple of miles. There must have been some big storm because he said they came on a slide area and the path, the trail was completely gone. After they got passed that they came around a gully and found a herd a cattle dead."

Colton sat up straight. "Indians?"

Dixon shook his head. "Nope. No arrows. No ponies. Just about forty beef cattle laying over on their sides in a bloody mess. Now here's the odd part. The group of riders thought they had come up on someone's secret slaughter yard, but nobody came out of the shadows. The horses started shying back away from the carcasses."

Lola asked, "No campfire? No gear?" She had an incredulous look on her face.

Dixon took in a deep breath and let it out slowly. "No. Nothing. Now here is the odd part. The cattle bodies, still warm." Kelly stared at the storyteller.

Dixon ground out the little stub of his cigarette on the sole of his boot. "One of the men said that when they got into that slide, muddy area, they must have gotten turned around and wandered onto someone's land. They mounted up and rode away from what they said was a slaughter canyon. He never forgot that strange feeling of seeing them dead cattle with no one around."

Colton shook his head and then looked at Lola. She shrugged and shook her head and looked at Dixon.

The old man yawned and stretched, then rubbed his eyes. "We were drinking in Santa Fe one night and I asked him about if he'd ever ridden through there again and he said he'd go fifty miles out of his way to avoid riding back through there. He was the sort to do that, too. Another fella at the bar had another story about a slaughter canyon up in the Rockies." He stood up.

"I doubt I'll be here in the morning when you get up. I want to make some miles before that sun heats up the air and makes traveling hard. I got eleven miles to go before I can take off my boots and relax." He smiled at the children.

Just inside the front door, Colton took Lola's arm. "Is he okay, Lola? I like him. I don't want anything to hurt him." Lola listened to her brother for a moment and then turned back to look out into the darkness.

She smiled. "No. He's okay. He's just tired. We'll see him again, honey."

Kelly laid in her bed and looked at the stars through the window. Another day had come and gone without word from their father. She still fought the urge every day to saddle up with supplies and start riding east to see if she could find him. More than one person had persuaded the young woman that the west was a big place and the odds were that she would miss him completely. They reminded her of her responsibility for her brother and sister. She pulled the quilt up to her chin and closed her eyes.

***

Tuesday had been put on the calendar as hunting blind day. Tracks and deer scat had been found along the trail. Clover shoots had been nibbled and the salt lick had been used.

Tall, straighter alders had been cut and then strapped with leather bindings up to the thicker alder trees. Six trees were reinforced with the additional posts and then Lola had carefully wound trailing vines over the trees to hide the ties.

When the children first asked Clay Dunagan about a length of iron chain, he had been skeptical about it being used up in the tree. On the anvil, the blacksmith custom cut iron spikes, u-nails and fasteners once he understood the design of the blind.

Between each tree, braces were positioned to stop the swaying. The chain was looped between each tree higher up at fifteen feet and tied off with wet leather strands. Moss and vines hung from the chain to disguise the construction.

"We'll have to adjust it bit by bit as we use it. It is good enough for now." Colton gestured to the trail to the west. "We're sure to see something come walking up that trail."

Kelly nodded. "Are we done here? I'm tired and I want to get some reading done before we go to sleep tonight. We've got a busy day tomorrow."

"Town day!" Lola did a little celebratory dance. Colton laughed. The three gathered up the tools and walked back to the house. Birds in the trees sang and cackled. Honey bees flitted amongst the wildflowers.

***

The next day at the stables they dismounted and Clay Dunagan came out to help unsaddle and turn the horses into the corral.

"Twice in the same week. You Stolters are becoming regular townies." He chuckled and ruffled Colton's hair. The girls laughed.

"We need a few things from the general store and Colton needs a haircut. I'm not so good at scissoring so here we are." Clay rubbed his chin.

"Well, it just so happens I need a shave and a haircut, too, Colton. What say you and I mosey on over to the barber while the ladies shop?" Colton nodded with a grin.

The general store door opened. "Are you Kelly Stolter and Lola Stolter?"

Kelly looked up from the tray of buttons to see a tall, thin man with long straight gray hair and glasses looking at her. "Yes, we are."

"I'm Dave, from the telegraph office at the hotel. Mr. Boardman told me to bring this wire over here to you and wait to see if you have a reply." He put the paper into Kelly's hand.

Kelly's mouth dropped open. "It's from Pa. He's okay. He's alive!" Lola read the short telegram and shrieked flinging it into the air.

**

"Headed for home. All safe. Nick Stolter"

**

"Run this over to the barber shop! I'll stay here and get the things we need. I'll come over there when I'm done." Kelly nudged Lola towards the door. The younger girl took off running out of the store, down the steps and across the square.

"Good news, Kelly?" Amy Kerner smiled. The young girl squeezed Kelly's hand.

"Yes, we've been waiting on word from Pa and now we know he's okay. This is good news." The smiling store clerk wrapped brown paper around the parcel and Kelly paid him.

When she walked into the barber shop, Colton sat with a long cloth around him while snippets of hair fell to the floor.

"Pa is coming home!"

The afternoon air was full of Stolter chatter as they walked the horses back to Flint Hills Ranch.

***

The next morning, the buckskin filly easily moved around the corral. Kelly had worked on her for three weeks before the move. The horse had remembered a lot of the training. She was a smart one and willing to learn.

The hour went by quickly. Out of the corral, Kelly rode the east path. Three miles up, she came to the slide area and just as she was about to clamber up to the mesa, Kelly saw horse tracks in the slide dirt.

Kelly smelled the air for wood smoke but there was nothing. She dismounted and led the filly up to the rim of the mesa. Back up on the horse, she casually walked her over to the descending trail. As she started down the rim, Kelly glanced farther east. There was no one at the old camp.

Kelly galloped the filly along the east road and then up the driveway. After unsaddling, she rubbed down the animal and turned her out to the pasture. Turning for the house, Kelly ran.

She ran in and found Colton and Lola eating jelly sandwiches in the kitchen. They looked at her.

"I need you guys. I just rode the east path with the filly. Horse and rider tracks came over that slide recently. Those tracks look fresh." She gasped to get her breath.

"Really? Someone came through there?" Colton stood up talking with his mouth full.

Lola took a drink of water. "Was there anyone at that camp?"

Kelly gestured towards the outside. "No. But I need you to see if there's any tracks leading away."

"Okay. Let me get my boots on. I'm sure my rifle is loaded. I'll be down to the barn in a few minutes." Colton took the rest of his sandwich up the stairs.

Lola stood up and wiped off her face. She put the cups in the bucket of soapy water. "My boots are right here but I need a sweater and my gun. Just a minute."

The black colt was more headstrong and tossed his head as Kelly saddled him. He tried to buck twice and Kelly had to rein him over hard to stop him. He was bigger and stronger with a force of will found in older horses.

Once out of the corral and down the driveway at a trot, he seemed to settle down. Lola led the way onto the east road followed by Colton and then Kelly. Four miles of running had the colt breathing heavily. She walked him around in circles at the path cutoff.

"I'll hold your reins. You guys go take a look." Kelly held out her hands. Lola and Colton jumped to the ground and after they gave the reins over to her ran into the brush. The black colt started shifting his weight and tossed his head.

It was ten minutes before they came back. Colton had a dirt smudge on his forehead and his blue jeans had dirt on the knees.

"You're right. It was a horse and rider that went across the slide. They didn't stop at the old camp or go up onto the mesa. They headed southeast. If we'd been up in the blind, they would have walked right past us." Lola and Colton mounted up.

Colton gestured for them to follow. He urged the dun mare across the loose earth of the slide, letting her pick her way over to solid ground. Lola waited until Colton had reached the other side then her black mare cautiously walked through the dirt. Kelly's black colt balked. Twice she tried to urge him over the sliding dirt and he refused.

Colton called out, "You want me to come get you?"

"No, he's got to learn this one way or another. I'll lead him over." Kelly eased out of the saddle and took the reins ahead. She sank up to her ankles in the soft dirt and kept having to climb up to get across. The colt was tense with the whites of his eyes showing when he reached the other side. Kelly fed him a couple of the new carrots from the saddle bag.

Along the trail they walked and Colton watched for the shoe marks in the clay. Thirty feet past the hunting blind, the trail turned southwest and Colton stopped.

"Look! They went off the trail here and up the hill through the brush. See how the limbs are broken and the grass trampled?"

Lola said, "There's another trail going up over that hill about fifty yards on down the path. Why wouldn't they take that?"

Kelly patted the neck of the black. "Because they can be seen by us at the house. If they cut up over the hill right here, they can't be seen by us."

Lola twisted around in the saddle. "Let's go up the trail we know and cut back to where this one comes out. If someone is going cross country, I don't want them to see they are being followed."

"Good idea." They walked their mounts down to the wider path that climbed up the steeper trail. At the top, they turned back north and Colton stopped them where the tracks came over the ridge. When they looked down the hill, there was a horse and rider drinking in the river. The rider stood up and waved. The three of them waved back. Kelly led the way down the hill.

It was a young man with reddish blond hair and striking blue green eyes. "Howdy, I'm Ray Ladd. I was hoping I'd get to meet you folks."

Kelly held the black's reins tightly as she stepped up to shake hands. "I'm Kelly Stolter. This is my sister, Lola and my brother Colton." Blue green eyes with dark lashes, a white easy smile, and a foot taller than Kelly.

Colton said, "Those are probably your tracks in the loose dirt back on the trail." Ladd nodded with a smile and stopped abruptly.

"Yes, those are mine. I've been using that little path all my life. It cuts miles off the ride home. I hope it's alright if I use it." He looked questioningly at Kelly. She blinked as she nodded and he looked visibly relieved.

Lola said, "We've been keeping an eye on it. Up on the mesa to the east, there's an old campsite. We're trying to figure out who has been using it."

"That would most likely be Ginger Whelihan's campsite. I had heard that before Glen passed away, he had asked Ginger to keep an eye on the place. He wouldn't stay in the house or even in the barn. He camped out up there on the mesa."

The three children looked at each other. Kelly could feel Ladd watching her. She felt fidgety and cleared her throat. "Our father is bringing in new stock from Phoenix. When he gets in, I'll let him know we met. I'm sure he'll want to reacquaint himself with the Ladd family."

"Very good. I've been away myself. I've been in school over in Los Angeles. I'm home now for the summer until school starts back up in September. I'm sure I'll see you all around the area at events," said Ladd.

Lola said, "In Yucca Valley, we had met another man who is related to you, Mr. Ladd. He is the son of Viola Ladd Sanderson. Jacob Sanderson."

Kelly looked at the broad shoulders and narrow hips. Ladd looked at the ground thinking. "Ah, Aunt Vi. She was aunt to my father, Grayson Ladd. I guess that makes me his cousin. I've got cousins everywhere."

Kelly mounted up and calmed the dancing horse. "You don't have to take your horse cross country anymore, Mr. Ladd. You can take the trail. It's okay with us." Colton and Lola waved as they headed back up the hill.

At the top of the hill she looked back to find him waving. She waved and then turned down the path leading to home. She frowned at the distraction of his eyes and how she had flushed warmly when he looked at her.

Later that night at the dinner table, Colton and Lola chattered on about the digging to be done the next day. Kelly remembered those eyes.

***

"Lola! Wake up! We got one!" Colton shook Lola and her eyes flew open. It took her a few seconds to look around and remember that she was in the barn hayloft. It had been campout night and they had agreed to bunk out in the barn for fun.

The half round edge of a yellow sun had just cleared the horizon and dust floated in the sunbeams.

"What? Where? We got one?" Kelly was gone from her bedroll.

"In the pit! On the other side of the spring! Hurry! It's that tall man with the slick hair in the pit." Colton hurried to the other side of the loft and disappeared down the stairs.

Kelly stood at the edge of the pit holding her revolver looking down into the hole. "You win, Lola. I didn't think this pit would ever catch anything, but here it is."

Lola beamed a smile to her sister and it turned to a frown as she saw the dead man impaled on the wooden spikes below. "Hmm. Here is what I get for reading the adventures of Genghis Khan and his merry band of followers." She turned to Colton.

"You sure this is the man you saw up on the trail?" Colton nodded affirmative.

"What about the other man? You said there were two." Lola walked around to the other side of the pit to get a better look at the contorted body down in the pit.

"Both of them had come up the trail and they were talking. They stopped and were arguing about something. I couldn't hear them because they were too far away. They turned around and went back towards the east road," said Colton as he peered into the pit.

"How we gonna get him out of my pit?" Lola had her hands on her hips. Kelly turned away and laughed at her sister's disgruntled demeanor.

"Lola, it's a dead man. I'm sure he is very sorry for falling in this hole. You will eventually have to forgive him for messing up your pit." Colton started chuckling along with Kelly.

"I'll go get a horse and a rope. Kelly, we'll need that long ladder that is hanging on the side of the barn. For God sakes, don't either of you fall in that pit," Colton said through his laughter.

An hour later the dead man lay in the dirt alongside the pit. "Rayford Ghery. This letter is addressed to Rayford Ghery." Kelly had rifled through the jacket pockets of the bloody dead man. Colton had unloaded the .45 revolver found in the pit and was examining a folding pocket knife.

"Mr. Ghery is going to be late for any appointments he has for the next couple of days." Kelly sat down to read the letter.

Lola had an exasperated look and pressed lips shaking her head as she knelt beside the edge of the pit. "He ruined five spikes. I'll have to replace those and I'm not looking for extra work in whittling spruce spikes. You know, I wouldn't be so put out if it had been a deer or a raccoon or rabbit. Something we could eat."

Kelly folded the paper pages back into the envelope and looked at Lola. "Well, honey, tell you what. Maybe this is a wanted criminal. A mastermind of evil genius that somehow, in all the world, managed to find himself in our yard. And here he died. So maybe, just maybe, there is a reward for him." Kelly looked at Colton who had burst out laughing. She tried to look sternly at the boy.

Kelly continued with Lola listening. "We'll put him over a horse and mosey ourselves into Bradford and ask the authorities if this is a wanted man. We'll demand the reward for capturing him. Then we'll mosey ourselves over to the general store and spend that reward on any little ole thing your heart desires. How about that?"

Lola perked up with a smile and nodded happily. Kelly picked up a dirt clod and threw it at Colton who was helplessly laughing on his back on the ground.

"We're sitting here plotting how to spend a reward that we don't know exists on a dead man who came here trying to hurt us. Do you know how stupid that sounds? Mother would have tanned our hides by now and sent us to bed or something," Colton's voice was a squeak when he tried to talk.

"What would Dad say, Kelly?" Lola stood up brushing the dirt off her jeans.

Kelly snorted and pulled out her handgun. "Dad would have done this," she said as she fired a shot into the body.

26 RAYFORD GHERY DELIVERED TO BRADFORD

It was a thirteen-mile ride in the afternoon sun to Bradford. They had rolled the body up in a bedsheet and tied it over the saddle of a calm mare. To anyone else seeing the three riders trotting up the dusty road they simply looked like a small family with a packhorse headed for town.

Directly across the dusty lane from Bruno Stenson's gun shop was the official Town Hall building where Mayor William Watley maintained his desk and files. It was close to three o'clock when the door groaned open on creaky hinges as Kelly walked in to find no one at the desk. She shouted a greeting to see if anyone answered and when nobody did, she went back out to the boardwalk. Lola and Colton flanked the mare carrying the dead man at the hitching rail and Kelly looked at them and shook her head.

"Can I help you, Miss?" Kelly turned around to find Doctor Baines. "Oh, hello Miss Stolter."

"Hello Dr. Baines," Kelly said and reached to shake his hand. She pointed at the body over the saddle.

"I believe this to be Rayford Ghery. We need him pronounced dead so we can collect any reward that is on him," Lola said matter-of-factly. Colton nodded. Baines stepped over and looked at the bedsheet tied around the body.

"Well, he does appear to be dead, but as you know, it is not official until I make out the paperwork," Baines said and then coughed into his handkerchief. He turned and looked at Kelly who fussed with her gloves.

"Miss, if he is dead right now, can you tell me how he got to be dead?" Baines mopped his brow and frowned. Kelly detected a whiff of whiskey.

"He fell into Lola's pit." Colton dismounted and stepped up onto the boardwalk alongside Kelly and looked at the doctor.

"He what?" The doctor looked at the shorter boy.

"Rayford fell into the pit. He probably couldn't see it in the dark. We did have it pretty well hidden. When he fell he landed on the wood spikes at the bottom. He probably bled out because there was a big gooey puddle of blood on the bottom," Colton said. The boy could have been talking about a caught fish on the riverbank.

Kelly said, "It was Lola's idea to build a trap pit to see if we could get any deer or rabbits and such. It has worked pretty good so far." The doctor rubbed his face with both hands.

Lola asked, "Who can we talk with to see if there is a reward on this Rayford Ghery? And where do you want us to put him?" The young girl had a dirt smudge on her cheek.

Doc Baines wrung his hands and looked at the young kids. "Well, let me open up my office door and you can bring him. No, wait. Colton, run over to Bruno's and get Mayor Watley. He should be standing at the bar, I think. The Mayor will have to send a telegram to see if this is a wanted man. And while you are there, see if Clay will come over and lend a hand getting this fellow off that horse."

Lola dismounted and tied her reins to the rail. The two girls looked at each other for a long moment and then turned to watch Colton run down the boardwalk to the saloon. About a minute later, six men came hurrying back up the boardwalk and stopped in front of the girls.

A broad chested burly man with a mustache said, "Ladies, I understand you've had some difficulties here?"

"No, Sir. He ain't giving us a lick of trouble, except for ruining a couple of wood spikes in the pit." Wide, round brown eyes looked at the Mayor who directed a couple of the men to take the body into the doctor's office.

"Who dug the pit? How did you know about the spikes? When did this happen?" Suddenly the questions flew at the girls and Kelly shook her head. She put up both hands in a halting gesture.

"This is why we avoid coming to town. Too many questions from too many people all the time." Kelly took Lola's hand and walked to the surgery, trailed by Colton. The huddle of men was left murmuring amongst themselves at the rail.

The dead man was put onto the wooden examining table. The doctor motioned for the children to sit on the wooden bench along the wall. He lifted an eye lid and then, with the little horn, listened for a heartbeat. He made a grumbling noise and then pressed his fingertips to Ghery's wrist. Again, the doctor made a grumbling noise.

Mayor Watley came in with a sheaf of papers on a small wooden board. For the next ten minutes, the children told about how they had found the dead man and the effort to get him out of the pit.

"This paper was all you found on him? Where is his gun?"

"Don't know. It's not in the pit. It wasn't on him." Lola gestured to the body. "Downright odd for a man to be walking around in the dark without a gun, don't you think?" The Mayor nodded with his bottom lip pushed out in concentration as he wrote.

"At this time, we formally make the claim on any reward that exists for capture of Rayford Ghery. Would you make a note of that, Mr. Mayor?"

"You want to what?" Mayor Watley blinked half a dozen times and then frowned. "How do you know to claim a reward?"

"We read it somewhere. We're going over to Merle Doyle's office in a few minutes and let him know to check with you about that reward. He must handle that sort of thing for us. We're children." The doctor chuckled.

Doctor Baines moved over to the small wooden desk in the corner and took out a clean piece of white paper. He dipped the quill in the inkwell and began scratching the statement. "This is the death certification. I do declare that Rayford Ghery is deceased. May God have mercy on his soul."

"Amen." They all said together. Kelly and her siblings stood up.

"If there is no further need for us, we should go find Mr. Doyle now." The doctor waved his hand to shoo them out.

***

When the children came out of the medical office, they found Bruno Stenson smoking a cigar as he leaned nonchalantly against the porch rail. Kelly nudged Lola who nodded. The children stepped up onto the porch.

"Good afternoon, Mr. Stenson."

He took the cigar out of his mouth and blew gray smoke into the air. With a smile, he looked at them. "The Stolters. I heard you had some excitement earlier today." Briefly, they told him about finding the body.

"We're on our way to find Merle Doyle. He's our attorney. He likes us to tell him about the things we do, the things we see. You know." Colton nodded.

Stenson said, "After you're done with your attorney, it would be my pleasure to buy you dinner over at the hotel. I'd like to hear more about this pit full of spikes." He raised his eyebrows questioningly.

"Oh, you don't have to do that, Mr. Stenson. We got the idea from the Roman Empire's guerilla warfare strategy. It was used by Quintus Fabius Maximus Verrucosus to stop the rear attacks on his army moving into Germania." Lola looked smug as she pulled on her gloves.

Stenson's mouth fell open. "Where in the world did you learn about warfare strategy?"

"Grandpa Glen's library is full of books on war. Battles, generals, all kinds of stuff. We've been reading some of it." Kelly gestured to the children. "It took us three days to dig the pit. One day to catch someone."

"We play war all the time. Nothing like being prepared in case a Roman legion comes marching through our east pasture." Kelly started to laugh. Lola and Colton began to giggle. Stenson frowned.

Lola wiped the corner of her eye. "Do you read books, Mr. Stenson?" She smiled.

"Not as many as I probably should. I mainly look at catalogs and manufacturer's specification sheets. Why?" He fussed with his cigar that had extinguished itself.

"There's a book in the library in the same section written by someone called Sun Tzu. We think it's in French because we can't read it. I learned some Spanish in school last year and I know it's not Spanish. You wouldn't happen to know how to read French, would you?" Kelly was surprised to see Stenson slap his own forehead with his hand.

"Oui, je sais comment parler et lire le français."

Lola's mouth fell open. "You know how to read and speak French!" She hugged Colton and danced around gleefully. Kelly shifted her weight and grinned, waiting for the gunsmith to explain.

"My mother was French. She used to curse at my English father all the time. I had a mixed-up time growing up. Thinking in French and speaking English and vice versa." Stenson shook his head. "Next time you come to town, bring that book and I'll help you with it. Well, unless it's something that children shouldn't be reading." He winked.

Kelly fidgeted with the edge of her shirt. "Yes, we've found a couple of books in the library that I'm sure he never meant for kids to see."

"You know what you might do? Send a telegram over to Mike Cushing. He's in Los Angeles right now. See if he'll stop at a book store and pick up a French dictionary for you. He might do it for you. For a price, of course." Stenson winked.

Kelly nodded. "We've learned that everything with Mr. Cushing has a price. But I think he's been fair with us. Sometimes he'll cut the price if we let him water and pasture his horse overnight at our place."

"We're sorry to have taken up so much of your time, Mr. Stenson. We need to go see Mr. Doyle now." Stenson's eyes jerked to the right and Kelly turned to see the attorney stepping up onto the porch.

"I heard my name." The attorney held a lit cigar between his fingers.

"Nothing like this ever happened up in Yucca Valley. We never had excitement like this. Living here is like living in the Wild West, just like in the newspapers!" Colton doubled over laughing which made Lola start giggling. Kelly put her hand over her face trying to stifle a chuckle and failed.

Lola put her hands on her hips and dug one toe into the dirt. "Kelly wanted to drop off Rayford at the Faraway Inn. I said no because I think it would be good to talk with you and see if you have heard anything from Pa.

Colton doesn't care where we brought Rayford to because as long as cake is there, it is all good for him." The sister winked at the brother who giggled.

Kelly looked at the attorney. "So here we are. Have you heard anything from Pa?"

Doyle cleared his throat and looked from child to child. "You three better come up to my office immediately. The authorities are going to want a full account of what happened." The gunsmith waved his hand at the children as they turned to follow the attorney.

***

It was later that afternoon when Kelly, Lola and Colton turned off the Flint Hills road. Colton stood up in the stirrups. "There's a wagon up at the house, Kel. Somebody's there."

"Halloo!" Mike Cushing stood up from his seat in the shade. The unhitched big Percherons were drinking from the water trough. Thick ropes crisscrossed the canvas load on the heavy freight wagon. The faces of all the children lit up with smiles. "Howdy, Mr. Cushing."

"You kids are getting bigger each time I stop in here. And you, Miss Kelly, are the spitting image of your ma," Cushing said with a grin.

"We're just getting back from Bradford. We were told that you were in Los Angeles."

"Yes, well, I'm supposed to be in Los Angeles, but I got sidetracked and here I am."

"Let us get unloaded and we can tell you all about our excitement and adventure," Colton waved and jumped down from the mare.

"Excitement? Adventure? Sounds like my life!" They all laughed.

"I found a couple of big rugs in Los Angeles that you were asking about last month. A hotel was replacing these and I snatched 'em up for you. In winter those wood floors will be cold."

Cushing helped unload the packhorse and set everything up on the front veranda. Cushing removed the ropes off the load and they tugged out the ends of the rolled-up rugs. There was a green rug with a bronze and rust pattern, a gold rug with a black swirl pattern and a chocolate brown with a gold and green leaf design.

Colton claimed the green rug for his room, Lola rubbed her fingers into the piles of both rugs and then finally decided on the gold rug.

"Well, that makes it easy for me, Mr. Cushing. I get the dark brown rug," Kelly said with a laugh. Cushing chuckled.

Kelly admired the thick rugs. "What do you want for these?"

"I was thinking fifteen dollars, but if you let me park here overnight and my horses graze, I'll knock off five dollars. How does ten dollars sound?" Cushing looked hopeful, but business was still business.

"I've got eight on me. Bradford cost us a little more than I thought it would. I've got two dollars in the house. That okay?" Kelly fished out eight dollar coins from the leather pouch.

"Tell you what. I'll take your eight and if you feed me dinner, we'll call it even." The round, red face of the freight man beamed.

"We can feed you. Miss Georgianna sent us home with a roasted chicken and a small ham," Kelly said with a grin.

"Lola, will you start a fire in the stove? We can heat up dinner while we get these rugs into the house."

Over dinner around the table, the children told the junk dealer about finding the dead man down in the pit and the trespasser that died on the other side of the river. Cushing felt a shiver race down his spine listening to the story and silently gave thanks that he was not inclined to curiously snoop around the property.

It was after sunset when they took a couple of candles out to sit on the porch while Cushing smoked. Lola and Colton leaned against the porch railing and Kelly curled up on the bench cushions.

"We don't have any pictures or drawings of Charlie. We don't know what he was like, Mr. Cushing."

"Charlie was probably six months old the time I came through hauling an upright grand piano. Your mother played beautifully, like an angel and when I found it in Tucson, I thought of her first. Took four men to get it up onto the wagon and braced and covered."

"He was a happy, smiling baby. He had that reddish blonde hair like your pa along with those dark eyes of your ma. I wore a beard back then that he liked to pull. He'd coo along with your ma when she sang to him. Your pa rode him on the front of his saddle from time to time. It always made me laugh to see that little fella riding along." The three kids were quiet as they listened to the description of the brother they never knew.

"There wasn't a piano in the house when we got here. Someone must have taken it after Grandpa Glen died. There wasn't much here when we first got here." Colton looked at Kelly.

Cushing nodded. "I'm pretty fair at finding things folks need. You just tell me and I'll keep my eyes open for things. I'm headed for Los Angeles and I won't be back here for about a month. I got friends over on the coast that I want to visit with and stay awhile."

The next morning as Cushing hitched up his horses he promised to watch for any word on Nick Stolter. "I know he was headed the other way but if I hear of folks talking about him, I'll find out what they know. Chance for me to be a nosey Nellie." They all laughed.

That afternoon wore on slowly for the kids. The chores were done. Kelly sat with Lola reading on the cushion bench on the porch, but neither one could concentrate for very long. The mail man was not due to stop until the following day. There were times when all they did was watch time go by.

Colton and Lola decided to go hunt for rocks up in the sandstone wash on the north side. The yellow lab followed along behind them as they climbed over the fence headed east. Kelly decided to do more sewing on the shirt for Lola. She had been gathering scraps for the quilt for their father. Even though she was only fifteen, there were times when she felt decades older.

It was after dinner when they had all gone out to sit on the porch when Lola had looked up at the stars.

"Do you think that Dad might be looking at the same stars we are, Kelly?"

"He might be. He might be wishing on a star that we are safe and healthy. He will find us, honey. He will come home. You have to have faith that he will," said Kelly.

Lola stood up, stretched and yawned. Colton followed her into the house. Kelly took one last look up at the dark heavens dotted with the shimmering diamonds and hoped that her father was looking up, too.

***

About one o'clock the next day, the mailman brought a letter from Henry Elliot. Kelly sat on the fence and read the letter telling the kids that he has been searching for their father and trying to find out what happened. The letter said that Elliot would be headed to Los Angeles at the end of the following month. He promised to stop by the Flint Hills Ranch. They laughed out loud when they read the part about to please not shoot him when he rode in.

After lunch, they gathered their rifles and knives and headed out on foot. The east path was in the shade by that hour and it was an easy walk to the new blind. Kelly, Lola and Colton used grasses, moss and plants along with sticks, twigs and limbs to construct the deer blind. Aside from the usefulness of the structure, it had kept them busy for three days.

They had been perched in the blind for a little over an hour. "There's someone coming, I can hear them," Colton said. They all held their breath and listened. Small rhythmic crunching noises got louder signifying footsteps. Kelly saw a tall, thin man with stooped shoulders from the heavy pack on his back come into view walking up the narrow clay and gravel path. Tall brown muddy boots, dark denim jeans. He wore a green and black plaid shirt and walked with dark gloves with a walking stick. It was a pained expression on his gaunt face framed by long, shoulder length dark hair.

The man circled up onto the ridge path and they watched him disappear over the rise into the trees. Twenty minutes later Kelly turned to Colton who stared at the trail where the man went out of view. "Did he come back?"

"No, he kept going. He didn't stop. He wasn't sneaking around. He didn't care about the sound he made either. He was thinking about getting to where he wanted to go." The boy shrugged.

Kelly lowered her voice. "Both of you, stop and think. On the trail drive down here, in Bradford, at that community dance, do you remember seeing that man?" They shook their heads and looked at Kelly.

Lola took in a deep, gasping breath. "He's hurt. Something is wrong with him. It is like he doesn't dare stop. He's hurt bad."

Colton looked at Kelly while he fidgeted for a moment. "Do you want me to see where he went?"

"Yeah, you might want to track him and make sure he kept on going and didn't double back on us," Kelly nodded.

"Here." Kelly checked the chambers and handed the Colt revolver to the boy. "You know what to do. Take your time and don't put down any tracks that would bring someone back here."

Kelly and Lola watched Colton climb down the back tree and pick his way through the brush. Only once did they hear a snapping twig and then it was silent again.

Lola squeezed Kelly's hand. "That trail starts between two boulders up on the San Felipe River. You have to know where to look before you can even climb up that riverbank onto the trail. A horse and rider can't get to it. It is a footpath, not a riding path. It took me and Colton a couple of hours to drop two trees across it so it was hidden."

Kelly leaned back against the tree bark and squinted. "That trail was here before we were so whoever walks it, has to have known about it for a long time. There must have been a flood or something last winter that wiped out the trail on the other side of the river."

Kelly sensed that Lola had gone quiet and still. The younger girl stared at the trail from the direction where the man had come up the trail. Together they listened and then slowly Lola relaxed.

"Maybe just a deer or another animal. There was something there coming this way and it stopped." Colton was not a boy who played surprise games with them even if he had wanted to circle around them. Lola shook her head.

She whispered. "We'll have Colton go look when he gets back."

"Looks like we have an interesting spot for our blind," Lola whispered. They heard a special bird call and carefully turned to look for Colton. About fifty yards out the young boy crept through the underbrush and then climbed back up to the blind.

"He crossed over onto the Ladd Ranch and went down into the valley.

He didn't look behind himself once. He was going somewhere and wanted to get there." Colton rubbed his face and got comfortable. Lola told Colton about hearing something else on the trail moving toward them but it had stopped.

Kelly frowned. "This is our land and people are cutting across it. I don't like it. I guess I'm not in a sharing mood today."

Colton reached over and slid his hand into Kelly's. "On the other side of the gully there is a small ledge in the sandstone where it's smooth like many feet have been over it. About thirty feet on farther it broadens out into a trail and winds around the hill. If you don't know where to look for that ledge, you'll walk right on passed it. Dusty found a pretty big cave in that hill when we were out one day. We'll need torches because it goes back quite a ways. That trail goes right to that cave."

Kelly nodded. "After you left to follow the man, Lola said there was something coming up the trail. We need to go see what that is." The three of them moved slowly and watched where they put their feet and stayed off the main path.

They found the first man's tracks clearly in the slide dirt. As Colton had said, he didn't seem to care who saw the prints or who heard his walking. The second set of boot marks stopped in the middle of the slide dirt. Lola could see where the walker then skidded about forty feet down to the bottom. There was no movement and no noise.

Kelly knelt and sifted a handful of the dirt through her fingers. "It's like they just vanished."

Colton carefully looked over the ledge. "It doesn't look like they fell. More like they simply chose to slide down the dirt."

Lola said. "We'd have to climb down there and look for signs so we could track whoever it was. I didn't bring any rope so we could get back up out of there."

Kelly said, "I don't think women have feet that big. Those were big boots. So, it's a man. A walking man who suddenly changed his mind right here and went in another direction."

Colton said, "Was he following the first man for some reason?"

Kelly said, "I don't think so. I think we should track him. If he decided to go in our direction, it could be a problem."

"Alright. Who wants to wait here and who wants to do the tracking?" They all looked at each other.

Simultaneously Colton and Lola both said they would track. Kelly looked around and then sat down in a small grassy area off the path. She watched them carefully slide down the loose dirt and gravel. After a few minutes, they crept into the bushes to the northwest and then they were gone.

Kelly could smell the plants and earth. The faint scent of sage drifted by.

Off to her left back towards the blind a twig cracked and snapped. She took the leather strap off the revolver and went up on one knee. Everything went quiet again and she relaxed back to sitting. Ten minutes later, both kids appeared on the other side of the slide.

"We found three little animal trails. Rabbits, foxes, squirrels and such. Tiny paw prints. The trails went in underneath brush. Not big enough for a grown man."

"Nothing. Not a broken twig or limb. Not even a crushed leaf. Like he lifted straight up into the air." Lola laughed.

Kelly stood up and dusted herself off. "Okay, we've got an hour of daylight before sundown so let's go see if we can get us a deer."

In the darkness, Kelly could just make out the pocket watch time of 8:00. "Let's go home. I'm tired and want coffee. We can try again tomorrow, if you want." It was a long three-mile walk home.

After all the lamps were blown out, she tried to roll onto her side in bed to get comfortable. Something was keeping her awake. She felt exhausted and jittery at the same time. Finally, she wrapped the quilt around her and went downstairs to sleep on the sofa in front of the fireplace. The crackling, wood burning noise helped to block out her other thoughts and she drifted off to sleep.

The next morning at the mailbox, Kelly tore open the cream-colored envelope and took out the folded card.

"Mr. Raymond Ladd requests our presence at a dinner party at the Ladd Ranch." She handed the card to Lola who shared it with Colton. They started walking up the driveway.

Colton asked, "What is a dinner party? Is that like eating dinner with a lot of folks you don't know?" Kelly nodded.

"Do we have to wear fancy clothes and get cleaned up?" Kelly frowned and tried to remember if she had a long dress.

Lola asked, "When is it for? We gonna go?" Kelly handed her the card again.

"Is this the kind of party where Ma used to cook something and take it with us and we couldn't have any?" Colton tried to grab the card from Lola but missed.

Kelly shook her head. "No, honey. That's a potluck dinner. This is a dinner party where they have all the food there."

Lola said, "I'd like to go. Maybe they'll have cake!" Lola and Colton cooed at each other and fell over in the grass tickling each other. Kelly shook her head with a groan at her young siblings.

Half an hour later, Kelly yelled down the stairs. "Both my dresses and my one long skirt are too tight. I think I might have grown." Lola giggled.

Colton said, "I have one pair of black jeans that I haven't worn in the river. They look pretty good and they fit. I can wear those. I just need a good shirt." Kelly laughed to herself about her brother wearing anything in the river to find gold.

"I'm not a sewing person, Colton," said Kelly. "I'm a horse person. Ma was the sewing person. We'll have to make the ride to Bradford and buy you a shirt and me a skirt."

"Why can't I wear my slacks and a sweater?" Lola swung her foot as she sat in the chair.

"Because ladies get skirts and dresses for parties. They get their hair cut and curled so they look nice." Kelly made a note to see if there was a hair salon in Bradford.

"Oh, my gosh. This sounds like a lot of work." Lola pretended to be exhausted and fell on the floor. Colton giggled.

"Is it any more work to crawl around in the brush for a couple hours tracking someone? You'll do that before I can even finish the sentence, Lola." Kelly nudged the silly girl.

Colton said, "I had forgotten about going to parties. We used to go to them all the time when we lived up in Yucca Valley. Maybe people here just don't have parties."

Kelly winked at her brother. "Alright. Tell you what. When Pa comes home, we'll throw a party and invite everyone. Even that Texas Ranger, Henry Elliot." Lola sat up with her hair disheveled.

"If we're going into Bradford, can we get the gold weighed so we can see how much we have?" Colton nodded. "I think we have more than an ounce. I don't know how much it's worth either."

Kelly thought for a moment. "Yes, we can get it weighed. We'll have Mr. Doyle do it very quietly because we don't want to wake up and find fifty people out in the river panning for gold."

Colton thumbed his nose and lowered his voice down like an older man. "I'd have to run them varmints off with my blunder buster." Kelly doubled over laughing.

"It's called a blunderbuss, you silly," said Lola. "And it's bigger than you are. Probably take you a week to load it." Kelly had tears in her eyes from laughing as she held her tummy. Lola shook her head.

Kelly wiped her eyes. She walked to the desk to get a piece of paper and a pencil. She began writing down the things they would need and the errands to do in Bradford.

"On the way to town can we stop at the Faraway and have a piece of pie? Amanda makes good pies." Lola got back up in the chair and went back to swinging her foot.

Colton piped up. "And while we're in Bradford, can we stop at the hotel to see if they have cake?" Kelly groaned.

"Is that all you two think about? Pie and cake?"

Lola rolled her eyes in exasperation. "According to the West Point Cadet manual, an army fights on its belly. You take an army to war, you better take food along with them. They get hungry, them fightin' men are going home for beans and ham hocks." Kelly burst out laughing again. She held out her hands palms up to stop Lola.

"Don't tell me. Grandpa Glen has an official copy of the West Point Cadet manual in the library?" Lola nodded.

"And I've been reading it. The West Point way of doing things is a lot different from the way we run this ship, missy." Colton giggled with a mock salute.

"This ain't no ship," Kelly said indignantly. "Lola, stop reading all those books in Grandpa Glen's library. They're putting strange thoughts in your head."

"No. We are an army. We're fighting the war of life. And armies need food. So, let's stop for cake!" Colton cheered and went to dance around the room with Lola.

***

During the next few days, the children alternated times during the day in the hunting blind. On Thursday afternoon, it was close to sunset when Colton heard the crashing sounds of an animal running fast through the brush and trees. A buck skidded down the clay and gravel bank of the creek about twenty-five yards from the blind. Its eyes were wide in panic and its mouth was open, panting and gasping as it ran. Rather than contend with a scared animal, Colton held up his shot and waited to see what was chasing the buck.

A few minutes later a couple of men came trotting up the trail carrying ready rifles, scanning the surroundings as they went. Once they got close enough, Colton caught a few words when they stopped almost directly underneath the blind.

"You see it?" Shaggy black hair with a mustache and a hunched shoulder.

"Nope, it must be on ahead." Heavy jowled, chubby red-faced panting with streams of sweat down his face.

"It's here somewhere." The taller man with the greasy, lank longer hair took out a canteen and drank. Then he handed it to the other man who drank. Colton watched the shorter, heavier man scratch himself and adjust his trousers.

"About two miles west of here there is an abandoned old stone ranch house. I stayed there a couple of times when I came through here. We can go check it out if you want lay low for a while," the gravelly voice said.

"Nah, my belly wants food. Let's go after this buck and get some meat. After we've eaten, then we can go look at this place you are talking about," the shorter man said. Colton listened for the stumbling running gait of the buck but everything was quiet. Either it had picked up speed and gone down the other side of the ridge or it had hunkered down and was waiting for these men to walk on by it. Colton watched the two men walk single file on up the trail and only once did the shorter man turn around to look behind them.

Back at the house, Colton laid the rifle on the rough wooden table inside the door.

"We might be having company. There were two men chasing a good-sized buck up the trail right before sunset," the young boy said as he took off the holster.

"Do you know who they were? Seen them before?" Kelly wiped her hands on a towel and walked out of the kitchen to stand next to the table.

"Nope. Once of the men said he knew of an old stone ranch house about two miles away that they could lay up in. Said he had been there before. He was talking about our house. He don't know we are here, Kelly." Colton leaned both hands on the table and silently watched Kelly.

Kelly looked down at her hands frowning and she bit her lower lip. "If they come here and give us any trouble, we'll have to give 'em trouble right back. So far, we have been lucky in people leaving us alone. Maybe our luck is about to run out, I don't know."

"Where's Lola?"

"She's laying down in the bedroom sleeping. She doesn't feel too good and maybe she just needs some sleep." Kelly lowered her voice. "What did they look like, Colton?"

While Colton described the men, Kelly poured a cup of coffee and sat down at the table. Mary had given them a forest green tablecloth and Marianna's blue vase held wild flowers in the center. It gave them a familiar peace during meals but that was about to be disrupted.

"Like Dad always said, do we see trouble coming?" Kelly looked at her younger brother. In the last year the boy had gone from being a happy, playful child to a quieter child who looked at people with intelligent eyes and had become aware of his surroundings.

"What trouble?" Lola walked in rubbing her eyes. Her long, dark blonde hair was tangled and her face was puffy and rosy from sleep.

Colton said, "I saw two men that talked about our house."

Kelly stood up. "I've got beans, stewed beef and corn, if you are hungry, Lola." The younger girl nodded. While Lola ate, Colton told her the details about the buck and the men.

"If they've been here before, they'll know the house and the barn. They could surprise us in the middle of the night and I don't like that." Kelly poured a glass of milk for Lola and then refilled her coffee cup.

Lola looked up from her plate. "We'll have to trap them. Fix it so they do themselves harm before they can get to us. That lawyer man is going to get mighty fussy if we kill someone else." Kelly nodded and looked at her coffee cup.

"We might want to sleep a couple nights out in the barn up in the loft, just to be out of the way in case they do come here. I can leave Dusty in the house and he'll bark if a stranger tries to get in." Colton walked to the wash bucket and knelt rolling up his sleeves to clean his hands and arms. The boy dried his hands, put hot food on a plate and sat down beside Lola. The children talked quietly for another hour and then Lola went to sit near the fireplace and read. Kelly cleaned the dishes and stored the meal away.

An hour later the three siblings stood back in the shadows of the upper loft over the barn watching the darkened house. Their bedrolls were laid out in the soft hay and each had brought a rifle and a revolver and ammunition. They were never without their knives and the scabbards so each child was well armed. Colton was the first to lay down into sleep under the heavy quilt. A few minutes later, Kelly kissed Lola and hugged her and then went to lay down for the night. It was Lola who knelt and breathed deeply in the night air at the edge of the loft door.

Her eyes could see the thousands of twinkling diamonds in the inky night sky. Each breath brought the scent of earth, horses and sage. The crackling leaves of the cottonwood brushed against the back of the barn scratching at the wood. The young girl guessed it was after midnight when her senses had dulled and she could no longer fight sleep and finally laid down onto the blankets and closed her eyes.

***

The next morning found the yard covered in heavy dew. They carefully examined the ground in the yard for boot marks. There were none. Nobody had come to interrupt the calm.

After chores, they saddled up and walked towards Bradford.

The drapes were open in the windows of the dressmaking shop. The whitewashed porch had three colorful flower boxes, a wooden bench and two chairs for relaxing.

The little bell over the door rang when Kelly, Lola and Colton walked into the shop. There were tables stacked with stripes, polka dot and plain fabrics. Large jars of buttons and hooks sat on the counter. Pincushions, scissors, needles and measuring tapes were neatly in small wooden trays.

"Well, hello there. I'm Dawn White." She held out her hand to Kelly who struggled to get her glove off. The main room was thirty feet by forty feet with polished wood floors and scattered rugs. The back wall was filled with cubby holes of fabrics, laces and threads. On the south side, three large windows framed with lace curtains let in streaming daylight.

"Hello Miss White. I'm Kelly Stolter, this is my sister, Lola and my brother Colton. How are you?" The dressmaker was a stout, full-bodied woman with hazel eyes, and a reddish-pink complexion. The natural waves in her reddish-brown hair were still visible even though she had twisted the glossy strands around her head. She had a pretty, white smile.

"Very well, Miss Stolter. What can I do for you Stolters today?"

"I seem to have grown out of every long skirt and dress I own. Lola needs a long skirt." Dawn nodded.

Colton said, "We've been invited to a party and we want to look nice."

"Oh yes. Of course. Well, I might have blue dress that would go well with your coloring, Kelly. I think it might need to be hemmed up for you, though. Let me go look. Do you have gloves?"

"Not the nice white dinner gloves, no." Kelly watched the pretty woman open baskets as she hunted through the store. From the back room, she brought out a large wooden hanger swathed in paper. She unpinned it and held out the dress towards Kelly.

It was a shiny turquoise dress with small silver buttons in two rows down the front. The sleeves were elbow length and decorated with the same silver buttons.

Kelly smiled nervously. "I need to wipe my hands off before I touch it. It is very pretty." Dawn handed them a small brown towel and they all wiped their hands.

"It's so soft, Kelly," Lola's eyes were big as she ran the fabric through her fingers.

"It reminds me of ma's green dress. Remember? That shiny, dark green dress she used to wear?" Kelly nodded.

Dawn smiled and asked, "Would you try it on so I can see how much it should be hemmed?" Kelly nodded.

When Kelly came out from behind the screen, Lola's mouth dropped open. Colton stared. "You look like ma when she got dressed up." Lola hugged Colton. Dawn smiled.

"You're fifteen or sixteen, Kelly?"

"I'm fifteen. Why?"

"Well, the dress is a bit loose on you. You are a slim young woman. It doesn't fit as snug as some women like to wear them. But you have a couple more years to grow. It might be a good fit on you next year." Dawn uncovered the full-length mirror and let the young woman look at herself.

She didn't recognize herself. It was another girl in a pretty blue dress in the mirror. Her fingers lightly ran over the dress. She could feel her own mouth drop open. These last months she had been thinking of the ranch, the family and the stock and forgotten about herself.

"I'd say you would be very pretty with your hair up, a pair of nice earrings and dinner gloves. Do you like it?" Dawn stepped back while Kelly turned around.

"Yes, I do like it. It is too long though and will have to be hemmed. I'm not used to walking in dresses and I would hate to fall down and ruin it." Dawn chuckled.

"It would take me two days to hem it. I don't have any other dress orders right now so I could do it for you. Do you want to buy it?" Kelly nodded. Dawn handed short white gloves to Kelly to put on.

"I honestly didn't think that I'd find a dress to wear, Miss White. How much are you asking for it?"

"The price is eight dollars for this dress. The woman that ordered the dress took ill recently and she declined to go through with the purchase. She never got to try it on after it was done."

"I'll buy it. The party isn't until a week from Saturday so there is no big rush on hemming it." Kelly smiled.

"Very well. If you'll step up onto the small wooden stool I can put in the pins for the hem." She smiled a white smile.

Ten minutes later, Kelly gently slid the dress off and handed it to the dressmaker. From the leather wallet, Kelly laid the coins on the counter.

"Is there a charge for doing the hem, Miss White?"

Dawn shook her head. "No. I always include it in the price." She turned her attention to Lola.

"Well Miss Lola. Were you looking for a dress like your sister or would you prefer a skirt?" The young girl smiled.

"I have a nice long-sleeved white blouse at home. I would like a long skirt for the party." Kelly gestured for Lola to stand up and Kelly sat in her chair.

"A denim long skirt would not be dressy enough for a party. Neither would gingham or plaid," she said as she turned to the shelves of fabrics. She pulled out bolts and then shoved them back. Twice she turned and looked at Lola.

From the lower shelf, she pulled out a stack of velvet fabrics. She unfolded deep rust, forest green, jet black and royal purple lengths. "One of these with your white blouse would look nice, Lola. But you might be prettier than your sister at the party though." She grinned. Lola laughed.

"I like the rust color, please."

"Very good. I like that color, too. Very few women wear it."

"If you'll stand up on the stool like Kelly did, I'll measure you." Dawn gestured to the stool.

After Kelly paid for the skirt, they waved goodbye and left.

"That wasn't as hard as I thought it would be. All these years of Ma making our clothes, I had no idea there was someone who did that in a store." Lola mused about her purchasing experience while they enjoyed cake at the Bradford Hotel restaurant.

***

The note on the calendar marked the visiting day for Mary Rideout. Kelly handed the hot cup of tea to Mary as she sat on the sofa at the Flint Hills house. The afternoon sun streamed in the windows and the light curtain lifted and floated on the warm breeze. Mary took a sip and then sat the cup onto the side table and looked at the children.

"My Phineas was a stone cutter. It sounds so unusual that he could look at a rock and stone and can tell you how it grew or was made. I don't know the right way to explain veins and seams in it."

"It was in the spring, if I remember rightly, we had come up over the Layton Hills pass and noticed a campfire up in the trees back off the road. We could see smoke from a mile back on the road. When we got closer, we saw two raggedy looking men watching us go by in the wagon. I didn't recognize them and Phineas waved trying to be friendly, but neither one waved back."

Kelly asked, "Were there a lot of people camping out along the road like that?"

Mary smiled and patted her hand. "No, it wasn't unusual to see people camped out like that. Ginger Whelihan had a couple of favorite spots around in the hills that he used quite a bit. We used to see him from time to time. I'm surprised you haven't seen him more often. But if he's out with your pa somewheres, that would explain it."

Lola looked at Kelly and then frowned. "I wonder if Pa will still let Mr. Whelihan camp out up on that ridge. We found an old campsite up there so that must be where he stayed." Kelly nodded to her sister.

Mary seemed to ignore Lola's comment. "When we'd get over this way we always stopped in to talk to Glen for a few minutes. Phineas and Glen were good friends, it was like listening to a couple of biddy hens the way they used to talk. You would have liked listening to your grandpa's voice as he told stories about being young."

Colton sat up abruptly, smiling. "I would like to have known Grandpa. We only have one picture of him."

Mary nodded. "To the north of your ranch, on the other side of the old mine, there is a half mile wide outcropping of flint stone. Most people know it's there and help themselves. Phineas wanted to get a couple of good chunks for some stone work he was doing. Flint is part of the quartz family and most of the flint around here is the black or gray kind. In the south, you can find the red and yellow flint. It's very pretty, but it's scarce."

Mary's eyes brightened as she talked. "Anyway, we are at the flint quarry and Phineas had gotten the wood wedges pounded into an upright slab so it would break off in one piece. It was about seven feet, and he had to use the ladder as the face of the stone was too smooth for any footholds. He planned that seven-foot piece to fall to the hard rock below it and shatter into useable pieces. He liked to let the weight of the stone do the work for him.”

Colton said, “It sounds dangerous. He must have been very careful.”

Mary nodded quickly and went on. “I'd picked out a cool, shady spot and set out the food I'd brought along for our picnic. Phineas always said that working with the stone gave him a good appetite. So, I'm sitting there watching birds fly in and out of the grass and listening to Phineas' hammer when I hear a gun cock.”

“Well, I turned around and there was one of those raggedy men standing there, pointing a gun at me! So, I yelled for Phineas.”

Mary had a look of surprise and exasperation on her face. “The man yelled at me to sit still. How dare him! Gun or no gun, there's no cause to be rude. I looked at Phineas and he saw what was happening and do you know what he did? No, you don't, so I'll tell you.”

Mary lifted her arms up in a fanning motion. “Phineas turned back to the flint and gave the wedge another big whack and then dropped the hammer and motioned for me to come over to him.”

“By this time, I'm frightened, I'm exasperated, I've been insulted and I just know that Phineas is going to be upset that his picnic was ruined.” She winked at the children.

Kelly asked, “So what did you do?”

Mary put her hand on her throat and opened her eyes very wide. “This man hadn't shaved in maybe a year or more. He had a very crooked nose, like it had been broken. You know those men who like to drink too much liquor and then pick fights. I read the stories in the paper about rowdy men like that. Oh, and bad teeth! He was missing two in the front and the ones he had were awful.” The children giggled.

Mary cringed as if in fright. “Well, I stood up even though he was waving that gun and calmly walked over to Phineas, expecting to be shot in the back with every step. And that raggedy man followed me all the way over there! Well, now I'm standing with Phineas right in front of that tall slab and I can hear it crackling and that means it's getting ready to fall.”

“Well, the man tells Phineas that he wants our money and our gold and my jewelry and he's gonna take the horse and wagon. He's gonna take the picnic food, too! Well, I start to give him a piece of my mind when Phineas shushes me and moves to put me behind him. Then Phineas told me to take off my little heart of gold necklace.”

Mary put a sad frowny look on her face. “Now I loved that necklace. We got it in Saint Louis one year when I went with Phineas to work on the marble in the courthouse. That necklace was just the prettiest thing I owned. Well, I had a couple other pieces, but I really liked that one.”

Lola said, “I'd like a pretty gold necklace in the shape of a heart.” Kelly smiled and nodded.

Mary waved her arms as if she were falling backward. "Well, Phineas threw the necklace at the man with the gun and then pushed me back when he moved backwards. I thought I was about to fall! When the man stepped to bend down to pick it up, that flint slab broke loose and fell right down on him. Squished him like a bug." The children cried out in horror.

Mary made a horrendous, ghastly face. "Oh, it was horrible. I didn't want to stay there all alone with that squished man and I was crying so hard I didn't think I could ride all the way into Bradford to get the sheriff. It took Phineas over an hour to break up the flint to get the dead man out. Twice I had to look away as all the blood made me dizzy. I brought down the blanket out of the wagon to cover him up. It took me forever to help Phineas get him into the wagon."

Lola made a sour face. "Icky." Kelly still had her hand over her mouth.

Mary said, "Nobody in Bradford recognized the man, well, what was left of him. Several men when they looked at the body turned away and ran to be ill in the bushes. The sheriff said that he was probably just a drifter, no account vagabond desperate for money and food."

Colton said, "What about the other man? The second raggedy man?"

Mary nodded to Colton. "You know I told the sheriff that we saw two men out there. Maybe there was another man hiding somewhere going to try to hurt other folks for money and food. The sheriff told me not to worry about it anymore as someone was going to ride out there and take a look around for that other man."

Mary clasped her hands as if in prayer. "And I wrote a dozen letters to my friends and family all about this raggedy man who tried to hold us up. I think writing all about it so many times helped me get over this dreadful event that happened to us."

Lola looked at Kelly. "Death by flint. Can you imagine?" Kelly cringed away.

Colton asked, "Did the other raggedy man try to hurt you and Mr. Rideout?"

"Oh no. Nothing like that ever happened again. We had many more delightful picnics there at the flint quarry. Phineas was very careful to even break up the flint where the man had been squished and I couldn't even find it now if I tried."

Kelly smiled and fidgeted with the edge of her shirt. Mary stood up and set down the tea cup.

"Thank you for letting me stop by and visit you. I'll most likely see you next month over at the Grange dance in Beatrice." She stopped and looked at them. "You are going, aren't you? It is the big social event of the county every year."

Kelly grimaced and slowly shook her head. "We have been sticking pretty close to home waiting for pa. If he is home and able to go, I would think we would go. But if he comes home sick, we need to stay home and help him get well." Mary gripped her hands together and nodded.

The three Stolters stood on the patio and waved as the creaking black buggy wobbled down the drive. Colton and Lola murmured to each other and then sauntered down the path towards the barn. Kelly turned and went back in to clear the dishes and heat water for coffee.

***

On Saturday, the big clearing between the main barn and the second barn had been raked smooth. Lola had laid out borders on the edges and tiny twigs fashioned into people had been set up in a group at one end. Kelly stood holding the big book and frowning at the twenty by twenty-foot clearing.

"Okay, Colton. You have your pages and you know what to do?"

"Yep. Me and my legions are going to come down over the ridge on our heavy horses and trample everything in the path. Your puny arrows will not hurt us at all. A couple of my horses die, but my fearless legionnaires will march on." Colton raised his eyebrows questioningly.

"Kelly?"

She cleared her throat and read from her paper. "My advancing hordes will charge straight on at the legionnaires, suddenly split in half to the left and right and attack from the sides. Many of them will die because they are using wooden weapons and yours are iron and steel."

Colton asked, "Where are the trumpeters? The book says there were trumpets heralding the battle." Kelly held her closed fist up to her mouth and squeaked out a noise. They all laughed.

Colton said, "So when all these armored legionnaires died, did they just lay there and rot, or did someone bury them?"

Kelly asked, "And flags? Where are all the banners and flags?" Lola groaned.

"You don't hear me complaining because I don't have any cannon, do you?" Lola got down on her hands and knees and repositioned several of the figures.

"Well, I don't see how you can a drag cannon around in a battle. They have to be situated somewhere so the cannonballs can be shot into the fight." Kelly put in three large round rocks at the perimeter. She smiled and nodded.

"So, the legionnaires are marching along in smart lines with their weapons. The hordes are running on horses and on foot anywhere they want. Those are more like the guerilla fighters, right? They run in and stab and then run back out and ride on." Colton moved five of this horse-like stick figures along the sides.

Kelly moved a few more of her stick figures straight ahead. "This wasn't over in an hour. The book said it took almost a week. They must have stopped on account of darkness every day. That would give them a chance to bandage up their wounds and stuff."

Lola helped Colton move the legionnaire figures in the middle of the clearing. "The book says it took a month. I'll guess, and say that so many died only a few were left that could fight, some ran away. I still don't understand what vanquished means." She shook her head.

Colton said, "The Germanic horde was only a few dozen people. The book makes it sound like they had no chance. If you're a king, emperor, or ruler, why send in a thousand legionnaires to smash two dozen people?"

Lola sat back on her knees. "That is what the book is trying to explain. The legionnaires weren't just there killing the hordes. The legionnaires were going on to conquer the main Germania area. They were going to smash all the hordes, not just this one." Colton rolled one of the bigger rocks over a scurrying beetle, squishing it.

Kelly said, "That must be what vanquished means. To squish 'em like a bug." Lola and Colton nodded as they moved stick figures and made little explosion sounds as the rocks thudded in the dirt.

The tops of the cottonwoods and oaks ruffled in the breeze. Small birds darted in and out of the long grass on the other side of the fence. The rich, dark earth was warm in-between Kelly's fingers. She breathed in the scent of the animals, the land, and the trees.

"I understand now." Kelly looked up at Lola and Colton scooting figures around in the dirt. Colton dusted off his hands and looked at his older sister.

"The Richardsons moved here and settled this land and came to love it. I can see why Ma felt the land loved her because of all it gave to them." Kelly gestured to the clearing with the stick figures.

"The emperor of Rome wanted more land to love, to make a bigger Rome and make a grander life for all Romans. That's why he invaded Germania and conquered it." Lola nodded and went back to scooting the horse.

"Well, all this invading and vanquishing is making me hungry. Would you go start dinner and we'll put these away?" Colton rubbed his tummy with a grin. Kelly laughed and nodded. She walked over to the fence and retrieved the book.

"Kelly, someone is in the barn. I heard the bells." The children had suspended five cowbells on a slender rope from the rear double doors and draped the rope over a bundle of tall reeds. If anyone hit the reeds or somehow got tangled in the rope, those bells were heard clearly up at the house.

Kelly had been laying across her bed reading by lantern light. She looked up when Colton stepped inside the door. "You sure? Maybe it's an animal."

"They clattered and clanged twice. Someone got tangled up in the rope. Best put your shoes on and turn out that lantern. Where's Lola?"

"I think she fell asleep in her room. It's been a long day and it sort of wore her out. I'm not gonna wake her for this if she is sleeping. You and I can go take a look." Colton nodded and ducked out the door.

The children crept behind the trellis in the garden and scooted low along the rail fence until they got to the apple tree. Twenty yards out they heard a heavy thump in the barn and then Kelly recognized the sound of someone knocking over the garden tool rack.

She whispered, "If I spook 'em out of the barn, can you knock 'em down but don't kill them? Just hurt 'em so we can get a rope or two on them?" Colton nodded and patted the big Colt.

"Why isn't Dusty barking? Where is that dog?" She hissed a whisper.

"He took out this evening, right before the sun went down. I called him and he never came in." Colton shrugged. Kelly shook her head.

They scampered past the water trough and just as they started to climb through the rails, someone lit a match inside the barn and the light flared up. For a second they saw a man's face with a black mustache. Kelly looked at Colton who slowly shook his head. He gestured for Kelly to move to the barn. Colton knelt on one knee next to the trough and hunched over to blend into the shadow.

Two minutes later, the man's form came backing out of the side hatch door. Colton took a deep breath and then fired off the round hitting the man in the right thigh, making him scream and grab his leg. About the same time, a knife embedded itself into his left chest and he wobbled on his feet. The man in the dark stumbled, swearing as he limped around the side of the barn and headed for the tall grass. Colton saw him jerk the knife out and drop it.

Before Colton took a step after the man he paused, knowing the shot would have woken up Lola, and looked back towards the house to see if there was any movement. Everything was silent and still. He stayed near the grass as he ran low to the far side of the corral. The wood floor inside the barn creaked softly once and then off in the darkness someone groaned.

In the dim light Kelly signed with her upraised crossed arms for Colton to come to her. She nodded her head in the direction of the south valley.

"I put two knives into him. He's shot in the right leg. I don't think he'll get very far, unless he's headed for a horse." Colton listened to his sister whisper close to his ear.

"I'm going up to get Lola to track him. I know that shot woke her up and she's probably pacing back and forth like a caged animal," Kelly whispered. "Get up in the loft and stay there. If he comes back, shoot to kill, honey." Colton nodded.

Lola was waiting for Kelly inside the front door. "What happened?" She listened as Kelly took her by the arm and led her out the back door and down into the garden in the dark.

"He's hurt bad so he ain't thinking straight. Just give us an idea on which way he went and we'll get a rope on him." Lola nodded.

Colton came down out of the loft to kneel next to Kelly while Lola looked around. "He's headed for the river. You'll need a horse because he's on foot. You're right. He's hurting something awful, Kelly."

Kelly looked out into the darkness. Her voice hissed in a whisper. "Who is in the corral? I'll get a bridle and a rope. If he gets in the river, he'll float south. We may have to fish him out at the bridge if he gets that far." A chestnut mare grunted as the bit slid into her mouth and Kelly gripped the mane and swung up onto her back.

Lola watched Kelly trot down the driveway and disappear into the darkness. She then looked at Colton. "Give out two whistles if you run up on him. Wait till we get there, because you know wounded animals are scared and mean. Wounded people are worse." The boy nodded and his bare feet were silent in the grass as he followed the route the man had taken.

An hour later, Kelly walked the horse back up the drive and into the corral where she took off the gear. Colton and Lola sat curled up under a quilt on the bench on the front porch in the dark. The oldest sister sat down next to them.

"He didn't go by in the river. He might have made it all the way across somehow and if he did, he's gone. He'd be one tough man to get that far, as bad as he was hurt." Her whispered voice had disappointment in it.

Colton yawned. "We can look for him tomorrow in the daylight. I'm bushed. I want to go to bed." Lola nodded.

"I don't like looking for things in the dark. I'm not very good in the dark. I want to go to bed, too." She stood up and walked into the house. Colton followed his tired sister.

Kelly put the wood brace across the inside of the front door after she locked it. All three windows where closed tight and the wood stops positioned to keep them from being eased open. The four bolts in the heavy split Dutch door in the kitchen were shoved into place. The inside doors were shut and locked before she went up the stairs in the dark.

***

An hour after sunup the three Stolter children walked past the barn and headed towards the long grass in the valley beyond. All three carried a pistol, a machete, rope, and a knife. They were careful to stay off the trampled path that was made by the stumbling, injured man. To the three tracking senses, it was as if someone had painted a line leading away from the barn.

The ancient cottonwood leaned out over the water as the river flowed by. Lola knelt and looked at the reddish black drips in the dirt. "He made it this far. Better look a couple of yards along the bank on down the river." There was no sign that the man had tried to escape down along the water line.

"Okay. He had to have gone across. I don't see where he tried to get back to the road or cut out over the sandstone," said Kelly.

"It's almost a mile down to the bridge. We'll cross over and come back up the other side and see." a dog barked on the other side somewhere in the tall grass.

"Dusty." Colton nodded as he looked at Kelly with a smile.

"He's barking' like he's got something." Lola nodded.

"Alright. Let's figure he found the man. We need to saddle up so we can take him on into Bradford. Dead or alive I want him off the property." Kelly put her knife down into its pouch and relaxed her shoulders.

Lola nudged Colton as they walked alongside each other on the way back to the house. "If we're going to Bradford, I want to see if the hotel restaurant has any chocolate cake." The boy giggled. Kelly shook her head with a grin.

By the way the body laid in the grass, the man had floated about twenty yards downriver and then crawled up on the bank. He'd crawled around behind a couple of big boulders and that was where he died. Dusty had been laying down next to him and stood up when the horses came near.

Colton got down off the horse. "Is this where you were all night, boy? Hanging around dead people?" He ruffled the dog's neck and patted the head. The yellow lab's tail wagged happily.

"Lola, check those back pockets before we roll him over." Lola grimaced and tugged at the pockets.

"Colton, you see where there was a horse around here? Did it wander off?"

"If he had a horse, it's gone. He might have staked it over here and then walked in from the bridge. Seems an awful long way to walk, though, just to rustle through the barn."

Kelly and Lola rolled over the body and found a folded letter in the shirt pocket, a small pocketknife in the front jeans pocket and six dollars in coins. Lola slid the coins from hand to hand and winked to Colton.

"Cake money!" Kelly sighed at her brother and sister's insensitivity. They had grown and matured since coming to Flint Hills, but were still small children.

Lola had sat down, unfolded the letter and bit her lip as she read. "It is a letter of apology. It is not addressed to anyone. It's in crooked writing, not like Ma's nice handwriting." She lifted it up to hand it over to Kelly.

As Kelly read her eyes got wider.

'I am more sorry than words can say. I never should have said those things and I know they hurt. Someday I hope you can forgive me. I do love you.'

They looked at each other for a moment. Kelly folded up the grimy page and shoved it into her back pocket. "Alright. Let's get him up onto Colton's horse. Sweetie, you can ride with me into town." Kelly held out her hand to Colton.

It was on the east road that Kelly frowned and looked over at Lola. "What if he was looking for something that he put in the barn a long time ago and he came back to get it?"

Lola looked thoughtful. "The ranch was abandoned for a couple of years. We saw that the house was in pretty bad shape when we visited the first time."

Colton said, "Why hide something there in the barn? There must be a dozen other places better for hiding things." He shook his head and twisted around to look at the body tied over the saddle on the horse behind them.

Lola said, "There's something else to think about, too. Maybe he was putting something there for someone to come get. Maybe he didn't know that we lived there now. He didn't come up to the house so he wouldn't know in the dark."

"Well, I think he is about to be someone else's problem in just a few minutes." Kelly pointed towards the buildings of Bradford.

When the three Stolters had tied up in front the doctor's office, a small crowd had started to assemble. The front door opened and the gray-haired physician with rolled up sleeves came out wiping his hands on a towel.

"You children bring me the most interesting things." Experienced fingers felt for a pulse and lift an eye lid. The doctor opened his mouth to say something but Lola piped up.

"We know the process now, Doctor. We just need him officially pronounced dead so we can collect the reward."

A man in the crowd yelled, "There's a reward? Who is he?" Kelly grinned as Lola shrugged.

"Don't know, but the reward is ours!" Colton beamed.

One of the bartenders offered to buy the children a drink just as Merle Doyle, attorney at law, came around the corner and stopped as he saw the children. Kelly grinned as she saw a look of suspicion on his face and his shoulders tense. The children said goodbye to the doctor and followed Doyle back up the stairs to his office.

An exasperated attorney glared at the children from behind his desk. "You killed someone?"

"We didn't kill him completely, Mr. Doyle. If he would've made it to his horse, he might have ridden in to town and found the doctor. Who knows if he would be okay," said Colton who was inspecting the glass cases against the wall.

Lola tugged at a knot in her hair. "We didn't send out any invites for him to come rustle through our barn, Mr. Doyle. He was there trying to help himself to things." Doyle cleared his throat.

"How do you know that?" The thick eyebrows bristled together.

"We talked about that on the way into town. He might have been putting something in the barn to leave for someone else. He might have been trying to find something that was left there by someone else for him. He had no way of knowing we moved in. It is a mystery." Kelly shrugged her shoulders and nodded at Lola.

"Where do you children get these ideas? Did it ever occur to you that maybe you should just lock the doors of the house and wait for him to leave? You know, avoid trouble?" The attorney grumbled as he took out a sheet of paper and the top off the inkwell.

Kelly made an exasperated grunt. "We read a lot, Mr. Doyle. You told us yourself that our grandfather Glen had great respect for the word of the law. We do, also." Kelly stood up and dusted off her slacks. "So, in the meantime, if this unknown trespasser has a reward out for his apprehension, kindly request that reward be collected by The Stolter Family. That can be added in along with the other rewards."

Doyle stood up. "If there is a reward, I'll charge a fee!"

"Two dollars?" Kelly looked hopeful.

"I charge five dollars," said Doyle as he unwrapped a cigar. Kelly saw him make a furtive glance in her direction to see if the bargain was made.

"We'll be in the restaurant at the hotel in case you need us in the next hour, Mr. Doyle. Thank you for your assistance." Colton walked over and shook the attorney's hand, which left him with a surprised look.

***

It was the following week that three Stolter noses pressed against the glass case in the gunsmith shop. Rifle barrels and revolvers gleamed with blue black shine from the cleaning. Stenson had lain out a colorful red, green and yellow striped blanket on top of the counter with the business end of the guns pointing at the wall. Kelly leaned to look at the Colts and remarked on the difference in sizes.

Stenson prided himself on being at the right place at the right time with the right weapon of choice for any conflict large or small. The smell of gun oil, steel shavings and cold iron permeated the interior.

The broad plank floors were polished to a dull gleam and the fumes of gun oil and cold steel hung in the air. A glass case of tiny to large blade knives not suitable for kitchen use caused many to stop and stare.

On the south wall was a long ornate iron and glass case that sat up on six black iron thick legs and under the polished panes were knives that ranged from thin to thick.

Two dozen Sharps and Winchester rifles hung on the walls. If another war ever came, Stenson was ready. Mounted on all four walls were Winchester, Sharps, Talbott and Burnside rifles along with several lesser known firearms.

"Any word on a reward on that fella you brought in?" Stenson wiped his hands on a gray towel as he watched Lola peering into the knife case. Part of him was amused by her fascination and part of him was disturbed by the memory of a young girl with a fondness for slender knives.

Colton brought in the burlap wrappers and the leather pouches for carrying the rifles. "Did you figure out which ones belonged to Grandpa Richardson, Mr. Stenson?"

Stenson raised his eyebrows at the young boy and then grinned. "Yes, I did have records on some of Glen's guns. There are two pistols and three rifles here that he had brought in for cleaning and repairs." Stenson picked up the Sharps rifle and held it by the stock.

215

"I replaced two sights on this rifle. I believe these are the same ones, but I can't be sure as I didn't write down the parts I used, just the repair." Colton held the heavy rifle and examined it.

"We'll have to find something to shoot with it so we can say that all the family shot that rifle," Lola commented. Kelly nodded and motioned for Colton to wrap it up. Stenson then shook his head and carefully picked up the Remington rifle at the end of the counter.

"I replaced the stock on this Remington for your Grandpa, Colton. It is a "Common" rifle and there were quite a few made. Some of the old Home Guard used to carry these rifles. The old maple stock had cracked and splintered and Glen picked out this red oak stock. The oak stock came from a ranch out at Beatrice where there is a grove of red oak trees. The man that carved out that stock was a good friend of your Grandpa's," Stenson said as he handed the rifle to Kelly.

"So that's why it feels that way," Lola stepped over to Kelly and let her hand drag from the barrel down to the stock.

"It must be the stock that made it always feel like an old person's rifle," Lola said as Kelly smiled at her.

"What do you mean about that rifle being for an old person, Miss?" Stenson had leaned on the counter and was looking directly at Lola.

Kelly stammered, "She means that the rifle must have belonged to other people before Grandpa Glen got it." Lola held her eyes for a couple of seconds on Stenson's and then slowly turned away to the knife cabinet again. Kelly handed the rifle to Colton who began wrapping it up in the burlap.

Kelly stepped into Stenson's line of sight and interrupted his stare. "You said there were three revolvers that belonged to Grandpa Glen, Mr. Stenson. Did any of them need repairs?" Stenson stood up straight and blinked a couple of times to steady himself.

"Yes, these three down here at the end were his. There is a Colt Walker, a Colt Dragoon and Colt Paterson. They're all in good shape." Stenson furrowed his eyebrows together.

"Have any of you children fired these guns?" They all nodded and Stenson scratched his head.

Kelly said, "That Paterson has a heavier kick than the others. I have to wear a glove when I hold it because it wants to jump when I fire. Colton has to use both hands to hold it and even then, it kicks up over his head."

Colton lifted the pistol off the counter. "I used to sit on Mother's lap while she held it so I could fire it at targets. There is a little dimple cut in the barrel. That's how I know it was Mother's. It was in the bottom of an old trunk under her dresses."

Stenson rubbed his face again and began wrapping up a rifle. "I put two boxes of shells for each revolver and rifle into those saddlebags you left.

"I'm taking the Walker." Colton picked up the shiny revolver and wiped it off with the soft cloth. It slid into his holster.

Kelly slid the Colt Dragoon into her holster. "Lola, do you want the Smith and Wesson? It's your favorite, I think."

"No, I have a knife. That's good enough to get home. Just wrap it up, please." Lola walked over to the glass case and tapped her knuckle on the glass.

"Kelly, I want this black handled machete."

"Lola, you already have two machetes at home."

"Yes, but I want this one. It wants me, too."

"What?" Stenson frowned and cleared his throat.

"This will make three machetes so we can all have one when we chop weeds," Lola pleaded with Kelly. The older girl let out an exasperated sigh.

"How much do I owe you for cleaning the guns, Mr. Stenson?"

"It's a dollar for each one, so fifteen dollars. Another eight dollars for the ammunition so twenty-three altogether, Kelly." From a small leather pouch, the girl counted out twelve bills and eleven dollar coins.

"What are you asking for that machete?" Stenson realized that all three children were standing very still staring at him unblinking.

"Uhh..well. Twelve dollars."

"Lola, that's twelve dollars we don't have. Maybe it will still be here if we get that reward money."

"But what if he sells it before the reward comes in?"

"No, not today."

"Mr. Stenson, I need a favor, if you'd oblige me, please?" Kelly slide off her right-hand glove and fished two dollar coins out of her jeans pocket. Stenson was visibly curious about her holding the coins.

"What's that, Miss?"

"Would you step over to Bert Goldman's Saloon and buy a bottle of his whiskey, please? We don't have any alcohol out at the ranch and that whiskey cleans cuts and scrapes really good. You know, medicinal purposes?" Kelly held out the two coins and Stenson blinked a couple of times and rubbed his face trying to decide what to do.

"You kids aren't.."

Kelly held up a hand to stop him. "Mr. Stenson, we saw what drink did to our father. Too much and it turned him into another person. We aren't going to go through that." Stenson slowly nodded and turned to walk down the boardwalk to the saloon. Five minutes later he came back with a narrow muslin sack holding the whiskey bottle.

"Bert just took this out of the still. I think he thought it was for me. Don't get it near a fire, Kelly." Stenson's voice was low as if he were telling a quiet secret. Lola had mounted up alongside Colton. Kelly took out a length of the cloth from Dawn White and wrapped it around the whiskey bottle. She shoved it down into the saddlebag and pulled the loop tight.

Stenson stepped to the rail. "You sure you're all gonna be alright out there by yourselves? I know grown men who don't like to make that ride during certain times of the day."

"We'll be just fine, Mr. Stenson. You cleaned all our weapons. Anyone bothers us, we'll give 'em a war." That remark made the gunsmith's brow furrow.

Kelly, Colton and Lola all touched the brims of their hats nearly at the same time and then began a slow walk towards the edge of town. Stenson turned a small coin over in the fingers as he watched the children ride away.

Bert Goldman walked out of the saloon and saw Stenson watching the children ride past the stables. He leaned up against the rail alongside his friend.

"Those the Richardson grandkids, Bruno? I've been wondering if they're anything like Glen. They sure are growing up."

Stenson slowly shook his head and then turned to look at the saloon keeper. "You know they trapped and killed a man out at the ranch? I didn't see a tear or a fuss from any one of them. There's something about them that I wouldn't want to mess with, Bert."

"They are not sheltered, protected children, Bruno. They were raised by two champion rodeo riders who believe in hard work. They were taught how to take care of each other. Looks like that is what they are doing." Goldman cleared his throat and rubbed his eyes.

Goldman saw the odd concern on Stenson's face and frowned as he watched the four horses walk to the other side of the square. They disappeared around the corner.

***

"Oh my gosh, Kelly! You look beautiful!" Colton exclaimed as he watched Kelly turn around in the dress. The hemming was done perfectly, barely grazing the floor.

"Once you put your shoes on the dress will be about two inches off the floor. You look very nice, my dear. You are certain to get attention Saturday with that dress on." Dawn White smoothed the sleeves down. Kelly could feel her cheeks redden.

Lola came out in her white blouse and rust velvet skirt and twirled around with a grin. "I feel like I'm a dressed up pretty girl!" Kelly grinned.

"We don't do this very often so we are going to enjoy this as much as possible," Kelly said. Dawn took down a tissue wrapped item and set it on the counter. She looked at Colton.

"I thought you also might like to look dapper on the night of the party, Colton. So, I made this for you." She held up a small, rust colored velvet bowtie. Colton's eyes got big.

218

"I've never worn one of those before. I've seen men wearing bowties but not fancy like this one." He walked over to the counter and picked it up.

"Would you like to try it on? I think it might be a good fit without being too tight." Dawn smiled softly. Colton nodded as Kelly and Lola came nearer.

Dawn carefully brought the tie around Colton's neck. "There is a small clasp in the back to adjust the length of it so as you grow you can make it bigger." Both Kelly and Lola cooed at the tie. Dawn held up the mirror so Colton could see.

"I had a few extra inches of fabric and it was easy to make. Only took me a few minutes. I'm glad you like it." She smiled.

"Thank you, Miss White. I like it very much." Colton smiled.

After Kelly had changed out of her dress, she tucked her shirt into her jeans and sat down to pull on her boots. "Miss White, we have a pile of clothes that we have grown out of. We'd like to find someone to turn those into a quilt along with one of our mother's old dresses. We don't sew. Can you help us find someone to sew up a quilt?" Dawn nodded.

"Yes, of course. I can supply the underside fabric for the quilt. The clothes will become the top. There are a couple of ladies over at Beatrice who make quilts. They are the best in the county with their tiny stitches. They win ribbons at the fair for their quilts so I would say they would be a good choice." Dawn took out a large brown piece of paper and designed out a large square.

For the next few minutes the children watched as Dawn drew out a design. "I'll be in Beatrice this Friday. I'm going out to finish a dress. I'll stop in to Mrs. Lombard's house and talk to her about starting the quilt for you. I don't know what she charges for her work, but I can assure you, it is worth every penny. Any quilt that she makes will last long after your children are born." She winked and the children grinned.

"It's going to be mainly for our pa on his bed. He's going to be sad when he comes home and maybe this will help him not hurt so much," said Lola. Dawn hugged her shoulders.

"Watch for my letter in the mail so we can make arrangements for the quilt." Kelly lifted the paper wrapped dress, Lola carried her new skirt and Colton had tucked the bowtie in with Kelly's dress. Dawn opened the door and they waved as they walked out.

***

"We're going to meet people we've never met before. Lola, that means keeping your comments to yourself until we get home. Please." Kelly looked at her sister as she brushed out the burnished brown hair. After it was twisted into a long strand, Kelly wrapped it around in a tight bun and stuck in four pins to hold it. Small silver ball earrings went into Lola's ears and a matching bracelet around her wrist.

"Go look." Lola went into the big bedroom where her father's things were settled. There was a tall mirror in the corner.

"I don't look like me." She giggled. Colton came in holding the bowtie and looked at Lola.

"Who are you and what have you done with my sister?" They laughed. Lola helped Colton fasten the bow tie and they both took turns looking in the mirror.

Kelly smoothed the soft fabric down over her chest and tummy. Her fingers fastened the buttons. She brushed out her long brown hair and twisted it up into a bun like Lola's. A pair of small silver hoops went into her ears. In her father's room, she nudged Lola out of the way of the mirror.

"Do I look alright?" Colton stood with his mouth open, staring.

"You look like ma, sort of. When she used to wear her hair up on her head." Lola stared.

Kelly twisted and turned looking in the mirror. "We can't swim the horses across the river wearing these clothes. We'll have to go up over the ridge and cut west down to the bridge. It's about four miles that way."

Lola said, "Coming home it's gonna be colder so be sure and put your sweater in your saddle bag." Colton ran out the door to his room.

They turned down the lamp, closed all the windows and shut the front door leaving Dusty inside. It was an easy trot to the Ladd Ranch. There were six horses tied at the rail and three carriages parked when they arrived. A man in a black shirt and jeans came out to meet them.

"Good evening, miss. I'm Del. I'll take your horses over to the corral when you're ready." He touched the brim of his hat.

"Hello Del. I'm Kelly Stolter, this is Lola, my sister, and that's Colton, my brother." They dismounted and Kelly wrapped the white crocheted shawl around her shoulders.

"Kelly! Lola, Colton!" Ray Ladd bounded down the steps of the house and ran out to them. Kelly looked up to see smiling eyes and she grinned.

"I'm glad you came over tonight. I was afraid it would be all the grownups." He shook hands with Colton. Even though he was the same age as her, he towered over Kelly.

"Hi Ray. Thank you for inviting us." Lola and Kelly looked at the broad veranda on the two-story house.

"Well, come on in. I'll introduce you to folks and get you a cup of punch. Without the whiskey." He stopped and looked at Lola and Colton. "You don't drink whiskey, do you?" He grinned, and they laughed.

"No. We haven't had a drink of whiskey in," Lola looked at Colton. "A couple of months now." Colton tried to nod with a serious look but burst out laughing. Ray nudged Colton and they all walked up onto the porch. There were several men at one ending smoking and talking quietly.

Inside the front door, Kelly and her siblings stepped into a large, high ceilinged room. "Kelly, Lola and Colton Stolter, this is my father, Grayson Ladd. Pa, these are the Stolters from Flint Hills Ranch."

Salt and pepper straight hair cut just above his ears. A slightly crooked nose and full lips. His mustache was also salt and pepper. He reached to shake hands with Colton first.

"Mr. Stolter, I was hoping to meet your father tonight. It looks like he hasn't made it home yet."

"No, sir. We're waiting on word every day. We hope he comes home soon." Colton smiled.

"Kelly, Lola. It's my pleasure to meet both you young ladies. Ray told me about meeting you up at the river a few days ago. It sounds like you've had quite the adventure." An older woman with blonde hair done up in a French roll came to stand next to Grayson Ladd.

Ray said, "Mother, this is Kelly, Lola and Colton Stolter from Flint Hills Ranch." Mrs. Ladd reached out her hand to Kelly.

"I'm so pleased to meet you." Kelly felt a cool, strong hand in hers. She was also aware of Ray's eyes on her.

"Thank you, Mrs. Ladd. You have a beautiful home."

"Please call me Dottie. Everyone does." She smiled.

Ray said, "I want to introduce you to my cousin, Bonnie. She's here visiting from up in the Sacramento Valley. She's a hoot." The three children followed Ray to the far end of the room where a girl was paging through a book.

"Bonnie, these are the kids I was telling you about. Kelly, Lola and Colton Stolter, please meet my cousin, Bonnie Pickering." Bonnie closed the book and gave them a big smile. She was a taller young lady with wavy dark brown hair and eyes. She was tanned from the sun and wore her hair up in a ponytail.

"I'm so glad to meet you. Ray has told me you train cutting horses." She gripped her gloved hands together.

"One day next week, would it be alright if Ray and I came over to see your horses? I'd like to see how you do some of that training. I'm having a heck of a time working with a pinto colt up in Sacramento."

Kelly nodded. "Sure. I train every day because repetition helps them remember. Thursday might be the best day, if you want to come over." Just then a heavier man with a glass of whiskey stepped near.

"Who do we have here?" His brown eyes crinkled up when he smiled. Thick through the neck and shoulders, his snug tweed jacket made his physique seem powerful.

Bonnie said, "Father, this is Kelly, Lola and Colton Stolter from Flint Hills Ranch. It's the next ranch over to the northwest from here. This is my father, Garrison Pickering." Colton nodded and reached out to shake Mr. Pickering's hand.

"Ah. My pleasure. Flint Hills is the old Richardson place, isn't it? You all are related how?"

Kelly said, "Pleased to meet you, Mr. Pickering. Our mother was Marianna Richardson. Glen was our grandfather." Pickering nodded swiftly. He shook hands with Kelly and Lola.

"Please allow me to express my condolences on the recent passing of your mother. I never met her but heard that she was quite charming and talented with horses."

Lola said, "Thank you, sir. We miss her lot." Ray came back with three small glasses of punch and handed them out.

Pickering rocked back and forth on his heels. "That must have been quite an undertaking bringing those head in from Yucca Valley. I know that area up there. It's beautiful at the foot of those mountains."

Kelly took a sip of the fruit punch. "Yes, sir. We had five local hands come help us bring the herd into Flint Hills." Just then a light gong sounded. Pickering offered his arm to Bonnie who led the way. Kelly was surprised to see Ray offering his arm to her and she held it lightly as she followed him into the dining room.

The room was centered with a long, wide table covered in a white tablecloth, silver candelabra and flatware. High backed chairs with royal blue upholstered seats were at each place setting. As Ray held Kelly's chair for her, he said quietly, "You look very pretty tonight." Ray held the chair for Lola on his right, and she sat down. Colton sat down on Kelly's left.

She said, "Thank you." She saw that the two men from the porch sat across the table to the left. They both carefully unfolded their napkins and listened.

After she sat down, Grayson Ladd got Kelly's attention. "We heard an interesting story about a deal with Vic Helton on the way down from Yucca Valley. Would you tell us about that?" Lola and Colton laughed. Kelly felt her chest, neck and face flush with warmth.

"Mr. Ladd, I'm afraid I'm not a very good negotiator. I had been in the saddle for three days following my horses and we pulled into one of the Helton north pastures. I was exhausted and just wanted to eat and drop into bed. Vic Helton tried to undercut what I thought was a fair price. I got to the point that whenever he opened his mouth, the price went up five dollars." They all burst out laughing. Kelly looked at Colton and he just shrugged.

Two waiters came around with dishes, and Ray offered to fill her plate. She nodded.

"I've been wheeling and dealing with Vic Helton for years now. I always felt like I was paying top dollar for those Angus steers," said Ladd. "I'm glad someone got the better of him." Kelly saw a quick wink from Dottie and she chuckled.

After she had taken a bite of her dinner, Kelly was conscious of one of the men in the black jackets across the table staring at her. Out of the corner of her eye, she saw Ray chatting with Bonnie's father. Kelly leaned forward slightly and looked past Ray to Lola. The younger girl swallowed her bite and then put her left hand flat on the table as she looked at Kelly.

Bonnie smiled and said. "Is there a school nearby? What are you studying right now?"

Lola said, "No, there is not a school nearby. We've been looking for a tutor who will come out to the house and help us. We've been studying Rome's expansion into Germania as well as the French translation of Sun Tzu." The sound of a clanging fork against fine china jerked everyone's attention.

It was the first man in the black jacket with the short dark hair and narrow jaw. "You're studying what? You're just kids. What are you reading that for?"

Kelly felt herself stiffen. Colton started to stand up and Kelly gripped his arm. Lola put down her fork and wiped off her mouth with the soft white napkin. "Excuse me, sir. We haven't been properly introduced."

"Uh, I'm sorry." Ray Ladd stood up nervously. "Kelly, Lola and Colton Stolter, please allow me to introduce Cornel Wilson and Scott Groves. Mr. Wilson and Mr. Groves are law enforcement officers. They're here helping my father."

Slowly, Kelly, Lola and Colton stood up and looked at the men across the table. Grayson Ladd stood up and put his napkin alongside his plate.

"Mr. Wilson and Mr. Groves are in the county investigating unbranded stock. Several of the local ranchers have missing stock. I called them in to investigate."

"I'm sorry, Kelly. I should have introduced them to you earlier. Please sit down." Ray turned to Lola and asked her to sit down.

Grayson Ladd smiled briefly. "Yes, please sit down. There is no need for anyone to be upset. Shall we just enjoy our dinner?" Lola nodded to Kelly and together they all sat back down.

Dottie got the waiter's attention. "Kelly, Lola? Would you like coffee or tea? We have punch and lemonade also."

Kelly said, "Thank you, Dottie. I believe I'd like a cup of coffee right now. Colton will have lemonade." Dottie looked at Lola, who had been staring at Cornel Wilson.

She pulled her gaze to Dottie and smiled. "I'll have lemonade along with Colton, please."

A light conversational buzz started up between Pickering and Ladd. Ray put his hand on Kelly's arm. Bonnie was talking quietly with Scott Groves who had put down his napkin and picked up his whiskey glass.

Kelly looked at Colton who had gone back to eating his dinner. She turned and looked at Ray who looked back at her nervously.

She leaned and whispered in his left ear. "Grownups do stupid things from time to time. It was their turn tonight." Ray let out a sigh of relief and chuckled lightly. He sat back in his chair.

The dinner plates were cleared away. Cornel and Wilson stood up to go out to the porch to smoke. Colton happily selected the chocolate cake from the dessert tray offered. Lola took a small slice of yellow cake with chocolate frosting. Lola talked with Dottie about the baker and technique.

"Ray, I'm taking a wild guess here. Please hear us out." Kelly whispered as she put her hand on the boy's arm and Ray nodded as he leaned closer.

Lola said, "Mr. Cornel and Mr. Wilson are not what they say they are. That's their names. But they are not law enforcement officers."

Ray asked, "How do you know?"

Lola said, "We don't know. It's just a feeling. They don't act or seem like other law enforcement officers we've met."

"Just a minute. What are you talking about?" Bonnie crossed her arms over her body. "I saw their badges. They tried to impress me."

Colton stepped closer to Bonnie and with a lowered voice said, "When you looked at their badges, did you see a number? All law enforcement badges have numbers. It's how they keep track of their officers." The boy pretended to bend and brush something off his pants. Bonnie looked confused.

Lola put her hand on Ray's arm. "Get a good look at them. The way they comb their hair, any scars, limps, mannerisms. If you were walking down the street in Denver and one of them passed you, would you be able to say it was him? Make sure, please?" Ray looked confused.

Ray stood up straight and wrung his hands. "I don't know what to think of this. I don't understand why you'd say such a thing."

Kelly took a deep breath. "Ray, there may be nothing wrong here. It just pays to be careful. If you want me to, I'll speak to your father or Mr. Pickering about this. These two men are on your land. On your ranch. Looking at your stock. Ray, protect what you have."

Ray grimaced like he was in pain and looked at them. "Please, come with me. I'll take you into father's study. You can speak privately with him there." Bonnie followed them into the study where they sat down on the leather sofa. Grayson Ladd and Mr. Pickering opened the door and came in.

"What is going on here? Why did you want to see us?" Ladd frowned as he went to sit behind his desk. Pickering stood next to the fireplace with his cigar.

Kelly took a step forward. "Mr. Ladd. Mr. Pickering. As children left alone by the death of one of our parents, we've come to trust certain individuals who want nothing but the best for us. One of those individuals is Texas Ranger, Henry Elliot." Lola stood up from the sofa and went to stand next to Kelly.

She gripped her small gloved hands together and said, "Mr. Elliot taught us what to look for when someone is being truthful with us and when someone is trying to trick us. We've had to learn the hard way how to watch out for our family. Knowing how to protect our family and to keep us safe is very important to us." Pickering started to speak, but Colton stood up and said, "Mr. Ladd, we see something wrong here. You are our neighbors and a well-known family of honor and respect. It would be wrong of us to not say something about this." Colton went to stand next to Lola. The two men looked at each other with their mouths open. It was Bonnie who spoke.

"Lola, what is this about the numbers? Why should that be bad?" Bonnie spoke with a shaking voice. Pickering moved to put his hand on her shoulder.

"What numbers? What are you talking about?" Ladd shifted his weight in the chair.

Kelly nodded to Lola who said, "Mr. Elliot told us that all law enforcement men have numbers on their badges. It's how the government keeps track of officers. Bonnie could not remember seeing numbers on their badges. Those badges might be fakes. And that means the men are fakes."

Ray said, "So if they are here under false pretenses, why are they here? Where did they come from?" He looked at his father.

"One of the hands recommended them. We're running over five hundred head on the ranch and I was just trying to stop the losses." Ladd stood up shaking his head. He brought his eyes up to Kelly's. Before he could speak, Lola stepped forward and tapped the polished wood desk with her left hand.

"Just by looking at them, they seem like any two men we might find in a restaurant or on a stage. Those two men, Cornel and Wilson? They don't seem as they say." Lola turned and went to sit next to Bonnie who took her hand with a smile.

Ray said, "Lola, you said something to me earlier that made me think. Pa, this is why I came to get you." He gestured with his chin towards the young girl. "She asked if I was walking down the street in Denver and one of them passed me, could I say it was him for sure.”

Pickering looked at Ladd. “What are we supposed to do? Ask for their badges?” Ladd waved a hand.

“Ray, take them out to the living room. Show them the ribbons or something. Just say that we were talking about the possibility of buying a couple of head. Just act like we were talking about stock.” Ray nodded and offered his hand to Kelly. After he had opened the door, he called after the boy.

“Ask your mother to come in here for a minute, would you?” Ray nodded and followed Bonnie out.

Cornel and Wilson were not in the house. Ray let go of Kelly's hand and took a heavy wooden box out of the cabinet. They gathered around the table and watched him described the ribbons. Out of the corner of her eye, she saw Dottie walk carefully into the study and close the door.

Kelly picked up a large, purple, first place ribbon and, stepping next to Ray, held it up as if to discuss it. She whispered, “I'm sorry, Ray. I wanted tonight to be special and happy.” Ray took the ribbon from her hand and laid it back in the box.

“Me, too. Maybe next time, okay?” He smiled and nodded. She grinned.

The study door opened and Dottie came out smiling. She put a hand on the table. “I know you young people don't drink brandy or smoke cigars. Can I get you coffee or more lemonade?” They all laughed.

Kelly said, “Actually, Dottie. I'd like to see your kitchen if that would be alright.” The woman nodded and gestured for them to follow her.

Around the big wooden table, Dottie looked at Colton. “The men are seriously considering what you talked about in the study. I just wanted you to know that.” She smiled and winked as she poured three cups of hot coffee. They idly chatted about the kitchen design and then spent some time going over the heavy French cooking stove.

“Are you alright to get home tonight? I could ride with you, if you'd like.” Ray leaned against the counter with his arms folded over his chest. Kelly turned to look at his muscles and then at his blue green eyes. She lowered her eyes self-consciously.

“No. Considering the situation, we'll swim the horses across the river and cut up the hill. We've ridden that trail over a dozen times and know it fairly well. We'll see anyone following and double back on them.” Kelly took in a deep breath and let it out slowly.

Dottie had a surprised expression. “Oh! You'll ruin that pretty dress! Both your dresses! What a shame.” She pouted.

Lola smiled. “I'm sure that Miss White can fix whatever we mess up. We're not the daintiest of girls so we're used to getting dirty.” Bonnie laughed out loud.

“Pa said this was the first time he's seen me in a dress in months. I'm always in my jeans and sweater and boots." Lola laughed with her.

They all talked and drank coffee. When Ladd and Pickering came in from the study Kelly thanked them for a nice dinner. Ray and Bonnie walked them down to the barn where several lanterns illuminated the yard.

Bonnie called out, "We'll be over next week. I want to see how you work those yearlings, Kelly." Ray held the black mare while Kelly folded the shawl and took out the black sweater. Lola and Colton had put their jackets on and stood as they buckled on their guns.

"Oh! You carry guns!" She watched them as Kelly climbed up into the saddle. Carefully, she buckled the gun belt around herself.

"Yes, pa always said that if anyone tries to kill us, we should try to kill them right back." Colton grinned.

Ray looked up at Kelly for a long moment. "When you live in the west, you live a life of iron and rawhide, I guess."

"That's right. Very right. Thank you again for a nice dinner, Ray and Bonnie. We look forward to seeing you next week." Kelly, Lola and Colton waved as they walked their horses towards the road.

***

The next morning Colton brought in a bound paper pouch and laid it on the table.

"Mail must have come yesterday while we were at the party. This letter is from Mr. Jessup, the man who sold Windy Ridge to Pa."

**

Dear Kelly, Lola and Colton,

I hope my letter finds you all healthy and safe. I've often wondered about you living all the way down there on that big ranch. I hope you have friends to help you with every day things. I have some mail for you that came out to Windy Ridge. You'll have to tell people your new address down there so folks can get in touch with you.

Write back to me and let me know how you are doing.

Sincerely,

Rosamund and Carter Jessup

**

After Kelly read it out loud she handed it to Lola who began reading it. The older sister built up the fire in the stove and put the kettle on to heat water. Lola handed the letter to Colton who laid it on the table and read it carefully.

Kelly looked at the three penny magazines and then handed them to Lola. Lola started to giggle and then she winked at Colton.

"These penny magazines are written by folks in Chicago or New York who have never been past the Mississippi. They don't know what the real west is like. We do. We know." Kelly shook her head as she put loose tea into a mug and poured the hot water in. From a glass jar, she spooned out a heap of sugar and stirred.

"Tomorrow is wash day. If we get the washing done in the morning, it would be dry on the line when we got back home in the afternoon. What other chores need done tomorrow?" Lola looked at Colton and then Kelly.

"I was gonna bake cobbler tomorrow but that can wait. I was thinking of pulling the weeds in the garden but I'll put that off. I need to work those three colts this morning. I feel better when I spend time out with the horses." Kelly looked at the dark liquid in the cup.

"I was going to read more in my book. I was gonna go up to the wash and look for some of those pretty rocks. Nothing important like what you have to do." Lola shrugged.

Colton sat up as he folded up the letter. "Could we stop at the hotel and see if they have any chocolate cake?" He grinned.

"Ohh, cake!" Lola perked up. "I want chocolate cake."

Kelly took a sip of her tea and then set the cup down. "I'd say let's ride in now but I don't like riding home in the dark. Plus, I think we have two dollars in cash right now. Unless we do something to make some money, we'll have to ask Mr. Doyle for money."

Colton stood up and rubbed his face with both hands. "I'll go get the apples if you'll make the pie today, Kelly. I want to get outside for a while."

"Thanks, honey. Yes, I'll make the pie today. I need to work those colts again today for a couple of hours. Right after that, I'll get the crust ready." Kelly smiled at her younger brother and watched him walk out onto the porch.

***

That afternoon the mail man dropped off things into the mailbox.

"Kelly! We have a letter from Dawn White. The lady that made your dress."

Colton yelled as he walked into the house. Kelly trotted down the stairs and held the yellowed envelope.

**

Hello Kelly, Lola and Colton:

I hope my letter finds you well. I talked to Mrs. Lombard out at Beatrice. She charges ten dollars for making the quilt top. Please bundle up the clothing items you want in the quilt. Mike Cushing will deliver your bundle out to Beatrice.

Mrs. Lombard said it would be approximately two weeks to complete it. She will measure, cut and sew the fabrics together. She understands how important this is to you.

Thank you for letting me be a part of this treasure.

Yours,

Dawn White

**

Kelly looked at Lola who sat on the sofa reading. "When is Mike Cushing due to stop by?" Colton ran to the kitchen.

"The calendar says he stops tomorrow on Friday. Where are we going to get ten dollars?"

"I don't know where that money is coming from. We'll have to check on the reward money next time we go to town. I' m sure Mr. Doyle can give us ten dollars but I would rather not ask for any money from him," said Kelly as she put her hair up in a ponytail.

"Alright. Colton, any clothes that are too small for you, bring them down here. That includes anything you've torn up and we cannot mend." Kelly looked at her sister. "Lola, you too. I'll go get two of ma's dresses for the quilt."

In one of the big trunks, Kelly pulled out the tissue papers and the small leather pouches, laying them aside. With a flood of emotion, her hands held up the faded, light yellow dress with small pink and green flowers. It was paper thin. At that moment, Kelly realized that her mother had been going without buying a new dress or making herself another.

Colton came in and sat down on the floor next to the trunk. "Ma used to wear that one on wash day." Kelly nodded.

"You're right. I remember now." Kelly thought for a moment. "You know, honey. She wore jeans and slacks when she rode and worked with the horses. But here in the house, she always wore a dress." Colton nodded.

"Which other one, Colton? There are five dresses here. You pick the other dress for the quilt."

Colton shook his head. "I want to put in two of her shirts. There's the black and red plaid shirt she used to wear when she rode. That's a good one. And that dark green one she wore when she worked out in the garden. Use those instead of the dresses."

"That's a good idea." Lola walked in and leaned against the bed frame.

"That way, Kelly, if you ever want to wear one of ma's dresses, they're still there for you."

Kelly handed the long-sleeved, forest green shirt to Colton. After she hunted in the right side of the trunk she pulled out the worn red plaid shirt. "I've never thought about wearing one of ma's dresses. I've thought about saving them, but not wearing them." Lola nodded.

"As long as we remember her, she'll never be truly gone, Kelly. A little bit of her lives on in all of us, because we are her children," said Lola with a hushed voice. Kelly smiled and hugged Colton.

Faintly, they heard Dusty bark a few times and then go quiet. Then he barked again. Colton and Lola trotted down the stairs while Kelly put everything back into the trunk and shoved it back up against the wall.

***

When Kelly came out onto the patio, she could see Colton and Kelly running towards the front gate. Kelly stepped up on the column to see a man on a horse holding a large envelope up in his hand. He talked for a few minutes and then Colton turned and started running back to the house.

"It's a special delivery letter from someone in Mississippi. It cost a whole dollar, Kelly. We have to pay before he'll give us the letter." Colton's face was flushed and his eyes were wide with excitement. Kelly went into the kitchen and took the small jar down from the cupboard. He put four coins into Colton's hand and the boy raced out of the house and back down the driveway.

Kelly could see the rider accept the coins and hand the envelope to Lola. The man rode away and Kelly became impatient watching the two siblings walking slowly back up the driveway. They were grabbing the envelope back and forth.

Lola called out, "It's a big, long name of an attorney in Hattiesburg, Mississippi. It looks important." At the top step Lola handed the envelope to Kelly. The letter was addressed to Nicholai Stolter, Kelly Stolter, Lola Stolter and Colton Stolter.

"Can we open it or does only Pa open it?" Colton climbed up onto the back of the stone bench.

Kelly frowned. "It is from a lawyer. There is probably something in here that we don't understand." Lola snorted.

"In case you don't understand, Kelly. We have one of the best libraries

231

in the west in this house. I'll bet there is a book in that library that can explain anything in that letter we don't understand."

"Who do we know in Hattiesburg?" They were all quiet in thought for a moment.

"It can't be any of ma's family. They were all from here. That Clay Richardson was from St. Louis," said Kelly.

"Stop." Lola had a troubled look on her face. Her eyes were wide. "Kelly, you and I know someone from Hattiesburg. We met him and he bought those two horses."

Kelly's face lit up with recognition. "Dunbarton. Mick Dunbarton. He said his permanent home was in Hattiesburg. But why would an attorney be writing to us about Mick Dunbarton?"

Colton played with a small twig in his hands. "Should we ride into Bradford and let Mr. Doyle open it and tell us what it means?" Kelly nodded.

"I think so. Folks don't like trying to explain complicated things to kids like us. But Mr. Doyle is our attorney and he is obligated to explain stuff." Kelly nodded. "Come in the house. Let's open it up. We'll see who wants what."

In the study, they gathered around the table. With a sharp knife, Lola carefully sliced open one end and slid out five sheets of crisp white paper. She spread them side by side on the table.

"Alexander Hylton Lamotte, esquire, attorney at law. What does that mean?" Kelly looked at the letterhead. "Alright. That's our first question, Lola. Find out what esquire means behind someone's name." Kelly grinned.

Colton peered at one of the sheets and asked, "What is a last will and testament?"

Kelly said, "That's like when someone dies, it tells everyone what to do with their things. Who died?"

Lola shoved one of the sheets to Kelly. "Read the letter! Tell us what this is!" Kelly began to read out loud.

**

'Dear Mr. Nicholai Stolter, Kelly Stolter, Lola Stolter and Colton Stolter:

It is my sorry duty to inform you of the untimely passing of Mr. Winchester McKinley Dunbarton. Per his requests in his recently changed last will and testament, I must notify you of the following.'

**

"Mick Dunbarton died!" Kelly's face had a look of shock and her mouth hung open. She exchanged a look with Lola who also looked stunned.

"He's dead?" Lola sounded incredulous.

"Notify us of what, Kelly? Read it." Colton nudged Kelly's shoulder.

"Mr. Dunbarton passed away without a spouse or heirs. Per his last will and testament, Mr. Dunbarton has ordered certain distributions from his estate.

**

"Essentially, the children, Kelly Stolter, Lola Stolter and Colton Stolter are now owners of the lands and properties from the estate of Mr. Winchester McKinley Dunbarton.

Mr. Nicholai Stolter is hereby appointed guardian and trustee of and for Kelly Stolter, Lola Stolter and Colton Stolter until at which time they gain majority. At the time of their majority, each child will receive one third of the real estate holdings from the estate of Mr. Winchester McKinley Dunbarton."

**

"It lists out five places I've never heard of. We get to figure out those, too." Kelly showed Lola the list.

Colton said, "Wait. Mick Dunbarton died and this paper says he is giving his things to people? Is that what a will is?"

Lola said, "I don't understand what one third means. I don't know what majority means. This is making my head hurt. I've got too many things to look up now." She rubbed her forehead.

"The letter ends with telling Pa to contact Alexander Hylton Lamotte, esquire, attorney at law to receive all the details."

Kelly laid the sheet down and stared at the will and the lists. Why would Mick Dunbarton include them in his will? What land and properties?

Lola said, "There are a dozen books on law in the library. Maybe I can find a dictionary or encyclopedia on this. Colton, come help me so this will go faster. And Kelly, there's something else I just remembered."

Kelly grimaced and rubbed her face with her hands. "What did you remember?"

Lola frowned. "Mary Rideout knows a lot more about Mick Dunbarton than she wanted us to know. I could feel it. She almost screamed when we said his name. Something happened between Mick Dunbarton and Glen and Anna-Marie. Mary won't tell us. We'll have to have Mr. Doyle go talk to her and ask her what she knows."

"You're right. I remember that." Kelly nodded. "What if she won't tell?" Lola looked at the floor.

"Then we'll never know what she knows. We'll just have to go on from there. Mr. Doyle seems like he is very thorough. If we have questions, he'll try to find answers." Kelly looked at Lola looking back at her. "Kelly, go put water on to heat for coffee. We might be a while finding some answers.

The rifling of books and encyclopedias brought nothing but more questions and frustration. Finally, they saddled up and trotted down the road to Bradford.

***

It was close to two o'clock when they tied the horses up in front of the two-story building. The door to the attorney's office was locked. Colton tried to look under the door but the interior was dark.

"He's not in there."

Kelly said, "Okay, let's try the hotel and then the saloon."

It was at the bar in Goldman's saloon where they found the attorney talking with another man. "Excuse us, Mr. Doyle. We don't have an appointment but we'd like a few minutes of your time." Doyle looked at them.

"What's this about? You don't have another dead body, do you?" Doyle, the bartender and the other man laughed and then saw the children were not laughing.

Lola squinted, "Not exactly." Doyle let out a big sigh and fished a coin out of his vest pocket. After he put it on the bar, he walked towards the door.

"Come with me."

They stepped off the boardwalk into the street and moved towards the two-story building. "What is this about?"

Lola said, "We want to find out more about Mick Dunbarton."

Doyle abruptly stopped and looked at them. "Dunbarton? The man who bought those two horses? What do you want to know?"

Doyle slid the key to his office door into the lock and they went in. Dust mites floated in the streams of sunlight that shone in through the window. The children went to the long leather sofa and sat down. Doyle looked at them and frowned.

Kelly took off her gloves, "Did you know that he died recently?"

Doyle shook his head, "No, I did not. I don't normally keep up on deaths unless they are local. Why?"

Lola lolled a foot back and forth idly. "Would you tell us what you know about him?" Doyle frowned and sat down behind his desk.

After a moment, he drummed his fingers on his desk. "Well, right off the top of my head I can tell you that Dunbarton is a renowned building contractor. He takes on projects and builds them where other people won't even try. His company built the Edgefield Bridge over the Cumberland River. Beautiful bridge. He also put up that Frankfort, Kentucky suspension bridge. I know he built the big High Falls Aqueduct in New York State. That brings water down out of Canada, I believe."

Colton sat up and looked hard at Doyle. "So, he built things?"

"Yes, he did. The U.S. Army Corp of Engineers would go survey here in the west and Dunbarton's company followed behind them building the roads. I read a newspaper article where he was engineering for a bridge across San Francisco Bay. It was doubtful that such a long bridge should be built. Folks said that if anyone could build it, Dunbarton could do it."

"So, he also built bridges?" Colton again watched Doyle closely.

"He had a company that put up tall buildings. New York, Chicago, St. Louis. His bridge companies did the bridges. He also had a roads and highway building company. That's just here in America. He built roads and bridges in Scotland, England, and Germany. He even worked with the Mexican government to build that big road from Sonora up through Angels Camp."

Doyle held up both hands. "Stop. Now you tell me what is going on here. Why the inquiry on Mick Dunbarton?"

Kelly looked at Lola and Colton. She stood up and took out the long envelope from the inside pocket of her jacket and handed it to Doyle. He immediately frowned at the address and slid out all the papers. It was only seconds after he read the third page.

"God in heaven."

Doyle's face went wide in surprise. The children were silent as they watched him read through the pages twice. The attorney looked at them strongly and then read the sheets again.

Before Doyle could utter a word, Kelly held up a hand. Slowly and carefully, she told the attorney about their suspicions and the odd reaction of Mary Rideout. Doyle nodded as he straightened the pages and put them back down. He shook his head and rubbed his face.

"You children are old enough and smart enough to understand a lot about what I'm going to tell you. If you don't, just stop me and I'll help. Understand?" Doyle stood up and went to the cabinet and brought out three shining clear glasses. From the covered pitcher, he poured water for them and gestured for them to take the glasses.

Doyle took in a deep breath. "Mick Dunbarton believed you three to be his last blood relations. His grandchildren. That's the only explanation that fits this. His estate is worth millions of dollars and it looks like most of it went to charity, not to strangers."

Lola asked, "What does that mean?"

"It means that your mother's father was not Glen Richardson. It was most likely, Mick Dunbarton. I don't know why Anna-Marie did not marry Dunbarton and ended up marrying Glen Richardson. All the people who know the answers to these questions are dead now. Well, except Mary

Rideout. And unless Anna-Marie had secretly confided directly to Mary Rideout, what she knows is pure supposition. A guess, in other words."

Kelly said, "So we are both Mick Dunbarton's grandchildren and Glen Richardson's too?" Doyle shook his head.

"The law says that when a baby is born in a marriage, the husband is the legal father. Legally, you are all descendants of Glen Richardson. However, Mick Dunbarton has declared that you are his last blood relations and claiming you as his grandchildren. That means that Anna-Marie had to have told him that your mother, Marianna Richardson, was Dunbarton's daughter."

Colton said, "So why did nobody tell us?"

Doyle leaned back in his chair. "It would have caused a scandal for the Richardson family. It would have brought shame on Anna-Marie and Marianna. They would have been shut out from the local community. People would have talked behind their hands about Glen. Nobody talks about this sort of thing in a family. It was kept quiet."

Kelly rubbed her forehead. "In one of ma's small boxes in her trunk, there was a letter with a picture of a man. It said to find a man named Mick Dunbarton and ask him to tell you about himself."

Doyle nodded. "I would say that probably when Anna-Marie knew she was about to die, she had time to tell your mother, Marianna, about her natural father. Your mother would have known all these years. That letter was probably written by Anna-Marie to your mother."

Lola said, "So for us to run into him on that stagecoach at that time was pure accident. With all the thousands of miles of roads in the west, he ended up within ten feet of us that day."

Kelly sounded sad. "And right then, to find out that we were in fact, his grandchildren. That must have been a shock. No wonder he wanted to talk to us for so long."

"I was within arms' reach of my grandfather and didn't know it. And I'll never get to see him again. I just had one of the best chances in my life go right on by and I didn't know it." A tear slid down Lola's cheek. Kelly hugged her shoulders.

Doyle went to a built-in cabinet and brought out folded, white handkerchiefs. "I believe that Mick Dunbarton was never able to acknowledge his daughter, Marianna, in life. But now in death, he can not only acknowledge her, but provide for his only grandchildren, you."

Kelly wiped her eyes. "What do we do now? I feel changed somehow. I'm confused."

Doyle tapped the sheets laying on the desk. "The three of you have just come in to land, properties, bank accounts, businesses and I don't know what all. As soon as everything is settled in a court of law, I'll bring it all out to the ranch and make sure you understand about it. I need to send a letter as your attorney back to Hattiesburg to this attorney and let him know we received it. I'll send that out by courier on the train today. It will get to Hattiesburg in three days. I'll get a disposition on the rest of the estate and find out what is being done." Doyle sat down on the front edge of his desk.

"Let me say this. I want you to listen carefully. You are still the loved children of Marianna Richardson Stolter and Nicholai Stolter. Your family loves you very much and wants the best for you. For all intents and purposes, you are still Richardsons, and legally, the descendants of Glen Richardson. That will never change."

Colton asked, "What are these real estate holdings in the letter? What are those?" Doyle paged through the stack and pulled out the list.

"There is his personal home in Hattiesburg. It is a farm and a ranch with several hundred acres. It will have to be surveyed before we know the exact size. The Triple Flush Ranch north of San Antonio is a large cattle ranch. By large, I mean five thousand head of beef on the hoof. There is also a hacienda style estate north of Santa Fe and that will have to be surveyed. I've read reports that it is an operating horse ranch, but I'm not up to date. There is a house listed in Los Angeles and a house listed in San Francisco." The attorney watched them for a moment.

"When your father comes home, we will go over all of this and make any needed decisions to protect these properties," said Doyle. He cleared his throat and took a drink of water.

"Mr. Doyle, our mother died. And now we find out our grandfather died. This is too much death." Lola rubbed her eyes.

"Yes, I know. But your father is still alive. And, he is on his way home. That's the important part. He is alive and coming home. Everything will get a lot better for you once he comes home. Just remember that."

Colton stood up. "I want to go home." Kelly nodded. Lola stood up.

Doyle said, "I'd be happy to buy you dinner at the hotel before you ride home, if you'd like."

"I want to stop at the Faraway Inn and talk to Max. I want pie." Colton picked his hat up off the table. Doyle nodded.

Doyle put his thumbs into his vest pockets. "There's another thing I want to warn you about. I'm sure someone will go snooping around this will of Mr. Dunbarton's and see that you three are named as beneficiaries. Once someone dies, it's not private anymore. You may get folks coming out to the ranch and trying to sell you things or get you to sell those properties to them. I want you to do me a favor, if people show up." Doyle started to chuckle.

"Please don't shoot them. Just shoot over their heads and scare them off. Play like you don't know what they are talking about." Kelly shook her head with slight smile.

At the door to the office, Doyle said, "And you'd be smart to not discuss this with a lot of people. You can avoid questions that make you uncomfortable if you keep this to yourself."

Colton shook hands with the attorney. "I'd like to know how he died, Mr. Doyle. And where."

"The minute I get more answers for you, I'll come out to the ranch." The attorney put his hand on Colton's shoulder. "Be strong for your sisters, Colton."

That evening, the three of them sat in front of the fire in the outdoor fireplace, quietly thinking. Kelly watched the trees gently wave in the late breeze. A flock of small birds darted in and out of the grass near the yard fence.

It had been less than an hour in his presence, yet as she thought back over the encounter, Kelly remembered the genuine friendliness in the eyes and in the smile of Mick Dunbarton. She resolved to hunt through his businesses and find a portrait that could be hung in the house next to her mother's.

Two days later, Colton came running into the house. Kelly looked up from the table at the boy. "There's two men at the gate asking for Glen. You better come," he said panting. Kelly pulled her boots on. Lola ran after her.

"Miss, my name is Montana Clayton and this here is Jefferson Sterrit. If Glen Richardson is home, I'd like to say hello." Clayton's jeans were faded black and patched. They were tucked into tall run down tan boots. Sterrit wore torn and mended denim jeans. The sleeves of his red plaid shirt were torn off at the elbows and soiled black and brown gloves covered his hands.

"Howdy, Mr. Clayton. My name is Kelly Stolter and this is my sister, Lola and my brother, Colton. My mother, who passed away recently, was the daughter of Glen Richardson. I'm sorry to tell you that Glen died almost nine years ago now, Mr. Clayton." Kelly shielded her eyes from the bright overhead sun.

Both men's shoulders slumped and they looked at the ground. "I'm right sorry to hear that. He was a good man, miss. Hard at times, but fair and I trusted him. I'm sorry for your loss."

Sterrit said, "Glen was more than fair to me. Seemed like he was always helping me out of one jam or another. I was hoping to see him again." The man's grizzled beard hung in tattered strands. His icy blue eyes held a steady gaze.

"Thank you, Mr. Clayton, Mr. Sterrit. Please, water your horses at the trough by the barn. We don't have a lot, but you are welcome to a plate of chili and cornbread if you are hungry."

Clayton took off his hat in thanks. "That's right kind of you, Miss. We'll come to the house after we see to the horses." His light brown hair was trimmed short.

Kelly and Lola brought out two plates with bubbling hot chili with beans and set them on the round wood table on the porch. Colton put down the pate of cornbread and went back into the house. The young boy brought out a small pot of coffee and two heavy ceramic mugs and poured the black liquid.

Lola asked, "How far have you traveled, Mr. Clayton?"

Clayton took a sip of the coffee and swallowed. "We spent the winter up in the Imperial Valley working a big horse ranch. It was good not to freeze in the ice and snow for a change. Before that we were up in the Pacific Northwest working on a timber crew with a team of draft horses. We saw the geese flying south so we left with them."

Kelly, Lola and Colton began telling them about life in Yucca Valley. Sterrit waved his spoon. "I seen your ma riding a champ cutting horse up at the Denver Rodeo one year. There was maybe four young women who were all neck and neck racing for the ribbon. Your ma won it. Glen was rightly proud."

Lola said, "That was the year she met my pa at that rodeo. They used to tell us those rodeo stories." All the children smiled.

The children spent more than a few minutes describing how the tall stranger came in one day and talked Nick into going out on a job. Kelly frowned as she watched the two men look at each other sideways and then look away. Lola was the first to speak plainly.

"Mr. Clayton, Mr. Sterrit, we lost our ma. We know there is a good chance our pa may never come back. We don't know where he is or even if he is dead or alive." The two men turned and looked at Lola. "But we are smart and have good folks helping us."

Colton spoke up. "Our ma and pa taught us how to keep a roof over our head and food in our bellies. On the morning she died, ma told us that pa would move heaven and earth to get back to us. So, we must believe that he will come back. Someday. Somehow." Sterrit and Clayton leaned back to listen to the young boy.

For a few minutes, the two men stared out into the darkness. Sterrit grimaced and rubbed his face. Just as he opened his mouth to say something, Kelly spoke.

"Folks have told us some troubling things about the man my pa rode away with. Other folks have told us that our pa could not be safer with anyone else." Kelly walked over to the railing and looked out into the darkness. She fidgeted with a button on her shirt and then turned back to look at the men.

"You can bed down in the old bunkroom in the far barn when you're done with dinner. We've got a couple of spare quilts you can use. Please don't go wandering around in the dark as you might fall down and hurt yourself." The men looked puzzled.

"If you're gonna be here tomorrow, there are a couple of things we'd appreciate your help with." Both men stood up as they wiped their mouths off on the soft blue cloths.

"We were aiming to stay up at the camp up on the ridge that I remember from years ago. I'll say though that a bunkroom sounds a bit more comfortable than hard ground." Sterrit nodded.

Clayton stopped and caught Kelly's eye. "Thank you for the hot food, Miss. We can stay and help you out with whatever chores you got, Miss. We sorta owe Glen that. We don't got to be anywhere until October and then we should be in Brownsville, Texas for the winter." The man's words came out in a nervous spiel.

Kelly smiled and then gestured to the table. "Colton, take the lantern out to the barn so these men can see what they're doing. Lola, go get those two quilts out of that upstairs bedroom and take them down to the barn. I will clean up the plates and put things away for the night." Later, when Colton came in the front door, Lola asked him if the men had said anything to him.

The boy nodded. "They said they were sorry they didn't know Grandpa Glen was dead. You got a feel for them, Lola?"

"It is kind of sad. They are just two old men who knew Grandpa many years ago. Like old people know other old people. They're moving on. They'll go to Texas and stay there until they pass away," she said. She frowned with a grimace and then shook her head.

Kelly held a damp towel from the dishes. "Anything else?"

"They've been everywhere. They have seen the great rivers, snow up in the mountains, and herds of elk and moose. They've seen both oceans. They have been wandering mostly their whole lives," Lola's voice broke and lowered as she turned away.

Kelly sat down at the table and watched Lola. "Is something wrong with them, Lola? Are they sick or hurt in some way?" The younger girl shook her head.

"They've done everything that I want to do. And I'm not old enough to go do those things. Yet. Kelly, I'll tell you this. I love you and Colton and Pa, but there will come a day when I pack up my horse and go. Just like those men have done. There are things that I want to go do and part of me is afraid I won't live long enough to do it all."

Colton hugged Lola. Kelly smiled watching her brother and sister. Deep inside her, she had known that there was something ma called wanderlust inside of Lola. But it was years away.

The next morning was spent bucking up length of downed alders, spruce and birch on the east hills. Five wagonloads came down to the south side of the barn where the splitter awls and axes were sharpened. A half cord of firewood was stacked against the barn by midday with the short logs piled to one side.

Colton said, "We should put in a dozen more posts into that corral near the small barn and enlarge it. It's the strongest, I'd say." Kelly nodded.

Sterrit and Clayton went out and helped tear out the rotten posts and marked with new posts should be put in. After the meal on the patio the twenty post holes were dug out and the straight alder posts sank for the new corral south of the barn. Sterrit went with Colton up to the hunting blind to help secure it and reinforce the plank trestle. He showed the boy where to set rabbit traps and how to loop the snares.

Clayton caught and killed one of the chickens which Kelly cleaned and put into the oven to bake along with root vegetables. They baked an apple pie. When Sterrit came in the front door he held a small leather packet in his hands.

He showed Kelly how to divide the sticky dough in half, wrapping the saved part back up in the leather pouch. To the small portion he added more flour, a few drops of water, a little butter, salt and an egg.

"Ma used to make bread every Saturday. I never paid much attention. We just sort of got along without when we moved here to Flint Hills. It's funny, too. Because when we go to Bradford, we like to eat all the bread in the hotel restaurant with butter and berry jam," said Kelly.

Clayton's dark eyes twinkled when he chuckled. "I used to eat the same thing all the time when I was staying in one place. I'd find the best tasting thing to eat and just stick with it. You need bread, though. Sometimes there's nothing like a good piece of bread."

Lola said, "Ma used to put butter and a sprinkle of sugar on a slice of bread and send me outside to eat it. I'd be a pest to her and she'd give me bread to get me out from under her feet."

Colton smiled and said, "I remember Pa putting a big piece of bread on his plate and ma pouring that beef gravy over it. He used to sit there and get it in his mustache and beard. I'd laugh at him and he'd wink at me." The kids grinned at each other sharing the memory.

Two days later all the chores had been done and Clayton and Sterrit sat up on their horses just before sun up. The three children sat on the stony ridge on the patio.

Clayton waved. "Keep a loaf of that bread on the counter. We might ride through again sometime." The children waved as they watched the two men walk the horses down the driveway towards the road.

***

The next day the mailman handed over three newspapers, two magazines, and one letter. It was a grimy, brown envelope with scribbled handwriting.

**

Dear Kelly, Lola and Colton,

I've made it to Yuma with the horses. I had some trouble and I'll tell you all about it when I get home. I'm in one piece but banged up and I could sleep for a week. I've made some good friends, gotten help from folks and caught a couple of lucky breaks.

I got your telegram about moving to Flint Hills. I don't know why you did that and don't understand what led you to that decision, but I'm sure you will find it is your home. We will all be happy there.

I've got 14 good horses that I'm bringing with me. They will need to be put in a big corral until we can get them branded so make those preparations. There is a lot of work to do with them.

I'm sorry beyond words about your ma. I've lost the love of my life and it will never be the same again. I just hope she was not in pain and had time to tell you the important things.

I'm going to put this letter on the stage headed to Bradford. Someone will bring it to you.

Remember to take care of each other and that I love you and I'm coming home,

Your loving father,

Nick Stolter

**

"He made it all the way to Yuma. How long is it gonna be before he gets here?" Colton danced around the patio.

Kelly said, "I would say six days, if he can make fifteen miles a day with those horses. That means we've six days to put the supplies in for those fourteen head. We'll need grain, hay and plenty of water."

"We'll need to fall six of those fir trees and make posts. We need to make rails. This is a job for Clay Dunagan. We can do a lot of it, but the heavy stuff will have to be done by someone who is stronger. We need to figure out the waterholes between Flint Hills and Yuma. Clay can help us with those, too.

"So, can we get a telegram to Pa? Is there some way that he'll get it?" Lola held the letter in her hand.

"I don't see how. We plain have to wait. We stay home, get ready, and keep watch. He is counting on us." Kelly looked at Lola and Colton, then walked into the house followed by her siblings.

In the study, she pulled out a sheet of the rough brown paper and began a calendar list. She put the pencil down and took in a deep breath, letting it back out slowly. Their lives had changed beyond her imagination. And it was changing still.

They had bought another sofa, chair and several rugs. The house seemed like they had always been there. In such a short time, it had gone from being just a house to live in to a home where they lived. Now that her father was so close to riding through the front gate, it was even more of a home.

***

The three children leaned on the corral rails and watched Dunagan heat a horseshoe in the glowing red forge in Bradford.

"We don't have an outside chute at the corral. There probably was one there at one time, but I don't even see where it could have been. I don't know how to build one. We've got a dozen good fir posts, but need the boards and rails."

Dunagan put the shoe into the bucket of water and steam hissed off the surface. With the back of his left hand he wiped off his cheek. "So, you want a chute that leads to the pasture, not to another corral?" Kelly nodded.

"The letter we got from pa. It says for us to prepare for him to come home with a herd. He's bringing in fourteen head and I'd like to get them looked over before they mix in with our horses." Kelly watched the blacksmith fish out the shoe from the tub and lay it on the anvil. Dunagan fidgeted with the heavy pliers for a moment.

"There is one problem, Mr. Dunagan. We're out of cash right now. So, I was wondering if you would consider taking one of the horses as payment." Kelly held her breath.

Gray blue eyes flitted from child to child. "I can come out tomorrow and get the posts set in for you. Out here alongside the shop, I've got a stack of some knotty boards that were milled for a house. They weren't good enough for a house but I'd say they'd be right good on that chute."

"We'll settle up after everything is done. I can always use another horse around the stables." The man winked at Kelly.

Kelly felt as if a sack of grain had been lifted off her shoulders. She said, "Thank you, Mr. Dunagan. I'll make sure to have those posts stacked close to where that chute will be."

The tall, lean man shifted his weight to his other foot. "I was over to Yuma last month. It's a ninety-mile ride, give or take. You got something to write with? You need to take this down," Dunagan gestured to Lola. The young girl went to her saddle bag and pulled out a small notebook. She walked back and boosted herself up onto the wooden table and took out the pencil.

Dunagan reached over and quickly tweaked her nose making her laugh. "Coming out of Yuma, he'll most likely stop at Jasper Carr. Outside of Yuma there are camps set back in the trees, back up into the hills where people stay. Jasper Carr might be the safest for him." Dunagan directed Lola to draw a line from the far-left hand side to the right edge and make black cross lines along it.

The grimy finger tapped the rough map. "His next stop might be a couple of small waterholes on the south of the road. One is a camp used by the Mexicans that ride through. If he doesn't stop, he'll move the herd on to La Jolla Rojo, the red jewel. It would be a good place to bed down for the night."

Colton asked, "Is La Jolla Rojo a ranch?"

Dunagan nodded. "Used to be. It was abandoned years ago."

"Wait a minute. On the way down from Yucca Valley, we came through a couple of water holes. Set back to one side was a Mexican camp with a family. They were travelling. Is that what you mean?" Again, Dunagan nodded.

"If he can push them horses good enough he can roll into Nuevo Vargas right after dark. It depends on if he gets up and rides at daylight. What do you think your pa would do?"

Kelly was quiet for a moment as she turned over a small stone in her fingers. "He'd still be four days out so he won't push the herd. If he's hurt, he's going to stop right there. I just don't know how well he remembers the road."

Dunagan took the pencil and made a long wavy line to the next cross mark. "The road from Vargas to Camino Pequeno is full of twists and turns. There's a lot of trees and brush grown up on both sides of the road. When the stages come through that stretch they tell the passengers to arm themselves and be alert. I'm not saying that it's dangerous, but that is the one place on the road where he might run into trouble."

Colton said, "When we brought the herd down from Yucca Valley, we came through a couple of places where the road was only wide enough for a single wagon. There was a lot of thick brush along there."

Lola held out her hand to take back the pencil. She drew in a wavy circle on the north side of the road. Dunagan nodded.

"From Camino Pequeno, he'll veer in off the desert and move up onto a set of mesas. He can see for a couple miles in all directions. He'll be able to see if anyone is coming up behind him. He just has to watch that the string doesn't start stretching out. Some of them horses will like to slow down and want to stop. He'll have to push 'em."

An older woman walked her horse to the corral and dismounted. Dunagan went to help her. Kelly leaned over Lola's shoulder to look at the small map. The blacksmith came back and rinsed off his hands in the bucket. He paused to roll a cigarette.

Dunagan blew gray smoke up into the air. "From your place, going east on the road nine miles, there's springs that broaden out into a water hole on the south side of the road. Folks have been clearing it out and maintaining it for years. Your pa knows that waterhole is there because he used to live here. He'll pull those horses in and make sure they get plenty of water."

Kelly asked, "So you think he'll put them into a run straight to the gate?" Dunagan nodded.

"It's been fifteen years since he was at Flint Hills. It might be dark or close to it. You can make it easier on him and mark that gate with some whitewash. Maybe put up a couple torches on those posts. Let him know that you're there and ready." Dunagan put his hand flat on the little map to get their attention.

"Now here's the touchy part. If anyone has been reading your telegrams back and forth, they know he's headed for Flint Hills. He may have been in a fight and be wounded somehow when he comes riding through that gate."

Lola sat up straight. "So, we should prepare bandages in case he's hurt?" Dunagan nodded as he exhaled smoke.

"Yes, ride up on the mesa and cut up a couple of those aloe cacti for the salve. There ain't nothing you can do if he needs stitches. The doctor will have to take a look at him."

Kelly rubbed her forehead with a grimace. "Lola, you and Colton can ride up there and get a dozen pieces of that aloe vera plant." The kids nodded and scribbled down notes.

Dunagan sat on the edge of the table next to Lola. "I've seen it happen where outlaws will chase someone right up into their own yard. Gunfire, shooting, lassoing. On Friday morning before dawn, you'll want to position yourselves down near your front gate. Someone rides in after your pa shooting, you gotta shoot to knock them down. I'd say your pa is counting on you being ready that way." Dunagan shrugged.

Colton said, "That's it? That's all we can do?"

Dunagan nodded again. "He wouldn't take those horses off the main road. It would slow him down. Now, you three, get yourselves some food and ride for home. I'll be over tomorrow early and we'll get those posts in."

Half an hour later the Stolters trotted east, headed for home.

***

True to his word, Clay Dunagan pulled into the yard right as the first rays of light hit the tree tops around the house. The long wagon carried the lumber and building tools. Kelly and Colton ran down the steps and guided Dunagan out to the barn. The builder walked back to the house and accepted a cup of hot coffee as he laid out the drawing of the chute.

It was noon and all the posts had been set into the rich, dark earth. Dunagan showed them how to start nailing on the boards, starting at the bottom row. The tops of the trees were burning red and gold in the last gleams of sunlight. The heavy iron hinges were nailed on for the gate.

After a dinner of beef stew and cornbread, Dunagan hugged Colton. He tried to put on a serious grimace as he shook hands with Lola and Kelly and then ended up hugging them tightly.

"I've come to know you kids a bit better than I know some adults around these parts. I'm not gonna sugar-coat my words here. There's a good chance you Pa has run into trouble coming home. In fact, if he's been riding through from Tucson, he's probably caught the eye of an outlaw or two." Dunagan coughed and wiped his mouth.

Colton said, "We thought the same thing, Mr. Dunagan."

Dunagan nodded and ruffled Colton's hair. "Take your guns into Stenson tomorrow. Get them cleaned and make sure they are all ready. Make sure you have fifty, sixty rounds for each weapon in case you get into a gunfight. Your pa is going to need sleep and rest for a couple of days. Don't make him have to get up and go out to do chores."

Colton rode with Dunagan on the wagon down to the gate. Dunagan stopped the horses long enough for the boy to climb up onto the fence. Kelly stood on the patio and watched her younger brother waving as the blacksmith drove away.

***

That morning, Kelly found Lola and Colton wrapped up together in a quilt on the patio near the crackling fireplace. They stared at the front gate where nothing moved but a couple of tall cypress in the light wind.

"How long have you two been down here?"

Colton rubbed his eyes. "I had nightmares. I couldn't sleep. I asked Lola to make a fire out here for me." Lola shrugged and turned back to watching the gate.

Kelly pulled her heavy sweater tighter around her. She put another two pieces of wood into the fire and watched the flames lick around the wood.

"People have tended to leave us alone in the last few weeks. Is something or someone coming, Lola?" The younger sister yawned then frowned.

"No. It's all quiet out there. North back to the ridge. East out to the mesa. Even south up over the hill and down to the river. Nothing is moving, except the grass in the wind." Kelly twisted around to look at her sister.

"According to the books of Lewis and Clark, there was a time when there were no more than five thousand people west of the Mississippi. They were all scattered over the territories all the way to the Pacific." Lola unwrapped the quilt and stood up. Then she turned and wrapped the blanket around Colton. The young girl went to stand next to the fire with Kelly. She put her arm around her sister and pulled her close.

"People were alone here back then. There were no towns or buildings. Weeks and months could go by without seeing another human being," Lola said with a quiet voice. "Right now, right here, maybe this is like it was back then."

"And it will never be that quiet again. The stages bring them. The trains bring them. They get off ships in the harbors. More people, more noise." Lola watched the fire burn for a few moments.

"Years from now, we'll remember back to this hour. The quiet, the feel of the wind, the smell of the fire burning as we waited for pa to come through that gate. We may be right here or we might be on the other side of the world. Something will remind us of this time right here, right now," Lola said.

The darkened sky had begun to lighten. Gray became a shade of blue, then lighter with pink streaks as the day claimed the horizon.

"I'll start coffee. I think we have a couple pieces of ham and a few eggs, when you're hungry."

Colton turned around. "Can you make pancakes, Kelly? It feels like pancakes this morning." His sister nodded.

"Yep. I can make pancakes." She smiled and went into the house.

31 KEEPING BUSY

The morning was spent hauling in three downed trees. Kelly strapped the heavy harness on the dun gelding and dragged two alder and part of an old oak to the small barn. Dunagan had shown them how to use a set of steel wedges to split the logs at weak points. They managed to stack half a cord into the wood shelter.

They pulled weeds in the garden and braced the small fence. It took an hour to put all the tools away.

In the early afternoon, the delivery wagon from the store arrived and they unloaded the sacks and supplies into the barn and the house.

"This is probably going to be the last chance I get to dig in the river for a while. Is there anything else you want me to do? Any other chores?" Colton leaned against the kitchen counter. Kelly shook her head.

"No, honey. I think we've got done as much as we can. I can't think of anything else. Go dig in the river." Kelly patted his shoulder.

Colton took a couple of steps towards the door. "What're you gonna do?"

"I've have two of my shirts to mend. Lola ripped the hem in one of her nightgowns. I'm going to make coffee and get that done." Kelly grinned.

"Lola's reading. She's almost got that French book done. I guess it's harder than she thought it was." Colton shrugged. Kelly watched the boy lift the small canvas bag of tools off the porch and trot across the yard.

Kelly went to get the sewing basket. Two of her shirts needed rips mended and buttons replaced. With a cup of coffee, she sat at the kitchen table guiding the slender silver needle into the fabric.

It felt like a storm approaching, but the sky was clear. They had tried to prepare for a big change coming to their lives and done everything they knew how to do.

That night as she laid in bed, her eyes would not close to sleep. She tossed and turned and every small sound in the big house made her sit up and listen. It was the hoot of an owl jerking her awake that let her know she had finally fallen asleep.

***

Right before noon the three children stood back and admired their handiwork.

"It looks like a pile of brush," Colton said.

"Yep. Looks like a burn pile." Lola grinned. "It is good to know how to make camouflage."

Since sunup, they had nailed together limbs and boards to build a low-slung blind near the front gate. Set back about fifteen feet, it would give Kelly a clear line of sight for her rifle down the dusty county road. Several arguments had broken out about the strategic positioning for tree bark and grasses.

"You should be able to pick off anyone chasing after Pa and the horses, Kelly. They're gonna ride right up to you and they won't know your rifle is there." Colton had walked fifty yards down the road and tied a strip of white cloth to the brush on the south side. She aimed in on the rag and agreed.

Kelly crawled out of the blind and looked at the disguised shooting platform. "Don't be waiting on me to start the festivities here. You see 'em, you shoot 'em. These folks will be trying to take Pa's life. They come in your range, Colton, you knock 'em down." Colton nodded.

Lola said, "You have everything ready up on the barn? I heard you up there hammering on something yesterday."

Colton nodded. "Handholds, footholds and a couple of braces for the rifles. I can move ten feet to the left and right if I have to get a shot off." The young boy grinned.

Kelly rubbed her eyes. "What else do we have left to do today?"

Colton said, "Only the fun part. Whitewash the front fence."

"We cleared back most of the grass and weeds from the fences yesterday. There are some good berry vines that I saved so later in the year we can have blackberry pie," said Lola as she licked her lips. Kelly chuckled as she shook her head.

"We're always thinking about dessert in this family." Colton giggled.

"Okay, right after lunch we'll get the fence painted. Lola, you have the

250

best printing so you get to carefully write in the letters on the sign with that can of black paint. If I tried to do it, the letters would look like a chicken walked all over it." Kelly laughed at her own wiggling fingers.

One hundred yards of pole fence shone in flat white in the afternoon light. Colton had smears on his forehead and cheek. Kelly had white rings around both wrists where her gloves had slid down.

They braced up two wood ladders with a long plank between them against the fence. Kelly carefully lifted the cans of white and black paint. Lola climbed up and walked between the ladders.

"Kelly, do you think that the sign looked like this when Ma lived here?" They watch Lola dip the small brush into the can and work on the letter outline.

"It's the only sign on the ranch, honey. It has to be." Colton nodded as he watched Lola finish the last black letter.

"You remember Ma telling us how Grampa Glen liked to keep his home and ranch in tidy shape?" The boy nodded.

Lola said, "I saw where the fence had been whitewashed a long time ago. Most of it was gone but I could see where someone had repaired the fence with new poles and slathered on the whitewash. Someone took good care of it."

Kelly said, "Well, we're going to take good care of it, too." They all nodded and admired the new Flint Hills Ranch sign.

They were all quiet at the dinner table that night.

"Do you think he'll look the same, Kel?" Colton twirled his fork in his fingers.

"Yeah, his hair might be longer. He probably has a couple bumps and scrapes, maybe a scar. Maybe he didn't shave and let his beard grow out. Wrangling a herd of fifteen horses alone is a big job. I don't think I could do it without getting at least one rope burn or getting my foot stepped on." Kelly put her fork down and rubbed her temples.

The siblings looked at each other. "It's still Pa. He's coming home to us to take care of us. We won't be alone any more. He'll protect us and make sure we are safe from now on." One by one, the heads nodded.

***

The morning sun was hiding below the eastern horizon. The corral was built and the water troughs filled. Sheaves of hay waited in the feed buckets. All the ropes were braided, coiled and hung silently on the fence posts.

Lola ran from the slate patio down the sloped driveway. "Someone's coming in from the east. They're coming in fast! It's gotta be Pa!" Her eyes darted from the hills and back to the road.

Kelly stood up from the blind and yelled towards the barn. "Colton! Lola says they're coming! Get ready!" Her eyes detected the brief flitting of the small red signal flag.

The telegram said fourteen head. Her pa would be in a hard run coming in through the front gates at the front of the herd. There were no more changes to be made. There was nothing more to be done. Either they were ready or they weren't.

Kelly could hear the thundering hooves of a running herd. Her eyes searched the road, but nothing yet. Lola waved a calming hand from her position near the front of the house.

A man riding low on the neck of a big red roan swung the powerful horse up the drive and off to the right. Pa! A tightly packed herd was on his heels. Kelly counted five, seven, ten head. Then she heard the crack of the rifle and saw that her pa had tumbled from the roan near the first water trough.

A rider came into her sights and Kelly fired. It rocked the man in the saddle and a second shot knocked him to the ground. Colton had fired, too.

Another rider behind him in a black hat fired a pistol. At ten yards, Kelly fired nearly point blank and the man fell from the saddle into the tall grass.

A man's voice called out from outside the front fence. "Moss, I'm shot! Moss?"

A heavier man in a crouch ran to the cover near the fence, pulled his revolver and shouted, "Harry! Can you make it out? Harry!?"

Kelly brought up her rifle and let out her breath and pulled the trigger. Another shaggy haired man had started to climb over the top rail, then fell into the brush just inside the gate.

"Harry will be late for dinner, Moss." It was a small murmur from Kelly's lips as her eyes found another man squeezing through the fence rails. It was only a split second, but something looked familiar about the man. She fired and missed. Another shot rang out and she saw the man collapse to the ground and not move. Colton.

There was no movement near the fences. In the distance, she could hear the fading hooves of a running horse.

"We're clear. Three down. Two rode away," shouted Colton. "I'm coming down!"

Lola came walking out. "That's what I counted. Three down. Two gone. Where's Pa?"

The gruff voice called out, "I'm here!" They turned to see their father struggling to drag himself from behind the trough. Lola let out a shriek and broke into a run.

Kelly stood up from the blind and dusted off her jeans. In the dawning light, she could see the herd had smelled the water and feed and walked through the open corral gates.

Colton made it to their father first. "Pa!" It was a screech of joy that came from Lola when she ran to hug her father.

Anger and joy raged through Kelly as she laid down the rifle and picked up both Colts. Her skin still crawled in the anger that someone had tried to breach their home. The crumpled form of one of the shooters laid on the other side of the drive. Her brow furrowed as she rolled the man over with her boot.

The deep faded scar from above his ear down to his right jaw.

Kelly snickered. "Where's your red plaid now, mister?" The Colt bucked as she put another bullet into the already dead man just for good measure.

It was when she got close enough to Pa she realized that he had risked his life to get back to them. Back to his family. That was when she broke into a run to him and came sliding to a halt to hug him tightly. He had a bloody gash along his left cheek that had soaked his beard, a bandaged hand, and he favored his right leg.

Colton had not turned loose of Nick. Lola had tried to put one hundred kisses on his face. Stolter looked at his three children and sighed with relief. He kissed their foreheads again.

Stolter grimaced in pain when he tried to move. "I've got a gunshot in my hip. I need a doc to get the bullet out." It was a deep, shuddering groan that escaped him as Kelly and Lola helped their father get on his feet.

"Was that man still alive down there, honey? Why'd you shoot him?" Nick saw the tear-filled eyes of his oldest.

Kelly's throat was so tight that she could barely speak. "Red plaid." Nick had a look of shock on his face when Lola burst out laughing.

Nick wiped his mouth with the back of his hand and spit out blood to the side. "Who or what is red plaid? Never mind that. I've got plenty of questions for you three, but first things first."

Kelly nodded. "The doc is due here at noon, Pa. I told him you were coming home with stitches and he said he'd be here. Let's get you into the house. We've got a thousand days of things to tell you about."

Together they began the long walk to the house.

The End

Playlist – People ask about the music I listen to when I write.

Def Leppard - Pour Some Sugar on Me

Depeche Mode - Perfect

Green Day - Boulevard of Broken Dreams

Howling Wolf - Back Door Man

Jimi Hendrix - Red House

Jimi Hendrix - Hey Joe

Joe Bonamassa – Django

Joe Bonamassa - Quarryman's Lament

Johnny Cash - Ring of Fire

Katy Perry - Dark Horse

Kings of Leon - Sex on Fire

Led Zeppelin - Kashmir

Mark Newport - Nightgrooves 2013

Muddy Waters - I just Wanna Make

Nickelback - Burn it to the Ground

Philip Glass - Mechanical Ballet

Ralph Vaughan Williams - Fantasia on a Theme

Rascal Flats - Bless the Broken Road

Samuel Barber - Adagio for Strings

Sia - My Love

ABOUT THE AUTHOR

Lee Anne Wonnacott grew up enamored with the struggle and adventure of men and women living in the 1800 U.S. At thirteen, it felt as if she had suddenly awoken to hear that space was the final frontier. Eventually, she came to realize that is was the human imagination that encased the new frontier.

Lee Anne believes it was the stories of others who ignited her novelist imagination. Neighbors recited trials and tribulations on trains. Elderly relatives brought forth memories from diaries and letters. A lonely stranger in the Zurich train station revisited deep scars.

It was the prodding, nitpicking, and pushing from one determined high school English teacher who showed her where to jump into storytelling. Lee Anne's secret to crafting the moving story is that if the story is not working, just kill off a character in a horribly painful death. Her passion is authoring and promoting her western adventure novels. Author of fiction titles Newton Cutter, Iron and Rawhide, Rage at Rancho del Oro, and Nick Stolter.

www.leeannewonnacott.com

Lee Anne Wonnacott cooks, knits, hunts for sea glass, and howls with the neighborhood dogs in Oceanside, California

CONNECT WITH ME

Smashwords:

https://www.smashwords.com/profile/view/forsennata

Goodreads:

www.goodreads.com/author/show/8092849.Lee_Anne_Wonnacott

Facebook:

https://www.facebook.com/leeanne.wonnacott

Twitter:

https://twitter.com/lwonnaco

Google+:

https://plus.google.com/100292242352070178630

Pinterest:

https://www.pinterest.com/lwonnaco/

Instagram:

www.instagram.com/lwonnaco

LinkedIn:

https://www.linkedin.com/in/leeannewonnacott